D0118934

SICILIAN
BLOOD

ALSO BY DARRYL LONDON:
Respect (also published as *A Man of Respect*)

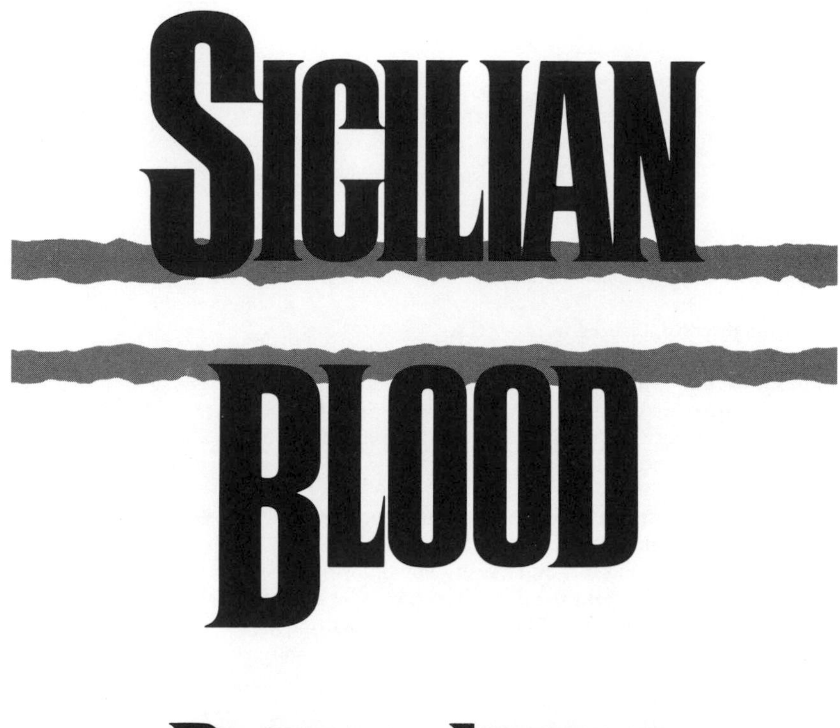

SICILIAN BLOOD

DARRYL LONDON

KNIGHTSBRIDGE PUBLISHING COMPANY
NEW YORK

Published in the United States by
Knightsbridge Publishing Company
255 East 49th Street
New York, New York 10017

Library of Congress Cataloging-in-Publication Data

London, Darryl.
Sicilian blood / Darryl London. — 1st ed.
p. cm.
ISBN 1-877961-29-9 : $19.95
I. Title.
PS3562.0485S5 1990
813'.54—dc20 90-31005
CIP

Designed by Stanley Drate/Folio Graphics Co., Inc.

10 9 8 7 6 5 4 3 2 1

FIRST EDITION

For Rosie

A hundred years
after a Sicilian dies
he still remembers.

SICILIAN
BLOOD

Prologue

1939: Boston, Massachusetts

A bright light glared out of a kitchen window overlooking Fishermen's Wharf. It was at the foot of Fleet Street. The old man, Gustavo Menesiero, sat on a wooden chair facing his youngest grandson, Bephino.

The ten-year-old boy stared into the eyes of his grandfather as tales and fables, mixed with truths and wisdom, were passed down through the reflections of blood-ridden history—a moment of closeness for both the man and the boy.

Gustavo was short, stocky, and powerful. His white hair, brown eyes, and unshaven face gave him an innocent look. The young boy's red lips and absorbing eyes were set off by a nest of curly brown hair. He watched and listened silently and with fascination as the old man casually stopped to puff his twisted black cigar, which emitted a harsh smell of burning seaweed. Like all immigrant grandfathers, he talked about his youth in the Old Country.

It was a Friday night, after the customary Italian fish dinner overly complemented with the rich thickness of homemade wine. Gustavo was proud to be the baby sitter and the one to get his youngest grandson's undivided attention for the evening. He began to cut a pear, and in between laughs fed a slice into the young lips of the boy, who seemed to be adoring him. Sixty-five years of wisdom were being funneled into the young boy's mind. Gustavo's voice penetrated the young boy's soul. A passing of the wisdom was important to the old Sicilian, but it had to be passed on carefully. A heavy Sicilian tone filled the room as the old man spoke in broken English.

"Remember, *figlio mio,* in Sciacca, a Sicilian must have honor and respect to be a true Sciaccitano. You must be loyal to your people. There should be only *uno padrone, uno presidente,* only *uno capitano, ah capito?* Understand, Bephino?" he repeated, demanding the boy's attention.

"Si, io capeesh, Nonno."

"Fai il buono, figlio mio. Buono." The old man rewarded the boy with another slice of pear. Then he whispered, as if he were telling a secret to his grandson, "The men and women of Sciacca, theya obeya the unwritten law in one worda." He raised his voice. *"Ah respecto* means respect and loyalty to our people." Exposing his tobacco-stained teeth, he grinned at the boy.

"Ah respecto," the boy repeated in a low voice. *"Ah respecto* means respect," he whispered. It was Sicilian slang for *rispetto.*

"Grandpa, Grandpa, did you ever fight with other men in Sicily?" he asked, chewing his fruit. "The older boys told me you fought a lot in Sicily."

The old man's thick lips pulled back, once again revealing his stained teeth as he smiled at the question. In a rough but gentle voice he replied, "Yes, Bephino. I fighta, but only when my honor and *rispetto* were being taken from me; then I fighta very hard. I fighta to win, never to lose. But otherwise, I avoida to fight. But sometimes we need a good fight to cleara the air, to keepa respect. Don't let people confusa your goodness with weakness. They do that very easy, you know. And thatsa very bad."

"Grandpa, are we in the Mafia?"

The old man's eyes widened at the question as he sipped his wine. He asked harshly, "Who tella you Mafia? Why you talka Mafia?"

"The kids in school, they say I'm Mafia. Am I in the Mafia, Grandpa?"

"You're ten years old, *figlio mio,* you're a . . . a young boy. What kids in school saya that to you?"

"The Jewish kids. They call me Mafioso. What does that mean, Grandpa?"

The old man's face flushed with anger. He thought for a moment, then whispered to himself, *"Eh, ejewda.* The Jewish boys." Raising his voice, he said to Bephino, *"Ejewda,* they lika to teasa you. You tella them you gonna be the *presidente* someday. You tella them you gonna be . . ." He hesitated, then looked into Bephino's innocent eyes. "Sometimes, Bephino, you gotta smacka their face to keep them boys nice. *Ah capeesh,* Bephino?"

"Si, io capisci, Nonno."

Gustavo slipped another slice of pear into his grandson's mouth.

A moment later, the boy spoke again, "But, Grandpa, I would like to know . . ."

The old man, afraid of the next question, quickly interrupted him, reaching into the pocket of his well-worn work pants. "I got something for you today, Bephino. Special for you."

Bephino's question remained unasked as he waited in eager anticipation for his surprise. His eyes followed his grandfather's hand searching deep in his pocket.

The old man pulled out a few coins, hoping to find a shiny nickel. "Ah, see what I gotta for you? Special for you, Bephino. A shiny nickel with the Indian and buffalo on it."

The boy's eyes lit up. "Thank you, Grandpa. I'll save it. Thank you very much." The boy hugged his grandfather with a loving affection that passes through one's life so quickly—a love that becomes a memory, like a dream that ends too quickly. The old man kissed the boy's forehead, his unshaven face rubbing against the smooth skin. A spark of love ignited in both, a moment only death can obliterate.

Gustavo, tired and trying to stay out of the line of questioning, told Bephino, "Put the radio on, Bepy. There's a fight tonight. We listen to it."

"What station number, Grandpa?" Bephino asked, moving toward the large wooden radio standing in the corner of the room.

The old man sprawled quietly on the sofa. "You searcha, *figlio mio*, you searcha."

WEDNESDAY, JANUARY 10, 1977, 9:00 A.M.

NEW YORK FEDERAL BUILDING, FOLEY
SQUARE, MANHATTAN DISTRICT COURT

TRIAL IN PROCESS; THE HONORABLE
CHRISTOPHER SOLOMON PRESIDING

UNITED STATES GOVERNMENT V.
[REPUTED MAFIA HIT MAN] BEPHINO MENESIERO

The cross-examination was in progress. Bephino's attorneys allowed him to take the stand. The defendant lowered his right hand.

James Oewton, the U.S. prosecutor, a large-faced, heavyset man, stood nearby and squinted as he watched the swearing in, rolling his lips anxiously as Bephino Menesiero spoke the final words, "I do." The prosecutor moved toward the witness stand. "Mr. Menesiero," he said in a loud voice that echoed through the thirty-foot-high ceiling of the federal courtroom. "Did I just hear you swear to tell the truth, the whole truth, so help you God?"

"You did," Bephino Menesiero replied softly.

"I did?" Oewton screeched back. He smiled while glancing reassuringly over at the jury. The prosecutor then turned back, facing Bephino. "Then, sir," he shouted, "state your name and address, and please speak loud enough so the jury can hear you." Smiling slyly, his eyes shifted back over to the jury. With a wide smirk he repeated, "Yes, please speak up, so the jury can hear you!" Leaning on a railing dividing the spectators and reporters from the trial participants, the burly prosecutor, dressed in a sport jacket and thick sponge-soled shoes, began grinning confidently in the direction of the judge. Bephino hesitated, watching the prosecutor's smooth actions. "Go ahead!" Oewton called. "State your name and address, we're waiting. . . ."

"My name is Bephino Menesiero. I reside at El Covallo Ranch, Little Falls, South Carolina."

Holding up a sheet of paper, the U.S. prosecutor asked, "South Carolina? Is that so?" scratching the side of his chubby face as if in thought. "That's strange . . . we have here your address shown as being in Georgia! Will you explain this sudden change to the court?"

"It's nothing serious," Bephino replied firmly. "My ranch fronts on two state lines. I pay taxes to both South Carolina and Georgia. I can use either address if I wish to. I pay quite a lot of taxes," Bephino said, nodding his head.

The prosecutor did a double take at Bephino's tax remark, shook his head, and frowned. Holding open a folder, he began glancing over his file papers. Oewton walked slowly, while reading, to consult with his staff of federal attorneys sitting at the prosecutor's table. Their heads moved back and forth while consulting one another, some looking directly over at Bephino. After a few moments, Oewton returned to confront

Bephino. "Mr. Menesiero," he said, displaying a displeasing smirk, "you openly say you pay exorbitant taxes; well, we think that's very commendable. And I'm sure the United States government and its citizens are surprised, to say the least, but in any case we appreciate the gesture very much. But for the record, Mr. Menesiero, I want you to know this is a very serious magnitude of crimes you are being charged with. While the government realizes you are fighting for your organized-crime existence, we . . ."

The prosecutor continued. Bephino lowered his eyes, his thoughts vivid. It wasn't so long ago that New York's ailing Boss of Bosses—Emilio Sequso Morrano, *capo di tutti capi,* the Boss of Bosses—decided he would push the New York council to make his good friend Bephino an independent Mafia don, a boss recognized by all as a man of respect. The year was 1973, Bephino was forty-four and wealthy. Hoping to turn away from the carnage of the Mafia's business, he planned to retire. But Morrano had called the five heads of the council to a meeting in Zito's Club Room in downtown Brooklyn and had pushed feverishly for the council's unanimous approval. Opposition was evident. When one don, Alberto Cirrillo, had voted no, Morrano had to negotiate to convince him otherwise. After staring across the famous wood table and asking the uncooperating don how his young grandson was, Morrano got his wish: a unanimous vote of yes. Two months later, Alberto Cirrillo was shot to death in Atlantic City and left in the trunk of a car.

Bephino thus became known as Don Dante, a Mafia boss accepted by all the men of the Mafia. But Bephino didn't care to be known as "Don Dante," and asked his closest friends not to call him by that name. Besides, Emilio Morrano had since died, and though Bephino, now forty-six, was surrounded by his childhood friends—the Old Blood—and a small army of thirty or so imported Sicilian hit men—his family soldiers—things were not what they used to be. And there was a new Boss of Bosses.

So, after over three decades, Bephino chose to leave his beloved New York. He sold his Staten Island home to Don

Rocco Boretti, the new Boss of Bosses, and moved to a two-thousand-acre ranch near the state lines of South Carolina and Georgia. There, he planned to retire and enjoy the absence of scrutiny. But one beautiful fall South Carolina day in 1976, he received a call and then a visit from the FBI. Turned in by a Brooklyn Mafia informant, Bephino was arrested and charged with seventeen murders. He was extradited, processed to New York City for trial, and jailed. His attorneys battled the court proceedings and fought vigorously for bail. Because he had never previously been arrested, U.S. Federal Judge Christopher Solomon ruled against the federal prosecutor's request and granted Bephino bail to the tune of two million dollars.

Now, after six months and several postponements, Bephino's attorneys had agreed to this trial date. And Bephino knew his destiny lay not in the hands of his attorney, but in those of his main soldiers, Ben and Monkey.

The next day, at 10:00 A.M., federal agents hid on rooftops and in alleyways around Foley Square and some sat idly in unused taxicabs, observing the public's movement. There would be several days of caution on the cold, snowy streets of New York City for both the FBI and the Mafia's soldiers.

Nervous button men glared through the tinted windows of their passing late-model automobiles, moving slowly down Park Row. Bephino's mobsters, disguised as priests, were crossing the square, watching for a clue to the whereabouts of Frank Caputo, the government's star witness. Time was running out; Caputo was to take the stand on the third day. And Bephino Menesiero would then surely become just another number in Atlanta's federal prison.

Ben ("Don't Call Me Benny") Del Ponte and Aldo ("the Monkey") Pastrona sat quietly sipping hot chocolate in a rear booth of a coffee shop about half a block away from the courthouse and the old Columbo Hotel. Monkey had grown up with Bephino in Bay Ridge, Brooklyn. At five-foot-eight, with straight black hair, dark complexion, and round shoulders, his nose resting high above his lips, Monkey was a proven hit man and Bephino's gifted partner. Now forty-seven and a capo in the Menesiero mob, he owned and operated several Hero sandwich shops and had made a small fortune in Bephino's stock manipulation schemes. "Whata ya think?" he asked Ben.

Ben, Bephino's consiglieri and underboss, was a short, wiry man with dirty-blond hair and off-color gray eyes that affected the deadly calm of a smiling cobra.

"I think we're gonna lose Bepy if something don't break," Ben worried. "We got at least ten guys watching the front of the Nineteenth Precinct and ten more watching the rear. It's the only place I figure they could keep a witness safe. When they call for Caputo, the marshals will probably take him out with an armed squad patrol. Mikey and Vinney Renaldi got about twenty boys out on the street. They're all set around the courthouse. They got two grenades each. It's the last resort. It's becoming a fuckin' Chinese suicide mission for us. It's gonna be hell in these streets if we don't get lucky." Ben rubbed his chin. "When the cars and vans roll out at the precinct yard and approach the courthouse, it's gotta be then or never, about forty grenades will hit them. In the confusion our people should be able to get away easy enough. The whole place will be in shambles. I got Fat Arty calling his pigeons in. If the Fat Man's info comes in time, we may get lucky and be able to make the hit inside a building or some other way rather than use grenades in the streets. We gotta clip Caputo before they get him on the stand," Ben rubbed his forehead. "He's gotta be in that precinct, there's no other . . ."

Monkey's eyes widened. "Hey, Ben, look, there's a guy going into the phone booth." Monkey nudged Ben's arm. "We need the phone clear." Ben jumped up and moved to the rear of the busy breakfast place. He addressed a man who was reaching for a coin and about to enter the booth.

"Excuse me, but we're waitin' for a very important call on this phone. Can you go next door in the cigar store and use that phone?" Ben asked.

"Who's we?" the large blond man, half in the booth and half out, asked with a sneer. Phone in hand, he stared down hard at little Ben.

Ben opened his jacket and exposed a leather shoulder holster containing a 9mm pistol. "Me and this black bastard,"

Ben whispered. "Now get the fuck out of here before we get crazy."

The large man eloquently squirmed out of the booth and tiptoed out of the coffee shop. Ben looked to the front of the busy shop and waved over at another man he knew, who was busy behind the food counter. When the dark-haired worker in his early forties, unshaven and wearing a white shirt and apron, hurried over to Ben, the consiglieri put his arm around the man's neck and began talking busily into his ear. The man nodded frequently as Ben spoke. Ben then returned to his table and sat down with Monkey. The man with the white apron picked up a roll of tape and began affixing an out-of-order sign on the phone booth. He then turned, winked at Ben and Monkey, and walked back to his busy counter.

At 10:45 A.M., the phone rang. Ben jumped up and moved quickly to answer it, closing the booth's doors. Monkey's eyes watched Ben's anxious face through the glass doors. It must have been Fat Arty, their banker. Ben turned, as if listening hard, facing out of the booth. Suddenly his eyes opened wide as important words passed through the telephone wires. He put the receiver down hard and climbed out of the booth. He rolled his eyes at Monkey as he moved quickly back toward their table.

"Guess what?" Ben snapped, curling his lips. "Fat Arty's pigeons are in. They got Caputo in the fuckin' old hotel. In the fuckin' *hotel,*" he whispered in a harsh, deep voice. "Not the precinct! Could you imagine that? Fat Arty just got word from his man in the bureau in Washington. The feds are holed up in the fuckin' Columbo Hotel. Would you believe that! And we're lookin' in trucks and garbage cans, and they're tucked away nice in the hotel. Unbelievable!" Ben grunted, "I never thought they would use the hotel. It would have been too easy for us to figure that. We could have been there already."

Monkey stared at Ben for a while; then he said, "We gotta move quick. How much time we got?"

"According to Hal Rosenberg, he's putting Bephino on the stand today just to buy us time. Fat Arty told me they're gonna guard Caputo with the best they got. He's the only witness for them," Ben replied.

Monkey shrugged. "We don't know what room they're in. How we gonna find them in time? It'll take days to scan that hotel." Ben slammed his hand on the table and stared, thinking.

"There's gotta be a way we can get to him in time." Ben shook his head from side to side in disgust. At that moment a young Hispanic walked by with a box of take-out orders. Ben watched him for a moment, then walked over to the area near the dark-haired man with the white apron behind the service counter. He made eye contact for him to come over to the back to talk. The unshaven man stopped what he was doing and quickly followed Ben to the rear, holding a wet terry-cloth rag in his hand. "Sonny," Ben whispered, "do you know anybody with rank at the Columbo Hotel?"

Patty ("Sonny") Garbo shook his head confirming he did not, then said, "No, the joint's run by Yankee Wasps. We only use the place to bang a new waitress or a customer, when we catch a live one who's in heat. The hotel always charges us full price, them rubbers, they got no respect; they never heard of half-day charge—no comps, nothin'. They're all fuckin' Wasps," he sneered, rubbing his five-o'clock-shadowed face.

"Sonny, I gotta get into the joint. They got the canary held up in one of them fuckin' rooms; we gotta get in to clip him. Maybe we could make believe we're deliverin' some orders and we could wander through the building. Maybe we'll get lucky and run into them."

Sonny passed his hand over his face "Are you sure they got him in there? It's a big fuckin' hotel. You could spend days going through that joint."

"I know, I know, that's why I gotta get in and find out which room they got the bird in. It's my only shot." Ben stared at Sonny.

"I don't think I can help you, Ben," Sonny shrugged. "I'm sorry, I don't have that good a contact with the manager. He'll open up to the coppers if we start wanderin' around his hotel or talkin' like that to him. If we start asking about the feds, the witness, things like that, the guy's gonna run scared. The whole neighborhood is crawlin' with cops, you know that. I'm sorry, Ben, you know if I could help . . ."

"Sonny, you're Sicilian like us. We need your help." Ben stared. "Get us in the fuckin' building with some cover. We don't have to tell them why we're in there."

"Ben," Sonny whispered in a parched voice, "if I could, I'd do it in a minute, you know that, Ben." He grabbed Ben's arm and pleaded in a soulful voice. "What kind of cover can I give you guys? I can't afford to send your guys in the hotel pretendin' they work for me—it won't work! They don't know me that well. I only send the fuckin' spick in with orders, that's all."

Sonny returned to his counter. Ben said to Monkey, "We got problems; Sonny won't help out. We gotta remember this bum in our will."

Suddenly, at that moment, Sonny came rushing back to Ben and Monkey's table and sat down. He leaned over to Ben. "We just got a phone order to deliver three late breakfasts to the Columbo Hotel," Sonny said, raising his brow at Ben. "Whata ya think?" he asked. "You can make the delivery yourself and look around the building. See what you can see," he grinned.

"What did they order?" Ben asked.

"Two scrambled egg sandwiches, coffee, dark pancakes, jelly donuts, and I think an extra-cold milk."

"If it's the feds," Monkey said, "why didn't they order from the hotel restaurant? This is the second day they're up there, why today?"

"I'm not sayin' it's the feds who ordered the food," Sonny said. "I don't know who the food is for, it could be for anybody. It'll get you up in the room area carrying food, that's all. Once you're in, you could scout the floors. Anyway, it's a long shot. You wanted cover, so do you want it or not?" Sonny asked. "I gotta know."

Ben jumped up. "Gimme a minute, will you, Sonny? Go get the orders ready. I gotta make a fast phone call, something just entered my mind." Ben walked to the phone booth, closed the door, and deposited twenty cents. "Operator, gimme the number of the Bay Parkway Social Club in Brooklyn." Ben got the number and dialed the club. The phone rang four times.

"Hello," a man answered in a heavy voice.

"Who's this?" Ben asked.

"Who's this?" the man asked back.

Ben frowned. "Is Chubby Fusaro there?" Ben asked.

"Yeah, hold on. Hey-y-y-y, Chubby, it's for you."

A few moments passed. Then an out-of-breath voice came over the phone. "This is Chubby speaking, who wants to talk to me?"

"Chubby, listen to me and don't talk," Ben said with the tone of Brooklyn authority. "Just answer my question carefully, *a capisce?*"

Chubby became quiet; his nervous mind wondered who the caller might be. He tried to control his heavy breathing. "Go ahead, I'm listening," he mumbled.

"Chubby, a fuckin' pigeon is gonna sing like a canary today, *a capisce, bellezza?*" Ben asked, using the Brooklyn Italian slang that would give Chubby the cue that this was a caller who should be given respect.

"Si, io capisce," Chubby answered softly, cautiously.

"Chubby, the canary comes from Bay Parkway. Before the canary flies away on me, what does the bird eat for breakfast? Does he eat bird seed or does the bird eat *cazzo* for breakfast or what?" Ben scowled into the phone. "This is very important, fat one; please think before you reply. I'm interested in his breakfast habits only," Ben repeated in a raspy voice, speaking closely while cupping his hand over the receiver.

Chubby became silent, as if in deep thought. "If you're talkin' about the scumbag I think you're talkin' about," Chubby replied, "he eats wholewheat pancakes sometimes, buckwheat sometimes, jelly donuts, and always ice-cold milk . . ." Click, Ben hung up.

"Hello, are you there?" Chubby asked, looking into the phone.

Ben rushed back to the table where Sonny and Monkey were waiting. "That's it, a fuckin' million-to-one shot—we win again!" he whispered hoarsely. "That's the fuckin' breakfast order for the room where they got Caputo. The pancakes are for him. Are the pancakes wholewheat?" Ben asked Sonny.

"Buckwheat," Sonny replied.

"Fantastic!" Ben yelped. "That's it! You're beautiful,

Sonny! We'll never forget this, Sonny, believe me," Ben promised, looking right at him. "We'll always remember this," Ben repeated. Sonny grabbed Ben's arm and gave him a warm, wide grin of understanding.

Back in the courtroom, allegations were still being read to Bephino by the prosecutor.

"I object," Bephino's lawyer leaped out of his seat. "Your honor," Rosenberg shouted, "I object to this unethical method used by the government to discredit my client. This is the second day, and the U.S. prosecutor is still making allegations against my client. The government has not established that my client is involved in organized crime."

"Objection sustained," the judge ordered sharply. "Keep your presiding comments in perspective," he warned, looking over his silver-rimmed glasses at the federal prosecutor.

The U.S. prosecutor moved awkwardly in his buff sponge shoes toward Bephino. Bending over and leaning on the railing, he glared passively up at Bephino. "OK," he smiled. "As I was saying, Mr. Menesiero, the allegations against you are for murder, racketeering, brutality, reckless endangerment of American citizens, consorting with members of organized crime, and causing fear in society. That's a whole catalog of asserted criminal activities that are impossible for the average American citizen to comprehend. And you are also being charged with seventeen counts of mu-u-u-rder," the prosecutor announced, his voice echoing throughout the courtroom with emphasis. "You have terminated the lives of our fellow, law-abiding citizens. In a word, Mr. Menesiero," the prosecutor lowered his voice, his eyes flashing from Bephino to the jurors, "this is actually war. It's the people versus the Mob, and you are going to the chair." Oewton turned, his eyes darting at Hal Rosenberg, who seemed ready to leap from his seat at any second. Oewton began speaking faster and louder, trying his best to get the words out before Rosenberg caught on to what he was up to. He turned back to Bephino and called out, "It's the people versus the Mob! That's it!" he yelled uncontrollably. "The people versus the Mob! This is the real thing here. . . ." Oewton shouted hysterically, wiping his large face with his handkerchief.

"Your honor!" Bephino's attorney interrupted as if gasping for air. "My client is receiving injustice right here in the halls of justice! I object to this outrageous, backhanded, cheap shot at my client's expense. The prosecutor is already predicting the conclusion of my client's trial to the jury. This episode is totally unethical. It has not been proven that my client committed a murder. I can't believe what I'm hearing!" Rosenberg shouted. "This sounds more like an unlawful final summary taking place here," he continued. "I want my objection logged into the trial records. I'll file for a mistrial if this jabbering is allowed to continue!"

"But I'm not finished jabbering with the defendant yet, your honor," Oewton shouted back. "As a matter of fact, I'm just beginning." Oewton grinned as he walked back to his table, picked up a folder, and glanced pointedly over at Rosenberg. "I'm only just beginning," Oewton loudly reminded him.

Judge Solomon removed his spectacles and looked sagely at both attorneys, and as his eyes focused on Hal Rosenberg, his face paled. In a deep voice he growled, "There's nothing unlawful going on in my courtroom, counsel. You may file for a mistrial if you wish. In the meantime, please sit down! Your objection's been noted and overruled." Judge Solomon then addressed Oewton, placing a pen to his mouth. "Please continue, Mr. Prosecutor. And let's not be so presumptuous; the defendant, in this country, is innocent until proven guilty. And cut the vaudeville tactics. You're overacting."

"Yes, your honor," Oewton replied, his satisfied eyes quickly scanning over the jurors. His face then turned sourly at Bephino. "Mr. Menesiero, would you please state your date of birth, place of birth, and the address you lived at during your New York teen years, plus your last legal address known in the State of New York."

"You sound like you're beginning to realize you may have the wrong man, Mr. Prosecutor," Bephino answered with a shy grin.

The entire courtroom erupted with laughter. Even the judge smiled briefly. Widening his eyes and raising his thick, hairy brows, he looked over at Bephino and said neutrally, "You are directed to answer the federal prosecutor's request, Mr. Menesiero. He needs this information recorded into the trial records. It's a formality. Please proceed," the judge ordered.

Bephino paused and looked over to his attorney, who nodded for him to continue. He shook his head easily for a moment, then began to speak. "As you already know, my name is Bephino Menesiero. I was born in Boston, Massachusetts. As an adolescent I lived in Brooklyn, New York. I then moved to 1400 Sea Horse Drive, Staten Island, and I now reside in the southeastern state of South Carolina. I served two years in the U.S. Army and was honorably discharged. I have never been arrested or in trouble in my life."

"That's enough!" Oewton yelled out. "We don't need your resumé or your medical history." Passing his hand over the top of his head, he pounced. "Just tell the court how well you knew Mr. Eugene Bolanski of Beverly Hills, California."

Bephino raised his eyes. "I didn't know him at all," he replied.

"Did you ever meet with Mr. Bolanski or his wife, Sonia Bolanski?"

"No."

"Did you ever see them on TV or in newspapers or magazines?"

"No."

"Are you telling me you don't know what they looked like?" the prosecutor shouted incredulously.

"I'm not telling you nothing, Mr. Prosecutor. I'm just answering the questions yes or no. Isn't that the way it's supposed to be done? Yes or no?" Bephino asked.

"Not always," the prosecutor responded. "But if yes or no is your thing, we'll play it your way," he said, turning slowly toward the jury, his eyes making contact with a juror before darting for the ceiling as he started the next question. "Have you ever been in contact with Mr. Bolanski or his wife by telephone and/or other means? Answer yes or no."

"No."

"Then why did you kill Eugene Bolanski?" the prosecutor screamed.

Hal Rosenberg leapt from his seat. "Your Honor, I object to this line of questioning. The prosecutor is badgering my client, and those questions are misleading the jury. My client, in his pretrial hearing of the grand jury, stated he killed no one. It's up to the government to prove my client committed a crime such as murder."

"Objection sustained," Judge Solomon ruled. Turning to the stenographer, he said, "Strike those comments from the record. Continue."

"OK, now." The prosecutor, clasping his hands, smiled and exposed a set of large yellow teeth. "Did you ever commit murder, any murder, Mr. Menesiero?"

Hal Rosenberg jumped up again. "Your honor, I object. We have a specific crime that my client is on trial for. This line of questioning is irrelevant to this trial."

"Overruled. Answer the question," the judge instructed Bephino.

"No," Bephino replied.

"No?!" the federal prosecutor screeched, once again briefly looking over at the jury. "Are you saying, Mr. Tough Guy, you never pulled the trigger on anyone? Not even a little old lady?" Oewton grinned at Bephino.

"That's right," Bephino answered. "I never killed anyone, especially not a little old lady—ya fuckin' sickie," Bephino added under his breath. Oewton's eyes widened as he contemplated what he thought he'd heard.

"Aren't you a hit man for the Morrano family of Bensonhurst, Brooklyn?" he called out loudly, so the entire courtroom could hear him.

"No."

"No?" the heavyset prosecutor whined in question. Spinning around to face the jury, he picked up a piece of paper and began reading from it. "Do the names Pete Lungo, Vince the Hawk Gacolido, or perhaps Pete, Sam, and John Grimaldi of Bel Air, California, mean anything to you?"

"No."

"How about their murders—did they mean anything to you?"

"They mean absolutely nothing to me."

"Not anything?" the prosecutor leaned forward, pounding his fist upon the stand. "Not even just a little murder?" he persisted with a deceiving smile. "Just a little one?!" he prodded, hoping to irritate Bephino into saying something stupid. "I want to remind you, Mr. Menesiero, you're under oath in this courtroom, and aside from murder I also will now prove perjury." Turning and walking toward his peers for a briefing, Oewton looked back at Bephino and called across to him, "You're under oath, and don't forget it."

"I won't," Bephino answered in a calm voice.

"Your honor, I object, I totally object," Rosenberg said in an exhausted-sounding voice, waving his arms. Without asking permission, he began walking toward the bench. "The Government is badgering my client." Pointing to Oewton, Rosenberg said in a whisper, "He's playing games, he's putting on a fucking show for the jury, and I want this on record."

"It's on record. Your objection is overruled. Now let's get on with this trial."

"OK, now," the prosecutor said cheerfully, standing off to the side, listening. He grinned at Hal Rosenberg, and as Rosenberg walked by, their eyes met. Turning to Bephino, Oewton continued. "OK, now. Let's see if the name Don Dante means anything to you." The burly prosecutor leaned forward as he knowingly dropped the bomb. "Does it?" he repeated to Bephino with a sly grin.

The feds knew it all; the next thing he expected was for Oewton to come out and call him Sciaccitano. They had all the information they needed to put him away for keeps, and the federal attorney was really just going through the motions, performing for the jury, building up his questions to bring about a triumphant climax. He intended to win a guilty verdict with only one witness, a Mob stoolie, a witness with no credibility waiting in the wings to testify for the government—a hoodlum witness, Frank Caputo, an ex-soldier in the Morrano family. Caputo had turned state's evidence to save his own ass, and in so doing had given up Bephino, a boss, in exchange for a life sentence that with this particular cooperation would revert to a new life under the protection of the Special Government's Witness Program. Caputo had given the FBI everything they'd needed: hits, names, dates. If this government witness held up, Bephino would be good for two hundred years in Atlanta. Hal Rosenberg, in his pretrial estimates, had said the trial would be a quickie, maybe a few days or so at the most. But Hal Rosenberg had put Bephino on the stand as bait early in the trial, knowing the prosecutor would jump at the opportunity to grill and question him and try to discredit him. Ben needed time to act, and Rosenberg understood this—and Bephino understood it also. Bephino had only one shot left, to clip Caputo before he got up on the stand.

"Answer the question. Does the name Don Dante mean anything to you?" the prosecutor repeated. "Just state yes or no. . . ."

"Donald Dante, if I recall, lives at 105 Market Street, Newark, New Jersey," Bephino replied.

"Just state yes or no!" the prosecutor shouted. "Yes or no?"

"Is that who you mean as Don Dante?" Bephino, refusing to say yes or no, asked naively, playing on the federal prosecutor's nerves.

The prosecutor's face paled. "And Donald Duck lives in Hollywood and you're a damn liar, Mr. Menesiero," he whispered hoarsely. "We got a strong live witness who will prove you a liar. We'll have you so damn good in a few hours, you'll be talking to yourself. This will be the quickest murder trial in New York history, Mr. Mafioso."

Bephino smiled, leaned forward, and whispered low in return to the prosecutor. "You got bad breath, you know that, Chubby? I'm sorta psychic, did you know that?" Bephino grinned widely. "And about an hour ago I could swear I saw flashes of your live witness at the Bronx Zoo, being fed to Leo." Bephino then widened his eyes at the prosecutor, winked, and said, "Whata ya think, Mr. Prosecutor? Are you taking this case too personal or what?"

The judge heard the furtive whispering and turned in awe when he realized there was—unthinkably—a private conversation actually taking place between Bephino and the prosecuting attorney. Looking over his bifocals, he raised his thick brows and rapped his gavel. "Are you two people finished?"

The federal prosecutor propped himself back up and began backing away from Bephino. His thick, fast-moving spongy shoes bounced awkwardly about on the tiled courtroom floor, and his eyes bulged wide. He glanced up at the judge, then walked to his table to meet with his colleagues. After a few moments he called out in a reckless voice, "Your honor, I would like to approach the bench!"

"After I take a thirty-minute recess," the judge growled, "then you may approach the bench," he answered while getting up.

"But your honor," Oewton spoke out. "The Government would like to recess until Monday."

"Thirty-minute recess," the judge growled again, "and no one leaves my courtroom."

Judge Solomon stormed out of his courtroom and into his chambers.

About half an hour later the judge returned and addressed the courtroom and the jurors. He then began to confer with the federal prosecutor while Hal Rosenberg listened cautiously and Bephino sat wide-eyed on the witness stand. "What's your reason for requesting such a long recess of this trial?" the judge asked.

"Your honor, I believe the federal government will need such a recess. My witness and my briefs must be entered simultaneously. We need another few days." The judge stared hard. "And I also believe the life of the Government's witness could be in danger here today at this courthouse." Oewton glanced nervously about, like a man who had just had a bad dream. The judge's eyes tilted cautiously over at Bephino.

Bephino returned the judge's look and smiled, raising his brows at Solomon.

The judge hesitated, then said, "All right, we'll reconvene Monday at 9:00 A.M. Recess is granted. Court dismissed."

"Thank you, your honor," Oewton said.

While walking off and away from the witness stand, Bephino approached the prosecutor. "Mr. Prosecutor," Bephino said with a grin, "if you find I don't have to show up on Monday, give me a call, will you? I'm at the Hotel on the Park, Suite 901."

The prosecutor sneered, "It's unbelievable you made bail while this trial is in process, but soon you'll be playing basketball in a federal park. So, Mr. Mafioso, enjoy your Hotel on the Park while you can. I have great plans for your future." Oewton slammed his briefcase closed and shouted, "Now get the fuck out of my way! Your kind make me sick!"

Later that evening during dinner, sitting alone with Ben Del Ponte at a Manhattan East Side restaurant, Bephino asked in a low voice, "Where is he now?"

"We got lucky at the last moment," Ben grinned. "Believe me, we almost blew it! A million-to-one shot and we win again! They had him locked up tight in the Columbo Hotel across from the courthouse. All the time we thought he was in the precinct around the corner. Thank God for Fat Arty! We made contact with Fat Arty at Sonny Garbo's coffee shop, over the phone. A wild card paid off. They ordered their breakfast from Sonny's coffee shop down the street from the Courthouse. You remember Patty Garbo, they call him Sonny after his father, the hairy guy with all the broads. You remember him, he's from the East Side; he owns the joint." Bephino nodded; he knew the Garbos. Ben smiled his sly cobra smile and then said, "They fucked up when they ordered them breakfasts from Sonny's place. Sonny had a strange feeling when he got the phone order from the hotel. They ordered breakfast about 10:45. To check it out, I called Caputo's old hangout on Bay Parkway. I got that fat bastard, Chubby, on the phone. Fat Chubby opened up fast. He told me Caputo loves his buckwheat pancakes and ice-cold milk. It matched up perfect with the order Sonny Garbo got. So we drugged the coffee and the scambled egg sandwiches. The food was brought up by Monkey. We figured we'd put the feds to sleep so we could get in the room. At 11:30, we opened the door to the room with crowbars and found the feds snoring like two mutts, and Frank was sitting on the bed watching 'em. Me and Mikey entered, took all the drug-tainted food left on the paper plates and flushed it down the bowl. We even took all the paper dishes and empty cups with us. We left nothin' behind—no prints, nothin'. Frank got up, put his hat and coat on and said, 'I knew I'd never get in that courtroom.' I pumped two into his head real quick. We picked him up and put him in a mattress-cover bag. We left the room in three seconds flat. We dumped Frank headfirst down the hotel laundry chute. Monkey and Pauli were in the basement, waiting for him to land. When he landed he looked like a sack of laundry. They wheeled him out in a laundry hamper, put him in the station wagon we stole, and took him off to the schoolhouse.

"Did you put any cash in the feds' pockets?" Bephino asked, sipping wine from a crystal goblet.

"Yeah, in their pockets, in their ass, and even under the bed. They gotta have some explaining to do with all that cash on hand. It looked like somebody bought the witness from them and they pretended to be drugged and played dead. The drug that Mike came up with don't show up in the blood. Mike uses the drug on broads he wants to daze, so the feds got no real excuse and, like I said, a lot of explaining to do. It went easy, Bep. We owe Sonny, he stood tall. He deserves respect. He got us in there. They sure underestimated our skills!"

"They never figured you would be able to get to him under FBI guard so close to the courthouse," Bephino said.

"We got lucky. I thought sure we were gonna have to blow up Foley Square to hit Caputo. Oh, that Fat Arty was great." Ben smiled. "He got all the necessary information for us. I tell you, he's got a fuckin' parakeet in Washington, that's for sure! We always knew they were stashed on the street, but we had to wait for the actual location. We didn't know where they had him."

"Did you make sure none of his blood hit the rugs or around the laundry chute area?"

"Yeah, everything was left spotless. We stuffed his holes with gauze, you know, like those medical sponges the doctors use, only we used tissue, plain ol' toilet paper; we packed him good, soon as we hit him. We plugged him up tight so no blood hit the floor. I assure you, everything's left clean. Not a drop of blood anywhere. No noise, nothin'. We used a silencer."

"Sounds good. What about the body?"

"We took him over to the schoolhouse to see that German custodian. You know, the crazy guy I knew from Staten Island. He works over at the high school, downtown Brooklyn. They say he used to work the ovens in Germany." Ben grinned slyly. "You think it's a joke, but we used this guy before, years ago. He turns them to dust for five G's, so we gave him five grand and he stuffed Caputo in the coal furnace all by himself. We hung around and watched. After an hour of cooking, we opened it up to add more coal. Caputo was totally gone. Dust to dust."

"Good," Bephino said, raising his goblet. "Dust to dust. I like that expression." Then he smiled at Ben. "After all these years, you finally did it perfect for me. This sounds perfect," Bephino nodded. "All the years we've been together, I always had faith you were a real pro, and now you proved it."

Tapping their glasses, Ben said, *"Salute."*

Bephino whispered, "Thanks, Ben, I owe you."

"You owe me nothin', we're together. We've been together. Whatever it takes, it takes."

Bephino smiled, then grabbed Ben's arm warmly. "You did it good, Ben. Believe me, it really sounded good."

Two days later, back at his hotel suite, Bephino sat with Ben, Monkey, and Alan Stone, the Menesiero family's loyal and trusted advisor. At 1:00 P.M., Bephino got the important call he was waiting for from his attorneys, Rosenberg, Gottlieb and Weiss. Morris Gottlieb spoke. "Did you read the morning papers? The witness took a walk, he escaped, the feds say. They found unexplained money all over the place. It's under investigation, but somebody got bought off, they think. Mr. Caputo must have left the witness program, perhaps on his own accord—it's all speculation at the moment. But you don't have to show on Monday. It's all over. The judge has to dismiss the case. Hal just called; he's at the office preparing the necessary final papers. The feds agreed to sign a no-show order. They have no case. No witness, no case! The charges against you are dropped. Mr. Menesiero, not only don't you have to appear on Monday, but the beauty of it all is they can't schedule a new trial, because amendment 1215 prevents them from doing so. It's over, Bephino; it's like you've been tried. They're finished, they blew it. The feds came up empty," Morris repeated. "Your bail will be returned to you within twenty-four hours by certified mail."

"Thanks, Morris, and thank Hal for me. And thanks for getting me out on bail while the trial was going on. That was really somethin', how you pulled that off. You fellows did a great job."

"Good luck, Bephino. Keep in touch."

"OK, Morris, I will." While hanging up the phone, Bephino turned to his friends. "I'm checking out. I'm leaving for the farm tomorrow morning. It's over. The feds gave me a year of grief. They kept Caputo under lock and key, but they still fucked up at the end: They ordered breakfast from a Sicilian." Turning to Ben and Monkey, he said, "Thanks for lookin' out for me. Oh, yeah, Ben, see that Sonny Garbo gets twenty-five grand, and thank him for me personally. Tell him if he ever needs a job, he's got one. Let him know we got respect for him."

Ben smiled, "They thought they were dealing with some punk guys from Brooklyn." Ben laughed, "They didn't know they had a Staten Islander in this crowd." Ben shook his head and looked over at Alan Stone, Bephino's close and respected friend. A man of chosen words, Stone was the majority shareholder and owner of the El Banco Hotel in Las Vegas. Now sixty-five, he resided in the hotel's posh Presidential Suite. His tight, wavy, silver-gray hair was kept neat and short. A short, wide gold chain with Hebrew lucky charms hung casually from his neck. His clothes were Palm Springs flashy, his teeth a perfect pearly white, his skin a deep Hollywood tan. He wore heavy-rimmed glasses and spoke Jewish slang at strangers through a thick Teamo cigar.

Bephino turned toward Alan, who was quietly puffing on his cigar, and motioned for him to join him in the bedroom. Bephino began to speak. "Alan, tell me something . . ."

About twenty minutes later Alan and Bephino returned to the living room, where Ben and Monkey were sitting.

"Oh, yeah, I almost forgot," Monkey said, lighting up a cigarette. "Don Rocco wants to see you."

"Rocco? What the hell does he want?" Bephino asked.

"I don't know. He sent some goon over to the club early this morning lookin' for you. I told him you were at the hotel sleepin'. He said to tell you Rocco wants to see you at Zito's at ten tonight. It's very important."

Bephino narrowed his eyes and said to Ben, "What the fuck does he want?" After a moment he sighed, "OK, Ben, you and me, we'll go over tonight and see what he wants." Turning to Monkey, he said, "You, Mikey, and Pauli look after everything. Keep things nice. Keep all our men under control. Alan, thanks for coming. I'll call you in Vegas in a few days." Bephino embraced Alan Stone warmly, then did the same to Monkey.

Later that night, Bephino and Ben went to meet with Don Rocco Boretti, who was not only the new head of Brooklyn's notorious Morrano family, but also the new reigning Boss of Bosses of the New York Mafia and the entire country. Once known as Rocco Borelli, the don had decided, due to a close IRS encounter of the indictment kind, to permanently adopt his a.k.a., Boretti, for purposes legal, commercial, and familial.

As Bephino and Ben entered Zito's back room, they observed a long table. Sitting with Rocco were Mob bosses Anthony ("Tony Boy") Cafaci from Bath Avenue, Brooklyn; Angelo Marandala of Queens; John ("Bad Johnny") Tortoricci of Staten Island; and Gataneo Gaeta of the Bronx and Manhattan. Their respected capos from each of the Mafia families also sat, assuming the second position at the table. Bephino and Ben walked cautiously into the back room.

"Hey," Rocco yelled excitedly to the others. "He's here now. Congratulations on your court case, Don Dante. You really walked away like a champ."

Bephino returned a disbelieving smile around the table to all the men and began to focus on the situation.

"Yeah," Tony Boy said, in his deep, raspy voice, "you did good. You even make witnesses disappear, hah, Dante?"

Bephino, detecting the falseness of their compliments, replied, "Yeah, I'm like Houdini the magician." Then, with an icy smile, he looked over at Rocco and asked, "What's up? Why are we meetin' tonight?"

Rocco raised his hand to cover one side of his mouth in order to exclude the others. "We got important business to discuss with you. You'll hear about it shortly. Relax." Rocco Boretti reached over and touched Bephino's arm reassuringly.

"OK, let's all sit and get this thing over with," the oldest don, Gataneo Gaeta, said, while tapping on the table. "It's no good for us to hang around too long together," he grinned. Then, when all present settled down, he looked directly at Bephino: "We got somethin' important for you to do, Bephino, and it will pay you very well."

Bephino glanced quickly around the room; silently he watched each man's eyes. Gaeta repeated, "We have something real special for you to do." Bephino had always detested Gataneo Gaeta; ruthless and without concern for others, Gaeta had been a whoremaster and pimp all his life. But more important, Emilio Morrano had never trusted Gaeta; Bephino never forgot that. Bephino's facial expression changed smoothly from concerned to actively annoyed. He watched as the dons of New York's largest families all nodded their heads at each other in what clearly was a prearranged agreement. Don Gataneo Gaeta continued to speak, but suddenly Rocco Boretti interrupted, leaned forward, and began giving Bephino careful instructions on what seemed to be a murder contract he should not refuse.

Bephino listened, staring down at the tabletop and barely suppressing his impatience. After a few moments he looked directly at Boretti and said with a smirk, "Whata you giving me, Rocco, an offer I can't refuse? Ben and I walked in here and nobody even offered us a drink. Now you're telling me we gotta do this, do that. Whata we having here, a sit-down or what?"

Rocco smiled at Bephino's words. He looked at all the men in the room, then turned to Bephino and growled, "Whata ya talking about sit-down, we're giving you an opportunity to bring credibility to all our American families. The hit, as I just told you, will take place in Europe. Your man lives in Vienna. He has ties to our people in Sicily, Milan, Rome, Naples.

"We do this for our friend Generro Polucci, the *capo di tutti capi* in Palermo. Polucci controls thirty families in Europe, he's our people. The man that's gotta go is a guy by the name of Count Del Rego." Bephino's eyes flashed at Ben. Rocco continued without acknowledging what Bephino might be thinking. "We understand he's involved in some political dealings with the Communist Party operating in Italy," Rocco said. "I don't know all the details on what's going on over there, but Generro Polucci wants this Del Rego guy *morte.*"

"So why don't this Generro Polucci put his people on it? Why do we get involved?" Bephino asked Rocco. "We're in America. Let Generro's people in Italy handle their own problems." Bephino glared at all the men around the table and grunted, "And if this guy in Sicily is the Boss of Bosses, he controls thirty families, right?" Raising his voice, with a deeper glare in his eye, he said, "Let Polucci do it himself. He's got plenty of men!"

"No!" Tony Boy called out, "we owe Generro Polucci a favor from years ago when Don Geno sent his kid to Sicily. In those days, Polucci had to do our people a lotta favors. Now that Don Geno is *morte* and his family is mine, we gotta do the respect. Generro Polucci asked Gaeta here to take care of this small favor for him. Gaeta accepted on our behalf."

"What you're saying, Tony, don't make a bit of sense to me." Looking over at Gataneo, Bephino continued. "Let Gataneo Gaeta here send one of his top guns to Europe and make the hit. Simple as that; Gataneo Gaeta accepted it, so he should handle it. Why should I have to go?" Bephino shrugged. "I got my own problems. I just spent a year out on bail. Just got finished with my problems and you guys give me another one. In Europe, no less!"

"Who the hell do you think you're talkin' to, you young punk," Gataneo snarled across the table. "I was a don when you were still suckin' the tit," the seventy-eight-year-old Mafia boss said, banging on the table. "I made the commitment to our friends in Palermo." His wizened, hollowed-out features and large dentures seemed to make his ugly face glow in the poorly lit room. "I singa the songs and you dance to my tune, Mr. Menesiero," Gaeta snarled again across the table. "You're still a glamour boy from Bensonhurst." Gaeta motioned, waving his hands as if dismissing Bephino. "You're the son of a pushcart fisherman, a Sciaccitano," Gaeta huffed, looking away as if in disgust. Pausing, he then looked back across the table. "We owe you no respect-t-t!" the old man scowled, pounding both hands on the table. "You just carry out the council's orders."

Bephino's eyes widened, then darted nervously around the room. Bile had risen in his throat. He shot back, "So was Emilio Morrano a Sciaccitano, and he was the son of a fisherman, you old bastard!" Bephino yelled. "What's wrong with fisherman, hah?"

"*Morrano e morte,*" Gaeta spat out. "He's with the dead!"

Bephino shot up. "He's with the dead! You sound like a fuckin' Indian. He's with the dead!" He shouted in agitation. "*Morrano e morte.* . . . Where do you think you're going, hah? You got no respect for the dead, old man, and I earned my rank, so let's get that straight!" Bephino shouted. "I paid my dues! So cut the shit with the Sciaccitano stuff or you're gonna be—" Bephino stopped suddenly and shook his head from side to side. Turning to Ben, he said, "Come on, Ben, let's get the fuck outta here before things begin to happen. These bastards think they're gonna intimidate me. They got another fuckin' guess comin' to them."

Ben got up, keeping his eyes on every capo in the room. Ben was packing and silently ready for action.

All the other men quietly watched Gaeta watch Bephino.

"Gentlemen, gentlemen," Rocco said, breaking the silence. He stood up and grabbed Bephino's arm, motioning him to sit back down. "We are all becoming upset for no reason. Let's talk, let's go over the details once again so Bephino knows what is expected of him," Rocco said, looking at Gaeta. But the conciliatory smile on Rocco's face did not fool Bephino. Clearly, Rocco was reassuring everyone in the room that an accord had been reached, only now they had to convince Bephino of it.

Rocco continued, "Look, Bephino, I'm gonna be honest about this. The council has already decided on you—not one of Gataneo's buttons, but you! We want to show the ultimate respect to our friends in Palermo. We are sending a don to make the hit—not a soldier, but a don—and they will know of this in Sicily. We expect you to cooperate and make this hit one of your best, because you *are* the best. So make it something nice, *a capisce?*" Rocco winked at Bephino and grabbed his shoulder.

"Don Rocco's right," Tony Boy Cafaci said curtly as all the men around the table busily grunted, nodded, and shook their heads in agreement with one another.

Bephino's eyes moved from person to person and then settled on Ben, who was back sitting quietly next to him. After a few moments Bephino puffed out, "Look, fellows, I just had a year of aggravation from the feds. I just went through a damn murder trial, I'm only off the hook one day, and now you're askin' me to go to Europe to make a hit, in Vienna no less! I haven't been well lately. I got high blood pressure. I'm not that sound anymore. And when did you guys decide on me? It looked like I was surely headin' for Atlanta. When did you people decide it should be me to go to Europe?" Bephino asked again.

"Today," Gataneo Gaeta spat across the table. "Today I decided."

"I got high blood pressure!" Bephino yelled. "It's over one hundred on the bottom."

"Stay off the salt," Tony Boy Cafaci barked back, laughing, looking for a laugh from the others.

"Hah, we all got high pressure," Angelo Marandala said, sitting up and arranging his tie. "It's part of our makeup. See my face, how red it is? My pressure goes up every day. It's going up right now, as a matter of fact." Staring at Bephino he said, "Sicilians are born with high blood."

Bephino breathed in, held it for a moment, and then puffed out in disgust at what seemed to be a losing battle.

Rocco continued. "So all the information will be given to you by our good friend Nimo Guiliano here. He works for Gataneo." Nimo, sitting next to Gataneo, nodded to Bephino from across the table. "Nimo has all the details of this contract. When you return, you can pick up the hundred grand, your contract fee, from Nimo." Rocco raised his brows at Bephino as if the matter were settled.

At that point Bephino stood up once again. "Just a minute, Rocco, this is too hard for me to swallow. I want it on record that you made me this offer, and I want a yes or no vote by all the dons at this meetin'. I say I don't go to Europe on this thing. I say you send a button that needs a hundred grand, not a don. I paid my dues. I want a vote for or against my acceptin' this contract."

"Why?" Rocco asked curiously.

"Because you and I made an oath when you took over Morrano's spot, remember, Rocco?" Bephino said, his eyes flashing around the room. "I'm sure all you people remember *bocca e faccia,* the oath from the Old Country that Rocco and I made on Morrano's deathbed, that all our enemies will be both our enemies. Well, now I call for a vote to go or not to go, and then I decide if I accept you all as my enemies, and my enemy will have to be Rocco's enemies, *a capisce?* And if Rocco wants to break the oath, he must cut off his fuckin' finger and give it to me *now, right here!*" Bephino blasted, quickly turning to Ben while addressing the others. "You guys make Sicilian blood seem like piss, so we gotta go by the rules here! The Sicilian rules, the rules we all agreed on many years ago, the fuckin' oath! Ben, be my second!" Bephino barked. "Call the vote."

Ben, caught off guard by Bephino's fast-talking request, jumped up. "I see six dons at this table," Ben said, snapping to it, pointing at each member. "Don Marandala, Don Cafaci, Don Gaeta, Don Tortoricci, Don Dante, and, of course, *Capo di tutti* Don Rocco Boretti. Who's in favor of having Don Dante havin' to take the hit?" Ben asked. All dons except for Bephino raised their hands, quickly voting yes.

"OK, that's it," Ben said, turning to Bephino. "Five out of six votin' yes, Bephino. You must accept," Ben's voice got gentler.

Bephino's eyes stared at Ben, then focused on all the dons as he remembered, not so many years ago, the last Boss of

Bosses, the late Emilio Morrano, saying these words to him: *The same men in this room who voted you Don Dante and embraced you may be your destruction.* Bephino now spoke his thoughts while affixing a stare on Rocco Boretti, "You, the great men that made me a don, now treat me like an errand boy."

Ben swallowed deeply at Bephino's declaration, knowing what was coming. His thoughts raced back in years, when they first met on a hit in New Orleans. He remembered how young Bephino was and how sure of himself he always acted. And how Bephino suggested to kill Don Santoro of New Orleans, and his suggestion that if they had any bad luck, he and Ben would have to kill both Santoro and their own boss, Don Emilio Morrano of Brooklyn. Ben remembered the southern voice of the New Orleans don warning them that if they goofed up it was do or die. . . . And now, so many years later, Ben watched and listened as his friend defied all the New York Mafia bosses, an exercise that seemed unsurvivable.

Bephino maintained his stare at Boretti and then said, "You sleep in the same house I slept in, your children play in the same rooms my children played in, we share life together, Rocco, and now you disrespect me in front of all these men." Rocco looked away. "And now, Rocco, you turn your face to me!" Bephino looked up. With dead calm he declared, "These men are my enemy."

Rocco knew what was coming. He leaned over to Bephino and whispered in his grumbly voice, "Are you sure this is what you want?"

"Are you sure this is what *you* want?" Bephino whispered back in a thick, strained voice.

Rocco said no more. He knew he had to show strength or face humiliation. He got up and moved away from the table, talking closely with his second-in-command.

Gataneo Gaeta looked over at Bephino. "You bit off more than you can chew tonight, *figlio mio.* I see a man committing suicide before my eyes. You will be sorry for this disrespect you brought upon us tonight."

"We'll see about that, you horse-faced bastard," Bephino spat out viciously across the table, moving Gataneo Gaeta's bodyguard to flex his muscles and break his sitting position.

"Sit down, ya fuckin' mutt," Ben growled harshly at Gataneo's man.

Rocco reapproached the group. Quietly he sat back down and placed his left hand across the old wood table, as if to show everyone he was willing to give up a finger to settle himself on the agreement he had once made with Bephino. His second, following closely with a knife, stared at Bephino with what seemed to be the eyes of death, as they prepared for the dismemberment of Rocco's own finger from his left hand. Both Rocco and his second fully expected Bephino to call it off. They had decided in their huddle to call Bephino's bluff.

Bephino nervously glanced around at all the dons as they feverishly watched Rocco displaying his enormous courage. Breaking a long-forgotten oath had obligated him to cut off his own finger and offer it to Bephino, and he was prepared to make good on it. Bephino looked down at Rocco's waiting hand, then glanced over at Ben and whispered, "Is this bastard righty or lefty?"

Ben stared at Bephino in surprise and whispered back, "What the fuck do I know? I think he's righty."

Bephino broke the silence as everyone watched the consequences of breaking *bocca e faccia* for the first time in American Mafia history. Even the children of Rocco and Bephino would be affected by such a curse. Bephino watched Rocco's eyes, then leaned forward. "I want this finger from this hand," Bephino said dryly, pointing to Boretti's righthand index finger.

Rocco's eyes spread wide. He was willing to give up a finger from his left hand to break the oath with Bephino, but not the right. He knew the code allowed for it to be Bephino's choice, but he was hoping that Bephino would not invoke that option. He expected Bephino to back down; surely the man knew that to go through with it would constitute a death move. But Bephino persisted, pointing to the hand and the finger he wanted.

The room erupted with contemptuous murmurs in Italian. "*Neinto rispetto!*" The Sciaccitano was romancing death, he heard another whisper in Italian. But Bephino defied them all, and stared at Rocco expectantly. Rocco looked to his second-in-command, then smiled sneeringly at Bephino and nervously whispered, "Is this really what you want?"

Bephino raised his eyebrows. "It's up to you, Rocco."

Rocco turned to his second, and the second handed him the knife. Rocco Boretti, suddenly realizing it was going to happen, became awkward and clumsy. He had to cut the index finger off his right hand and do it himself, using his left hand, with what seemed to be a butcher's boning knife, and then he had to respectfully present the finger to Bephino immediately after the self-dismemberment, without an outcry or even a grunt. All must be done in true Sicilian style. Rocco and Bephino both knew this was the only way the Sicilian oath they had taken at the time of Emilio Morrano's death would be no more. And everyone in the room, being of Sicilian heritage, understood that.

Bephino's eyes moved from man to man. This was a do-or-die decision, and it had to be enacted without fear or regret of any kind. Appearances were everything.

He still had the option to accept the contract, even though he had broken the oath with Boretti. His thoughts raced for the proper conclusion. He knew that in just a few seconds, Rocco would be handing him his finger. He also knew that everyone in the room would view him as their enemy. But he decided that by accepting Boretti's finger without remorse and then going ahead and accepting the contract, he could buy himself some time. Yes, he could buy time to stay alive, recoup, and make future retaliation decisions on his enemies' behalf. The men around the table were ready to put out an immediate open contract on him, he was certain. Bephino looked across at the dark-skinned Angelo Marandala, and then at the loose, puffy eyes of Tony Boy Cafaci and over to the distraught, cracking face of Gataneo Gaeta. Bephino broke the silence.

"I want you all to know I change my mind, I accept the contract you men have offered me. I leave for Europe tomorrow, and you will have your Count Del Rego!" The men began to grin, nodding their heads in satisfaction at Bephino's wise decision. Bephino kept stern and silent. After a long moment, turning to Boretti, Bephino smiled slowly, and raising his eyebrows, he sat up farther in his chair.

Everyone in the room was expecting him to call it off. He had accepted the contract, so why make enemies? they thought. Rocco had already raised the knife, but after hearing Bephino's acceptance lowered it to the table without hesitation.

Bephino appraised him with cold, wicked eyes. Leaning forward in his chair, he urged, "Come on, Rocco, I'm in a hurry."

Everyone at the table howled with surprise. Rocco widened his eyes, then nodded a deadly grin at Bephino. Bephino had balls, there was no doubt about it. Rocco couldn't help a hint of respect creeping into his glare. Then, *thump,* Rocco chopped; the blade came down hard on a joint. But the finger didn't come off. Rocco paled but remained silent. He then cut crosswise, into the joint, until the seemingly dull blade finally released the finger from his hand. Rocco's second, Tony Mancuso, quickly tied the blood-spouting hand up with a handkerchief. Rocco uttered no sound, but his face was white as milk. He was strong, and everyone in the room sensed it. Rocco Boretti looked at Bephino and silently handed him the two-inch piece of flesh, the cut-off side toward Bephino.

Bephino took it without flinching. "Take this with us," he whispered to Ben. "We're gonna put it in white vinegar." Ben's usual sleek, cobra-style smiling face was finally without expression; his feverish eyes remained serious as he prepared a clean handkerchief in which to store the bloody finger.

Bephino stood up, motioning across the table to Nimo Guiliano. "Give me all my instructions right now, tonight, because I leave for Europe tomorrow to do this filthy job of a soldier. You, the great men of our Mafia, disrespected my rank tonight," Bephino admonished. "You send me off like an errand boy to another world to fill a job that any of our soldiers could have done." Then looking down at Rocco, busy squeezing what was left of his finger in a blood-soaked handkerchief: "I received my pound of flesh, and when I return . . ."

"*If* you return!" large-bellied Tony Boy Cafaci screeched out, pounding his fist on the wood table. "*If* you return . . ."

"I'll return," Bephino replied steadily, "and you look out, Tony. Don't bust that hand, you're gonna need it." At that moment Rocco's man began helping the Boss of Bosses out of his chair and walked him slowly to his car. They left silently, without further comment, probably to the nearest hospital. It was obvious to all in the room that the amount of blood he was losing necessitated speedy medical care.

Bephino and Ben followed shortly. During the drive home conversation was at a low ebb. Finally Ben turned from the wheel and said, "You really took a fucking strong stand there tonight. Are you really leaving for Europe tomorrow?"

"No, I just told them that so they'll think I'm away. I'm going, but when I'm good and ready. Count Del Rego will have to wait. I gotta get my head together. When I do go, I'd like to make a stop in Palermo and whack that fuckin' greaseball Generro Polucci. Imagine that bastard, he calls in a favor to New York for what he done for Don Geno. Geno's been dead for years. His only son is living in California in a fuckin' movie world. He's a fuckin' dopehead mogul in recluse, he lives with wall-to-wall cunt. The guy's got it made in L.A., and a fuckin' million-to-one shot, I wind up with the father's contract! I'm a don—a boss in New York City—and they order me to make the hit. I knew it was an offer I couldn't refuse. I did a lot of damage tonight, calling for Rocco's finger. I made the biggest enemies in the world, but I couldn't swallow it. Did you see their faces? They all knew, they all agreed before we got there tonight. Gaeta stunk of garlic from across the table. That smell drives me wild. Tony Boy kept burping away like a Cafoni—I hate them guys—and I just got finished with my own problems. I was facing two hundred years in Atlanta. By the skin of my teeth, thanks to you, I'm free only one day and these pricks make a decision on my behalf because they heard we took out Caputo and knew I'd be free again. That rotten scumbag Boretti, the two-faced bastard, really thought he was gonna send me on an errand three thousand miles to Europe and I was gonna let him off the hook so easy. I bet his fuckin' stump is hurting him real good! It must be beating like a drum."

"Whata ya gonna do with it? I got it wrapped up."

"I told you, put it in a small jar of white vinegar and hold onto it."

"You're really serious with that vinegar?"

"Yeah, I want it so I can look at it once in a while and remember Rocco, the Boss of Bosses, and how he gave me the finger."

Ben smiled, raising his feverish eyes at Bephino. "Maybe I'll put a fuckin' bay leaf in the jar for atmosphere." They burst into laughter. "Yeah, we're laughing—meanwhile, they're probably making plans to hit us right now. Open contracts all over Brooklyn are out on the street already," Ben said, shaking his head. "We committed suicide in there tonight."

"Relax, they won't try that until Del Rego is dead. They want Del Rego hit first, and with my style; that's why they ordered me to do it. They figured I would make it exotic, something special. They figured I'd go all out tryin' to impress them, like in the old days, when I was a kid. Well, they figured wrong." Bephino thought a moment, then said, "No, Ben, they won't come after us yet. They want Generro Polucci from Sicily to be satisfied. They want the old ties with Palermo to stay intact. It's a matter of Old Blood ties and respect."

"Yeah," Ben grinned, "you sure showed them some respect tonight. You cut the finger off the old man. The council's gonna make a decision on all of our guys for this. It's gonna be a total mess someday. Their eyes had blood in them tonight. You made them look like old douche bags."

"They are old douche bags," Bephino sneered. "They gotta worry about us, because I'm makin' plans for all of them right now! And they know our capabilities, better than anyone. You think them guys are comfortable with this situation?" Bephino asked with a shake of his head. "Pig's ass, they're all confused as shit over this. They don't know if maybe they were better off dealing with someone else on this thing, because it's just a matter of time now before I start pluckin' them out of their beds, one by one. Oh, and Benny, don't panic our people. Keep our soldiers quiet about this. You can tell the Old Blood only, but none of the others. Odds are in our favor. When I return from Europe, they won't know I'm back, and we'll begin knockin' them off. Meanwhile, I'll fly over the ocean, kill some time in Europe, and when they hear I made the hit, they'll think I'm soft, trying to do the right thing for them. When they drop their guard, we kill them all!"

Ben caught a glance at Bephino's face, then said seriously, "Don't call me Benny, Bep! It sounds cheap. Call me Ben, ya fuck." Ben stared. Bephino grinned at Ben's request. "I can't believe that fuckin' Gataneo Gaeta and that fat slob Tony Boy!" Ben laughed, shaking his head. "The balls on them bastards! I'm gonna whack them two out myself. They were the troublemakers. Rocco coulda been swayed by them, Bep. He probably never believed you would break ties with his family. You been with the Morrano family since you were fifteen. Now you're cuttin' fingers off of them. Unbelievable!" Ben exhaled. "Now we gotta kill them all."

Bephino looked thoughtfully at Ben but did not speak. After a while he said, "Well, tomorrow I'm going down to my farm, and when I'm good and ready I'll go to Europe and make the hit. I gotta get in the right mood for that shit. I'm gettin' old. Right now, I wanna see my cows."

Ben smiled. "See your cows! You're nuts, you know that? With all this shit in front of us, he wants to see his cows!"

Bephino smiled. "Yeah, I got nice white cows."

2

JANUARY 28, 1977, 2:00 P.M.

EL COVALLO RANCH, LITTLE FALLS, SOUTH CAROLINA

"Whata ya doin'?" Ben's voice asked over the phone. "How's the cows?"

"They're OK," Bephino chuckled.

"Whata ya doin'?" Ben asked again.

"I'm sittin' around by the pool, enjoyin' the beautiful atmosphere and cheekin' my blood pressure."

"Ain't ya supposed to go do that thing?"

"Yeah, when I'm ready. Right now, I'm runnin' 180 over 120. I'm still boilin'. When I calm down to about 104 over 90, then I'll go do it. It's beautiful over here. I'm relaxin' and waitin' for my passport to be made up. Oh yeah, Ben, I'll tell ya the name of the guy I'm travelin' with before I leave."

Ben became quiet. After a moment he asked, "Are you feelin' all right, Bep? Don't you think we should go do this thing together?"

"Nah, I'm fine, how about you? Are you all right?" Bephino giggled.

Ben became quiet again. It didn't sound like Bephino, he thought, he sounded kind of upset and trying to hide it. "How's Dana and the kids?" Ben asked.

"They're all fine, but Mrs. Roselli, our housekeeper, she's got bad hemorrhoids and Joey D's feet are botherin' him." Joey ("Joey D") Desporto, also known as Sabu, was a six-foot-tall, dark-skinned, prematurely graying man with a small, insecure chin and deep, beady eyes. Although he wasn't considered Old Blood, Joey D was a loyal soldier. "Otherwise," Bephino continued, "everybody's OK." Bephino laughed again. "I'm babysittin' for Mrs. Roselli and Joey D. Would you believe that, Ben? Joey D's got the gout and she's got inflamed hemorrhoids. They're both walkin' around like fuckin' zombies. This farm looks like a rest home."

Ben began to laugh a little. "That fuckin' Joey D is useless, ain't he? He's always got some kinda problem. He should be takin' care of you. Instead, you're takin' care of him, the worthless bastard," Ben mumbled.

"That's the way life goes, Ben. Things pop up. There's a surprise every day for us, you know that. You saw it yourself two weeks ago with them droopy-eyed bastards."

"Bephino, I know we can't talk too much on the house line, but I'm comin' with you. We'll go on that vacation together. You need company, and I need a vacation."

Bephino smiled. "You're beautiful, Ben! I'm grateful, but forget it. You got the business to look out for. We got about forty sandwich makers to keep busy. We're gonna need them guys later in the year."

"Yeah, I know, but Monkey, Pauli, and Mikey can look out for the store while we're away."

"Ben, please, I gotta go on vacation alone. I knew you were gonna ask to come, so this is not a surprise to me. Please, forget it, OK? Alan Stone was told today he deals only with you on all our Vegas interests. And you deal with Fat Arty, our banker. Keep things nice and legal, so we don't have problems. Make sure all our people pay their taxes."

"Hey, Bep," Ben said with a chuckle, "you want another surprise? I got a good one for you. This one will shock you good. But you gotta come to New York for this. We'll go eat scungilli like old times on Mott Street, and then we'll go to the fights over at St. Nick's Arena. I gotta big surprise for you."

Bephino thought for a while, then in a cautious tone said, "OK, I need a good surprise, but I can't stay long; I gotta leave in a few days. Pick me up at Newark tomorrow. I'll take the noon flight; it'll get me in at 1:40."

"OK, I'll be waitin' for you."

"Boy, these scungilli are hot," Ben laughed the next evening. "I ordered everybody's appetizer with the hot sauce," he grinned, reaching for the ice water. "So tomorrow, you're all gonna burn good!"

"Whata ya crazy, all with the hot sauce?" Monkey yelled. "I got ulcers. We ain't got the stomachs we had years ago. This hot stuff destroys me for two days."

"Remember how Alley Oop used to love the linguine fini with the thick, extra-hot sauce, smothered with scungilli and calamari? He even used to put the black mussels on top, like a jumpor'ta, remember, Bepy?" Crazy Mikey said. Mike Lastrano was a three-time-divorced Sicilian American from Bensonhurst. As a kid, he beat his own father with a stickball bat, thus becoming known as Crazy Mikey. At forty-seven, he remained a deadly force in the Menesiero family, powerful, handsome, with black curly hair, cupid lips, piercing black eyes, and a strong, square, slightly dimpled chin.

"How could I forget?" Bephino sighed. "I remember everything about Alley Oop. I'll never forget the Oop. It's like yesterday when I think of him. Just like yesterday."

Afredo ("Ally Oop") Opolito had once lived in Bay Ridge, Brooklyn. Born in Trevelina, Sicily, he'd been a large-boned gorilla of a man whom everyone in the Mob admired. The Oop had been killed years back while he and Ben were attempting to fill a contract out on the West Coast. The first of the Old Blood to die, he lived on in the minds of his friends.

Ben lowered his head. He kept eating quietly as he listened to the boys bring up old memories of Alley Oop.

"Wait till you see what we discovered, Bepy. You're gonna shit when you see it," Mikey said, busily chewing on a raw clam.

"I hope it's good, because I need a coupla laughs in my life. I just finished a trial, I been disrespected by the board, and when I got back home to my farm, some pig-faced cowboy shot a couple of my breeding bulls. My housekeeper, Mrs. Roselli, is sick, she shuffles around holdin' her ass, and Joey D is walkin' around like the bride of Frankenstein. My wife claims she misses New York, and my kids are off going around with Hollywood people. I'm really having a fuckin' time this year. I'm glad I came to New York. You guys make me feel good again. Too bad Alan Stone couldn't be in New York today. I called him last night and asked him to come, but he's busy with the engineers on the new wing they're adding to the hotel. They're putting sprinklers in the entire hotel now, since the fire at the Strand.

"Yeah, guys," Bephino said after a brief pause, "Old Blood like us always feel good when we're together."

"Old Blood is Old Blood," Monkey said, grabbing at the platter of half shells. "Ay, the clams is the only thing that don't have that hot sauce," he whined, looking at Ben.

"Where's Little Pauli, how come he's not here tonight?" Bephino asked, twirling his fork in a plate of linguine. Pauli ("Little Pauli") Segura had been a Menesiero soldier since 1948. Now forty-seven and still unmarried, he was smooth faced and poignant looking. At six-foot-two, he wore his black, straight hair flat back and always smiled softly while arranging to be an indulging partner in marital relations—usually other people's marital relations.

"He's got a date with that Johnny Romano's wife. Remember that guy, Romano? The guy who flys the pigeons on 14th Avenue? Pauli's had his eye on Romano's wife for a long time. She's some beauty. Romano left for a hunting trip, so Pauli's gonna pork the wife for a few days."

"I hope Pauli's careful. If I remember right, Romano gets a little *pazzo* when it comes to her," Bephino said, raising his brow at Mikey.

"Yeah, but Pauli's smooth as silk," Mikey laughed. "He'll fuck her so gentle, Romano will never know she's been touched."

Turning to Ben, Mike asked, "What time we gotta be at the fights?"

"Nine o'clock," Ben answered, chewing on a large shrimp.

Later that evening, everyone was seated at St. Nick's Arena, waiting for the first match to start. The crowd was excited and talking loudly when the bell for the first round sounded.

"You know, this fight is bein' televised." Monkey raised his voice over the crowd's roar.

"Yeah, I saw the sign when we entered. It's on channel 3," Bephino answered.

Halfway through the third bout, Bephino asked, "Where's the surprise you guys talked about?"

"It's next up," Ben smiled. "The next fight on the card."

Bephino looked down at his program and read the names of the fighters for the next bout—Vernon Johnson versus Alley Boy Murphy. He looked up and smiled. "Whata you guys, nuts or what? Johnson versus Murphy sounds like two people I could never have an interest in."

"You wanna bet?" Monkey asked with a grin.

Bephino's eyes focused down at the card again. "Are we talking about the same match, Johnson versus Murphy?"

"Yep," Monkey said. "A nigger against a white guy."

Bephino shook his head in confusion. He leaned over to Ben. "What's going on? How could a Johnson or Murphy concern me?"

"You'll see. It concerns all of us," Ben shrugged, curling his lips. A few minutes later the third bout ended.

The fourth match of the evening, a light heavyweight bout, was about ready to start. The fighters were making their way down the isle. The fighter wearing the red robe was a black guy, Vernon Johnson, and the other fighter in blue was white, Alley Boy Murphy. Both fighters climbed into the ring.

Bephino focused on both of them. Ben, Monkey, and Mikey's eyes zeroed in on Bephino. Bephino just stared straight ahead and watched quietly as the ring announcer introduced the fighters. He looked up and down at the black fighter, then his eyes scanned back to the white boy. As he looked him up and down his eyes kept focusing on Murphy, then slowly moved over to his three friends. "Where'd he come from?" he asked dryly. Not waiting for a reply, Bephino said, "This guy, Alley Boy Murphy, he looks just like Alley Oop."

Ben smiled. "Last week we went to collect a few markers at the Eastside Gym on Third Avenue, and this kid, Murphy, was working out on the heavy bag when we spotted him. He's a fuckin' duplicate of his father."

Bephino's eyes were locked back on Murphy. "Whata ya mean, his father? Are you telling me he's Alley Oop's son?"

"That's right. That kid's Alley Oop's boy."

"How could you be so sure?" Bephino asked sharply.

"Does he look like Alley Oop?" Ben asked.

"Yeah, he's Alley Oop all the way," Bephino admitted.

"Well, when you see the mother later, you'll be one hundred percent sure, like us. Alley had a goomada we never knew about—but the fight's starting, we'll talk later," Ben said. "Let's see what this kid's got in him, then we'll take him home and you can meet his mother. You know her," Ben grinned.

The bell rang and both fighters met in the middle of the ring. Johnson hit Murphy two hard lefts, then followed up with a right, then another left. Johnson backed up and began to showboat, winding up with a bolo punch. Murphy, a slow, sluggish fighter, his nose already bleeding from the two lefts that had caught him cold, stepped in awkwardly and clinched. While clinching, he put his left arm around Johnson's neck and began pounding with his right hand. The referee yelled break, but Murphy held on and kept punching. The more Johnson tried to back up and break away, the more Murphy kept stepping into Johnson in a grossly awkward style and hammering away at his head. Suddenly Johnson just fell to the floor facedown, his body jumping with muscle spasms. Alley Boy stood over Johnson, and the referee shouted for him to return to his corner. The referee then counted Johnson out. Murphy won in the first round.

"He's like his father!" Monkey yelled, "a fuckin' steam-roller."

"The kid is good but needs a lot of polishing," Ben said excitedly. "He needs a lot of work, he's green." Then, with a chuckle playing on his cobra smile, he yelped, "What a fuckin' puncher! Holy Christ, can he hit!"

"Is that Alley Oop's son or what?" Mikey yelled out to Bephino.

"He sure looks like him. He fights like the Oop—same style: slow, sluggish, and deadly, like a steamroller."

"Hey, Bep," Ben laughed again. "Get ready to meet Alley Oop's old girlfriend, the kid's mother. Wait'll ya see her—that's the finale, you're gonna be shocked. We'll leave soon as the kid's showered and ready to go home." Ben got up. "I'll be back in a little while. I'm gonna go wait for him in his dressing room."

Monkey slid over next to Bephino. "You're surprised, hah, Bep! We were too. We couldn't believe our eyes when we saw him. We found out his address, and when we went to his house to meet his mother, we couldn't believe who she was. You're gonna be shocked."

"Who is she?" Bephino asked, looking up at Monkey.

"You'll see later. I don't wanna spoil it for you. She's expecting us for coffee and cake."

Bephino smiled. "I can't believe this! Alley Oop's son! Does the kid know his father was Alley? What's with the name Murphy?"

"Unless his mother told him his father was a Sicilian, he sure acts like an Irishman. We didn't say anything," Monkey said. "We wanted you to see him first. We weren't sure how you'd wanna handle this. I wonder if he knows he's got an Italian grandmother still living in Bay Ridge," Monkey said. "If he don't know, he's gotta be told, right?"

Bephino stared, deep in thought over the unbelievable words he was hearing.

"Alley Oop's mother will go nuts over this kid," Mikey interrupted, "and he's got plenty of Alley's fortune from our stock deal comin' to him if he's the son, right?" Mikey looked over at Bepy and Monkey.

"Yeah, but don't mention those kinda things yet. Don't fuck up his mind with money talk. Let's see the kinda kid he is first," Bephino warned. "The kid might be nuts, for all we know."

About a half hour later, Ben returned with Alley Boy Murphy. They were pushing their way through the crowd and down the aisles.

"Look at his shape. Look at the fuckin' head on that kid. It's like a coconut, like Alley Oop's head," Monkey laughed. "His legs are like two tree trunks. His mother told us even his cock is like Alley Oop's," Monkey hooted. "He's a dupe of his father."

Bephino grinned. "His mother said that about his dick?"

"Yeah, she sure did."

"Christ, this sure is a surprise to me." Bephino puffed on his cigar. "Wait till I tell Dana and the kids about this. They'll crack up over this. A million-to-one shot, and we win again. The son of Alley Oop shows up sixteen years after conception, like a fuckin' dream," Bephino laughed.

"Yeah, amazin'; like the son of King Kong, the giant ape returns," Mikey said.

Later that evening, a four-door black sedan pulled up to 462 Livingston Street, a downtown Brooklyn tenement house. Everyone in the car was quiet except Ben, who chattered constantly into Alley Boy's ear. "You did good tonight, kid, but you take too many punches. You're too slow. Practice movin' around; you're too slow. And your name, Murphy, sounds bad. You need a respected name, something not so, so . . . Murphyish."

"I could take punches, it don't bother me, and I like my name. My grandfather's name is Murphy," Alley Boy responded.

"Oh yeah, you could take punches, look at your nose. It's got a fuckin' bandage over it like a shadow roll on a racehorse. You bled. The fuckin' coon hit you hard, he caught you two good raps. You never wanna get hit so much before you take them out. You'll get punchy. Block, keep your left up, block them punches. Then knock their fuckin' heads off. Use your brains," Ben scolded the heavyset boy. "Use your brains, ya big fuck, then your brawn!" Ben reiterated. "How old are you?" Ben huffed.

"I'm gonna be seventeen," the boy grinned.

Bephino, puffing softly on a cigar, watched and listened quietly at Ben's enthusiasm over the boy.

"Us Irish can take a punch. I'm Irish, you know," the kid said, smiling over Ben's obvious interest in him.

Everyone in the car exchanged glances. Monkey proceeded to park the car. Bephino shrugged at Ben, then shook his head in thought. After a long drag on his thick cigar he said sharply, "Let's meet your mother, kid, and see just how Irish you really are." Bephino raised his eyebrows directly at Alley Boy.

A few moments later, they were in the apartment, being greeted by Murphy's mother. Moderately heavyset, she was busty but neat, a pretty-faced woman, smelling heavily of cheap perfume. Her hair was graying prematurely. She seemed to be in her early forties.

Bephino removed his coat and fedora. As the woman took them she smiled broadly at him. His eyes nonchalantly looked her up and down as he tried to remember where he knew her from. The other men didn't speak. They let nature take its course and Bephino lead the way.

"You don't remember me, do you?" she asked, continuing to smile at Bephino. "I got a lot heavier since the last time we saw each other," she said, pulling her sweater down over her bosom. Grinning shyly, she said, "We're both a lot older, aren't we, Bephino?"

Bephino's eyes focused on her grayish-colored hair; he couldn't see too well in the dimly lit apartment. Speaking through his cigar, he answered while removing it from his lips, "I know . . . I know you, I'm sure of that, but from where?" She continued to grin over his thought; then, while he gazed at her extremely large breasts, he suddenly recalled a scene from twenty-five years earlier. His visions were of his partner and old friend, Red—that's right, she'd been Red's secretary at the Hero company! She was the girl he called Big Tits. She was really something, that Big Tits, Bephino remembered, raising his hand to his chin. Red used to pay her two hundred bucks a week because he loved the way she sucked cock and because her beautiful big tits were so young and firm. Bephino stared for a moment, amused at the ordeal confronting him as he remembered the time he fired her and then found her late one night going through the files in the office. Oh yeah, Bephino thought slyly to himself, I remember you . . . You sucked me off that night and hung on until my legs began to tremble; and then you sucked Alley Oop off—but how did you bear Alley's child? You only blew him one time. Bephino pondered, rubbed his forehead, and then looked into her brown eyes. "You're Red's old girlfriend, aren't you?" he asked, smiling dryly at her.

"I guess you could say that," she replied, her face reddening with embarrassment as she realized he was confirming their last meeting. "But the fact is I was Alley Oop's girl years after I was Red's girl," she said, defending her past and shrugging shyly as the men stood listening to her.

Bephino grinned, amused at her defensiveness. "Tell me about that," Bephino said, turning to Alley Boy. "I'd like to hear how this fine young man we saw fight tonight came to be."

"Oh my gosh! With all this company, I forgot to ask my son if he won! How did you do, honey?" she said, turning to her boy.

Alley Boy grinned. "Piece of cake. I put the nigger's lights out in the first round."

"I still think he should stop fighting, it's too dangerous!" she said, turning back to Bephino. "Let's sit in the kitchen," she suggested, lowering her voice. "Is it OK if your friends and my son sit in the living room? I can tell you the whole story much better if we're alone."

"Sure." Bephino motioned to his friends.

"Make some drinks, Alley," the boy's mother yelled to him. Then to Bephino she asked, "How about a cup of coffee?"

"Sure," Bephino nodded, "coffee is fine."

"I guess you remember my name is Paula Murphy. But then again, you always called me Big Tits." She laughed, holding her hand to her mouth.

"I remember your name, Paula. I signed your check a few times. I'll call you Paula from now on," Bephino said, accepting a cup of coffee and sliding it toward himself.

"You take sugar and cream?"

"No, this is fine, I'm drinking it black these days, thank you."

After a restless moment, she looked at him, apparently bracing herself for the words she finally spoke. "Remember that night I did you and Alley Oop up in the office?"

"Yes, as a matter of fact, I do remember that night," Bephino whispered with a serious look. "The last words I heard was you saying, 'It's ugly,' and then you began to choke and gag on Alley Oop. So where did the kid come from?"

Paula glanced toward the kitchen's entrance, then lowered her voice and her eyes. "That night Alley Oop impressed me very, very much," she said in a parched voice. "You know, after I got to know the guy, I sorta . . . well, got turned on to him. I mean, the guy had something nobody had. That evening before he left, he asked me for my phone number, and I gave it to him only if he promised never to tell anyone that I was seeing him. I felt like a freak, going for a guy with a thing so big." She shyly grinned up at the ceiling at her own candid words. After a pause she continued. "I wanted him from time to time, but I didn't want to be seen with him."

Paula watched Bephino lower his eyes and slowly rub his chin as he considered her words. When he raised his eyes to her she went on. "So for several years, up until he got killed in California, I saw him from time to time. What he did to me no man ever did, and my son is the product of that affair. I never came to you, Bephino, because I was afraid after what I heard you and Alley had done to Red and Johnny Mac. So I decided to name my son Alley Clarence Murphy, after my dad. Even though Alley Oop's his father, I kept him Irish. My father is old; he and I grew him up the best we could."

Bephino shrugged, then spoke. "The kid looks exactly like

his father. He's all Italian, he don't look a bit Irish, but he thinks he's Irish." Bephino nodded. "And that's a shame, Paula; the boy's a Sicilian. He should know this, and be proud that he's a Sicilian. He's my best friend's son. You must realize we have great feelings for this boy. The kid thinks he's Irish," Bephino laughed, "and he acts so proud of it! That's not right," Bephino said, lowering his voice and repeatedly shaking his head.

"Well, he's half Irish, he is Irish," Paula responded, raising her brows at Bephino, trying her best to convince him.

Bephino frowned. "He's a Sicilian. He's gotta be told his father was from Sicily," Bephino said firmly, "and his name's gotta be changed right away. I know Alley Oop would want that done. Right away, tomorrow," Bephino insisted.

"But . . ."

Bephino interrupted. "Look, Paula, I'll take care of all the expenses and legal details, and I'll even tell the boy who he really is, so he don't think he's an Irish Murphy all his life. He's an Opolito, Alley Oop's son." Bephino was silent for a moment. Then he asked, "How do you make a living these days?"

"I'm a waitress at Chickford's."

"How much do you earn?"

"About a hundred forty a week."

"See, we were overpaying you twenty years ago. Two hundred bucks, remember?" he smiled.

"Yeah, but I was really worth it in those days," she grinned back at him.

"The kid, what does he do?"

"He works in the fruit store around the block. He loads and unloads trucks."

"A fruit store!"

"Yeah, it's a big place, open all night."

"His father used to work in a fruit store when he was a kid. Paula . . . Look, Paula, this kid, how come he's boxing? Where did he get that idea, from his Irish grandfather?" Bephino asked.

"My father had nothing to do with it. That's his dream. He

wants to be a champ. He tells everybody. He tells his grandpa he's gonna be a real Irish champ."

"Look, Paula, this kid is misguided with this Irish stuff. He's gonna be an Italian champ. His father was pure Sicilian. His great-grandfather's balls came from Palermo, not Dublin. He's Italian, so forget the Irish stuff, OK?"

"OK," she groaned finally in a choked-up voice, putting her head down.

"All right, now," Bephino huffed. "I hope we understand each other. I'm gonna talk to this kid very seriously and very fatherly in a moment. I hope he knows the meaning of respect."

"He's a good boy, like his father," she smiled.

"That's what I'm afraid of," Bephino scowled. "If he's like his father, he's liable to throw us all out of the fuckin' kitchen window tonight. Look, Paula, I want you to quit your job. You're back on our payroll. Starting tomorrow, you're back up to two hundred bucks a week." With a warm smile, he said, "You're still worth the two hundred."

"What do I do for it?" she smiled back at him.

"Nothing. Stay home and feed this kid steak. Do only what Ben tells you to. Ben will be his personal guardian and his fight manager. He will also pay your salary every week. Ben calls all the shots from now on. He's the man. Do what we expect, and you and the kid will be taken care of for life."

Paula looked startled, then forced a smile. "In other words, Ben's our Godfather," she murmured.

"I guess you could call him that," Bephino replied. "He's gonna look after you both. Ben's gonna see that this kid gets his chance in life."

"Isn't this Ben the guy who got Alley killed in California?"

"Look, Paula, Ben's a great guy, he loved Alley Oop. He's a self-made man. He didn't get there for his mistakes. We got respect for him, and we don't question each other's errors. Alley got a bad break. We're in a dangerous business. Ben will bring this boy along, so relax. The kid's young, he's probably got about six more years of hard training to get a title fight. Ben likes the kid, I could tell, and we will be instrumental and pave the way for his championship opportunities. If he proves worthy of a shot at the title, he'll get one; if not, then we'll see. Your job is to take care of him. He can keep his job at the fruit store until Ben decides otherwise. Now, call your son in here so I can tell him who he really is, and ask Ben to come in also."

Paula swallowed hard, then got up and walked awkwardly toward the living room. She returned with Alley Boy and Ben in tow.

"Have a seat, gentlemen," Bephino said sharply, directing the young, powerful man to sit up close. Their eyes for the first time officially and seriously met. The boy glared as he sat down, center stage. He looked strangely at Bephino, then nervously crossed his thick legs, dumping one across the other awkwardly.

Bephino, caught up in a moment of emotion, remained quiet. Ben watched Bephino scan the boy and sensed Bephino's feelings over the son of his lost friend. Ben asked Paula for a cup of coffee. She was happy to hear a request, any distraction from her concern over what Bephino was about to say.

She began to pour. "Would you like another cup, Bephino?" she asked softly, respectfully.

"No, thank you, Paula," he answered, not taking his eyes from Alley Boy.

Alley Boy grinned uncomfortably. "How come he keeps staring at me?" he asked, looking to his mother for an explanation.

"He has to tell you something, Alley Boy," she murmured, "and listen to this man very carefully, because what he has to say is the truth and things that you should know."

"I heard him say when we first walked in that he wanted to know how I came about. Is this guy my father?" Alley asked sheepishly, the big, strong ox of a boy blushing at his own words.

"No, I'm not your father," Bephino answered. "But I'm the next-best thing. Your father and me were the very best of friends. The very, very best. We were such good friends that I still cry for him. And I'm a tough guy, Alley Boy; believe me, son, I'm the original tough guy from Brooklyn. Still, I often find myself crying for your father. So that makes you and me close, very close. Your father's name was Alley Opolito. He was born in Trevelina, Sicily. Do you know where Sicily is?" Bephino asked with a grin.

"It's in Europe, ain't it?"

"Yeah, it's an island, part of Italy, a beautiful island. And very beautiful people live there, and they're Italians, not Irish."

Ben grinned and rolled his sleepy-looking eyes at Paula when he heard very beautiful people mentioned.

"Now, your real name is Alley Opolito, Jr. That's your real name, not Alley Murphy. That's your mother's name before she met your father. Do you understand me, son? They tagged you with the name Murphy by mistake."

The boy quickly looked over to his mother for confirmation. She nodded, holding a handkerchief to her nose.

"You are the exact image of a very great man. Your father was kind, generous, and everyone loved him. He was also a very fearless man. He was a man that could virtually kill if someone hurt his family or loved ones. Believe me, son, your father was a respected person."

Paula began shaking her head emotionally, still holding the handkerchief to her now tearing face. "Your father looked exactly like you, Alley, exactly like you," she said in a choked voice.

"So now," Bephino said, "what we gotta do right away is change your name the way it's supposed to be—Alley Opolito, Jr., not Murphy. You're not Irish; you're Sicilian, like your father. Remember that your blood is Sicilian and always be proud of that," Bephino said, looking directly at the boy. "Your mother does not have to work at the coffee shop anymore. Her only job is to take care of the house and you. If you wanna be a fighter and a champ, you gotta train hard and eat right. And not too many broads, OK?" Bephino winked at the kid. "Ben, here, is gonna be your closest friend. He's also my closest friend. He was with your father when he died. Ben will see to it that you and your mother have what you need. If you prove to us you are worthy of our interest and respect, then we will do what we're supposed to do for you. Now, you have a grandmother, plus two wacky aunts. They live over in Bay Ridge. Your father loved his mother and sisters, and they loved him. When they see you, they're gonna be so happy. They'll probably all shit their pants."

The kid burst out laughing, covering his mouth with his hand. His young, pimpled, pitted face was virtually that of Alley Oop as a teenager. Bephino just stared, then in a hoarse voice said, "You also have a lot of other friends that loved your father, like me and Ben, my wife and my children, and all the boys in our crowd. You have an uncle in Las Vegas. He's a Jew. His name is Alan Stone. He loved your father, and when he sees you he's also gonna shit and probably will start mumbling funny words in Jewish. Mr. Stone owns a large hotel in Vegas; he's our partner and you will meet him soon. He'll probably spoil you rotten. Now keep working hard in the fruit store. Train hard, and if you do a good job we'll send you to the El Banco Hotel in Las Vegas for a vacation, OK? As a matter of fact, we'll make you famous. We'll start a training camp in the hotel if you're a proven fighter, a good proven fighter—so you got good things to work for," Bephino smiled.

Alley looked up at his mother, who was awash in tears of joy at the attentiveness, the caring, being extended to them.

"Now, I gotta go away for a while," Bephino said. "When I come back from this trip, I'll be checking to see if you're doing the right thing. Ben will call you a few times a week, and he'll come over to see you once in a while. He'll arrange for a good, experienced trainer. The guy you got now can stay and pick up towels—you need someone who trains winners. Ben has no children of his own, so he'll enjoy working with Alley Oop's son." Bephino's eyes met Ben's in confirmation. "If you wanna be champ, you got a long way to go, you gotta do that part yourself. I saw you fight tonight; you got your father's punch, but you need a style to be a classy boxer. And Ben will see that you get a style and the proper trainer, and fights with the proper opponents, and the proper equipment—right, Ben?"

"You're right," Ben said. "If this kid does the right thing, he gets the royal treatment. If he fucks up, he gets the fruit store."

"I don't want the fruit store," Alley quickly interjected. "I hate it, I only do it for the money."

"OK, then, I'll see you when I return. Here's five hundred bucks for the both of you. Buy yourselves a hat each," Bephino said as he rose from the table.

Alley Boy's eyes lit up. When he looked up at his mother, he found her smiling gratefully at Bepy and Ben.

Ben reached into his pocket and counted out another five hundred. "Yeah, buy yourselves two hats each," he chuckled, and he slapped the money on the table.

"I'll take my coat now," Bephino said. "Our lawyers will contact you to start the name change. And Paula, explain to your father that this fine young man had a father, so he understands, OK?" She nodded.

"Oh, yeah, Paula," Ben said, "give me your phone number again, for the lawyers and in case I gotta call over here." Everyone hugged and embraced.

On the way home in the car, Bephino spoke to his friends. "I can't believe what I saw tonight—Alley Oop's boy!" Turning to Ben, Bephino said, "We get another chance! Take good care of them, give them whatever they need. If she plays it straight with us, she'll get more, but for now she gets two hundred a week. Take it out of the Hero shops' account. Put her on the payroll like she's a cashier, OK, Monkey?"

"Sure, Bep, that's two families we support now: Red's wife, Norma, and her kids, and now Alley Oop's Paula."

"That's good," Bephino said with a grin. "It's OK, we're doing the right thing. Ben, make the kid a winner," he nudged. "Get him the best trainer in New York. I don't wanna listen to excuses, no purple prose, no stories, *a capisce?*"

"I'll do my best," Ben nodded in agreement.

3

FEBRUARY 3, 1977, 6:00 P.M.

PAN AM FLIGHT 29

The giant silver-and-blue 747 roared out of Kennedy Airport heading for Europe. Bephino Menesiero sat quietly alone, sipping a vermouth on the rocks and thinking of Dana. Even now, at forty-four, his green-eyed, black-haired, oval-faced wife was a beauty. Bephino's childhood sweatheart, she had grown into a woman of genuine desires, a wife and mother above all else. She had stood by Bephino through it all—a life of riches combined with the anguish of a Mafia wife. She had fought with all she had to keep her family alive and together.

Bephino recalled how before his departure she had argued over his leaving for such an undetermined length of time and to a location he was unable to speak about. The strain in her voice was still clear in his mind. She'd argued sharply, just as she had at eighteen: "What the hell is this! Another fishing trip!" she'd asked. "Are you still going after Moby Dick, or are you taking some chippy to Mexico?" Bephino smiled over these protestations as he rubbed his newly grown mustache and considered his beloved's temper and style. Always honest, and as tough as she pretended to be, she still hurt so very easily. He smiled to himself again at Dana still questioning him as she did in the old days, when they were both young and newly married.

"Is this another one of those fishing trips," she'd asked, "that the whole world shouldn't know about?"

"That's right, Dana," he'd replied. "This is another one of those trips. I'm really sorry, I didn't think I would ever have to travel without you again. It's business, important business."

He'd kissed her beautiful oval face good-bye, and reminded her yet again to send his love to their children, despite the fact that he'd just phoned them at their respective places in California and Florida moments before. Then he hugged Mrs. Roselli, now nearly recovered from her hemorrhoids, and instructed his friend Joey D on what to do while he was away. Joey D had embraced him and whispered, "Hurry back. My head gets fucked up when you're away. I get lonely without you on this farm."

"Watch the football games and take care of the women," Bephino had whispered back, "and keep the ranch hands working."

Then, while walking out of the house to his waiting car, Bephino had turned to Dana and Joey D. "For any reason you need anything, just contact Ben. He will know all there is to know, and he will take care of whatever has to be taken care of." Bephino had winked confidently at Dana, Mrs. Roselli, and Joey D. Waving good-bye, he'd stood silent for a moment. His eyes gently focused on Dana. She detected something different about this trip; he seemed unsure and uneasy. Without speaking another word, his eyes sent the final message: *I love you, Dana.*

I love you, too, Bepy, her eyes softly replied to him.

The wailing roar of the plane's jet engines began to ease from its long climb into the heavens like a humpback whale. He smiled as he realized how close the 747 was to what Dana had had in mind—a flying, spread-eagled Moby Dick, moving gracefully to its destiny.

"Would you like another drink, sir?" the flight attendant asked brightly. "You'll be having champagne shortly, and dinner a while after that."

"I'll take another vermouth with ice, please," Bephino replied, casually reopening the envelope Nimo Guiliano had given to him with personal information on the man he was traveling so far to kill. Information he had already read several times before. Sitting back, he unbuckled his seat belt and studied the pertinent details of the contract.

Several hours later he was awakened by the voice of the captain announcing their final approach to Vienna. "It is 11:00 A.M. in Austria," the captain said. "The weather is thirty-three degrees Fahrenheit, or one degree Celsius, and clear. We enjoyed having you with us and hope you have a wonderful stay in Europe. All passengers are required to report to customs with their travel cards, passports, and baggage. Please have your passports and other immigration records available so that you may be processed without delay. It was a pleasure to serve you, and we hope you'll travel with us soon again."

After the process of luggage retrieval and a longer-than-usual customs check, Bephino hired a cab and went directly to his hotel, the Vienna Victorian, an exclusive seventeenth-century chalet-type building set high in the snow-capped mountains and surrounded by thick green pines. Several castlelike estates, set far apart from one another amid cliffs and dense forest, could be glimpsed from the hotel. One of these estates belonged to Count Phillipo Del Rego and his wife, Countess Lucia Del Rego. According to Bephino's information sheet on them, the countess was an ex-starlet from Milano and her husband a count from Rome. Generro Polucci, the old don from Sicily, had given the information to America in great detail, even down to the color and breed of the Del Rego estate's dogs. The estate was nestled somewhere in a snow-covered clearing, surrounded by thick black pines, not far from the Vienna Victorian hotel.

It was 3:30 P.M. and getting very cold as the winds began to howl. Bephino was in his suite sipping hot chocolate brought to him by a room-service valet.

"Mr. Charles!" the valet called to him in English across the large living room from the bedroom. Bephino released the sheer curtain he'd been holding aside at the terrace's french doors, as he'd stared into the distance at beautiful Vienna, wondering what the hell he was doing there anyway. Bephino turned to the voice of the valet and lowered his cup to a silver tray resting on a nearby serving cart. Hearing the name *Charles* directed at him and in such an unfamiliar accent still sounded strange, and his thoughts quickly turned to the valet calling for his attention. The guy spoke excellent English for an Austrian, he thought, as he walked toward the bedroom. Such a strange name, Charles, for a Sicilian like me from Brooklyn, he mused, but the name had come with the only passport made available to him by Jerry Hoy the counterfeiter in Philadelphia. Everyone in New York expected him to be traveling as Bephino Dante or Bephino Menesiero. Only Ben knew the truth. Bephino had thus molded his plan to travel as Mr. Joseph Charles, a land developer from Pittsburgh.

Bephino entered the bedroom, and the valet, bending over into the fireplace, looked up. "Is there anything else I can do for you, sir?" he asked while turning a thick log and stirring the newly lit fireplace. "It will fire up briskly after a while," he said, "and the hotel's woodsman will keep your wood closet full each day in both your living parlor and bedroom." Bephino handed the long-nosed valet ten U.S. dollars and thanked him for his services.

As the valet began to depart from the suite, Bephino had a second thought. "Excuse me, friend," he called out.

"Yes, sir," the valet promptly answered in a firm, crisp voice, nearly snapping to attention. "Can I be of further help, sir?"

"Yes, maybe you can tell me a little about the area." Bephino motioned and walked back toward the french doors.

The valet closely followed. Opening the doors to the balcony and speaking above the strong wind, Bephino asked, "Tell me, who owns those beautiful hilltop mansions I see hidden among the trees?" Stepping out on the balcony and gasping from the strong winds blowing at him, the valet said, "The villa you see far off to the left belongs to Baron Eli Styer, from München." Trying to keep his voice above the wind, the valet continued. "The one high up over there on the mountain is also belonging to a baron from Deutschland. I believe his name is Friedrich von Mueland . . . and that one over there to our left with the gray slate roof is belonging to the Count Phillipo Del Rego. He's from Italia, and his wife, the countess, was an Italian movie star before she married. The villa directly below us belongs to the owner of this hotel, Mrs. Helga Cohen. She rents it out; she's originally from Russia," the valet added, holding his velvet-vested jacket close to his chest in an attempt to keep warm. "If we move to the other side of your suite, sir, I can tell you who . . ."

Bephino, holding the doors from the wind's grasp, interrupted, waving him inside and closing the doors. "No," he said, "that's fine; it's getting too cold to stay out there. I was just curious about those lovely estates surrounding this side of the hotel. Thank you, that will be all," he said, handing the valet another ten dollars.

"If you need any further help, sir, just call down. My name is Klaus Varick."

"You speak English very, very well. Where did you learn it?" Bephino asked.

"I studied at the University of Kent in Great Britain for four years. I have two degrees in British business and two in psychology, sir," the pointy-nosed valet exclaimed with a broad grin.

Bephino raised his brow and nodded, impressed. "Well, thanks a lot, I enjoyed your help." Walking Klaus Varick to the door, he thought to himself how unbelievable it was: Four degrees, and the guy's a fucking bellhop! "Thank you," Bephino smiled, "I'll certainly ask for you if I need further help."

The door shut, Bephino walked back to the french doors,

pulled back the sheer curtain once again, and began scanning the Del Rego estate. After about ten minutes he returned to his bedroom and stretched out on the bed for a nap before the late-night dinner traditionally served in Europe. Several hours later he was awakened by a strong, strange feeling coming over him. Groggy and disoriented with jet lag, he jumped up and looked around the room. Here he was in Europe to kill a man for people he now hated. A political hit, no less, he mused, by a poor kid from Brooklyn once just trying to make a buck, who was now involved in Italy's politics. A hit involving communism. Like in the movies, James Bond—kill or be killed. Them fuckin' dons in Brooklyn didn't know when they were well off, he reasoned. They had so much money stacked away, they all should retire. But no, they still wanted to have the sit-downs. They were all seventy and eighty years of age and they wanted to kill people in Europe. They wanted to be involved in this shit all the way to their graves. Jesus, Bephino thought, they should be spendin' all the cash they got piled up in places like this, havin' a good time. Look at this room, he marveled: beautiful hardwood floors, twelve-foot ceilings, three hundred fifty bucks a day, and it's worth every penny.

Bephino walked toward the bath and filled the large European marble tub with hot water. They should bring their wives or girlfriends here to relax in Victorian style, he thought, shaking his head easily.

I'll soak for a half hour, he decided, and have dinner later this evening.

After several days of surveillance, Bephino began scouting up close and around outside the Del Rego estate. When the estate's electronically controlled gate opened, a small gray Mercedes would speed out and head swiftly down the hill. He noticed that there was always a woman driving, and she routinely came out at about the same time each day. On the seventh day, he parked his rental car about a block from the electronic gates, opened the car's hood, and waited patiently for the little Mercedes, hoping its driver would stop to inquire if he was stuck and needed help.

The gravel road was narrow and quiet—a mountainside estate road only rarely used by the public. Suddenly the sound of tires rumbling the gravel intruded into the quiet air. A larger car, perhaps a Bentley or a Rolls, quickly rounded the mountainside curve and pulled directly up to him. The dark-tinted window on the passenger's side went down electrically. A beautiful, winter-faced, red-cheeked woman in her late twenties stretched across the seat and put her head out of the English-made auto. "*Kann ich Ihnen helfen?*" she asked.

"Sorry, I don't speak German," Bephino called out with an apologetic shrug. "I'm American."

"Ah," the lovely blond creature responded cheerfully, "I loff Americans! Do you need any help?" she asked in a slight German accent.

Bephino, with one eye on her friendly face and the other on the Del Rego estate gates, hoped the little sports Mercedes didn't appear while he was talking to this stunning savior of the highway. "No, thank you, I'm just letting my engine cool down. I'm testing my new voltage switch. I'll only be parked here a few minutes."

"Vel, if you need a lift, I vould be glad to carry you," she said in a warm, refined voice. "Are you staying in the area?"

"I'm staying at the Victorian, but I'm sure I'll be OK, thank you," Bephino replied, glancing briefly up the road.

"My name is Giessler von Mueland . . . and yours, may I ask?"

"Joseph Charles. From Pittsburgh. If I may have the pleasure of buying you a drink one day," Bephino spoke quickly, his nervous eyes darting back and forth, "please stop over at the hotel. I'm registered. I would enjoy meeting someone from the area."

Giessler smiled. "You want to buy me a drink? I'm Frau von Mueland—Mrs. Friedrich von Mueland." She smiled for a moment, finding Joseph Charles's request amusing.

Bephino's nervous eyes kept darting back up the hill toward the Del Rego estate, while the lovely Giessler's continued to focus on him.

"To join you for a drink is not possible, Mr. Joseph Charles from Pittsburgh," she grinned broadly. "My husband vouldn't like that," she added with increasing warmth and friendliness. She seemed in no hurry at all to leave him.

"Well, in that case," Bephino replied with a broad, embossed smile, "being that you're married, perhaps we can have two drinks, one for you and one for Mr. von Mueland."

"I don't think ve should do that," she said, smiling wickedly at Bephino. "That vouldn't be zo nice. Two drinks means ve're old friends," she whispered sexily at him, "and that ve're not, Mr. Pittsburgh," she said, raising her eyes at him.

"Well, I'm registered at the Victorian. Don't forget, the name is Charles, Joseph Charles. I'll be in Vienna another week or so. I'm alone—without friends. If you care to join me, perhaps we can have a friendly dinner." Bephino backed away from her car. "Please call me, will you?" He quickly glanced back up toward the Del Rego gates. Giessler's eyes silently followed his all the way up the road. Suddenly she laughed, "Bye-bye," and quickly pulled away. Bephino had begun enjoying the conversation so much he'd temporarily lost sight of why he was parked on the cold, snowy mountain road to begin with. Soon, however, he restationed himself, this time on the car's fender, trying to appear stuck. For the next twenty minutes, he contemplated how friendly and attractive Frau von Mueland had been. Quite a morsel, he thought, raising his collar against the cold wind. The weather was again becoming gray, and snowflakes began to fall. He consulted his watch. A half hour had gone by. No one from the Del Rego estate had showed.

What if Frau von Mueland returned and found him still parked on the road, he thought, what would she . . . At that moment he heard the gates roll open, and the little gray Mercedes sped out. Bephino stood by his car, trying to look troubled. The car sped right past him and continued to crest the hill beyond, and then suddenly it came to a swift halt. The car backed up and the window on the passenger's side went down.

A mature, interesting-looking woman in her late fifties called out, *"Brauchen Sie Hilfe?"*

"Sorry, I don't speak German. Do you speak English?" Bephino asked.

"Yes, of course, most everyone does, no? Do you need help?" she repeated in his language, displaying a charming, refined Italian accent of her own.

"Yes, I do. Can you give me a lift to the Victorian hotel? My car won't start. I'll have to send a mechanic to pick it up."

"I'm going to the Victorian myself. Come on in," she invited in a friendly voice.

"Thank you, you came just in time. I was getting cold waiting there." Bephino got in quickly, and they sped off down the winding road.

"My name is Lucia Del Rego. I live at the Villa Italia."

"Yes, I walked up to the gates and I noticed the bronze plaque on the stone columns. It said ITALIA. My mother was Italian. My father was a French-English American," Bephino said thoughtfully.

"What is your name?" she asked.

"Oh, excuse me, I thought I introduced myself. I'm Joseph Charles III, from Pittsburgh. My family has been in the land developing business in Pennsylvania for many years. I'm on vacation. I plan on spending several months traveling in Europe."

"Well, you came to a lovely spot. Vienna is beautiful, but most of the young people are holidaying on the Greek Islands or Australia. This is the wrong time of the year for Austria unless you like to hunt or ski. Do you like to hunt or ski?" she askcd with a tilt of her head.

"I never did learn to ski. I always wanted to. As for hunting," he said with a grin, pulling at possible straws, "that's what I really like to do—hunt or fish, as well as horseback riding. But skiing looks real interesting, and someday I would like to try it."

"My husband, Phillipo, is a famous boar hunter in Italy," she smiled playfully at him. "As a matter of fact, he hunts now in the Milano area."

Bephino's ears perked up, but he was careful not to show interest in her husband. He observed a riding crop lying on the dash of the car, and thoughts raced fiercely in his head. . . . "Deer hunting's my sport," he said, looking straight ahead. "I really enjoy it, but of course I enjoy other things, too. We own a horse farm," he said nonchalantly, glancing out his window.

"That's my second love," Lucia cried out excitedly, turning to Bephino, "horseback riding! We have our own stables on the villa grounds. The trails go way up the mountain. It's so beautiful to ride through the Viennese mountains. You can see part of the world from up there," she said with a flush and a broad smile.

"I can imagine," he replied. "I see the mountain trails from my suite. Tell me, if horseback riding is your second love, what's your first?" Bephino asked.

At that moment, the Victorian hotel entrance appeared. "Oh, we're here already," she said, turning sharply into the grounds. "It seems time goes so quickly when one has fine conversation." Pulling into a large parking area, she hunted a space, parked, and turned off the engine. She turned to Mr. Charles and said, "You asked about my first love. It's strange that for a stranger you are bold enough to ask me something so personal, but you deserve an answer from one who purposely uses a 'second love' phrase. *Love* is my first love." Getting out of the car, she smiled. "See?" she said softly. "A bold question from a stranger always deserves an honest, bold answer. I enjoyed talking to you, Mr. Charles."

"I enjoyed talking to you very much, Mrs. Del Rego."

"Call me Lucia. The other sounds so . . . so attached and formal. I like people who like horses; they usually have good spirit like horses, and I like spirit."

"Good," he said with a broad smile, holding out his hand to shake, "and I like you. You are a straightforward person and a very interesting and beautiful lady. I wonder if I may be bold once again, and offer you a drink later this evening. Would you accept? Or—better yet, a late-night supper? Such a thing with a lady as charming and interesting as you would be fantastic for me." Bephino smiled, his white teeth glittering at her. "Would the lady consider being bold and joining me this evening? I'm alone," he pleaded, "and it's terribly unpleasant to dine alone." Lucia did not answer, but it was obvious she was thinking hard. "I hate to sound so presumptuous, Mrs. Del Rego," Bephino said, giving her his best sensual smile, "but I feel I would really enjoy talking to you much further. I also own horses in America and . . ."

The countess smiled shyly, then said, "You're a very nice man, but we just met. Maybe some other time, we'll meet again and . . ."

"Fine," Bephino said, smiling. "In that case, then, how about supper at the hotel tomorrow at nine? Then we can surely meet again. And if you would like to bring along a friend, that would be fine with me," he said, trying to buy some insurance and build up his credibility.

Her beautiful, matured face smiled with amusement. The mystical, alluring crow's feet in the corner of her eyes suddenly became warm and evident. "What fun would that be, if I brought along a friend!" she said, as her lips, thinning and suddenly quite sexy, parted in a smile. "OK, Mr. Charles, you win. Tomorrow at nine at the hotel's La Bistro. I'll be there. I'm sorry, but I really have to go now," she said. "I'm late." They both finally got out of the car and walked inside the hotel. "I have an exercise class here every day," she whispered to him, "and I'm always very late. *Ciao,* see you tomorrow!"

Joseph Charles walked to a corner of the lobby, his thoughts racing. The countess, he reminded himself, had purposely used a "second love" phrase—and he'd picked up on it. Good boy, Bepy! he congratulated himself. Then he called the valet to have someone drive him to fetch his car. He felt fine. Contact had been made.

The next day, he planned well and went into the city to visit the modern art museum and the Austrian museum of European history. Walking through the museums, he contemplated the hit. He knew he needed to be able to maintain interesting conversation on subjects other than hunting and horseback riding if he was to stay close enough to this obviously intelligent, elegant lady to find a way to approach her elusive, remote husband. Bephino knew he would have to penetrate the Del Rego household to get close to him and to do a job that would not seem political. It should perhaps be some kind of family affair, or an accident of some sort. This contract was different, really different, in a world about which he was largely ignorant. Here they were, the blue bloods of

Europe, Bephino kept thinking, and he was going to have to get close enough to kill one of them; he was actually going to have to be able to see the whites of Del Rego's eyes, and then be able to exit quickly and leave Europe without creating an incident. The wife of the count was probably the only available key.

That evening, Joseph Charles anxiously waited at the entrance of the hotel's famous La Bistro. Lucia Del Rego appeared on time. She was dressed beautifully in a long silk burgundy dinner dress, topped off by a magnificent pearl necklace. The bare-shouldered dress pulled at her body with every movement of her firm, plump buttocks. Lucia's hair was tied up quite elegantly in a large bun, spiked by a matching pearl hairpin. Joseph Charles eyed her appreciatively as she made her way toward him. She looked good enough to eat.

"Hello, Joseph," she greeted Bephino, smiling warmly, holding out her hand to shake in a delicate fashion.

"Good evening, Lucia. You look extremely beautiful," he said, trying to be charming and complimentary. "Your dress is stunning. I love that burgundy color. And you're on time. I appreciate a woman who is on time," he grinned warmly at her.

"I'm always on time for supper engagements—perhaps because I'm always famished by nine," she giggled.

"Good, then let's be seated and enjoy a lovely evening together, celebrating new friends, fine wines, and whatever else we can see to enjoy," Bephino said cheerfully, leading his lady by the arm.

Lucia smiled at his charm and enthusiasm. During supper they talked at length about Austrian art, European history, politics, Italian culture, horseback riding, her husband's wild-boar hunting trip, and of course just a little about sex. She never brought up her movie star days, and Joseph Charles felt it perhaps better left unmentioned. After the meal, while sipping a light sherry, Lucia was clearly very comfortable with her new friend. As they began to huddle close to one another like old friends and young romantics, a woman far across the dining room could be seen glancing over at them. Her face was not clearly visible in the dimly lit room. Lucia made no mention of it, but Bephino spotted her out of the corner of his eye and kept looking back over to her. A short while later, the woman, wearing a white silk dress that also fitted snugly from butt to bosom, got up and walked directly over to their table. As she approached, they both saw it was Giessler von Mueland, the blonde from the road.

"Well, hello there, Mr. Charles," she said with emphasis on the 'Mr. Charles,' exposing a sly sparkle in her eye surely caused by the rich wines served at the restaurant. "I see you are actually meeting the right people already, and in only one day! Is your auto runnng OK?" she grinned icily. Then, looking over to Lucia, Giessler smirked, "Well, Lucia, I see you also don't waste time, do you?" She nodded, casting a devilish grin at her neighbor and continuing in a tight voice. "You are ahead of me once again on the social level, actually having dinner with a man who previously invited me only yesterday!" The young blond German forced a wise smile as her face flushed a deep cherry red.

Bephino stared at Giessler von Mueland in total amazement and did not utter a word. How absolutely unexpected for such an elegant woman—in fact, a married woman—to behave so childishly, so inappropriately, to drop her little bomb so petulantly. After a few minutes of Giessler nervously moving her young body around in what seemed like oval circles, Bephino arose and held out his hand. "Would you care to join us?" he asked curtly, but with the utmost correctness. Giessler huffed and smiled falsely at him, her glassy eyes glittering sensuously at his strong, handsome face. She rolled her wet lips at him, without exposing a bit of remorse at her ill-spoken words. But she closed her eyes and shook her head in a bold no, as if to tell him he had simply missed the boat. Lucia closely observed Giessler's tipsy antics and impudent interference with Joseph Charles as if his dinner partner did not exist. But Lucia was also honest with herself. She could not deny how beautiful the young German looked, this outstanding natural blonde with a body that seemed taut and firm. La Bistro's dim light made her look dreamy. Lucia marshaled her forces.

"Are you having dinner with your husband tonight, or are

you dining with the chauffeur?" Lucia asked in retaliation.

Giessler summoned an oily smile, and then said archly, "I'm dining vith my husband tonight, but sometimes the chauffeur will do just as vell." Her bright face turned from Lucia to Bephino, her words directed at him as she more completely displayed her rudeness.

Bephino sat back down. He rubbed the side of his chin, then nervously flagged down the waiter. "Three brandies, please," he said hastily. Then turning back to Giessler: "Why don't you join us? Call your husband over. We'll have some brandy together," Bephino invited, trying to cut the chill in the air while keeping Giessler a friend rather than a foe. "Sit down, Giessler, have a brandy with us. Please be our guest," he insisted. And each time, Lucia's eyes twitched at his words. She hated Giessler for what she was doing to upset such a beautiful evening.

Giessler, without response to Bephino's invitation, simply turned and started to walk away. Looking back over her shoulder she said, "See you in our exercise class tomorrow, Lucia, if you legs vill be up to it." Grinning wisely, she waved. *"Ciao."* Then from a distance she called, "Bye, Mr. Charles, it vas so nice to almost meet you!"

Bephino's face flushed. Why had this gorgeous creature made such a spectacle of herself? Bephino, watching Giessler all the way to her table, sat back and shook his head in amazement.

"Wow!" he said to Lucia. "What the hell was all that about? She's a sassy young lady, isn't she?" he asked while accepting the brandy the waiter set down.

Lucia was pale. After a few moments of silence, she began to speak in a low voice, her eyes downcast. "She's a lot more than sassy. She's a collector of male penises—from all over the world." Bephino's eyes opened wide at her words. Lucia, still sipping from her brandy goblet, raised her eyes fully to his. "To be totally and perfectly blunt, Joseph," she said, placing her glass once again up close to her lips, as if embarrassed by her next words, "she screws any man who crosses her threshold."

Bephino almost choked on his drink. Such blunt candidness from his exquisitely charming dinner companion wasn't exactly what he'd expected. For a moment Bephino considered Giessler's beauty; she really was gorgeous. But then he quickly explained his position and relationship to the German girl. "I only met her on the road yesterday, shortly before you came along, and she offered me help," he explained. "At that time I still thought I could manage the problems I was having with the car myself, so I refused her help, but to be polite I offered her a drink. I really wasn't interested in her; I just wanted to thank her for her offer. I'm really more interested in beautiful Italian women." Bephino smiled reassuringly, then added, "The kind I heard so much about from my Italian grandfather." His smile deepened as he tried to restore the previous warmth of their evening.

"She wants you, Joseph," Lucia said gently, all the while staring into her brandy snifter. "I could tell she's after you, the daring little tramp, and she won't stop until she gets you."

Leaning over closely toward Lucia, allowing his thick black mustache to graze her smooth, milky face, he whispered, "She wants me and you got me, so what do we do now?"

Lucia did not reply. She seemed unsettled, but it was obvious she was considering Joseph Charles's words—all of them. Bephino pressed his wild-card move. "Why don't we go to my suite and have a cocktail, light the fire, and talk about senseless things?" he grinned. "Let's talk about us and forget about that ridiculous person coming and upsetting our lovely evening."

But Lucia's eyes were still on the young, sexy frau at the table far across the room. "That annoying German slut," she whispered. "She looked back at you even after she said *ciao*. She couldn't just walk away. I know this girl. She will be back." Lucia then softly dotted the edges of her mouth with her napkin and forced a hurt smile. "Did I hear you say something about senseless things, Joseph?" Her large brown eyes were now focusing seriously on Bephino; not smiling, just focusing. Without waiting for his answer, she suddenly stood up. Bephino looked at her, not knowing what to expect. As Lucia picked up her purse, her eyes stretched once again far across the room to the von Mueland table, then returned to Bephino, who was still closely observing her moves.

"Sounds fantastic, these senseless things," she blurted out. "Come, let's be senseless, darling."

During that night, Joseph Charles was awakened twice by a naked Italian countess crawling all over him, begging him for more love—all kinds of love. He had given her his love three times already, and he was tired, but the countess wanted more. She rested on her knees in the center of the bed. A small light in the corner of the room made her appear to glow. Her long black hair, unfolded and hanging over her bare shoulders, made her look unbelievably sexy. She was beautiful, no question about that. She called out to him, speaking affectionately in Italian. Bephino rubbed his face, trying to wake up. His eyes roamed her body, trying to find another reason to love her again. He began to touch her short-haired crack, her buttocks; she still felt very exciting to him. Lucia was so round and firm. Her body had a fine, tight, toned feeling for a woman her age, he thought. His hands reached and began to seek the total round of her, then back down to her cunt that was so sexy and moist. Lucia got into a squatting position. This began to excite him—the hairs, the lips, her ass, it all seemed so fine to him. She began to move passionately to his touch, rolling her buttocks at him with exotic movements. Although he still lay exhausted on his back, he began to rise up to admire her actions. He opened his legs wide, allowing the now approaching countess to move down between them. Bephino lay watching the mirrored wall adjoining the bed, which reflected her anxious tongue probing and flickering up close to him, touching his thighs, then his balls and thick penis with such a great, delicate, loving affection. Lucia began taking him slowly and easily, inch by inch, into her mouth. He felt himself enlarging again to the touch of her warm, delicious tongue. Bephino squirmed at the tantalizing feeling of that tongue flickering over the head of his penis.

"It's so beautiful, Joseph," Lucia whispered up to him. "You have such a fantastic-looking prick, so big and beautiful." She moaned, sucking wildly on him, licking hard.

What a nymph of a woman, she demands so much so often, Bephino smiled to himself. He knew he needed her continued companionship to get to the Count Del Rego. His fingers, not remaining idle, automatically went to work and did the right thing to her. They crawled once again over her beautiful breasts and then down her sexy belly, making her feel her beauty as he touched and rubbed. Mouth full, Lucia squirmed to his masculine touch and hummed in satisfaction with this man she was loving. The lady began moving into a better position for him to touch her below, lifting and placing his hands between her smooth thighs, encouraging his probing of her thick, posh pussy. After a few minutes, she dropped down; raising her up to face him, he whispered, "Easy, easy, with your tongue, honey, you're gonna make me come again." He leaned forward and touched her sensitive, taut nipples with his lips and flicked his tongue while systematically raising his hands from her crotch up to her waist; holding her just above her buttocks, he squeezed her. Lucia's eyes spread open wide at the way he manhandled her. Excitedly, she quickly began to dig gently at her own groin, moaning again and again as if a hot poker were entering her. Her hands between her own thighs, and her long black hair untied, hanging down to her hips, gave her an extremely sensual look. Bephino's eyes watched intently as she masturbated herself so elegantly for him.

It all seemed so bizarre, so unreal, but somehow so European. After a few moments of play, she raised her body up and mounted his strong, thick organ. Lucia climbed over him in a light, skillful style and directed his throbbing prick deeply into the darkness, toward her womb. Their bodies pumped with intense rhythm. Her moans became beautiful screams of love. Bephino then felt the beautiful woman's body tighten and grunt passionately. She shuddered hard as a flow of hot juices dripped down over him. He passionately responded and began to climax heavily into her body. Their bodies clung together as they kissed each other wildly. An aroma of spent lust filled the room as they both lay languorously in each other's arms. After a while, Bephino began considering just what he was involved in. Orgasm with this strange Italian lady was indeed something new and guiltily splendid. He turned his eyes secretly to Lucia. What a great experience of refined, savage lust, he thought to himself, like fucking an enthroned queen with the heart of an alley cat. Lucia lay silent, then suddenly turned to him.

"I think I love you, Joseph," she murmured, a little white lie into the air. "I must love you, my darling; you make me explode so often," she whispered in a childish voice.

Already she's in love, Bephino thought to himself with humor. Unbelievable. This was the first time all evening Lucia allowed her body to go limp.

"I must be in love," she continued to lie, speaking softly and touching his naked body, running her hand down between his thighs. "Yes, I'm sure I love you," she said as she closed her eyes.

Much later that morning, Bephino's eyes opened, peering into the bright sunlight glaring through the sheer fabric of the french doors far off in the corner of the room. He stared and listened to her calling out to him. "Joseph, *belle mia,* are you awake?" she asked as she approached the bed, smiling at him. "That was fantastic last night," she whispered. Lucia was up, smiling widely while running her hand over his tanned, hairy chest.

Breakfast was served in his suite. They sat and ate, sipped coffee, and smiled at one another. "You seem so Italian, Joseph," she smiled broadly. "You even look so Italian, and you make love like an Italian!"

He shrugged with a slight blush. "I told you my mother was Italian; she comes from Sicily."

"Ah, *Siciliano, va bene,*" she smiled, staring at him. "We're fond of Sicilians. My Phillipo sits in Palermo twice a month for our Republic Party." Then, touching his lips from across the table and rubbing his mustache lovingly, she asked, "Would you like to come horseback riding with me? We can ride through the great mountains of Vienna. The horses love to gallop through the hills high up. It's nice and cold outside." She smiled, waiting for his reply, then quickly added, "They gallop so well in the cold winter air, Joseph, so frisky. You may ride Il Sciacallo," she grinned. "He's quick."

"What about your husband?" he asked.

"Phillipo will be in Italy for the entire month. I will join him on the third week. Anyway, we usually have house-guests," she said, deepening her voice. "It's our way of life. My Phillipo understands this, and so do my servants; they are all very loyal to me. In any case, I want you to come to my villa for dinner," she said, puckering her lips.

For the next few days Bephino and Lucia rode huge black horses through the thick forest trails and along the ridges and mountain slopes overlooking the city of Vienna. Joseph Charles was dressed warmly and beautifully in a Bulgarian calfskin coat thickly lined with black lamb and trimmed with Russian sable. His boots were knee high, of the finest leather Italy had to offer. A posh sable hat matched his jacket. He looked like a prince from Budapest riding with a Russian czar's wife. All the finery came from the lavish wardrobe of Lucia's brother, Felini Marcata, who had been the same size as Bephino in his younger years.

"You look *magnifico,* Joseph," Lucia whined, speaking partly in Italian. "As you see, we still keep Felini's clothes intact," she grinned, "because we always have unexpected guests, and we have to dress some of the strangest-looking people." She giggled playfully from her horse, which was dancing about alongside him. With another giggle she kicked her horse and galloped away up the hill.

Bephino, riding the highly spirited colt Il Sciacallo, "The Jackal," owned by the man he was out to kill, kicked hard at his steed's side and galloped thunderously alongside Lucia. "Do you like to ride Il Sciacallo?" his companion asked excitedly over the blowing wind and the puffing of the horses.

"Yes, he's high spirited, and I like that in a horse," Bephino cheerfully replied, his horse prancing about as if wanting to keep on going. Suddenly, the Jackal reared up. When Bephino pulled down on the reins, the horse moved forward abruptly.

Bephino then pulled back hard, and the bit dug into Sciacallo's jaws, causing him to rear once again. "Boy, he's frisky today," Bephino yelped.

"The horses want to run," Lucia said excitedly. "Catch me," she screeched. "Let's run them." And like a young girl in love, she galloped off again.

The warm breath of the horses steaming and blowing in the cold mountain air, puffing their way up the mountain slope, made the lonely winter day become alive and beautiful.

Later that evening, Joseph Charles, alone in his hotel suite, settled in for a night of relaxation. Lucia was otherwise committed, which freed him to stay home and start a new novel by an up-and-coming author from California about the American Sicilian Mafia. Bephino eased into a thick, soft, feather-stuffed chaise lounge by the fireplace and picked at a platter of cold shelled crab and jumbo Portuguese shrimp in between sips from a goblet of chilled white wine, recommended by the house. As Joseph Charles began the first chapter of Larry James's *The Contract*, he became increasingly interested. Time passed quickly, and he was moving right along into the book's third chapter when the phone rang. Thinking it was Lucia, he hesitated momentarily. Bephino was afraid of her changing her plans and coming over, or else of her inviting him to the villa. He was nearly crippled from the week's horseback riding and frantically depleted from Lucia's sexual enthusiasms. There was no way he could manage the triple sessions she so boldly but elegantly demanded. So he determined to play sick if she should have somehow wrested herself from her other engagement.

"Hello," he answered softly.

"Mr. Charles?" a lovely voice asked.

"Yes, this is Charles."

"This is Giessler von Mueland . . ." After a short pause, she continued with an unsure, naive-sounding "How have you been?"

"Fine, Giessler, I'm fine, how are you?" he asked in total surprise, raising himself up from the chaise into a sitting position.

"I just called to say hello," she purred more confidently. "The way you answered the phone I thought I got the wrong room. It didn't sound like you. I feel zo terrible for acting like I did that evening we saw each other at your dinner table. That vas childish and very rude of me. I acted like a primitive, selfish young person. I felt I should apologize to you."

"That's OK, Giessler. No harm was done."

"You're so kind, Mr. Charles. But it's a shame no harm vas done. I'm still just a little jealous," she giggled.

"Call me Joseph, Giessler. 'Mr. Charles' sounds so formal for old friends like us. After all, for strangers, we have been through a lot together lately, haven't we?"

"You're right," she tittered. "In that case, I'll call you Joe. How's that? Joe, vould you care to join me for a drink? I'm down in the hotel's lounge."

"Giessler, I'm in my robe, relaxing by the fire. I hadn't planned on going out this evening."

After another long pause, she spoke again. "That's a shame, because I'm holding in my hands a bottle of Laventurieux 1946, a most spectacular French vine. Vould you like me to come visit you, Joe? We can enjoy this fantastic vine together. How about it, Joe?"

Bephino frowned in silence. It was feast or faminine. Either you spent a week alone in a hot tub or they sucked the fuckin' bone marrow out of you, he mused. After a few moments he said, "Sounds good, Giessler. I'm in suite 1213, parlor B. I'll be waiting."

"OK, Joe, I'll come right up."

A few moments later there was a light knock at the door. Waiting behind it with a big smile, wine bottle in one hand and fur jacket in the other, stood the tall, luscious, buxomy, blond Giessler von Mueland, the Baron von Mueland's wife. Her shoulder-length hair set off her beautiful face, with cheeks still red from the winter air. Her shape was like a magazine centerfold's. Her short wool dress hit her right above the knees; her high-heeled leather boots, just above her ankles. Bephino smiled. "Come on in, Giessler."

"See, I didn't forget you," she said in her lovely German-accented voice. She grinned sheepishly at him as she placed her jacket carelessly on the couch and then she began to prance around, exploring the living room and slowing down at the fireplace. "Oh, vhat is this?" she exclaimed, eyeing the serving cart. "It looks yummy."

"Cold crabmeat and shrimp. Would you like some? Or should I call down and order you some warm dinner?"

"No, the shrimp vill be fine," she said, as she held up a large morsel and took a bite out of it. "I'm not too hungry this evening," she said, moving her blond head and blue eyes about as if she'd known him for years. "I'd like some vine, if you please." She handed him the still-corked bottle and asked, "Vould you open it, Joe?"

"Sure, I'll open the wine. I have some white wine here, recommended by the house. If you care to . . ."

"I drink nothing, absolutely nothing, recommended by the house," she sneered, raising and lowering her eyebrows at him. "My vine vill be fine, thank you," she said, picking up a piece of crabmeat. After a moment, she asked in a slightly muffled tone, trying to chew and speak while keeping her mouth closed, "Can I play the radio? I like soft music. It makes me feel romantic." Shrugging prettily, she turned away and walked toward the shelf the radio was on.

"Sure, turn it on. Find us some relaxing music." He smiled as he poured her some of her wine, then walked over to the radio to serve it to her. He then returned to pour himself one.

Giessler, still turning the dial, looked over to him and giggled, "I'm having trouble locating my good music." Finally finding something suitable, she ambled over to his chaise and picked up his novel. "Vhat's this about the New York Mafia? Such horrible people you read about, Joe," she said, putting the book back down. "The cover looks so bloody," she murmured.

"Yes, I'm reading about a hit man from New York City."

"Vhat's a hit man, them crazy-guy shooters?" she asked, laughing and catching a cracker as it fell from her cherry lips.

"Yeah, them crazy-guy shooters," he replied, amused. "I like novels with action and fantasy."

"*Ja*, fantasy is OK. I like that too," she replied, raising her glass to him.

Within an hour, the two of them were lying before the fire, comfortably sipping from the last of Giessler's fine wine. Giessler stared and smiled deeply at him like a peach ripening on a tree in the Georgia sunlight. Bephino's eyes expressed amusement as he decided she was beckoning him to kiss her. He leaned over and began with her forehead, then her face, then her young, wet, natural-red lips. She responded smoothly and passionately to his caresses. Somehow, she seemed very different to him from Lucia. This was going to be a completely different ball game; he could feel it in her touch. As flashes of his Dana came to him, he tried desperately to clear those thoughts from his mind. After a while the mounting passion became effortless for them both. Giessler then excused herself and asked the direction to the powder room. He pointed to the bedroom, and she whispered, "Don't go away, I'll be right back with a big surprise for you." She grinned and turned, her boot heels clicking as she walked.

After what seemed to be a long while, Bephino, lying by the flickering flames of the fireplace, began to doze off. Suddenly came the clicking sound of Frau von Mueland's leather heels approaching him on the varnished hardwood floors. "Joe, are you ready for your surprise?" she asked impishly, innocently.

Propping himself up, he blurted out, "Yes, of course I'm ready," as he shook off his sleepiness. His eyes came to focus on a woman ravishingly beautiful and stark naked. Stark naked, that is, except for short, mink-cuffed high-heeled leather boots and a gold wristwatch. Giessler struck a sensual pose in the dimly lit room, the orange and black shadows of the flickering from the fireplace bouncing off her unbelievable, eye-startling body. He couldn't help notice her short hairs combed neatly and spread apart as if hand-fixed. Bephino's handsome, masculine face began to swell with anticipation. His thick, dark, recently grown mustache did not move a twitch. His eyes scanned her youthful body, very slowly and with great respect, as he appreciated how an hour-glass shape was indeed an hour-glass shape. Giessler then turned herself slowly, standing on her toes directly in front of him, and smiled the smile of a young, fresh-faced schoolgirl looking for approval. She patiently and silently turned like a beautiful exhibitionist. Her breasts were large and firm looking. The nipples stood taut, speaking out with lust. Her waist was small, and her smooth buttocks beckoned to be hugged. Both people were silent.

Then finally she spoke to him, smiling broadly while still spinning on her toes. "Do you like vhat you see, Joe?"

Bephino swallowed, then nodded his head in silent confirmation. His eyes were riveted on the amazing naked sight before him, the unbelievable shape of it, continuously smiling, continuously spinning! He shook his head from side to side. Another wonder of the world, he thought; never have I seen a girl do this before!

"You're an extraordinary-looking woman," he said with a soft rasp, as he observed her striking pose; it was as if a mannequin had come alive before his eyes. His eyes lowered, focusing on her dark-leather boots trimmed with soft, white mink fur, then rose admiringly to her knees and then back to the lush, neat, hairy patch between her smooth thighs. Her belly button—set just under her small waist—and curvy hips were proof she was God-made. As he lay by the fire, his eyes glided up to her full, bulging breasts and took a brief moment to admire once again the erect pink nipples that seemed to be sprouting in pleasure and testified to the ripeness of her intentions. Momentarily settling on her beautiful, smiling German face, he flashed to the small of her back and to her round, plump buttocks as she continuously spun, so robustly, like a ballerina, by his face in unbelievably even intervals.

"Do you like, Joe?" she asked once again.

"Yes, I do, Giessler. Very much so," he whispered thickly, "but you're gonna get dizzy spinning around like that."

"I'm going to give you something, Joe, you could never get in America," she said with a broad grin.

"And what may that be?" he asked, reaching up to touch her silky smooth body.

She stopped her spinning and looked down at him as he partially reclined by the fire. She stooped down and opened his heavy terry-cloth robe, spreading it wide and lowering it from his shoulders, exposing his chest. "I like your body," she whispered at him, "you're nice and tan and hairy. I like men like you," she grinned. "Do you know vhat I'm going to give you?" she asked. "I'm going to give you me, Joe," she said, pushing him farther down on his back. Then, squatting down and resting her bare bottom on his chest, grazing his face and lips with her fingertips, she whispered, "I'm going to give you me, and *that* you cannot get in America." She giggled like a young girl. "I'm going to fuck you, suck you, and lick you all over, because I feel so healthy tonight, and you are my pleasure."

Bephino stared silently, amused at this erotically generous beauty sitting on his chest as if it had been made solely for that purpose.

"I'm going to give you all of me, Joe. Vould you like that?" she asked, squirming softly on his chest.

Bephino quietly reached out with both his hands and grabbed her by both big cheeks. His strong, dark hands roamed the white-skinned round of her as he thought to himself, Here we go again, Bephino.

The next morning at eleven, Giessler still lay sleeping on her belly. The ruffled satin sheets crumpled between her thighs exposed her buttocks and very small waist. The bright sunlight peered through the french doors, reflecting off the bright snow-capped mountains. This natural light gave Bephino a warm, comfortable feeling while reading. All showered, shaved, up ahead of Giessler and ready to face the day was Brooklyn, New York's, most valued hit man. He sat about ten feet from the bed, reading a New York newspaper, complimentary for all American guests staying at the Victorian. In between reading, his eyes would casually seek out Giessler's half-naked body. After about half an hour, he found himself constantly focusing on her restless, unconsciously seductive movements. Giessler would casually and gracefully turn herself, propping her buttocks up, and catch his lazy gaze. What a woman, he thought, rolling his lips, what a night of splendor! This woman was born to be fucked! As Giessler continued to move her body about in beckoning moves as she slept, he found himself staring harder and harder. Finally he could stand no more. He got up and walked to the foot of the bed, and after a moment or two of carefully looking her over, disrobed and planned his reentry into her. Giessler silently moved again, very slowly, easily rolling her beautiful ass around and around. Finally she settled down to a fine and fitting propped-up position. Crawling on the bed quietly, so as not to wake her, Joseph Charles embraced her body with his strong hands around her tiny waist. He moved down and kissed her bare back with long, lush licks, then directed his huge, throbbing organ between the vaginal lips just below her buttocks and pumped easily into her warm, blond, womb. Giessler let out a sudden series of moans that seemed more sounds of relief than great sighs.

"I thought you'd never get to me, Joe," she gasped. "I've been vaiting for you." Bephino thrust deep into her, moving in and out and around. She began to respond in vigorous reverse moves, thrusting herself and raising herself up, spreading wide like a young mare, moving back into him forcefully. Giessler gave her abundant buttocks to him in a fashion that made the female body outdo itself. God, she's beautiful, Bephino thought, as he pumped deeper to the sucking sound of her body, raising her back up to him with long-lasting thrusts. He viewed her yearning face and large, astonishing breasts in the mirrored headboard in front of them and squeezed her feverishly. "You're unbelievable, Giessler," he whispered as he kissed her neck with passion, in a voice swollen with approaching climax.

"You, too, Joe. Oh, Joe!" she replied in the same swollen voice, moving her bottom in a way that no man could resist. "I come for you, Joe. I . . ." She attempted to say something else but instead began trembling hard. "Oh-h-h *Liebe,* oh *Liebe,* oh-h-h *Schatzie,* I have so much for you!"

Both of them began to shudder uncontrollably in ecstasy, Giessler reaching down in wild passion, raising herself up to him. As she felt his hot sperm entering her she actually turned in an effort to face him, to watch him shudder. Reaching behind herself, in a triumph of perfect timing, she grabbed his swollen testicles with a sensuous, squeezing touch that widened Bephino's eyes. Unbelievable pleasure flooded Bephino's thoughts as he continued to void his climax. Giessler continued squeezing him with gentle desire and unspeakable affection. Like a molded statue, they awkwardly positioned themselves as if locked together; they remained throbbing.

The next day while Joseph Charles was dining with the Countess Lucia Del Rego at the Villa Italiana, Bephino asked his hostess when she intended to leave Vienna to join her husband, Phillipo, in Milano.

"To be perfectly honest with you, Joseph," Lucia said, "I'm really in no hurry to join him. I am having such a wonderful time, I hate to see it end."

"I feel the same way, Lucia, I hate to see it end also; that's why I was wondering, if you're going to Milano, maybe I could join you and your husband on the hunt. I have never hunted wild boar. I think I would really like that. I could stay at a nearby hotel, you could come over when possible or when you desired, and I could join the hunt each day—of course, providing your husband wouldn't mind."

There was a moment of silence at the dinner table, then Lucia looked over at Joseph Charles, smiled, and said, "I was going to ask you this week if you would consider doing just that. I was hoping you would consider joining us in Milano."

"How about your husband, would he mind if I showed up with you?"

"Not at all, *belle mia.* My husband has a mistress. He's always had a mistress. She travels with him as his secretary. We are very complex, understanding, modern-day people. Men like Phillipo are expected to have a young woman for their pleasure, and while I'm not expected to do likewise, I very much enjoy doing likewise." Picking up a grape, she bit into it seductively and added, "With the right man, of course.

So that's settled, we both agree." She smiled, tilting her head at him.

"When will we leave?" Bephino asked, pressing to get nearer to his prey.

"We can leave in three days, Joseph, if that suits you. And you can borrow hunting equipment from Felini. He goes up and down in weight. He owns three full wardrobes, and we'll be staying at Felini's Villa Gabreali, not a hotel." She smiled. "We can make love right in the villa."

"Sounds wonderful," he said with a smile, sipping from his wineglass. "I'm really enjoying my European trip, thanks to you, Lucia."

"I'm glad," she said. "You're a very interesting man, Joseph Charles. I've enjoyed every minute of you. I can understand why that young frau, von Mueland, had her claws out for you. She wanted you badly, and I think you were aware of that." Lucia grinned strangely at him. "Yes, she missed something really special, didn't she?" Lucia asked, pausing for a moment. Staring directly at Bephino while selecting a pastry from a silver tray, she repeated with a slow, shy grin, "Yes, that German tramp missed out on something very, very special." Bephino returned a faint smile to Lucia, who seemed to be still observing him.

Three days later, upon arriving at the Milano airport, Bephino suggested once again that he stay at a hotel, but Lucia insisted he would be welcome at the mountain mansion of her appliance-manufacturer brother, Felini Marcata. "We are all staying there," she insisted. "It's a family-and-friends reunion; the boar hunt is a festive occasion. Lots of people will be there. The villa has seventy bedrooms," she said.

"How about Phillipo?" he asked, as they departed from the aircraft. "Will he mind if I show up with you?"

"Not at all, darling. I told you, he has a friend. He may be actually relieved," she replied airily, if not altogether convincingly.

"Will his secretary be with him?" Bephino asked.

"Always, she's always with him. A count in Italia always carries his secretary with him. It's not fashionable otherwise. And don't worry so much, Joseph, you will not be unfashionable with me. You will have a wonderful time and be respected by all at Felini's home. Felini will see to that."

Bephino smiled as he walked from the airport's corridors to the waiting limo. Grabbing at her plush fur coat with a warm gesture, he said, "That's good, Lucia; just as long as I'm respected, everything will be OK."

The limousine crawled slowly up the narrow, icy road. Bephino's eyes scanned the mountains of Northern Italy that extended all the way to Switzerland. After a forty-minute drive, the mansion's private road appeared to the right side of an even more narrow cliff road. A small sign that hung on a cobblestone column read VIA FELINI, VILLA GABREALI. The limo turned onto the heavy-wooded country road and began to climb steeper into the mountains thick with pine. After another ten minutes, the mansion appeared in a clearing.

Bephino became somber as the realities of making the hit began to move in on him. His thoughts went to the shabby Mob bosses back in Brooklyn, giving orders to kill someone who to Bephino seemed to come from people of a great monarchy. It was as if he were committing regicide, he thought to himself. Did those Brooklyn bosses ever dream what it would take to get close to someone like Phillipo Del Rego? They must have thought it was going to be as simple as fly over to Europe, walk up, hit him, and then leave on the next plane out. These wealthy, well-born people were like kings, and unavailable to the common person—well, to most common persons.

Bephino squinted, approving of his work thus far. He marveled at what he'd had to do to discover Del Rego's whereabouts without arousing suspicion. And the irony was, this would be a hit he'd never receive an ounce of credit for. No one would ever dream what it had taken to fulfill, he thought to himself. Look at that stone mansion! he said to himself, transfixed. It was like something from the movies, like a castle. Bephino gazed through the window at the mansion like a young boy admiring the Statue of Liberty.

"Are you getting out, Joseph?" Lucia asked, interrupting his thoughts, as she stood waiting outside the limo.

"Yes, I was just thinking about the construction of such a

beautiful building as this," he said, climbing out of the vehicle and breathing in the fresh mountain air. "Italians are great contractors," he continued, to cover an increasing sense of discomfort. "The way things are engineered in Italy is unbelievable." It was becoming more and more fantastic to Bephino that he was actually here, entering this opulent estate to stay with such affluent Europeans he did not even know—not to mention making love to such an otherwise unattainable woman as Lucia and then actually having to murder her husband, the father of her two children. This was shaping up into a scenario more suitable to a kind of horror movie he used to watch as a child in Brooklyn. Everything was suddenly becoming gray to him, uncomfortable, and very, very real. It looked as if the vacation was coming to an end, he thought to himself, as he walked through the huge mansion doors and was greeted by a tall, thin, balding Italian butler with a very pronounced stoop.

"Buona sera, signore," the long-nosed butler greeted him.

"Lucia!" a distant voice echoed the room, turning everyone's head.

"Felini!" Lucia heartily exclaimed as her brother entered the large room and warmly greeted her. They both embraced and spoke rapidly in Italian. Bephino listened and was surprised to understand most of what they were saying, considering how much of a challenge the northern dialect, spoken so fast, was to him. He did not dare to himself communicate with them in Italian, fearing that his Brooklyn Sicilian would clash with the delicate tongue of these blue bloods.

When Lucia's affectionate and high-spirited reunion with her brother had subsided, she turned toward Bephino, and while still speaking energetically in Italian introduced him. "This is my good friend Joseph Charles. Joseph is a very big land developer from Pittsburgh, America. Joseph builds big, big buildings. *Gran costuttore contraente,"* she repeated.

Felini greeted Bephino warmly, nodding amiably and saying, *"Bene, bene,"* to his sister's bragging.

After a few moments Lucia actually caught her breath enough to ask, *"Dov'è Phillipo?"*

As Felini responded as to her husband's whereabouts, Bephino's ears perked up. Phillipo was his man. He had to make contact as soon as possible and take him out. But if he hit him up on that mountain in the snow, how would he get off the mountain and be able to make his way to the airport and leave Italy without being detained? The mansion had to be at least fifty or sixty minutes out of Milano, high up in what seemed like the Italian Alps. This was going to be a very, very tough hit, he thought to himself. The atmosphere was against him. All of his luggage and belongings would have to be left behind, but he had no problem with that. And maybe he could take one of their cars to make his getaway. But what weapon could be used to kill the man? He had not wanted to risk bringing a weapon from America that might be traced or discovered in customs. He had to come up with a workable plan.

Felini Marcata was a short, stout, cheerful man in his early sixties who wore a dark gray suit and black tie even at home. After he explained Phillipo's whereabouts to his sister, she smiled with understanding. "Phillipo will be here tomorrow," Lucia said loudly, turning to Bephino. "He's away for a day on business, then everyone goes back out to the hunt on Thursday," she said in a somewhat edgy voice, entwining her arm through Joseph's in an assuring manner, as if he was greatly anxious to go hunting. Bephino was getting a sense of something he didn't altogether understand—or appreciate—in Lucia. As they walked, she continually reassured him in a geared-up and excited manner how absolutely fine everything was going to be, as if showing off or perhaps feeling self-conscious with her own family. Bephino politely confirmed that everything was in fact fine, and for her not to worry about his hunting ambition, while stocky Felini grinned agreeably at Bephino to his sister's promises. Bephino again became uncomfortable. He knew now that he was going to have to eat and run. The hit suddenly became even more of a priority.

The next day, Phillipo and Florentina arrived through the large mansion doors, shaking snow from their heavy mink-lined boots and doeskin coats. They removed the boots from their feet, donned their shoes, and arm in arm made their way to the main living room. The house was now as full of guests as Lucia had told Bephino it would be, and everyone was busy chattering and enjoying cocktails and hors d'oeuvres when the host and his secretary entered the large room.

"Ah, Phillipo-o-o," one of the guests sang out in a welcoming voice. Everyone looked up and greeted the entering couple. Phillipo waved to everyone as MacArthur did in the Philippines, and then he and Lucia warmly hugged and kissed one another, embracing more like old friends than husband and wife. Both began speaking rapidly in Italian and smiling affectionately for the guests at each other. "Have you heard from the children?" Phillipo asked his wife. After a few moments of conversation, Lucia finally glanced over at Florentina, who was patiently standing by with a swollen grin pasted across her face. "Ah, Florentina," Lucia said, greeting her with embraces in the same manner, as if a very old friend, but the strangeness in the show of affection was evident to all.

Everyone was joyous and acted charming. Italian was spoken rapidly, and wine flowed freely. Beautiful, exquisitely dressed ladies giggled and called out the names of distinguished-looking males with a sensual tongue: Gianni, Carlo, Felini, Aldo. Bephino heard a woman call out Bepi to a fine, dapper-looking fellow, who responded by kissing the woman's hand. Bephino smiled alone as he admired his namesake.

Joseph Charles stood alone by the huge stone fireplace and observed the glitter and the chatter and listened to the laughter of people to whom he in no way belonged. His outsider's eyes focused across the large room directly upon Phillipo. His mark was tall, gray haired, partially balding, about six-foot-three, perhaps in his late sixties, and clearly an Italian intellectual from one of the finest families of Europe. A handsome-faced man, impeccably dressed in a black sharkskin Italian-cut suit, black tie, and white shirt, Phillipo carried himself with the air of a king. And Florentina . . . Florentina was another story. An Italian beauty seemingly in her late twenties, she affected a look as matronly and conservative as possible and acted in every way like a woman born of society. But

Bephino detected something else under her portrayal; another commoner seemed to lurk within. Lucia walked through the large room, making sure the female servants were offering wine to all the guests. It seemed to Bephino as if Florentina was as lost as he was, present at the gathering only because of her beauty and sexual relationship with the count, and not because she was one of them. The smirk on her face and the appearance of her heavily veined hands told Bephino her family history. Bephino's eyes then followed Lucia, who spotted him watching her.

"Ah, Joseph," Lucia called out from the center of the room, as she juggled the various roles she was playing that night. Lucia tapped her husband's shoulder for him to join her, and now they both approached Bephino arm in arm. "Come, Joseph," Lucia called out to him, as though he were some kind of rare species. "I would like to introduce you to my husband, the Count Phillipo Del Rego." Lucia's introduction was brief and unaffected, and Bephino felt it hover over him like a light veil. He quickly perked up to play his part as a smooth, upscale businessman from America, worthy of being a houseguest to this glittering, titled European family. But instead he felt like a vacuum-cleaner salesman. The two men shook hands gracefully and smiled politely at one another. Bephino had him totally in his sights. Now, to put the whole act together: a hole in his chest the size of a plum and a quick getaway out of Europe, he thought. Bephino and Phillipo talked awhile about Italy, Europe, America, and then the hunt. After about fifteen short minutes, Phillipo rejoined the other guests. Lucia was busy circulating among her friends, so Bephino took this opportunity to roam about the mansion's halls, quietly admiring Felini's sumptuous art collections.

After a long while away from the guests, standing off alone in one of the far corners of the atrium's glass-domed rotunda room, Joseph Charles was marveling at a magnificent Spanish suit of armor when from the silence came multiple footsteps entering the large, marble-floored room. Turning quickly, he saw Lucia and Florentina approach him.

"Ohh, this is where you are hiding, Joseph," Lucia called pleasantly. "We were wondering where you may be. Florentina would like to be introduced to you. She claims she was the only one at the party who wasn't introduced. Florentina," Lucia managed curtly but deliberately, "this is my friend Joseph Charles, from Pittsburgh."

Florentina's young, pretty face flushed. Putting out her veined hand, she smiled and said in careful English, "Hello, Joseph Charles. I felt that since we are living under one roof at the moment, we should know each other. I am Florentina Cognetta," she said, stressing the family name that Lucia had not bothered to include in her introduction.

"You're right, Florentina, and I'm so glad to meet you," Bephino replied, and put out his hand to receive hers.

Florentina then coldly said, "Thank you, Lucia," and simply turned and walked away, her heels casting a long, lonely sound on the masonry floor as she disappeared through the double-glassed doorway.

Lucia shook her head, then said apologetically, "She insisted upon meeting you, such an insecure child. She must always show off her English speaking."

"She's young," Bephino answered reassuringly. Lucia purposely did not respond. Still in thought, she puffed in and out for a moment, and then, uttering a sound only she understood, looked up and moved directly in front of the silver-colored suit of armor.

"Who's this guy?" Bephino asked.

"This is an original, sent over from Toledo, Spain. It was once the property of a very, very great and kind man, Umberto Emanuel Aragello," she said thoughtfully. "He sent this to Felini as a gift when Felini was voted governor in 1937. It's an absolute original from the castle of El Cid in Toledo. Priceless," she murmured, while turning and folding her arm through his as they walked slowly toward another piece. Lucia looked up at him and whispered in a thick voice, "Joseph, tonight come to me. My room is only two doors away from yours, on the opposite side of the hall. It's marked 'Venti.' We're both staying in the east wing. After everyone settles down, come to my room, and we will make love."

"What about your husband? Suppose . . ."

Raising her finger to his mouth, she said, "My husband will be too busy watching her. Florentina has that special gleam in her eye tonight. I don't know who for," Lucia said, tilting her head and raising her brows. "But the gleam is there."

"Maybe you should come to my room," Bephino whispered. "It may be better that way . . ."

"Ahh, here you are!" a loud voice echoed off the great masonry walls of the mansion. The sound of husky leather heels clicking quickly on the stone floors confirmed it was a man approaching. Soon Phillipo appeared, with a benevolent smirk on his face. "I was wondering where you both were," the count said, forcing a smile.

"I was just showing Joseph Felini's priceless gift from Umberto," Lucia replied. Then she quickly and thoughtfully added, "Florentina insisted on being introduced to Mr. Charles, so I had to bring her to him for a special introduction."

Bephino focused quietly on both their expressions, sensing that Phillipo now had concern over Florentina's concern, and perhaps even over Lucia's concern.

"Yes, she just told me about that," Phillipo answered coolly. "So, Mr. Charles, are you enjoying yourself?"

"Yes, I really am. It's been a fantastic experience, meeting such fine people of Italy. I'm really anxious to go for the wild boar. Do we hunt in this immediate area?" Bephino asked, trying to change the mood of these modern-day people who claimed they didn't worry about their wives in the company of other men.

"No," Phillipo answered. "We hunt the boar about a four-hour drive from here, on the other side of Milano, heading north toward Penti-Milla. Are you familiar with Penti-Milla?" he asked politely.

"No, I can't say that I am," Bephino replied, looking from Lucia to Phillipo, studying their faces.

"Come, let's join the others," Phillipo announced curtly.

It was then that Bephino knew the kill had to occur the very next day. He could not prolong his stay in such a rapidly chilling atmosphere. The complimentary moves he had made all evening were clearly becoming useless. But now he had to try for the big one: to get close to him.

"Phillipo," Bephino asked ingenuously, "could I hunt alongside you? I would consider it an honor to be able to hunt with a man of your experience."

"Hah!" Phillipo grunted. "We do not hunt side by side," he declared firmly, looking straight ahead as he entwined his arm with his wife's as they continued slowly through the huge corridor. Bephino got the message and retreated. As he walked silently with them, feeling uncomfortable and out of place, his eyes darted nervously at the artifacts on display in the rotunda room. Soon they came to rest on a Portuguese knife on display in a closed-glass tabletop cabinet, a short, ancient, powerful-looking dagger with a blade only about seven inches long. Bephino was impressed with the stoutness of the blade and the grasp made of coarse fisherman's twine over steel for a handle. It seemed easy enough to conceal, he thought, as he returned to the room with its drinking and laughing guests.

Later that evening, Felini announced with some mirth that since the men would be leaving for the hunt at 6:00 A.M., it would be advisable for them to go to bed as early as possible. Breakfast for the hunters would be served at 5:00 A.M. in the main dining room. The party would arrive at the hunt site around noon or before, then begin the hunt later in the afternoon, around dusk.

Bephino approached the robust, amiable Felini and asked if he could borrow some hunting gear. Felini smiled warmly and assured Bephino that everything was prepared and waiting in his room. Moreover, a Browning bolt-action rifle awaited with the equipment aboard the van for him to use at the hunt site. Bephino asked about a skinning knife. Felini smiled and said, "We have boar bearers who do that for us. No knives are needed on the hunt."

For the balance of the evening, Bephino was unable to make any personal contact with Lucia, as she stayed solely in the company of Phillipo, Florentina, and another couple from Rome, the banker Renaldo Farbruzzi and his wife. So he assumed his presence during the night was still expected in Lucia's bedroom. Unsure and uneasy about his plans to kill Phillipo, he wandered around for a while, thinking about the kill. Then, excusing himself, Bephino announced he would retire for the evening. But before going upstairs, he slipped quietly back to the now-dark rotunda room, opened the glass cabinet, and removed the stout Portuguese dagger from its display. Bephino silently made his way upstairs to his room. His bed was turned down for him, a thick pillow and down-stuffed quilt laid over the neatly turned bed. It all seemed too tempting to his weary brain. A small brandy snifter, three quarters filled, sat waiting on his dresser. He undressed and entered a hot shower. As he dried off, he sipped the brandy in deep thought about the hit that he still had no specific plan for. When completely dry, he slid under the thick, feather-stuffed quilt, but not before consulting his watch. It read 12:30 A.M. He turned off the lamp and closed his eyes. Several hours later, Bephino was awakened by the sound of heavy rain, thunder and lightning, and the sound of melting snow and ice sliding off the villa's slate roof to the ground below. He switched on the light, and his watch told him it was after 3:00 A.M. Thinking of Lucia probably waiting for him, he donned his pajama bottoms and quietly wandered down the hall to her room. Looking around before opening her door, Joseph Charles listened for sounds, hoping everyone was asleep; then he quietly and easily slipped into the designated bedroom. Adjusting his eyes to the darkness, he moved slowly toward a dimly lit floor lamp far across the forty-eight-foot-long room and headed for her bed. Knowing what a sex maniac Lucia was, he felt sure she would be awaiting in eager anticipation. Bephino, barefooted and bare chested, felt like a gladiator in this dark arena. Moving slowly and cautiously on the oak-planked floor, he made his way toward the glowing bed. Suddenly, he heard a slurping and moaning sound. Stopping dead in his tracks, he began to focus on what seemed to be two dark shadows making love. The shadows turned into bodies wracked in passionate squirms, and then, to his utter amazement, revealed themselves to be two naked women! It wasn't a man! One body was Lucia's, and the other—in the darkness he couldn't make it out. Her long black hair partially covered her face, but she looked young to him. Bephino swallowed hard and thought to himself, Christ, the bitch really does play many roles! Remaining silent and still, he watched the two women kiss and tongue each other with lust. Bephino, amused, also felt strange. Who was the other woman? He stood and watched quietly. Look at them, he thought, their big tits rolling all over each other. Lucia's hands roamed all over the younger woman's body. Bephino's eyes focused once again. Was it Florentina? But her hair was all tangled in abandon. Finally, the woman tossed her hair back with a sensuous shudder, and Bephino saw it was one of the housemaids who had served the cocktails at the party! Bephino grinned to himself: She's got the fuckin' maid in bed! Unbelievable, he thought; it's that young, naive-looking one. . . . Yeah, that's the maid all right, the heavy-built kid with the wide hips and the sexy Greek nose.

Just at that moment, Lucia began to climb on top of the young woman, and, hovering abreast of her, began licking her taut, swollen nipples, then moved slowly, sensuously, down her belly. Licking amorously, Lucia swabbed around, then lowered herself once again between the thick young thighs of the girl.

Bephino stayed quiet, not a sigh released from his startled body. Gladiator, shit, he thought to himself; Lucia's the fuckin' gladiator! He remained standing, peeking through the darkness of the dimly lit room, looking directly up Lucia's spreading rear as she artistically worked her tongue thoroughly over the young woman's sprawled-out, now throbbing body. Bephino's eyes widened at what seemed to be very pleasurable loving for the younger girl. Lucia's busy head darted around up and down, probing and poking with her erect tongue, when suddenly the girl began to let out yelps and *ohhs* and *ahhs,* followed by sudden and continuous jerking body movements. The girl then recklessly pulled back her legs, holding her thighs apart with her hands. She continued to jerk forward, yelping with a strange, hiccupping sound. After a few moments, the girl settled down. He heard the two women whisper to each other passionately, speaking low but heartily in Italian. The maid's moist, heavily haired womb was now totally wet and fully exposed to Bephino, while Lucia, standing up, toweled herself off. After drying her face, she then adopted the sixty-nine position. Her head now faced Bephino but looking directly up the girl's ass. Lucia dug deep again into the woman's dark womb. Bephino, stunned, closed his gaping mouth and slowly started to back away across the room as both women, moaning out softly, began to stiffen with erotic excitement. They sounded to him almost like heavenly females singing out with joy. Reaching the door he stood for another moment, shaking his head in renewed astonishment. As he slowly opened the door, Lucia's head suddenly balked and spun up at the click. She noticed a person departing in the darkness. The door closed. Lucia's worried head continued upright and erect for a moment, staring strangely at the door she forgot to lock, before it returned down to what was awaiting her lips.

Breakfast was over. It was 6:15 A.M. Two stretch limos and a supply van moved down the mountain for the long ride to Penti-Milla. Bephino sat quietly in the rear corner of the black limo trying to fully awaken in an atmosphere that was filled with intellectual European morning people. Strange-sounding men in the morning, he thought, all laughing, giggling, and acting silly, speaking so rapidly in the northern dialect. Except Phillipo; he sat quietly staring out of the window to his left. Unaware that Bephino understood Italian, the men felt they were able to speak freely, and one fellow actually brazenly asked Phillipo what a man like him was doing as a guest of the Del Regos. Phillipo Del Rego did not reply, a clouded expression crossing his face as he moved about impatiently in his seat. But from the front seat next to the driver, there was a reply. Felini Marcata turned and answered sharply that Mr. Charles was his houseguest—not the Del Regos'. The man quieted to Felini's abruptness. Felini was a decent guy,

Bephino thought, as he wondered to himself yet again what he was doing there to begin with.

Then his thoughts turned completely to the hit. Looking to his left he peered at the man sitting between himself and Phillipo at the other end, busily clearing and looking through his foggy window. Bephino once again considered the tall, refined, elderly gentleman of Milan, highly distinguished—a count, a politician, a man of enormous wealth—who had been recklessly sentenced to death by a Sicilian Mafioso living in Palermo with contacts reaching all the way to the underworld in New York City and directly into the hands of Bronx Mafia boss Gataneo Gaeta and the New York council.

Suddenly, Bephino's thoughts froze. His face paled and his stomach clenched as he realized he had forgotten his passport—it was still in his luggage back at the mansion. The hunters traveled light for the few short days they would be away. But he needed the passport to get back to the States after he made the hit. *Damn,* he thought, I fucked up already. *Stupido.* I gotta kill this guy now, on this trip, or I may lose him altogether. All I got is my American cash and lire with me. How the hell am I gonna get back home? Shit, what a fuckin' screw-up! Them naked broads making love to each other last night messed up my head. I wasn't thinking too straight when I woke up this morning. Jesus, what am I gonna do? Shaking his head in disgust, he slouched down in his seat and closed his eyes. A few hours later he heard the men stirring.

"Ah, we're here," Felini announced excitedly as the cars pulled into the camp area. "Penti-Milla."

Bephino sat back up. "What time do we start the hunt?" he asked a man sitting in a jump seat opposite him.

"First, we unpack," he explained, "then we rest up, have a little lunch, then rest up again in the afternoon. Then about five o'clock," he said with a grin, moving his hands about as he talked, "when the sun goes down, we begin to take up our positions deep into the woods. The boar move around during the dusk hours and into the night."

Bephino looked over at the long-legged Phillipo, who was

now preparing to remove himself from the limo. Wetting his lips in deep thought, Bephino shook his head at what seemed to be a not very well planned hit. But considering the circumstances, he was still on target and very close to his prey indeed.

All the men got out of the car and began to stretch their bodies in the cold, fresh air. Felini motioned for them to enter the lodge building and get their room assignments. "Everyone be casual," he said. "After lunch we will relax until four o'clock, then we will load up and begin to leave for the hunt."

Bephino's eyes were virtually glued on Phillipo. Closely watching all his movements, he tried to determine the older man's capabilities—how much strength he had, what body movement possibilities prevailed, and when the best time would be to end his life. The use of a gun was out. It would cause everyone—including the ammunition bearers and boar skinners—to move quickly to the source of the shots. It had to be done with the knife, silently; then, after the kill, he would quietly leave the area and try to get away, far away, from Penti-Milla. Then he could contact Ben in New York and have another passport sent via the mails as soon as possible, perhaps to a new location in Rome. He would then be able to leave Italy as another person. His eyes followed the Count Del Rego's graceful movements. Bephino again considered his long legs, his half-bald head with its gray hair blowing in the wind. He was surely tall, Bephino thought, which would make it tricky to reach up and grab him. But he was also considerably older. . . . The men entered the hunting lodge. Bephino assured himself he'd be able to handle the man. Bephino stared silently, then smiled naively in the manner of an insecure hunter. The count walked past Joseph Charles without acknowledgement and left the lobby quietly, holding his room key. Bephino stared at the key and then observed the passive ways of the count as he moved about the hall heading for his room, and he began to lose respect for the man. He knew he needed time to get away, so killing him right in the lodge would not be feasible; the woods, he knew, presented the natural possibility that Phillipo might not be discovered until the next morning. If so, that would allow the entire night to get away.

Felini handed Bephino his room key. "We will see you for lunch in one hour," he smiled, trying to be a pleasant host.

"Thank you," Bephino said agreeably. "I'll meet you all at lunch," he nodded, looking at the others who were walking and smiling alongside Felini.

Bephino continued to feel out of place despite Felini's graciousness, and for good reason: he was an imposter, an outsider, and even if he hadn't been there to kill his host's brother-in-law, he would never have fit in; he knew that. But meanwhile, he still needed a plan to make the hit and get away to Rome, or perhaps Sicily. Then he would call Ben and have him send a new passport so he could depart from Italy as a tourist and get back to America. He knew it was a weak plan, not up to the standards of his usual hits. And without a passport and a car to get away, it would be difficult. But he also knew that if he didn't kill Phillipo soon, he might miss his chance altogether. What a mess, he thought. The odds were not good, but he had to do it right then, on that same day, one way or the other. Two and two were definitely coming up three for him on this.

He looked out the lobby window to see if there were any vehicles parked around the area. He was becoming anxious, and that was bad, but it was time to get the ordeal over with. Phillipo was acting too weird; maybe he had a bad feeling about him, Bephino thought. He spotted several cars in the lot. He would double back after the kill and get one and take off to Rome; that's the best he could come up with under the circumstances. He would kill Phillipo quietly with the knife and make a quick exodus. He noticed a small pickup truck parked by the side of the building, as well as a few cars alongside it. Rubbing his chin, he thought that if only he could get a vehicle during the night, he'd have the entire night to drive south. Bephino then left the lobby and went toward his room. Turning the key in the door, he kept thinking of Phillipo. A shame, Bephino thought, to kill this poor guy with an old knife—his brother-in-law's old knife at that. Living the life of a king, the guy had everything: a wife with a hot, wet pussy, a girlfriend less than half his age, and a castle in Vienna. It was a strange world, Bephino mused. "The count," he said to himself, "has no idea I rode his favorite horse, slept in his king-size bed, or fucked his wife in her ass, and now I'm gonna kill the poor bastard. What a world we live in. I gotta get out of this business of killing," he vowed. "I'm gettin' too old for this shit. It seems like it never ends, and them guys in Brooklyn, they never stop. They always got some kind of contract in their back pocket."

At 4:00 P.M. the hunters were fully dressed and standing outside picking up their rifles and ammunition at the supply van. All the men were dressed warmly in heavy, winter-piled coats, pants, and arctic snow boots. The night would be long—fourteen hours long into the morning hours, the coldest hours. Bephino, smiling and nodding politely to the other men as he let them get ahead of him, remained last in line. He waited and watched respectfully as he listened to Phillipo and his friends describe with excited hands their hunting style and adventures on previous excursions. Clutching the Portuguese knife in his pocket, Joseph Charles kept thinking of the kill. He was then handed a Browning bolt-action rifle by the ammo bearer. Felini, watching, quickly approached Bephino and told him that that was his favorite rifle, and that he had killed many, many boar with it. Bephino graciously thanked his host and removed the yellow tag with his name from its butt.

The men all loaded themselves onto a canvas-covered truck for their placement into the bush. Bephino would remember the route so he could walk back after the kill. Meanwhile, Phillipo's attitude toward Joseph Charles remained cool. He had not looked at or spoken directly to him since the previous night, nor had he reconsidered or even acknowledged Bephino's request to hunt alongside of him. The truck rumbled, for about thirty minutes, deep into the countryside, up dirt roads that led to the mountain region where wild boars were known to roam in packs. When the hunting party reached a certain zone, the boar hunt leader, sitting in the truck with the hunters, began to read off the names of the hunters as their posting positions came up in the bush. After the first few hunters were dropped off, the leader called out, "Count Phillipo Del Rego, please." Phillipo got up proudly, as if being called to combat, then awkwardly climbed off the rear of the truck. After a short wait the truck continued to wind slowly up the hill, its gears struggling and straining on its way to the top. The next position, one thousand yards away, was given to Vittorio Giangianelli. Vittorio jumped off, and the truck pulled away. The next name called out was Joseph Charles. Bephino moved to the rear and hopped off the truck. Felini smiled and waved good luck to him. Bephino waved back, but his eyes quickly sought the area where Phillipo had gotten off. He knew Phillipo would already be moving deep into the woods looking for a quality posting position, and so he had to move quickly, before total darkness, or chance getting lost in Italy's thick, black forest.

Bephino watched the truck pull away and fade into the distance, and then he walked back down the mountain toward Del Rego's area. Bephino's heavy boots squished in the deep, crystalized snow, amplifying his activity and presence. But he knew his snow-crunching steps had to come now, when all the hunters were themselves moving about in search of a good spot to post and the winding gears of the truck were still echoing through the mountains. Bephino kept looking around as he walked the long two thousand yards to where the count had been dropped off. But despite his vigilance, he failed to notice, about halfway to his destination, fellow hunter Vittorio Giangianelli crouching down, already posting behind a large stump. Vittorio's eyes silently took in Joseph Charles's progress as he headed in a direction opposite that which he'd been directed to. Vittorio watched Bephino quietly as the outsider opened his rifle chamber and loaded four shells into it. As Joseph Charles moved steadily through the snow in Phillipo's direction, Vittorio's eyes followed him in despair for as long as was possible, but Joseph Charles soon disappeared, covered by the brush, after another fifty feet or so.

When Bephino reached the area where he thought the count should be, he began searching for and soon found the footprints that would lead him to his prey. And sure enough, a few hundred yards farther into the woods sat Phillipo Del Rego on a large rock, waiting for the wild boar to cross his path. Bephino quietly continued toward him. Phillipo heard movement, the sound of someone approaching. He recognized Joseph Charles coming toward him dressed like an Eskimo. Bephino began to wave and smile at him. Phillipo stood up and shouted harshly, "Why you come to me?" as if he knew death was approaching.

"You're not supposed to move from your area!" Phillipo shouted. "Go, now, back to your position!" he demanded nervously.

But Bephino continued on his course, the hand in his pocket tightly clutched around the ancient dagger. He kept smiling and nodding reassuringly, as if about to speak. Both men, heavily dressed for arctic weather, were now up close to one another. Bephino dropped his rifle from his shoulder and lowered it to the ground. He moved forward calmly, then grabbed at Phillipo. Wasting no time, he quickly plunged the thick-bladed knife into the count's heart area, a hard, thrusting stab in the chest.

But Phillipo actively fought back. He began to wrestle with Bephino. Both men reacted clumsily, their heavy winter gear weighing them down. Bephino stabbed at him again, but the count continued his unexpected resistance. Phillipo was putting up a heroically vigorous fight for an old socialite who had already been stabbed twice, Bephino thought. Bephino was now wildly waving the cold steel. His eyes flashed over at the blade and noted that there was only about an inch of blood showing on it. He then realized that the heavy, arctic-type coat the count was wearing protected him from the full length of the blade. Bephino became confused, began crouching down like a wild beast, taunting his prey, this time trying for the neck. Phillipo began to shout in a voice drenched with fear. Suddenly, Bephino lunged at Phillipo with all his strength, slashing wildly at his face and dragging him to the ground. Phillipo screamed out one more time. A frightening groan for help sounded out in the cold air.

Both men lay on the snowy ground, with Bephino holding

Phillipo firmly, ready for the kill. His thoughts were of the Brooklyn Mafia dons waiting for the blood of a man they'd never met. He felt remorse for the struggling old man he was now ready to destroy. Holding Phillipo tightly, Bephino was wracked with second thoughts. Then he realized that if he didn't make the kill, his own wife and children would become vulnerable to the Mob. And with that realization, Bephino began to carve open Phillipo's throat, trying to work between the heavy lamb-pile collar of the count's jacket, directly under his jawbone. Bephino slashed away at his throat, like cutting open a giant cod, and Phillipo let out two more harsh, deep moans before he finally quit. His eyes went into shock. Bephino continued the deep slashing, going deep into and across the jugular, trying to spare Phillipo a prolonged death. He held him securely until he was sure the man had nothing left.

Still on the ground, Bephino felt the lowest of his life. His eyes stared nervously at Phillipo, who lay bleeding, dead in the snow. Catching his breath, he got up and began to visualize the oblivious old faces of the dons who had ordered the hit. *They don't know what we're doin'*, he thought to himself. *We're murderin' the wrong kinda people,* he mumbled in anguish and remorse, as he looked down once again at Phillipo's wide-eyed death stare. Bephino felt like death himself. He bent over and closed Phillipo's eyes, then made the sign of the cross.

Suddenly, he sensed that he was not alone. Turning around quickly, he caught a glimpse of Vittorio Giangianelli's horrified face. Bephino's rifle was lying on the snow, about twelve feet from him and the body. Vittorio seemed scared and frozen solid. Bephino, shocked and startled by Vittorio's presence, was quickly considering whether to go for his rifle, or to make a quick run for Vittorio and cut his throat, or to just plain make a run for it. Then, as Vittorio slowly became unfrozen and raised his rifle at Bephino, the decision was made: Bephino turned and fled, running down a hill dodging trees, sprinting as fast as he could. A bullet was fired and hit a branch next to his ear. Bephino threw himself down, then hauled himself up and proceeded to run once again. He kept moving and ducking behind trees, crouching down, trying to avoid catching a bullet. He then stood up and went for another downgrade and began tumbling and rolling down the hill. Another shot whistled by him, scuffing the snow in his face. Then another shot followed instantly. This one grazed him along the back of his neck, about two inches below his head. He was hit and hurt, but the bullet had not entered his body; it had just damaged a chunk of muscle on the back of his neck. Bephino, still alert and strong, desperately continued his flight as he rolled down the steep hill. Finally, near the bottom, pausing behind a thick tree, he stood up and felt hot blood gushing down his back and into his long underwear and pants. Bephino began to move again. It seemed endless; the weight of his boots and heavy clothing wore him down. The loss of blood made him weak. Suddenly, he heard the sound of squealing boars running past him. He ran until he reached a cliff overlooking a dirt road. He awkwardly slid down the side of the cliff to the road below. Utterly exhausted and losing blood steadily, he slipped into unconsciousness.

About half an hour later, a man driving by saw Bephino's body slumped over on the shoulder of the road and took him all the way to the mountaintop village of Santa Anna. Later that evening, already stripped of his clothing, Bephino regained consciousness just in time to see a doctor looking over him and four Catholic nuns praying. Covered only by a white sheet, he heard the doctor speaking rapidly. "We must operate right away to close the neck," he said to the nuns in Northern Italian dialect. "We must operate to stop the bleeding."

"Yes, operate . . . operate . . . operate." The word kept ringing in Bephino's ears as he was being positioned on a table with the bright lights of the operating room glaring down on him.

"Blood, keep giving him blood," the doctor ordered excitedly, preparing him for surgery, as the feeling of needles pricked Bephino's neck. "Be quick, we have only *cinque minuti,*" he pleaded with the nuns while scrubbing for the operation. Bephino's pulse was exceedingly weak; the blood would strengthen him for the surgery. The nuns worked very fast, hovering all the while over him. Forty minutes later, the operation was over and the patient was alive.

But while lying in the recovery room, Bephino slipped into a semicoma. The next day, he was still comatose and unresponsive in a cold, drab, ancient hospital room, green paint peeling from the walls, in the unused wing of the extremely primitive Santa Anna Catholic Hospital that had once been widely used by the German forces during World War II.

Later that afternoon, the doctor, making his rounds, stopped by Bephino's bed, placed his stethoscope to his heart, and listened. After a few moments, he rolled back his lips and turned to the assisting nuns. "His heart tells me he still strongly lives, but like *morte,*" the doctor shrugged.

"Come un morto," like the dead, the nuns repeated, turning to each other as they made the sign of the cross. Bephino could hear them talking but could not respond.

FEBRUARY 16, 1977, 11:00 A.M.

PENTI-MILLA, ITALY

The day following the murder was hectic for Felini Marcata and his hunting party. The Penti-Milla police began questioning the entire group of hunters, and called for the presence of the Countess Del Rego and Florentina to identify the body.

Vittorio Giangianelli moved his hands dramatically as he explained how Joseph Charles, the American, walked through the woods, straight to Phillipo. When Vittorio heard Phillipo's screams, he related, he followed quickly in the American's footsteps to the murder site. "The American was like an animal," Vittorio said loudly, squeezing his fist. "He was on the ground holding Phillipo and cutting his throat like a crazy man. Phillipo squirmed like a dying chicken," he explained excitedly. "The American jumped up quick, and he ran fast between the trees. He moved too quickly for me to see clearly." Vittorio moved his hands as if aiming. "I shot three times, but he was impossible to hit. We looked for blood down the hill, but no blood."

"Why didn't you help Phillipo?" the police chief asked. "Why didn't you use your weapon when you first saw him attack Phillipo?"

Vittorio yelled at the police chief. "Like I told you, I could not see him clearly; I shot at him but missed!" The Penti-Milla police, giving up for the moment on Vittorio, looked toward the others—including Lucia—for an answer.

They had no way of knowing that Bephino had indeed been hit, but that the blood from the wound had drained down his neck and into his clothes, and not onto the snow. And so the police figured Bephino must still be at large, uninjured, and most probably on his way to Rome or Milano or some other big city. Possibly he had already crossed the nearby French border or gone into Monte Carlo, only a short distance away.

After questioning the hunters, Florentina, and Lucia, the police began regarding Lucia as a possible suspect. She was questioned intensively about her friend Joseph Charles, and if the American had been her longtime lover. As her lover, he might well have also been her hired killer. Lucia was frantic at the wild accusation. What would her children think? They all had loved Phillipo immensely. She was in no way part of this savage slaying of her husband—she was innocent! She had always loved Phillipo! Felini Marcata attacked the police chief's presumption and defended his sister. Lucia sat, quiet and distraught, her complexion now a strange, pale gray. Florentina sat as well, bewildered, watching it all. The old chief of police asked Lucia outright: "Did you bring this American man here to kill your husband?"

"No!" she screamed frantically. "I loved Phillipo! I worshipped him! He was my husband!"

"Where are your children?" the chief asked.

"Away in Sydney, Australia, on a holiday with their families. I told you that already," Lucia replied in her Northern Italian dialect.

Felini Marcata regularly interrupted the questioning of his sister by threatening to have the regional governor himself chase the police captain out of Penti-Milla and back to the woods where he belonged. After a while it became clear that no further progress was going to be made.

"All right, Signora Del Rego," the chief of police concluded with a sigh. "We will let you go for now, but you are not allowed to leave the *provincia* of Milano, and this is an order. You may not return to Vienna. Please turn in your passport by 2:00 P.M. today to the Penti-Milla police clerk's department." He then turned away from her and stared angrily at Felini. After a few moments, the police chief's eyes returned to Lucia. Looking down at her with an impassive face, he said firmly, "At least stay in Milano until I finish my investigation of the brutal slaying of your distinguished husband. You may have to return to our region for more questions."

Everyone then left Penti-Milla and headed back to Felini's Milano villa. The next day, Felini immediately called his battery of attorneys, who rushed to the mansion for a private conference with Lucia and Felini Marcata. After the attorneys had asked their routine questions, Felini told them, "The police wanted Lucia to turn in her passport by two o'clock that afternoon, but she didn't. We had no time to send for someone to come all the way to Penti-Milla with it, a few hours' drive from our home," Felini said, raising his eyebrows expressively. "I told Lucia to speak to an attorney first."

The four attorneys grinned across the room at each other, confirming one another's contempt for the Penti-Milla police treating her so unprofessionally, asking for her passport but not holding her.

"Lucia," the head attorney, Guiseppe Fertinelli, reassured her, working his hands before her face. "The Penti-Milla police force consists of exactly three men, plus one woman clerk! They really have no serious contact out of Penti-Milla. They will try their best to forget the whole incident by tomorrow." Lucia began to cry, wiping her eyes with a linen. "Listen to me, Lucia!" Fertinelli growled, as he dropped his hands with a benevolent look on his face. "No sense to cry," he said, leaning across Felini's desk. "If you want my professional advice, pack your clothes and leave right now for your home in Vienna, before the Milano police really enter the case. The Penti-Milla police only act like they want to handle the investigation, which, of course, is in their jurisdiction—and that's good for us, because they don't know what to do, they don't know how to handle it. They already goofed up by letting their prime suspect leave Penti-Milla. Even the newspapers won't get a correct story from Penti-Milla, trust me; and Milano police will rather stay away from it. After a few days, it will be called a hunting accident. You have not been charged, so you have every right to leave the country. And the American, Joseph Charles, will be completely forgotten by lunchtime tomorrow. The police will be so embarrassed they'll be grateful to return to their school crossings and happy to forget that this Charles ever existed."

"Can they arrest me in Vienna?" Lucia asked.

"For what?" Fertinelli asked, shrugging and waving his hands. "For what?" he repeated. "You did nothing; you did not kill your husband in the woods. It was the act of a madman. Perhaps, at the very most, the act of a jealous American lover. Italy will never try to extradite a high-profile woman like yourself with such trivial evidence. It's too risky for them. Now go, today, back to Austria. They will never attempt an extradition on the request of the Penti-Milla police," Fertinelli assured her. "Trust me, Lucia, the case will fade into history by tomorrow. I've been Felini's attorney for more than thirty years." Fertinelli raised his eyes. "Your husband's body will be sent to his home in Vienna for the funeral, and it is only right that you be there to make the necessary arrangements."

"What shall we do with the belongings left here by the American?" Felini asked the group of attorneys.

"What belongings?" Guiseppe Fertinelli asked, walking to Lucia and delicately raising her from her chair, then purposefully, soothingly, escorting her toward the door.

As Felini, too, arose, one of the younger attorneys, Alberto Tomosi, caught his eye, motioning him to the other side of the room for a private talk. "Gather all the remaining personal effects belonging to the American and burn them right away," Tomosi whispered to Felini. "Do it now! Put them in the furnace," he emphasized. And then he walked away. Felini curled his lips and stared.

Later that week, a small article appeared in a Palermo newspaper:

JEALOUS LOVER SLAYS PARTY LEADER, COUNT PHILLIPO DEL REGO. Born Phillipo Marcello Del Rego, the son of powerful Mussolini supporters Benedicto Pocci Del Rego and Maria Chellino Del Rego, both members of the Italian Fascist Party of 1939, he was murdered savagely by an American tourist, asserted to have been the friend of the ex-movie star the Countess Lucia Sabella Marcata Del Rego. Count Phillipo, an active member of the Southern Council of Italy's Communist Party, was nominated by the Socialist Partisan Party for a stronger voice of communism in Southern Italy's District 109. Count Del Rego narrowly won his election over Renaldo Apolimi of Palermo, Sicily. Had he lived, Count Phillipo would have achieved . . ."

4

SATURDAY, MARCH 2, 1977, 3:00 P.M.

BROOKLYN, NEW YORK

Five men sat around a table in a Bensonhurst social club. Rocco Boretti, Boss of Bosses, conferred across the table with Ben Del Ponte, acting boss of the Bephino Menesiero mob, and Menesiero family capo Aldo ("The Monkey") Pastrona. Porky Capeto, a Boretti capo, spoke out.

"So where is Bephino now?" Porky asked.

Ben glanced briefly at Monkey, then shrugged at the three Boretti people. "That's a hard question for us to answer. We know he's someplace in Europe makin' contact with the count, but we don't know where he is. You guys gave him the instructions," Ben said. "You probably know more about his whereabouts than us."

Monkey quickly interrupted. "Hold it, Ben. Why do they wanna know where he's at?" Monkey raised his head at Rocco Boretti in question. "What's the difference where he's at?" Monkey's eyes darted piercingly back over at Ben, sitting alongside him. "Bephino's got work to do, he's busy over there. You guys are asking where he is like he's around the corner," Monkey scowled.

"Because we got word he was at the scungilli house on Mott Street not too long ago," Rocco said in a rough-sounding voice, "that's why." He looked back at Monkey, ostentatiously raising a cup of demitasse to his lips with the hand that was missing a finger.

"Yeah, but that was a few weeks ago," Ben said, frowning. "He's been away for a while, doing that thing for you, since then."

Rocco raised a good finger at Ben. "We just wanna make sure he's handling that item for us," he insisted smugly. "Because a lot of blood's gone into this job, *a capisce?*" Rocco said, reaching for his cup again. "We just want confirmation he's on the job."

"I wouldn't worry about him being on the job, because when Bephino goes to work, they gotta hurry and order their tux," Ben sneered back.

"You guys make me laugh. You think going to Europe's gonna be a quick, easy job?" Monkey huffed, shaking his head at them. "He's all alone over there. He don't know how to speak German or Austrian. He ain't got nobody with him, it's not gonna be as easy for him as you guys think. He's gotta make contact with that fuckin' prince. And it ain't so easy for guys like us to get close to them kinda people," Monkey reiterated.

"The guy's a fuckin' count, not a prince," Porky Capeto, Rocco's fattest wise guy, said. "He can get near a guy like that pretty easy. It's no big deal," Porky snuffed.

"Yeah? If it was so easy, why didn't you go and do it, ya meathead?" Monkey snapped, then added with a chuckle, "With a fat head like yours, they'd never let you get through the customs. They don't let Porks in or outta Europe," Monkey crowed.

Porky whispered to Rocco, "Would you believe this shit, a fuckin' Unkymay like this calling me a meathead?" He stared sharply at Monkey and said, "You're outta order."

Monkey stared back across the table. "Whata ya, supposed to scare me or what? I'm outta order? Go look in the fuckin' mirror, ya mutt, and go scare yourself. Your ass is hangin' half off the chair like a fuckin' pork store." Ben's eyes rolled with laughter, and even Rocco laughed at Monkey's rattling.

Ben chimed in with Monkey. "Bephino should have never been sent on that thing, Rocco," he said, chancing a blunt remark.

The Boss of Bosses' smile instantly drained from his face. "Yeah, why not?" Rocco growled.

"Because he's a don, not a button. He was your friend, you bought his house, he was loyal to you and Morrano . . . that's why! And you guys showed him that respect means shit, and you know it," Ben returned.

"Oh, yeah!" Rocco snarled, twisting his face in anger. "And you're not showing me *il rispetto,* right now! You're questioning me and my reasons!" Rocco glared at Ben impassively. "And I don't like that, Beoggio," he added softly, using Ben's Italian name to signify his seriousness.

Ben backed up three giant steps. "Wait a minute, Rocco. We always honored your position, and you know that. We've always respected you and Morrano," he quickly repented, "but we can't forget easily that Bephino was your friend. You and Bepy did great things together when Morrano was alive—and for respect, you sent him off to Europe, because Gaeta asked you to. It don't make sense to me; Bepy was your true friend."

Porky looked over at the guy sitting next to him and smiled. "Friend, my ass," he whispered.

Rocco held up his hand with the missing finger once again and said, "Yeah, I know we did great things together, and he was always supposed to accept my orders with the unquestioning duty of a true friend—but he didn't. So the next place we're gonna send him is China. Maybe he can do great things over there, like Marco Polo did. OK," Rocco snapped his voice, "you guys are better off going now." Rocco waved his hand like royalty, dismissing them. "Keep in touch. We wanna be kept posted when the 'man of respect' comes back, *a capisce?*" Rocco grinned at his people. "You tell Bephino all we wanna know is when and where our royal friend went to heaven, OK? And he can pick up the hundred grand for his services. Nimo's waitin' for him, tell him that!"

Ben rose from the table. "Nimo's waitin' for him?" Ben asked with a smirk and a knowing stare. "I'll tell him." Then Ben walked around and embraced Rocco Boretti, kissing him on both cheeks, showing the don of dons the utmost respect. Monkey merely watched and casually moved toward the door without saying good-bye or showing an ounce of respect to anyone. He opened the door and walked out of the club, buttoning up his overcoat. The 280-pound Porky got up from the table and headed for the club's storefront window. He leaned forward and stared out at Monkey and Ben walking away. His right hand reached back behind himself, pulling his pants out from the crack of his ass.

Later in the car, Monkey asked Ben, "How could you embrace and kiss that rubber?"

Ben turned to Monkey, who was driving. "Whata ya talking about, he's the Boss of Bosses," Ben answered adamantly. "We gotta show the bastard some honor and respect."

"I'll show him shit," Monkey answered. "He's gonna kill Bepy when he comes back, sure as my name is Monkey. I could smell it all over him, and from what you told me about the cutting off of his finger and all that shit, I could see it's gonna be a gruesome death. Rocco Boretti ain't gonna lose a finger in front of all the bosses in New York and forget it. He's gonna kill Bepy and even you—he's gonna kill you and me," Monkey insisted. "Whata ya think of that? A guy like that don't lose a finger for nobody. We better get ready for a fuckin' war!" Monkey intoned, hitting the wheel. "There's bad blood rolling around in that guy's eyes."

"I know," Ben replied, shaking his head. "I agree—whata ya think, I'm stupid? That's why I embraced him. I wanna stay close and friendly so I can embrace him again some other time with a fuckin' .38 to his chest. I wanna keep things nice for a while. We gotta be able to get close to him if we're gonna make arrangements for him—would ya watch your driving!"

Ben yelled suddenly. "You're in the other fuckin' lane! Slow down before you wreck this thing!"

"Don't worry about my driving, start worrying about Boretti. We better make his arrangements pretty fast, before he makes ours," Monkey puffed. "You're worrying about the wrong things—my driving! I could tell you right now, Ben, Boretti's gonna move on us."

"Fuck Boretti, for now," Ben said. "You better worry about Porky; he was watching us from the window when we left," Ben laughed. "He's really pissed off at you."

Monkey grinned back. "I love when that fat bastard gets upset. He's probably walking around right now pulling at the pants in his crack."

"I know," Ben smiled, "I could just picture him doing that. Hey! Let's go over to the Eastside Gym, the kid's working out this afternoon. I wanna see what kinda shape he's in."

"How's he comin' along?" Monkey asked.

"Real good; he's gettin' faster and faster. We booked him in Atlantic City for next week. He's fightin' some Puerto Rican. The Rican won his last one by a knockout. That makes him ten and 0. If Alley Boy beats him, that's five in a row for him. It should be the big breakthrough for the kid, if he wins! He'll go from a four rounder to a six rounder; then, in a few months, if everything goes well, to eight or ten rounders. He's young. I don't wanna take him up too fast, the guy he's fightin' is twenty-two years old. Alley's only about eighteen, I think. He looks much older, but he's only a kid. He don't have the killer instinct that I want him to have. He's homegrown, sorta mothered," Ben added. "The kid grew up in a different kinda environment than us. But that's OK, I got the ol' nigger, Pinky Williams, training him. Pinky knows his stuff, he's trained a lotta good fighters in his day. When we get through with him, this kid will be a driving force right to the heavyweight championship of the world. Alley Oop would have been proud of his son, believe me," Ben said, puckering his lips and sadly raising his brows to Monkey.

"I know," Monkey said softly. "Alley Oop woulda went nuts over having his own son. . . . When is Bephino expected back from Europe?"

"I really don't know, soon as he finishes with his work. It's already been a couple of weeks. Maybe he's fuckin' around on the French Riviera," Ben smiled. "You never know with him, he could be banging some French movie star by now."

March 4, 1977, 5:30 A.M.

Santa Anna, Italy

Three nuns prayed before Bephino Menesiero's failing body. Bephino's room was still in semidarkness. An I.V. tube with plasma was taped tightly to his left arm. Suddenly, during the prayers, the room's heavy oak door opened. In the doorway's light stood short, heavyset Mother Columbo Fabiano, the world-famous nun from South Africa, newly arrived to serve as mother superior to the Convent of Our Lady of Santa Anna. Behind her stood a pale, bland-looking, smock-wearing young Italian girl named Tattania, a nurse's aide. The mother superior entered slowly, her hands clasped. She waited, hawkeyed and impatient, for Sister Graciella, Sister Maria, and Sister Helena to complete their morning prayers. Her awesome shape in her parish dress resembled that of an enormous army tent, and her face was serious as an old owl's. Young Tattania also remained silent as the prayers continued, standing off to the side of Mother Fabiano, holding a pan of warm, soapy water. Finally, the three nuns completed their morning prayers. Making the sign of the cross, they turned and greeted their mother superior. "Good morning, Mother," all three said pleasantly, like smiling angels in the dark.

The mother superior only nodded, then whispered in a deep, raspy voice, as was her way when about to make her point, "In South Africa, we always washed and shaved the comatose first, *then* we began our prayers. In this case," she said with sour confidence, "I'll make an exception to the rule. Please complete your prayers by 5:30 A.M. I want this man to be shaved and bathed each morning at 5:30 sharp. He's dirty, unshaven, and neglected." The three nuns quickly nodded and left the room.

At that moment, young Tattania quickly moved to the patient's side, lathering up his face with the warm, soapy water. She turned to Mother Fabiano, and asked, "Should I leave his mustache?"

Mother Fabiano, standing still and solid, her old bird-face wrinkled and stern, stared and kept silent. Then, suddenly, she nodded. "Yes, on this man, we'll make an exception. Until we find out who he is, he will keep the look he came to us with."

The young girl began to rub the soap into his skin and noticed Bephino's scar. "Look, Mother! He has a scar under his neck," Tattania pointed out.

Mother Fabiano walked up closer, lowered her head to view the scar, and then left the room.

5

March 16, 1977, 9:00 p.m.

Vienna, Austria

"Where did you first meet the American, Joseph Charles?" Felini Marcata asked his sister one night on his first visit to the Villa Italia since the funeral. Lucia sat solemnly in a plush velvet chair next to a roaring fire. Her face was pale and chalky. Her rich, thick black hair hung down over her shoulders. She looked much changed—fragile and weak.

Felini, sipping white wine, stood facing the fire. Turning to his sister, speaking gently in Italian, he asked her softly, "Tell me, Lucia, where did you meet that madman?"

Lucia took in a shaky breath. "Outside," she shrugged. "Outside our front gates, on the road," she answered, pressing down on her stomach as if to tame its upset. Looking straight ahead into the fire's flames, she repeated in a soft Italian, "I met him on the road; he was stuck."

"Then what?" Felini asked.

"His car was broken down."

"So you helped him?"

"Yes, of course I helped him. I drove him to his hotel. He seemed very nice." She turned, looking at Felini. "He asked me to dinner. At first I refused, but he was persistent."

"And charming, I suppose?" Felini asked, raising his right hand to his forehead.

"Yes, and charming," she said puffing out, turning back quickly to face the fireplace. "You saw him, Felini," she said. "Would you think such a man would kill?"

"Lucia," Felini said, nodding in sympathy for his sister's nightmare and touching her shoulder with affection, "it's better we talk just a little bit at a time about it," Felini whispered. "It's no good to hold it in. . . . Tomorrow we will talk again, and eventually it will all pass for you." He bent over and kissed Lucia goodnight on her forehead.

The next evening during dinner, Felini and Lucia sat at a long table. Lucia talked about Joseph Charles once again, while Felini listened, sipping his wine. "He seemed like such a perfect gentleman," she said. "We had dinner at the hotel and after dinner we had a few drinks and I went home, back to the villa. Over the next few days we saw each other, went horseback riding, had dinner together—we really enjoyed each other's company. I can't believe this man murdered Phillipo," she said raising her eyes at Felini, "and for what reason? For what reason," she repeated, shaking her head and placing her hand to her mouth. "He did not know Phillipo. I can't believe this whole thing really happened," she said, shaking her head again and sighing deeply.

Felini nodded sympathetically, then gently shushed his sister across the table. "It's OK, darling," he said in a low, understanding voice. "It's OK; time will take care of your nightmare for you," he whispered, wiping his own wet eyes with his linen.

"What about Florentina?" Felini abruptly asked, in an attempt to change the mood.

"What about her?" Lucia questioned.

"What will she do now that Phillipo is gone?"

Lucia paused and thought for a moment. Her face suddenly seemed relaxed and calm. Then raising her eyes thoughtfully, she exclaimed, "Florentina!" exposing for the first time an unsavory grin. "Florentina will, of course, remain in my service, darling. What else is she suited for?"

Felini stared densely at his sister. His concerned eyes began to blink nervously across the table.

Nearly a month later, in April, Sisters Helena, Maria, and Graciella were making their early-morning rounds. Bephino continued to lie silent and still, his frail body nearly without breath, and very cold. The nuns came to his bedside and began the Hail Mary. Despite Bephino's semicomatose state, he could hear the nuns praying for him. It was like being in a straitjacket without being able to speak out, he thought to himself. The operation had gone fine, he'd heard the doctor say, until the spinal nerve in his neck leading to his brain had become overexposed. Now it was failing to send formal messages to the brain's directing systems. "I'm cold," he thought, "I'm so cold." The nuns were getting ready to leave, and they were making the sign of the cross over his body. "Give me a coupla blankets," he willed, hoping they would realize he was freezing. The nuns left quietly. "Look at me, I'm trapped in my own body! They only got a sheet over me. God finally caught up with me. I'm freezing to death!" Bephino's mind began to wander. Hours of loneliness, lying on his back, took him back many years to when he was a boy back in Boston, and then to New York City.

My grandfather is smiling at me. Look at him, he's like a bull, my Papa.

"Grandpa, are we in the Mafia?"

"Why you talka Mafia; you're only a boy, you're ten years

old. Figlio mio, *who tella you Mafia?" the old man asks, shaking his grandson.*

"The Jewish boys, Papa. They call me Mafioso."

The old man smiles. "Ah, the Jewish boys!" he says softly, "Eh ejewda, they like to teasa you. . . ."

"I want you to hurt this guy good," Don Emilio Morrano whispers to Bephino. "They call him Fat Man. He's from 4th Avenue, over in downtown Brooklyn. Can you handle it?"

"Yeah, I can handle it, Mr. Morrano, that's my racket. You want this guy Fat Man in a coma, right?"

"Ha, a coma, sounds good . . . a coma. Yeah, here's two hundred bucks, Bephino. Be careful you don't wind up in a coma yourself. Fat Man's a tough guy."

"Thank you, Mr. Morrano. You can order Fat Man's flowers now. . . ."

"You dance well for a cherry," Anita says, pressing her pelvis to his groin. "Let's dance again; the band's playing the merengue," she insists while rubbing his chest. Bephino cuts a thin figure on the dance floor, moving the smiling Spanish lady back and forth to him. "Come to Mama," she whispers, as she presses her pussy to him once again.

And then, thirty minutes later, "Come to Daddy," he whispers as he positions his long, thick prick between her naked, yearning thighs.

"Come on, fuck me again, baby," Anita begs, exposing her tongue while playing with her own breast. "I need you again; give it to me again," she whispers thickly in Spanish to Bephino.

"I gotta go," he hisses. "Your boyfriend is downstairs having cramps. I gotta get outta here before he starts shittin' . . ."

"Pete Lungo is dead, I killed him for you, Sally. He's dead. Peter is morte,*" Bephino tells Mafia capo Sally De Mateo.*

"Are you sure he's dead, you fuckin' young punk? Are you sure he's dead?" Sally asks.

"He's got a fuckin' hole in his head as big as your girlfriend's cunt," Bephino replies disrespectfully to Sally. Then Bephino yells, "Go tell Mr. Morrano I did everything for you tonight. I fucked your Puerto Rican girlfriend and I made the hit for you!"

"I'm gonna kill you, kid," Sally snarls at Bephino. "Maybe not tonight, but it's gonna happen."

"Not if I kill you first, Sally!" Bephino snarls back.

"Monkey, Alley Oop, Red, we're a team for life. We got a lifetime contract with a very important firm, and we gotta keep the board of directors happy. We're gonna get respect. We're gonna make hits for the big guys, and that means big bucks. . . ."

"Bephino, I'm gonna give you the contract you been waiting for. Big bucks, remember, big bucks," the Mafia don Emilio

Morrano, Boss of all Bosses, says to the Young Turk Bephino Menesiero. "I want you to kill Vince the Hawk Gacolido from East New York. The contract pays twenty-five grand."

"Thanks, Mr. Morrano, I sure could use the twenty-five thousand. . . ."

Ben stands smiling like a beautiful cobra, eyeing up Bephino. "We gotta go to New Orleans on this hit," Ben says, nodding at the kid.

"I'm good at those out-of-town hits. I work better under pressure," Bephino says, smiling back at Ben.

"We gotta hit a congressman. How old are you?" Ben asks.

"Twenty-one," Bephino replies. . . .

"Dana, where's the babies?"

"They're in the playroom, Bephino. They're playing with their toys."

"Bring them to me, sweetheart, I wanna kiss them a little."

"You always were good at kissing at the wrong time," Dana pouts. "I just sat down for the first time today, and now you wanna kiss the babies."

"Dana, I gotta go away for a few days. Don't ask me what I'm doing, it's business. Get the kids for me, I wanna squeeze them for a while."

"Rene! Patsy! Come in the den, your daddy wants to squeeze you. He's going fishing for Moby Dick again!" Dana squints her face at Bephino.

"I got bad news for you, Bephino," Ben says, shaking like a leaf.

"What kinda bad news? And stop that fuckin' shaking!" Bephino yells.

"Alley Oop is dead. He got killed by the nigger we were gonna hit."

"Alley Oop!!" Bephino screams out. "Alley Oop, my friend for twenty years! How could you let that happen, Ben, how could you? I want you out of this business, Ben, you're

through. I'm telling Morrano no more hits for you. You're out. . . ."

Bephino lay reminiscing, with no one to talk to, no one to warm him. Not even the nurse's aide had come today to wash him. It was another lonely day for Bephino Menesiero.

BROOKLYN, NEW YORK

One evening at the end of May, back in the rear corner of the crowded Thrao Sorella restaurant in Brooklyn, seven men sat around a large round table. Mafia chieftains Gataneo ("the Gentleman") Gaeta, Pat Salvatore, Rocco Boretti, Tony Boy Cafaci, Angelo ("the Butcher") Marandala, and buttons Bruno ("the Jock") Vitali and Darino ("Easy Trigger") Botti were all busy talking and chewing on special homemade beef tripe cooked in a very light tomato sauce.

"This place is under new ownership," Tony Boy said to the others while chewing hard on Italian bread. "We give him a little business from time to time. They're good people; the three sisters do the cooking and the brothers walk around with suits and ties, shaking hands with everybody." Tony grinned. "They stare at everybody's wife and make them feel important."

"You still enjoy to dip the bread, I see—hah, Tony?" Angelo Marandala teased as he stretched half across the table to grab for the basket of crisp Italian bread. "You took all the ends, I see, Tony," Marandala whined, looking in the half-empty basket.

Tony Boy grinned sheepishly. "Since I was a kid," he answered in his deep, husky voice, "I always dipped the ends of the bread in the sauce. I still love it. My wife gets mad when I do it. She says, 'That's not nice, to dip.'" Hump-bellied Tony Boy grinned around the table at all the men, then said with a broad smile, "But she never complains when I dip it in her! Ha! Ha! Ha!" Tony Boy burst out laughing and began a bout of coughing while holding a linen napkin to his mouth. He turned red. "Jesus Christ!" he said, gasping for air. "Every time I talk about my wife, I see God in front of me!"

Gataneo leaned forward, his sparrow face smiling passively across the table. Directing his voice toward Tony Boy Cafaci, he whispered, "You shouldn't speak about your wife like that, especially in front of other men." Gataneo Gaeta blinked and stared across at Cafaci. After a moment he lowered his old eyes and glanced over to Rocco Boretti for confirmation of his wisdom. Boretti's stern, cold face begrudgingly released a short grunt of acknowledgement. Gataneo then casually turned from Boretti to Darino Botti, sitting next to him. "Darino," the soft-spoken, thin-faced Gaeta said, holding his glass out for a refill, "pass me the wine, please." While waiting, the toothless Gaeta nonchalantly swallowed the moisture that had accumulated in his mouth. His skinny throat moved with the rhythm of his jaws as he quietly chewed on nothing. Darino, without hesitation, reached for the wine jug and filled the old don's glass to the top. Watching all this from across the large table, bald-headed Tony Boy Cafaci, still smarting over Gaeta's words, stared silently back at him. Gaeta felt Tony's eyes boring into him. He grinned to himself and repeated in a soft tone, "It's not nice to speak about *la sposa* like that, Tony, especially in the company of men." Gaeta smiled at Tony Boy, then lowered his eyes and began awkwardly spreading butter on a thick hunk of Italian bread. Gaeta kept raising his eyes to Tony Boy, his eyes flashing from the bread and butter to Tony. "After all," Gaeta continued, grinning, *"la sposa,* she's the mother of your children!" Then suddenly, as if dropping the subject, Gaeta raised his wineglass to the others. *"Salute* to *la sposa, buona fortuna,"* he said again in an Italian jest of good luck: *Salute* to their wives who, of course, were home and not present. Then, biting delicately into the bread, he sipped some red wine to help break it down in his toothless mouth.

"Salute, buona fortuna," all the men replied, raising their glasses back at Gaeta. *Buona fortuna* were special words used by their Sicilian fathers upon embarking from Sicily to the New World many years before. While eating and drinking,

Tony Boy kept his brown eyes fixed above his wineglass in a mixture of rage and shame at Gaeta's reprimand.

"Ah, si bella, questo vino," Gaeta's frail, confident face groaned as he sipped again of the dark red wine. As he turned and smiled at Rocco Boretti, his thin lips rolled with satisfaction, his gums bouncing up and down in his toothless mouth. *"Sono buoni."*

Rocco quietly smiled at the elderly don, amused at the way the old, white-haired man had softly scolded burly Tony Boy.

Tony Boy seemed uncomfortable. He mumbled to Bruno Vitali next to him, "*La sposa,* my ass. He thinks he knows everything, the old bastard." But as he felt Gaeta's eyes coming to rest on him, Tony Boy turned away and changed the subject. Nervously pointing to the owner of the restaurant, he announced, "See this guy, Larry Sorella? He's the one who makes the grape juice. Did you know that?" After quickly surveying the men around the table, Tony Boy lowered his head to his dish and scooped up a piece of tomato-covered white tripe. Busy sopping on the chewy white meat, Tony Boy added, "His father comes from my piazza in Palermo. Now the whole family lives on 84th Street and 14th Avenue. They make the wine right in the cellar. It's homemade," Tony said proudly.

"Andy could tell it was homemade the minute he smelled it," the frail-faced Gaeta offered to Rocco Boretti dryly. "Andy would tell you in two seconds it's homemade," Gaeta smirked, his Adam's apple sticking way out of his collar and his tongue slithering around loosely. "It's very rich," he blabbered, holding his glass up to the light. "It's not like the commercial junk they sell today," he reported to the group at large.

Tony Boy's face reddened once again, and his eyes shone bright with embarrassment. Looking back at Gaeta, he then surveyed the rest of the crowd around the table, still chuckling over Gaeta's subdued ribbing. After a moment, Tony asked loudly, "Who the fuck is Andy?"

"Andy? Andy's my dog," Gaeta replied straight-faced, sucking on a piece of bread dipped in wine.

"Whata ya got, your balls twisted tonight or what!" Tony screeched out at Gaeta, looking wildly over at Rocco Boretti and then around the table to the men who were barely able to contain their laughter. Tony, pointing his fork at Gaeta, said, "This guy fucked up a beautiful tripe dinner tonight."

"Sounds like he's after you tonight, Tony Boy," Boretti said in a muffled voice behind his napkin, stifling a laugh.

"Yeah, all of a sudden he's worried about my wife!" Tony Boy grumbled out loud. *"La sposa!* And meanwhile he's got his *la sposa* home talking to herself while she's wearing those fuckin' microphones on her ears, and he's out getting sucked off by his black hooker up in the Bronx. She blows his brains out. Look at him, how small he's getting with that banana nose. Why don't you wear your *teeth* when you eat with us!" Tony yelled. Then, turning to Bruno the Jock: "Look at him, he's all collar and tie. Look at him, the fuckin' nose on the old bastard! *Look* at him," Tony kept saying, "look at his face with the tripe hanging out of his mouth like a worm. *La sposa,* his fucking ass! Andy? I'll give you *Andy*!" Tony Boy exploded. Gaeta himself had to laugh at Tony's tirade. The men all joined in. Tony leaned over to Bruno, busy filling his face with tripe, and whispered, pointing with his fork, "He's a fuckin' expert on everything, the cheap bastard. I know for a fact he's got his first dollar still salted away. Whata ya think of that?" Tony Boy asked. Bruno lowered his head and quickly raised his napkin to his face to hide his own laugh. Then Tony chuckled, looking around the table. "You guys think I'm kidding? Watch when the check comes." He pointed at Gaeta. "When he sees the fuckin' check, he gets stomach cramps, and he goes to the backhouse. You watch!" Tony yelped. "You watch!"

After a while all the meat and Italian bread were consumed. The waiter came with a pot of espresso and a large bowl of fresh fruit. The men sat back, and between burps each of them casually began to unwrap their long, thick cigars.

"So you all know we got the news from Sicily that the Count Del Rego guy is *morte,"* Rocco Boretti whispered in a grave voice while lighting up.

"This Bephino Menesiero is really a good worker. Our people in Palermo said it was carried out with unbelievable style. He did it so well that the *polizia* even believed it was some kind of a jealous lover who did it. We heard Generro Polucci had nothing but praise and compliments for the guy who made the clip. The Italian newspapers hardly talked about it. They printed a few small articles. They called it a jealous-lover slaying. Bephino's unbelievable. What a fuckin' hit man. The guy's smooth as silk."

"It's a shame we gotta kill him," Angelo Marandala said, turning to Gaeta for acknowledgement. "He's been the best even when he was a kid. Remember how he took out Nick and them Grimaldis from L.A.?"

Gaeta shrugged while flicking ashes off the tip of his cigar. "It's not up to me, if we take him out; it's up to Rocco, it's what he wants to do about Menesiero. It cost Rocco a finger to deal with that guy."

"I say he's too good of a hit man to take out. He's a natural, and we could use him on other important hits that come up from time to time," Tony Boy said, looking over at Rocco.

Rocco paused, looked down, then said, "I agree with you, Tony; Menesiero is valuable. But he's also unpredictable and disrespectful. We have to weigh which is more important to us: keeping his services available to us or making an example of him."

"Why don't we let Menesiero live, and we take out one or two of his top men to show him we mean what we say," Angelo suggested.

"Whata ya, fuckin' botzo or what? Are you nuts?" Tony Boy asked incredulously. "Bephino's too tough for that shit; he'll strike directly at us if we hit his people. He's not gonna back off so easy. All hell will break loose in Brooklyn. He'll burn us in our beds. We better think good about this before we act," Tony Boy said, appraising the table for a reaction. "Either we take him out or we make peace; we got two choices. Anyway, is he back from Europe yet? Has anyone heard anything? Maybe he's on his farm, hah?"

Rocco waited silently and watched to hear if Bephino was

back or not. Everyone at the table looked at one another, but no one was able to confirm if Bephino was back. "I'll check it out," Rocco said. "I'll talk to his people. I'll keep pressure on Ben; he'll tell me, one way or another." Then looking at his finger, Rocco smirked, "If you wanna let Menesiero live, I'll go along with it. But the first one of them guys that rubs me wrong gets a miserable death. I gotta pass this thick bad blood I have in me. It's settling in my head."

"OK, so who's in favor of Menesiero still walking?" Tony Boy asked in a whisper. All four dons moved their hands. "Tortoricci couldn't be here tonight, but he says he goes along with the council," Tony Boy said through his cigar. "He's in the hospital with an ear infection, so it's our decision. So! Do we all agree to let Menesiero breathe?"

Everyone nodded in agreement.

"Good," Angelo smiled, waving his cigar. "Let's have a dinner for him when he returns to New York. Let's show him that we can forgive and forget. He did a good job for us, and he should be told he did well. Anyway, he's got a hundred grand coming to him for the hit. He'll be claiming it soon, that's for sure; when it comes to money, he's always available to collect."

"Let us know soon as you hear about his arrival," Tony Boy said to Rocco. "We'll make a nice dinner for him, maybe over here, the food is good. I like this place," Tony announced as he grinned and burped.

"Yeah, if I hear anything, I'll pass the word out." Rocco began removing the napkin from his neck and brushing off his expensive suit. "We'll do whatever we gotta do to keep the peace."

SUNDAY, JULY 30, 1977, 9:30 A.M.

LITTLE FALLS, SOUTH CAROLINA

"Hello . . ."

"Hello, Peggy, this is Dana. How are you?"

"Dana, we're all fine. How are you?"

"Not too good, Peggy, I'm havin' problems. Bephino's been away for a very long time, and I'm worried sick. The kids keep callin' home, and they're gettin' crazy with the thought that something has happened to their father. We're so upset down here, Peggy. I wanna ask Ben if he heard anything. It's a good thing I got Mrs. Roselli to talk to, otherwise I'd go nuts," Dana puffed. "She's been such a comfort to me. Livin' on the farm in South Carolina without Bephino is horrible. And now, the roaches are startin' to crawl out of the woodwork. Last night we had a disturbance."

"What kinda disturbance?" Peggy asked.

"Some skinny rebel gangster from Savannah, a guy named Bubba Reed, came on the farm late last night half drunk and tried to rape me."

"You gotta be kiddin'!" Peggy screamed into the phone. "Rape you!"

"Yeah, imagine that, the guy sneaked over the fences and came all the way up the hill to the house. It was a hot night."

"I'll say," Peggy mumbled.

"I was alone, sittin' out on my terrace," Dana continued, "thinkin' about my husband. It must have been about eleven, because I heard the news going on the TV in the bedroom. I always leave my TV playin' to keep me company, and it was then that this bastard sneaked up and scared the shit outta me. 'Well, hello,' I heard his voice comin' outta the darkness. I almost got a heart attack. Who the hell expected to hear a voice at that time of the night? It's always so quiet at night on the farm. I jumped outta the patio chair; I was shakin' like a leaf. He tried to take me into the bedroom. He said he wanted an Italian to make amour with. He'd heard Bephino was gone. He said he'd had dealin's with Bephino before, and that he came from Savannah. Imagine that bastard! The bastard smelled like a bar rag. After I got my nerve up, I punched him in his face. I hit him good and hard. He hit me back and knocked me down. Mrs. Roselli musta heard me yellin' at him. She came with a shotgun and cursed him up and down in Italian. You shoulda heard her! She almost fired it at him, but he saw the shotgun and ran."

"How about Joey D, where the hell was he?" Peggy asked.

"Joey left the farm a few days ago. He just packed up and left. He didn't even say good-bye. He'd been walkin' around, talkin' to himself ever since the word was out about Bephino bein' missin'."

"That fuckin' Joey D, he always seemed like a useless bastard anyway!" Peggy sneered. "He seemed like he'd run for cover if the hail came."

"Is Ben home?" Dana asked.

"Yeah, he's sleepin'. Should I wake him?"

"No, just tell him what happened."

"Hold on, Dana. I'm gonna wake Ben up. I think you should speak directly to Ben. You sound like you need to leave the farm and come back to New York. Hold on, baby . . ."

A few minutes later, Ben's voice came over the phone. "Dana, what happened?! Peggy just told me . . ."

"Ben, I don't want to repeat it. Peggy will give you the story later."

"Dana, I think you and Mrs. Roselli should come back to New York to live at least until we find Bephino. What happened to Joey D? Peggy said he ran off from the farm."

"Yeah, we saw him from the hill. He must of called a cab or car service. He was waiting by the main gates with his bags. He left and didn't even say good-bye to us."

"The stupid bastard; the guy turned into a real mutt. He couldn't hold out until we got some definite news. What a weak bastard. We'll settle with him later on. Whata ya wanna do, Dana, you wanna come back to the city? At least until we settle with this guy Bubba Reed, that fuckin' no-good rebel bastard."

"No, Ben, I gotta wait. Maybe Bepy will call on this phone. I stay by the phone day and night. I don't even go out to shop. We have everything delivered. We're so upset, Ben. What are we gonna do?!" Dana cried.

Ben's eyes shut with emotion. "Dana, I'm sending down a couple of guys, Fat Nickie and Petey Blue. Let them stay in Joey D's old house. They won't come up the hill, but they'll kill anyone that comes on the farm, believe me. You need our people on guard watching over you and Mrs. Roselli." Dana didn't answer. "Where are the kids, Dana?" Ben asked.

"Patsy is in L.A. living with that girl from the perfume company, and Rene is in Fort Lauderdale at the college. She's teaching classes there. Alan Stone calls me every day without fail. He stays in Vegas all year round, now. He's worried about Bephino," Dana said, taking a deep breath.

"We're all worried about Bephino!" Ben snapped back. "I know he'll return, I know him, Dana. He'll return. So Patsy Boy is still fooling around with the perfume tycoon's daughter," Ben said, trying to change the subject.

"Yeah, he lives with her in her father's Beverly Hills apartment. The kids call every day, asking about Bephino. 'Mom, did he call yet?' Patsy asks. Ben, I feel so unhappy. They love their father so much. I don't know what to say to them. I think we lost Bephino for good. It's been almost six months now."

"Dana, please don't get crazy. Bepy will be back. He's on a very tough assignment. He'll be back. I know him, I worked with him. He'll contact us, you'll see."

"I hope you're right, Ben. OK, Ben, you can send the men down, but tell them never to come up the hill unless it's an emergency."

"Don't worry, Dana, those guys are Old Blood, they got respect. They won't come up to the house."

AUGUST 22, 1977, NOON

MOUNT VERNON, NEW YORK

"You guys want lettuce and tomato on yours?" bank president Arty Argento asked Ben and Monkey while spreading a tablecloth across his office desk. Both men nodded yes. Arty motioned to his assistant to slice up another tomato.

"Not too thin, hah?" Arty rattled off to his man. Then, turning to Ben, he asked, "Have you heard anything?"

"Nothin'," Ben answered. "It's unbelievable. Bephino left for Europe seven months ago, and we've heard absolutely nothin', not a word. And all the dons act like they wanna know immediately when he gets back, like they wanna throw him a party. I can't figure them out. They never mentioned too much about the hit. They say nothin' other than Bephino met his man, but they show too much concern over Bephino's concern. It seems gawky, the way they ask. Somethin's goin' on. At least I do know from them the hit was actually made. I know Bephino got that far. Boretti's very tight-lipped, he thinks I know more than he does about Bephino. Dana and the kids are crackin' up over this. My phone rings every night. She keeps callin' me, and I don't know what to say to her."

Fat Arty handed both men their sandwiches on Italian bread. "Whata ya wanna drink? All I got is cream soda," he said apologetically. After a few moments of biting into the thick, crusty bread Fat Arty asked, his mouth still full, "So what's up?"

Ben leaned forward. "I want you to continue depositin' all the family's cash, just like Bephino set up in all the accounts. I also want you to continue payments to the two women Bephino's supportin', Alley Oop's family and Red's wife and kids. Everything stays the same, no matter what. The only people that can change things are me or Monkey here. If we both get hit, then you deal with yourself and Alan Stone. You call all the shots with Stone. Do what you think is right, because we got big problems comin' up. It could go either way for us. The odds are we lose," Ben said. "I gotta funny feelin'. I saw Tony Boy last week and he acted too happy to see me. I think hits are comin' down soon."

"You got it," the chubby banker nodded while still chewing. "I'll look after the cash, don't worry."

"I don't agree with that, Ben," Monkey said, placing his sandwich down neatly on a napkin. "We're gonna go underground if them guys make the slightest move at any of us. Then we'll make a clean sweep on them. We can kill ten of them to every one of us. We know exactly where they live. We'll wait day and night. When they arrive home, we'll storm them with automatic weapons. We'll hit their clubs, their houses, their businesses."

"Let's hope it never gets to that," Fat Arty mumbled, reaching for an olive on a plate in the middle of his desk. "Let's hope everybody has good sense. A war is the last thing all the families need."

"I agree, but Rocco Boretti lost a finger. He carries bad blood for us. He's gonna move against the Menesiero family sure as hell unless he's already buried Bephino. If he already buried Bephino in Italy, then he may drop this thing, and if you wanna know the truth on how I feel, I think Rocco had Bepy hit already," Monkey shrugged.

Ben curled his lips. "If he already buried Bephino, then we gotta bury Boretti, so either way there's gonna be hell to pay. We come, we go. Just like we came, dust to dust."

"Yeah, it'd be nice if at least we went in style," Monkey said with a smirk. "The way we're going, we're gonna wind up in plastic bags."

"Let's think of good things," Arty said, chewing. "You guys talk like the world's gonna end for all of us," he said, reaching for the plate again.

Ben looked over at Arty in disgust as the banker bit with swift delicacy into a large black olive. "If you take care of our financial affairs as good as you take care of your stomach, we should have no problems," Ben grumbled, putting his sandwich down as he stood up and brushed the crumbs off his clothes.

"We'll let you know about Bephino soon as we hear something. Come on, Monk, let's hit the road. I got *agida* watching this guy today. He don't lift his head for two seconds from them plates."

Fat Arty's assistant, the tomato slicer, was eating off to the side in the room. He burst out laughing. "What the fuck are you laughin' at?" Arty yelled. "You fuckin' bimbo, get the floor vacuumed up."

SEPTEMBER 26, 1977, 9:00 P.M.

A HOTEL SUITE OVERLOOKING CENTRAL PARK,
FIFTH AVENUE, MANHATTAN

"So what are you doing to find out about Bepy?" Alan Stone inquired, raising his eyebrows at Ben.

"I'm doing all I can do. I'm talking to every wise guy in New York," Ben replied, pacing the floor nervously.

"Is that everything? Talking to wise guys, while Dana and the kids are half out of their minds? You gotta do more, Ben."

"I can't do more. What I'm doing has gotta be enough," Ben answered, lowering his feverish eyes directly to Alan, who was sitting in a chair. "I can't do any more than I'm doing other than go to a fortune-teller."

"It's been almost eight months since we heard from Bephino," Alan said, removing his eyeglasses and rubbing his eyes. "I'm sure you can talk to Rocco or that Tony Boy What's-his-name. *Somebody* must know if Bephino's alive or dead," Alan insisted firmly. "Dana's going nuts, the kids are going nuts."

Ben sat down near Alan. "Boretti's people keep asking me where Bephino is! They keep calling *me* about Bepy! If Bephino's dead, they're the ones who ordered it done, so why should I continue to ask them while they are always asking me where he is? This thing smells, it stinks!" Ben said coldly.

"You gotta do something more," Alan politely repeated.

"There's nothing more I can do," Ben shrugged. "I gotta sit and wait."

Alan reset his bifocals comfortably on his nose, then flashed his eyes up above them to Ben. "Sitting and waiting is not the solution, Ben. You must become more investigative, be more aggressive, and get totally involved. You must find out if Bephino's still alive. To be honest, Ben, I don't think you're doing your best," Alan said coldly. "Maybe Monkey should become more involved in the inquiries."

"Did you come all the way from Las Vegas to tell me this shit?" Ben shouted.

"After all, it's almost eight months since Bepy left for Europe. We need answers," Alan insisted in a soft voice.

"You need answers!" Ben snapped.

"Yes, as a matter of fact, we do," Alan shot back.

"Look, you fuckin' Jew, cut the bullshit. You think I'm sittin' and shiverin' like you? I'm right in the middle of this fuckin' mess!" Ben shouted. "I got problems comin' up with that fuckin' Rocco Boretti. His eyes are still bloody, they didn't clear up; it's been all these months, they didn't clear up!"

"Look yourself," Alan replied, cold as ice. "I asked you a very serious question, Ben, and I expect an honest and just as serious answer in return from you, and the next time you call me a Jew, I'll . . ."

"You'll what?" Ben jumped up and shouted contemptuously.

Alan paused and then rubbed his fingers together, smiled briefly, and said, "Tush, Tush. For twenty-five grand, you could cease to be, Ben."

Ben stared wickedly at Alan and looked deep into his eyes. "Look, Jew," he whispered in a hoarse, strained voice. "I'll give you tush, tush! I'll give you a fuckin' funeral through Central Park that'll beat all funerals, if you keep fuckin' with me. I'll make Adolf Hitler seem humane if you fuck with me," Ben screamed. "I'll bring you back to dust. I got enough problems without you addin' to them."

Alan silently shook his head, but sat firm and looked most determined. Then he said, "You know, Ben, normally I'm a man that can be reasoned with. You're Bephino's choice, not mine. If he'd asked me who should run the family while he's away, I would have told him anyone in the fuckin' world but you. And if you keep up with the Jew talk, I'll . . ."

"You'll shit!" Ben screamed, moving about in a nervous, unfriendly fashion. "And since when does a Jew make choices for me?" Ben stared hard at Alan. "And what the hell are *you* doing to help find Bephino and get him back home, hah?"

Alan rolled his lips. "I pray, Ben, I pray every day."

"You pray!" Ben shouted in disgust. "No shit! Bephino's a Catholic and you pray in Hebrew, I suppose, hah?"

"I'm not in your end of the business, Ben. I can't squeeze the important people in New York. That's your business. The question is, are you doing enough with the dons to find out if Bepy's alive or not? We must know, Ben, we must know for Dana and the kids. I speak to them every day; they're miserable. Bephino's foremost on their minds. So I speak for them, for their sake, not mine." Alan's eyes began to water. "They gotta know something!"

Ben stood quietly, taking in what Alan was feeling. After a few moments, Ben curled his lips. "All right, Alan, you're still a Jew bastard, but to prove my respect for you, I'll try again. I'll call a sit-down with all of 'em. I'll put pressure on the entire council. I'll call those scumbags to a table and I'll let you know what happens. I'm sorry for calling you a Jew, Alan. You know I really don't mean any of those words. I don't feel right anymore without Bepy. Everything seems to be coming apart for us. I didn't mean to disrespect you. All we have left is each other. We're a small army facing a big war. It really seems like our work's cut out for us."

Alan nodded, wiping his eyes. Still in a choked voice, he murmured, "We had such good times together."

Ben rubbed Alan's back. "I know, Alan. I'll do my best to save some of those memories for us. I'll meet with them and get back to you in a few days."

"Thanks, Ben," Alan said, regaining his composure. Both men embraced, squeezing each other with warm affection.

"We're Old Blood," Ben whispered. "We can't let this thing break us apart." Alan nodded agreeably while wiping the lenses of his fogged-up bifocals.

Ben leaned forward toward Alan's ear and whispered, "Now cancel the tush, tush, OK?" Alan threw his head back and laughed, then hugged Ben hard.

Saturday, September 29, 1977

Brooklyn, New York

"Read all about it!" the paper boys yelled out to their customers. "Staten Island man thrown from Brooklyn roof. Read all about it!" The papers read:

> Ben Del Ponte, underboss of the reputed Bephino Mensiero New York City crime family, was brutally battered and then thrown from a four-story apartment building in the Bay Ridge section of Brooklyn. A police informant confirms Ben ("Don't Call Me Benny") Del Ponte was said to be confronting the council of all New

York Mafia dons on behalf of his close friend and protégé, Bephino Menesiero, asserted boss and long-time Mafia hit man. Menesiero, himself known to be a Mafia don from the Bay Ridge, Brooklyn, area, has been missing for nearly eight months and is believed by insiders to be dead. The police informant said Ben Del Ponte has been a longtime associate of Menesiero and a frequent thorn in the side of New York's five ruling Mafia families. It is believed Del Ponte had been ordered dead by the ruling council of the Mafia.

"Thrown from a rooftop but miraculously still alive," is the way police Lieutenant Paul J. O'Riley put it. "It's hard to kill these dagos," O'Riley chuckled to news reporters. "They fly like pigeons. Fortunately, his fall was broken by several sets of clotheslines."

Police reports also revealed that a young, unidentified man claimed to have been checking on his pigeons at 2 A.M. on his garage roof when he heard a struggle, followed by a man screaming out. Then the body came flying down, catching itself on and breaking three sets of clotheslines that stretched out across the alley. The young man was quoted as saying, "He kept grabbing at the air, bouncing around and yelling out. I called 911 as soon as the man landed. I'm glad I was able to get an ambulance there quick to save his life."

According to the papers, "The young man told this story as police took him in for further questioning. The youth's father was also held by police for questioning after an altercation with police for holding his son. Hospital reports indicate Ben Del Ponte has a broken collarbone, broken jaw, fractured skull, broken kneecaps, broken hips, and possible damage to his major organs. He is in critical condition at Bensonhurst Jewish Hospital in Brooklyn."

SUNDAY, SEPTEMBER 30, 1977, NOON

BROOKLYN, NEW YORK

"Hello, operator. I wanna make a long-distance call to Las Vegas, person-to-person to Mr. Alan Stone at the El Banco Hotel. If he's not in his office, please have him paged. It's important."

A few moments later, a female voice chimed, "El Banco Hotel and Country Club. Can I help you?"

"This is New York calling person-to-person for Alan Stone . . ."

"Hold on, please . . . I'll have to try the spa . . ." the hotel operator replied. "Who's calling Mr. Stone?" she asked, coming back on the line.

"Sir, would you care to give your name?" the New York operator asked.

"Tell him it's Monkey calling."

"Hold on, please . . . Did you hear that, operator?"

"OK, operator, I'm putting the call through to Mr. Stone . . ."

"Hello! This is Stone speaking."

"Alan, this is Monkey."

"Hi, Monkey, what's up?"

"Have you heard the news?"

"You mean about Iran?"

"No, about Brooklyn."

"What happened in Brooklyn, Monk?"

"Ben was hit last night at 2 A.M. They threw him off the roof after a sit-down with Rocco Boretti and the others. He sat down with the council alone. They turned thumbs down, and Ben went belly-up off the roof. They threw him off a roof right in Bay Ridge, four stories up. He's got more broken bones than Humpty Dumpty."

"Is Ben dead?" Alan asked, holding onto a spa railing.

"No, he's not. He bounced off the clotheslines. The lines broke his fall. He's all busted up, but still breathin'. They loaded him with morphine, then we flew him south this mornin', to a private hospital in Charlotte. Down there he may be safe. No one knows where he's at, so don't breathe a word. They'll come for him."

"Of course," Alan murmured, struggling with the words and his own composure.

"I figured you'd want to know this right away, Alan, because Ben mentioned you spoke words to him about not pushin' the dons hard enough about Bephino." Alan Stone did not answer. His already sweaty face had paled, and he began to have chest spasms. He quickly put two tiny pills under his tongue. "Alan, you still there?"

"Yes, I'm here, Monkey," he whispered softly. "I took some sleeping pills last night, and I'm still groggy from them," Alan said.

"I'll have to run things till Bephino gets back or until Ben gets well. Do you agree, Alan?" Monkey's voice asked, echoing through the telephone wires.

"Yes, Monkey, I agree," Alan echoed back faintly. "You run things," Alan whispered into the phone, holding his chest.

"OK, Alan, if you need anything, call me."

"Thank you, Monkey, thank you for callin' me. Please keep me informed."

"OK, Alan, good-bye."

Alan Stone sank down, putting his hands to his face.

"My *God!* What have I done?" he moaned, stricken. Two men changing their clothes in the spa looked over with a jolt at Alan Stone's sudden outburst. "What have I done?" he intoned again.

OCTOBER 1, 1977, 9:00 P.M.

VILLA ITALIA, VIENNA, AUSTRIA

A long dinner table hosted two beautiful women, Lucia Del Rego and Florentina, the young mistress of the late Phillipo Del Rego.

"I must compliment the veal tonight, Lucia," Florentina said, chewing delicately with a closed mouth.

Lucia, raising her wineglass in silent response, tilted it in a good-luck toast. With a sensual glance and a modest grin, Lucia then said, "You look quite daring tonight, *belle mia*. I just adore you in white lace."

OCTOBER 5, 1977, 6:00 P.M.

BROOKLYN, NEW YORK

"Mom, did you see on TV? They're still talkin' about Ben—Del Ponte, they call him—they say he's a Mafia guy and they mentioned the name Bephino Menesiero. Ben must be hurt bad. They said it again tonight on the late news. The hit men threw Ben off a roof. The Mob tried to kill him," Alley Boy Opolito spoke nervously to his mother.

"I know. I heard it several times too. It's been all over the papers and TV this week. I hope he don't die. Our dreams will die if Ben dies. He's our only ticket out of the slums," the boy's mother said.

"Mom, that's not what I meant. I like Ben, he's a great guy, he . . . he really plays it straight with me. I hope he makes it—for his sake, not ours."

"I hope so too, Alley, for Ben mostly, but for our sake also. I heard Bephino Menesiero hasn't been seen or heard of for almost a year. Remember, Alley, these guys are for real, and they play for keeps. Of course I hope they survive," Paula shrugged. "At the moment, it's our livelihood at stake. They say your father was the toughest of them all, and he didn't survive, so you figure that out."

"Yeah, but the TV said Ben's still alive, and no one knows where he was moved to outta New York. They took him out durin' the night. They don't want the Mob to find him. Oh, man, I hope he makes it," the boy said, clasping his hands, shaking them up and down in a nervous fashion. "Ben's a good trainer for me," he murmured. "He gives me reason to win. I respect him. He tells me things about my father, and that makes me wanna win for Alley Oop's sake."

October 6, 1977, 10:00 p.m.

Baptist Memorial Hospital,
Charlotte, North Carolina

"Can you breathe with all those tubes down your throat, honey?" Ben's wife, Peggy, asked while wiping his face with a damp towel.

Ben, half awake, nodded. Trying to speak, he only grunted; his jaw was wired completely shut. He managed to squeeze Peggy's hand affectionately.

"Yesterday was torture for me. Your operation took twelve hours," she murmured. "You're so lucky you're still alive. It took so many days for the swelling to go down, just so they could operate. Monkey told me to get you out of that Brooklyn hospital fast, because they would definitely come after you again. We flew you down here to Charlotte that same night. You were in terrible pain. They pumped you full of morphine. Honey, you been out on morphine for six days. I hope you get off it soon. I got you in a small private Baptist hospital. I know you'll be safe here."

Ben stared up at the ceiling and did not respond. The room was empty of flowers and friends. He closed his eyes. Peggy then curled up on a leather sofa chair in the corner of the room and watched her husband.

October 9, 1977, 5:30 a.m.

Santa Anna, Italy

"Hail Mary, full of grace. May the Lord be with thee." Like a hymn being sung by angels in the dark, the three nuns concluded their final prayer over the emaciated body of the once muscular Bephino Menesiero. He looked these days like cold death, his skin tinged blue from minimal circulation, his body temperature far below normal. The frail and thinning Mafia don heard the nuns depart his room, and then the sound of friendly, warm-hearted young Tattania arriving, ready to wash him. Pulling back the cover sheet, Tattania smiled and hummed as she began to sponge his cold, naked body. Tattania, considered by many to be a little bit slow, liked to sing. As she rubbed the warm, soapy water over her patient's body and genitals several times, she noticed that his penis moved slightly. This life response to her warm, soapy sponging caused her to look him over curiously. Keeping one eye on the door, she began to sponge him further in the groin area. Tattania could not believe such a sick man responding even slightly to her touch. It really seemed strange, she thought.

"You have no name," Tattania said, speaking nervously to Bephino, "so now I call you Puco. Puco, do you like the way I wash you every day?" she sang out to him. Lifting up his penis, she began to wash his testicles again with the warm, soapy water. Handling a limp but now full penis, she grinned. "Someday, Puco, you will answer me and you will get well, and you will dance at my wedding." Tattania began to raise his genitals again and dry him off gently. Then washing his feet and other parts of his body, she grinned. "You like when I wash you, Puco, I know that. I see you act well," she whispered with a sly smile, leaning directly over his body, speaking to him in dialect.

Bephino could actually hear Tattania, and sometimes he really felt the warm, soapy touch of the naive Italian girl. The warm water felt good until it began to chill in the cold, drab room. "Now she's calling me Puco. Sounds like some kind of a pet monkey," he thought.

"Tomorrow I shave you, Puco," she said, passing the sponge over his face quickly. "*Ciao,* see you tomorrow." She pulled the sheet back over him. Tattania walked toward the door. Suddenly she stopped and looked back. "You look so cold, Puco, maybe I get you a blanket," she said as she opened the heavy, oak-grained door and left the room.

"Did she say a blanket?" Bephino wondered. "I'd give a hundred grand for a fuckin' blanket," he thought to himself.

A few moments later the door reopened and Tattania came bustling in with two old army blankets under her arm. She hummed an Italian tune as she spread the blankets over his body and tucked him in. "OK, Puco, now you stay warm.

Because Sister Graciella said the Devil lives in this room and he keeps it too cold."

"God," he thought, "after all this time somebody finally realizes I was cold. She's all right, that kid. At least she thinks of me," Bephino thought, as he enjoyed the heavy feeling of warm wool over him.

November 5, 1977, 9:00 p.m.

Brooklyn, New York

All the prominent soldiers of the Menesiero family gathered in a Brooklyn apartment overlooking the Belt Parkway. Monkey stood by the window and held a curtain to one side as he watched the traffic move slowly along the highway.

"We got problems," he said, allowing the curtain to drop to its normal position while turning to the men in the crowded room.

The men sipped wine or scotch and listened quietly. "We got big fuckin' problems," Monkey repeated, his eyes focusing on the men around the crowded room, "so big that I, myself, have to leave town for a while. I gotta quit running the Hero shop business, the Shylock business, and our other operations." Monkey moved easily behind two men sitting to his left. "I gotta hide out and leave things to Black Augie, here, and Blubberhead to handle. All you men know Bephino's missing in action and Ben was almost terminated a few weeks ago. That means we are all their next targets. Augie here and Blubber are known around the neighborhood to be civilians. They always worked as cooks, so they shouldn't get whacked. Nobody in Brooklyn clips cooks," Monkey grinned.

Black Augie, a small, dark-skinned man, smiled at the men's laughter. Blubberhead, a crew-cut, swollen-headed man with a bad complexion, sat expressionless.

"Rocco Boretti's gonna wipe us out if he can," Monkey said more loudly. "He's gonna try to eliminate the entire Menesiero family. What we need is time, so I want all you guys to know that we are breakin' up our operations for a while."

Looking over at Pauli, Monkey said, "Pauli, as of tomorrow, turn the loan-sharking and numbers over to Augie and Blubber. They'll handle that stuff from the restaurant. And Pauli, you go on a vacation. Stay out of town. Forget the cunt in Brooklyn, OK, Pauli?" Then, turning to Crazy Mikey: "You go too. We all gotta lay low. I don't want you guys sneaking around Brooklyn, visiting other people's wives, *a capisce*? I'll tell Alan Stone and Fat Arty what we're doing. Boretti will hit the Old Blood first, so we three gotta scat." Monkey's eyes focused on all the men. "When I call you guys back, be ready for action, because I smell a big war coming. It could be the biggest war to ever hit New York." Then pulling back his lips, he glanced over the thirty or so men piled all over the room. "Let's hope Bephino's not dead. If he is dead, and if Ben's too sick to recover enough to work with us, then probably I'll officially take over and make the decisions for the family. But the main thing is to stay out of sight and alive. Everybody check in once a week, on Friday, at this number." Monkey handed out slips of paper. "If we need you, we'll tell you where to report. They hurt Ben real bad; we got no choice, we gotta protect ourselves and retreat for a while. I want all you soldiers to call in each week on this special phone number we got set up over in Jersey. Someone will answer and tell you what's going on each week, etcetera. Remember, we're not running from nobody; this is considered strategy. They can't hit what they can't see, so we lay low for a while. We need time to think, time to plan, time to stay alive so we can consolidate and put together a plan that we could continue to live with. Then, when the time's right, we carry out a major strike against the people who want the Menesiero family dead.

"For you buttons and you soldiers that are not considered Old Blood, if any of you consort with the other side, and we get wind of it, we're gonna turn on you and hit your old mothers and your wives and kids. No bullshit!" Monkey shouted in Sicilian, "If anyone of you fuckin' greaseballs from Sicily decide to cross over, your wives get fucked in their big, fat asses and the kids go down the tubes. This is the law of our jungle. It's our thing. We are experienced men, all of us. Them

Boretti guys gotta respect us just like we gotta respect them. We're small, and all we got is each other. We gotta be loyal to Bephino and most of all have respect for the family," Monkey said convincingly. Then, looking around at each of the men, he shook his head and said, "I know all you men are loyal, so I shouldn't have to repeat ugly words that have already been spoken. We got a bad war coming, and we're gonna go underground and win it like them fuckin' chinks in Vietnam, so you're on the winning side. We're gonna fight those bastards with all we got," he whispered in a deep voice. Everyone in the room mumbled support for Monkey. "I'm going to Los Angeles for a while to visit family and lay low." Monkey then raised his scotch glass and yelled, "But when I get back, be ready, because it's gonna be *dust to dust*!"

"Il rispetto," the men responded in what sounded like a war chant. *"Il rispetto!"*

DECEMBER 3, 1977, 2:15 P.M.

LAS VEGAS, NEVADA

It was surprisingly hot for December. The young temple-keeper watched the afternoon traffic whizzing along Las Vegas Boulevard. His sloping gray eyes zipped back and forth until they settled on one particular car, a white four-door Rolls Royce heading his way, and he smiled to himself. A few minutes later the white Rolls carelessly pulled up the cobblestoned street to the side door of the famous Reform Temple Beth-El. The beautiful white stucco building was usually locked up tight during the afternoon. The pale-faced temple *shames* stood patiently off in the shade and watched silently for his cash-paying visitor to officially arrive. The car finally rolled to a halt. Its door sprung open and a well-dressed older man in a light, cream-colored suit and royal-blue shirt and tie hastily climbed out and whisked past the temple-keeper, who was now holding open a side door to the stifling hothouse of prayer. Setting his own house rules, the visitor carried his shawl and skullcap in a velvet bag down the aisle to a front-row pew facing the ark. The shul's only light came from the shafts of sunlight seeping in through the large, curtain-covered windows. The desert heat seemed to crawl through the thick, stuccoed walls, releasing an aroma of stale, pasty air. The man unzipped his velvet bag, unfolded his belongings, and carefully placed his book of prayer before himself. He donned a little white yarmulke and a beautiful white tasseled tallith, a shawl finely embroidered with blue and gold letters of Hebrew faith. He then opened his leatherbound prayer book to a page he had previously marked and began to chant. He chanted loud and as well as any rabbi in the land. He hummed in a manner that sent chills up and down the spine of the only witness present besides God. The young *shames,* watching silently as he had every day for two months, stood to the rear. The Hebrew chant echoed clearly throughout the lonely temple, a fervent, mournful whine. Such a sound of human repentance! the young *shames* thought to himself.

The room was feverishly hot, and prayer filled the air along with the stifling smell of heat. The well-dressed man davened back and forth, perspiring into wetness that showed through his light-colored suit. A lonely place, and a lonely prayer, which seemed to be going unanswered. Thirty minutes later, the man closed his leather book, removed his shawl and cap, and, seemingly exhausted, walked slowly toward the side door. The young *shames* awkwardly pushed it open as a gesture of respect. The praying man's body was soaking wet. He walked out to meet the bright sunlight, and his wet eyes blinked sharply from the bright light. Quickly he put on his dark glasses.

After a breath or two in the fresh air, he turned to the shy-looking *shames,* who was staring quietly from his shady post off to the side. The man peeled off the usual fifty-dollar bill, stood for a moment, and then said, "Put the fuckin' air on tomorrow, ya schmuck. It's hot as hell in there."

Alan Stone then got into his car and drove off.

DECEMBER 31, 1977, 4:00 P.M.

LITTLE FALLS, SOUTH CAROLINA

"This is terrible. What kind of Christmas week is this?" Patsy Menesiero, the twenty-three-year-old son of Bephino, screeched out. "Where *is* he?" the young man asked his mother. "He must have said something when he left, he must have told you something, Mom."

"I told you, he didn't tell me a thing, Patsy. Your father never talks about his business, you know that. He just said he didn't know how long it would take and kissed me good-bye."

"Well, somebody's gotta know something! How about his friends in New York—Ben, Monkey, Lil Pauli, Mikey? Have you spoken with any of them?"

"I talked with Ben many times. Your father told me Ben would know everything, but Ben couldn't tell me much, and you know recently Ben was almost killed and is still recovering from broken bones. How could I keep botherin' him? He has his own problems."

Bephino's son stared morosely out the large picture window to the pastures of the farm. His sister, Rene, and his girlfriend, Stacy, huddled with Dana and Mrs. Roselli at the other end of the room. Patsy then turned to ask another question. "What happened to that mutt, Joey D; I don't see him around the farm. Where'd he go?"

"When he heard your father was missing, he packed and left the farm," Dana replied.

The boy's face turned red. "The miserable bastard. He left like a damn coward. If I ever see him again, I'll fix his ass. What happened to the respect and all that bullshit we've been hearing about all these years?"

Mrs. Roselli approached Patsy. "Don't be so upset, Patsy. Your father is strong. He's gonna come back. We don't need that stupid Joey D around. That man always walked around like he had bad feet or somethin'," the housekeeper said. "And remember, no news is good news. We pray every day to Saint Anthony for your father." She embraced Bephino's son affectionately. "Saint Anthony answers all my prayers," she whispered. "He never lets me down."

Patsy Menesiero raised his eyes over to his mother and sister, then glanced back down at the little old lady who was hugging him and gave her a warm kiss on her forehead.

The Menesiero home was just not the same. It was now two hours before New Year's, and 1978 was about to make its debut, but there was no holiday spirit. Patsy Menesiero sat quietly at the large walnut desk in his father's office, looking for a clue as to where his father could have gone. The young man remembered other holidays, when his father would laugh as he opened up bottles of fine champagne and encourage everyone to have a good-luck drink. But now the house was without life, as if the motor of a car had been removed from its casing and the car left sitting idle. Patsy picked up an old framed photo of Bephino holding him and Rene when they were young children. His father seemed to be hugging and squeezing them with all his heart. Patsy sat staring at the photo, remembering how strong and generous his father had always been to them. Suddenly the phone rang. He picked it up on the first ring. "Hello."

"Who's this?" a man asked.

"This is Patsy Menesiero. Who's this?"

"This is Ben. How are you, Patsy?"

"I'm OK, Ben. How are you? I heard you had quite an accident."

"Yeah, those things happen sometimes in our business. It comes with the turf. How's your mother and sister?"

"They're OK, Ben. We're all kinda shook up over my father. It's not like him to stay away for so long. He didn't call for Christmas, and now it's almost New Year's. This is the worst holiday I can remember."

"I know, kid, but you gotta stay strong. Your father would expect you to stand tall and be strong and hold the women in the family together."

"I'm doing that, Ben, but . . . I really miss him. I never knew how much I loved the guy," Patsy said emotionally.

Ben's own eyes quickly filled with emotion at the boy's pain. "I know, kid, I know just how you feel. I was very close to your father. We gotta continue to hope and pray. How's the girls?" Ben asked, changing the subject, as he realized "hoping" and "praying" didn't sound too credible coming from a Mafia underboss.

"I'm spendin' my New Year's with Rene, Mom, my girlfriend, Stacy, and Mrs. Roselli. I'm the only guy in the house. Even Joey D flew the coop. I was supposed to go to Stacy's father's party in Los Angeles, but I didn't wanna leave my mother and sister alone on the farm, Ben, without Bephino. The place don't seem the same. We miss his jokin' and bossin' us around, his teasin'—you know."

"I know, kid, I know," Ben answered. "Joey D did the wrong thing. We'll deal with him later. I sent a couple of our guys to guard the farm. I guess you met them already."

"Yeah, they stay down at the old house. My mother don't want them up here. She's funny that way. She sends all the holiday stuff down to them. They're gettin' fat down there. Ben, do you know where my father could be?"

Ben didn't answer Patsy.

"Alan Stone called earlier and spoke to my mother, my sister, and me," Patsy continued. "He wished us well for the New Year. He told me my father's suite is always available for us if we ever wanna go down to Vegas."

"Alan's good people," Ben replied. "The guy would give any of us the shirt offa his back. He misses your father, believe me, Patsy," Ben whispered. "Alan is sick over this whole thing."

"I know, Ben; Alan sounded like he was cryin' on the phone when he spoke with us. He's worried about you too, Ben. He blames himself for your accident."

"The guy's all heart," Ben replied. "He loves to blame himself for things. He's Jewish, he loves to suffer; it's tradition. He had nothin' to do with my accident."

"So where are you now, Ben?"

"I'm stayin' with my wife's brother in Maryland, just until my bones fully heal. Then I'm goin' back to Brooklyn to finish what them bastards started. You know, Patsy, guys like your father and me don't die so easy. See me, I flew like a bird offa the rooftop. I only broke my kneecaps, my hips, my thighs, and one arm and my jawbone. That's not bad for a Sicilian. Your father's the same kinda guy, so you relax and wait, *a capisce*? You'll hear from him, trust me."

"I hope so. And I understand, Ben. I know you guys are strong," Patsy grinned into the phone.

"My money says Bephino Menesiero walks in the door someday. Whata ya think of that?" Ben stated. "Give my love to your mother and Rene and your girlfriend. Tell your mother I'll be in touch, but don't tell anyone where I told you I'm stayin'. I'm not that popular at the moment. No one! Oh, yeah, and tell Mrs. Roselli I said to lay off the oregano," Ben laughed. "I'm like a little kid, learnin' how to walk all over again. Take care of the women, Patsy. If you need anything, ask your mother for my number. She's the only one who's got it. Happy New Year, kid. *Buona fortuna.*"

JANUARY 17, 1978, 3:00 P.M.

BOWIE, MARYLAND

Four men gathered around a warm fireplace in a large stone house in the East Bowie countryside. Little Pauli poured out four scotches straight up and then began to pass them out.

"You're lookin' much better, Ben," Monkey said with a half grin. Crazy Mikey and Little Pauli nodded in agreement. "Yeah, I look like a fuckin' movie star," Ben replied, gulping down his drink. "I got fake hips, plastic balls in my kneecaps, and an iron plate in my left thigh. They really destroyed my life, the motherfuckers. The only thing that still works right is my asshole," Ben said, shaking his head in distress. "I lived, I survived—but I'm nothin'. Look at me! I used to laugh at old crippled Philly, the guy sellin' shoelaces on the Staten Island Ferry when I was a kid. Now I'm like him, a cripple." Ben pulled back his lips. "Well, I may be destroyed, but in the end they failed, them scumbags. They ruined my legs, but they didn't get my heart or my trigger finger. So now I got nothin' to do but plan their deaths, one by one. Them rotten bastards, I could still see Rocco Boretti's ugly face smilin' at me when they dragged me up on the roof. I heard him laugh all the way up the steps. I'm gonna plan nice things for them people, you'll see. We're gonna hit them bastards when they least expect it, and we're gonna have no respect for them. We're gonna murder them in their livin' rooms in front of the TVs and their families. They sent Bephino to his death—I'm sure of that now—and they crippled me for life. Now we gotta pass the blood, the Sicilian blood. We gotta spit up the spoiled blood. This never ends until we kill all of 'em. Right in front of their fuckin' *kids*!" Ben raged. "Then the blood will be pure again."

Monkey frowned and shrugged at Ben's rage. "First get well, Ben. That's the important thing. Let 'em think we're on the run. I got all our people on furlough, they're on leave. When we're ready, we order them back to duty."

"Can we trust these guys?" Ben asked. "They ain't Old Blood, they know we're hurt; maybe they think we're finished, and they'll turn to Boretti."

"The men know if they sell us out we're gonna kill their wives and kids. I had to elaborate on that. We can't afford any of them to look for another family or turn to the other side. I had to put a scare into them. I agree we can only be sure about the Old Blood. All the other guys from Sicily we gotta keep under wraps. I think they'll heed to our warning."

"You did well, Monkey," Ben said. "You made good decisions for us. We all lay low for a while. When we're ready, we'll return to New York and gut them fat-bellied bastards. My doctor says I'll be back out on the street in a month or so. I'm doin' good."

Monkey glanced at Mikey and Pauli over Ben's words as Ben kept talking.

"He tells me in another month or so I'll be movin' around a lot better. By then we'll know one way or another about Bephino. If he's *morte,* we all lost a good friend."

Mikey reached for an ashtray. "Alan Stone feels bad about Bephino and about your terrible accident, Ben. He told me he was the one who pushed you into the situation with the council. Now he can't face you," Mikey said cautiously. "I was out in Vegas last week, and Alan was tellin' me it was all his fault that you sat down at a table with Rocco. He's sick over this. He wants you to know anything he owns is yours. Anything."

"It was my own fault, not Alan's!" Ben said sharply. "I knew better than to sit down with them. Rocco had bad blood to pass. I knew better, I was stupid. I walked into a hot situation head-on. The minute I stated my case, I saw it in their eyes. I knew right then at the table they were gonna hit me. I thought they would shoot me, but instead they punched me around and then threw me off the fuckin' roof headfirst. But they fucked up. They never figured I would grab onto the clotheslines for help. I was flyin' and reachin' out for anything to slow me down."

The three men's eyes focused on Ben's awkward, broken body. Ben was sitting with his metal canes by his side. The men said nothing. But their eyes said they knew what was coming: World War III in Brooklyn.

JANUARY 27, 1978, 5:30 A.M.

SANTA ANNA, ITALY

Three nuns prayed in the early-morning darkness. Their black-robed bodies leaned forward, half resting on the bed. "Bless it with thee, Bless it with thee," echoed the final words of the prayer. The sign of the cross was made. The nuns left the room. The lifeless body of Mafia boss Bephino Menesiero lay quiet and alone. It had been nearly one year that he had struggled to live.

Twenty minutes later the door opened again. Young, robust Tattania came in wheeling what appeared to be a metal cart. *"Buon giorno, Signor Puco,"* she announced in her sweet singsong. Something excited her; Bephino could tell by the lift in her voice. "See what I have here." She wheeled the cart up close to the bed and said, "That's why I'm late this morning; I had to set up my new cart. Now I don't have to carry basins of water from room to room. Now I can wheel this beautiful tank of hot water with me to wash all the patients," she said to Bephino, knowing he could not answer her. "You like my new cart, Puco? Alfredo, my boyfriend, made it for me. Isn't it beautiful?" she sang, touching her cart. "So now today, I have to wash you up." She pulled the old army blankets and sheet off his frail body. She touched his thin, cool thighs, feeling for some body warmth. "Ah, *bene, bene,*" she muttered. "You feel a little warmer today." Tattania began to fill a basin with warm water, drawing from her homemade spout hook-up. Adding soap and mixing the water with her hand, Tattania started slowly to sponge Bephino's body—ears, neck, arms, then legs and feet, and back up to his genitals. Before she began on his genitals, she turned, as was her usual nervous habit, and looked at the door. Tattania began to lather up Bephino's testicles with warm, soapy water. She used her sponge briskly on the head of his penis. After rinsing him off, her hands became the tools for her objective. Fondling him playfully, her eyes flickered nervously at the door. This rubbing action again caused his penis to expand as it had done on other similar occasions. Tattania was waiting for this. It began to grow right in her hands, and once again her eyes widened at the wonder of it. She grinned shyly and directed her beautiful brown eyes to the thick wood door of the shabby, green-walled hospital room. The young girl could still not believe that such a deathly ill man could show such life in her hands. Her eyes widened as he thickened further, exposing a vein. It seemed unreal to her. Tattania's thoughts ran wild in her head. The penis was still flaccid, but thickish and long, maybe nine or ten inches, she thought. Who could she tell of this new life in a comatose body? She couldn't tell the doctor or the nuns. She couldn't tell her boyfriend, Alfredo. The young Italian beauty nervously added more soapy lather and continued to rub under and around his testicles. After a while, she began again rinsing him off thoroughly. She dried his body well. Then she covered him up with a clean sheet and two khaki-colored wool blankets. She left the room dragging her cart awkwardly behind her, holding the heavy wood door to one side and pulling at the cart, all the while not taking her eyes off Bephino. Her eyes kept flashing back at Bephino's bed as if expecting him to rise up and call out to her.

Tattania the scrub girl saw life in a semicomatose man's body that she was unable to talk about.

6

February 3, 1978, 2:35 p.m.

The Eastside Gym, Manhattan

"Time! Take a break," a small black man wearing a gray sweatshirt yelled. But Alley Boy didn't stop; the son of late Mafia hit man Alley Oop stood erect, punching hard on the heavy leather bag. He pounded away, punch after punch, breathing in and out, exhaling profusely from his nose while continuously hitting the big bag. Trainers and boxers circled around and began to cheer. "OK, Alley!" The Negro trainer known as Pinky said proudly in a deep voice. "Go take a shower now, boy. That's it for today. Tomorrow, you're sparrin' with a heavyweight contender from Philly," he grinned. "And from what I see today, you're gonna look real fine, real fine."

"Who is he?" Alley asked, still puffing. "What's his name?"

"He's a number-five contender, a top ranker by the name of Tiger Cruise. Tiger's bad news," Pinky said, shaking his head. "He's so bad he needs half a dozen sparrin' partners tomorrow, and you're one of 'em. Don't fret," Pinky grinned, "you'll do fine. I signed you up last week. Stop by the desk and sign one of them sparrin' releases."

"Hey, Alley—phone call," the gym attendant yelled out. "Phone call for you."

Alley Boy removed his light leather gloves, handed them over to Pinky, and walked toward the wall phone.

"Pick it up over there and I'll hang up over here," the attendant called from the office section.

"Hello, this is Alley Opolito speakin'."

"You gotta nice name, Opolito," a man's voice said. "I like that. Alley, don't talk. Just listen," the voice said.

Alley hesitated, thought he recognized the voice, then said, "Is this you?"

"Yeah, it's me."

"Are you OK?" Alley asked in a cracked voice.

"Everything's OK. Let me do all the talkin'. Don't ask me questions over the phone, OK, kid?"

"OK."

"Startin' next week, the amount of money your mother gets is goin' to be three hundred a week. We're givin' her one hundred for you, so go ahead and quit your job at the fruit store. One hundred of the three hundred goes to you every week for your spendin' money. It ain't much, but it's somethin' anyway. I want you to double up on your trainin' hours. I want you to lift weights for three hours a day before your regular trainin'. Got that?" Ben asked sharply.

"Yeah, I got it. But what about old Pinky? He's been trainin' me like you told him to, and I know he needs some cash."

"I'm sendin' over four grand for the old man, but tell him not to blow it in one shot. Tell him I'll send him two grand every two months for your trainin' fee advance. That's what we agreed on. I'm callin' all the shots. I want you to lift weights for two years only. Tell Pinky I said that. I hear your body's still a little flabby. We gotta tighten you up. How's Pinky?"

"Pinky's been real nice to me. He knew you got hurt. He's not complainin' about the money. He's trainin' me hard every day. I'm workin' out real good. Tomorrow I spar a big coon. He's a top contender. I'm gonna knock him all over the ring," Alley Boy said, raising his voice.

"Good, kick the shit outta him, make a rep for yourself. I want the newspapers to talk about you. Keep up the good work, kid, and don't talk to no one about nothin'. I been laid up for a while, but I'll be in touch from time to time. If you do the right thing, you're gonna get a lot more dough, so be a good kid. Good-bye, kid, keep up the hard punchin'. I hear from the street you're lookin' good."

Click, the phone went dead. Alley stood silently for a moment with the phone in his hand.

"Hey, Alley!" a voice shouted out from the back office. "Are you finished with the phone? Hang up, we gotta dial out over here." Alley hung up and walked toward the office to sign a sparring release. After a few minutes he walked out and signaled Pinky with his eyes to a corner of the gym.

Alley leaned in to Pinky's ear. "Pinky, he just called. Your money will be sent over in a day or two."

Pinky smiled, and his white teeth shone with happiness. "I knew them boys would not forget old Pinky," he said. "They's good fellows."

"Pinky, I just signed that sparrin' partner release for tomorrow. You better tell Tiger Cruise to sign one too, because I'm gonna knock the livin' shit outta him." Alley Boy turned and walked toward the shower room. Before he got through the doorway, he turned and looked back at Pinky. Pinky's eyes were still following the kid. Alley winked over at him, then feinted a bit from across the room. "You know, Pinky," he said, "you're lucky, because you're trainin' the next white champ. And tomorrow, I'm gonna bruise Cruise."

Pinky squealed mightily, and then threw a towel at Alley Boy.

FEBRUARY 5, 1978, 4:00 P.M.

BROOKLYN, NEW YORK

"Don't put no sauce on my cutlet, Bruno, OK?" Mikey Obotza told the waiter. "I want it plain."

"I know how you like yours, don't worry; absolutely no sauce, and you want it on a seeded roll, correct?" The waiter then pointed at Pauli. "And this guy wants his cutlet like on the menu, *alla parmigiana* on a plain roll. You're both drinkin' beer, correct? Correct," Bruno snapped, answering his own question. "See, what's so hard about that?" he grinned, as he walked away. As Pauli laughed at Bruno, Mikey shook his head.

"The fuckin' guy's nuts with all them 'corrects,'" Mikey huffed. "I gotta lay off the sauce. My stomach's all fucked up. This dummy Bruno makes a big deal over everybody's order—a fuckin' san'wich, a pickle, and a beer, and believe me, he'll find a way to screw it up. All he's good for is 'Correct? Correct?' He's got the whole neighborhood sayin' that shit!"

"Did you hear about the trouble down at the gym?" Little Pauli whispered across the table at Mikey. "They say Tiger Cruise the fighter heard Alley Boy was bad-mouthin' him, so he butted the kid like crazy right away in the first round of their sparrin' match."

"Yeah, it's in the papers. I read it this mornin'."

"Alley Boy's really gettin' publicity by punchin' out top contenders. I can't believe what the papers said," Mikey grinned. "The kid knocked Cruise to the floor three times in one round. Cruise never expected the kid would be so rough."

"Imagine, Alley Oop's son a sparrin' partner for a pro like Tiger Cruise—floorin' the black bastard three times, no less. Cruise hit Alley Boy hard with his head, tryin' to dump him right away. Tiger then broke Alley's nose with a left hook," Pauli explained. "Then Alley Boy got mad and went to work. They say he crippled Tiger so bad, they carried him out on a stretcher. The kid broke three ribs on him. Cruise had a half-million guaranteed fight comin' up next week with the heavyweight champ, Big Larry Sims. Now it's all down the drain for

Tiger Cruise. His title shot has to wait till his ribs heal. I heard it from the street. Cruise's people approached Alley Boy at the gym that night. They were angry over the way the kid pounded Cruise. It's gonna cost 'em a fortune to postpone the main bout. The kid told 'em to go fuck themselves. He said he ain't takin' no shit from nobody. 'Tiger busted my nose,' the kid yelled at them, 'and I'm gonna bust his ass good again when he gets out of the hospital.' The kid takes after his father. He's got balls, that kid," Pauli grinned.

"Do you think them guys will go after the kid?" Mikey asked.

"Nah, I doubt it," Pauli shrugged. "They know he's with Ben. Them guys are nothin', they ain't with nobody big. Look at all the papers. They got it in big print in the sports sections. This kid's makin' headlines. He's even got the boxin' commission lookin' at him. Things could get serious for him, and he's just a punk kid. I think he's only fought about six or seven pro fights. The kid's got hardly any experience with the pros."

"Yeah, but he's got his father's punch, and Old Pinky Williams is trainin' him. Ben loves the kid. He's got a good shot to make it with them credentials."

"Ahh, here we go," Bruno the waiter said while recklessly dumping two plates on the Formica tabletop. "*Uno bianco* and the other with sauce. Correct? See how easy it is when we speak clear English to each other?"

"Ya know, Bruno, you're really a fuckin' brain." Mikey laughed. "I gotta give you credit. You're smart. You remembered we ordered two sandwiches and you forgot we ordered two beers. Go get the beers, ya crumb. With all them 'corrects,' you're incorrect, as usual. And change that dirty apron you're wearing," Mikey mimicked. "You look like an animal." Bruno left laughing.

"The guy's really nuts," Pauli said, biting into his sandwich. "You see the wide ass he's got? He looks like a kite. He's got the brain of a beached whale. And he tries to show everybody he's smart—'Correct? Correct?' Underneath it all, he's a fuckin' dummy. Even his wife couldn't stand him. She left him last year," Pauli said grinning sheepishly.

Mikey glared. "I suppose you fucked her too, hah, Pauli?" Mikey sighed. "She had some body, the bitch. She wiggled her ass all over the neighborhood." Mikey nodded at the thought of her.

Pauli smiled. "Nah, I never went near her. I couldn't touch her after she slept with that crummy guy. He always smells of pizza sauce. She must of smelled the same way. I can't stand a broad that's got a husband with a wide ass. She's gotta be as stupid as him."

Mikey leaned forward and spoke softly. "I gotta get down to Bepy's farm. Fat Nickie and Petey Blue are guarding the place since Joey D took off. Ben wants me to go check on them. Did you hear about Dana? Some fuckin' rebel from Savannah sneaked on the farm one night and tried to rape her. Imagine the balls on that guy. He heard Bephino was gone and he made a move on her. We're gonna kill him." The cold beers were brought to the table, and both men gulped quickly straight from the bottle. Bruno watched for a moment, grinned, and left shaking his head.

"Whata we gonna do about Bephino?" Mikey whispered to Pauli while wiping the brew from his lips with his hand.

"We got big problems," Pauli whispered back, shaking his head in disgust. "Rocco Boretti must have already had Bepy killed. It's not like Bephino to stay away from his wife and kids for this long without checkin' on 'em to see if they're OK." Pauli shook his head again. "It's been too long, Mike. He's probably already sleepin' with the worms."

"Yeah, and that's where we're goin' next, with the fuckin' worms, if we don't take Monkey's advice and lay low. We ain't supposed to be in Brooklyn. Monkey's orders, remember?" Mike said. "Maybe we better go to Florida for a few months until Monkey or Ben decides what they're really gonna do about this thing. Monkey thinks Rocco's gonna start killin' us one by one. If all the Old Blood are gone, our family goes down the drain. But I miss Brooklyn. I gotta keep comin' back every once in a while, like now."

"Yeah, me too. I love Brooklyn! And I can't believe Bepy would get caught off guard by some hit man. He was too sharp! He knew all the tricks," Pauli said, still shaking his head.

"Anybody could get caught off guard," Mikey said.

"They could have hired a broad to hit him. Who knows. Bepy enjoyed his pussy, we all know that. But when you're ordered *morte,* it's over, you're finished. That's how it goes. We been in this business since we were kids. It's gonna happen to all of us."

"Yeah, I know. But it's still too tough to accept the thought of the guns pointin' our way."

"We're outgunned by them guys, that's why we better lay low until we reorganize our people. I got the feelin' Ben and Monkey's gonna order a full-scale war in New York, and we're all gonna be hitting the mattresses. But I think they'll probably wait till Ben recovers fully, and by then we'll all know for sure if Bephino is *morte.* Nothing's gonna be the same without Bephino. He was always in charge. We always had a lotta respect for him. Remember when we were all kids together and Bephino got roughed up and thrown outta the poolroom by Pop's son, John? Bepy was underage and the old man that day was all fucked up in the head, and he began asking Bephino how old he was. He called Bepy a wise guy, and then John jumped Bepy and flung him out the door."

"Yeah, Bepy was embarrassed. But I knew Bepy was gonna do something back at them. When he opened the door and walked back in, the entire poolroom was silent, remember?"

"Yeah, I remember, we all waited to see what he was gonna do."

"He walked up to John with a grin, saying, 'Hey, John. I wanna talk to you.' I knew when he got up close as he did what was next."

"Me too. I still see Bephino as a kid holding onto John's shirt and kicking him in the balls three times. Boy, did he cripple John bad. John spent about two weeks in the hospital. The old man had to learn respect for Bepy the hard way."

FEBRUARY 23, 1978, 5:30 A.M.

SANTA ANNA, ITALY

The hospital halls in the old wing were dark and empty. Tattania stood at the end of the corridor, waiting for the three nuns to finish their morning prayers. She stood quietly, adjusting her cart and checking her supplies. The nuns walked out of Bephino's room and down the hall toward Tattania. "*Buon giorno,* Tattania," they nodded. "We're on our way to breakfast," Sister Graciella said, smiling.

"*Buon appetito,* sisters," she said, smiling back. Tattania's eyes moved nervously until the nuns were out of sight, and then she rolled her cart to Bephino's room, looking back over her shoulder as she did so. She opened the door quietly, walked in with her cart, and then firmly closed the door behind her.

Bephino lay like a zombie but aware nonetheless that young Tattania was coming to wash him. His brain, active and alive, was rendered useless without an intact spinal-cord system to work with it. Only Tattania knew how he responded to her therapy of warm, soapy water and lathered movements. But today Bephino could sense in Tattania's approach, in the squeak of the wheels of her cart coming slowly toward him, that something was different. Tattania was very quiet—too quiet—not like she normally was, robustly calling out a cheerful "*Buon giorno*" to him. Today she seemed serious and tense. As Tattania stood looking over him, her almond-shaped eyes flickered, then nervously turned to the large oak door, her breathing uneven. Yes, there was definitely something different today. Without a word, she suddenly pulled back the blankets and sheet and began to sponge down his genitals. The warm, soapy water once again caused his soft penis to grow and thicken before her eyes. Tattania looked at him as if expecting a smile to cross his face, but of course he did not move. He remained cold and lifeless except for his now husky penis lying in her tiny hands. Tattania began to fondle the circumcised head and pull gently on its skin. Her soapy hand squeezed it tight. After a while she began to rinse him off, her eyes constantly darting to the thick oak door. Then suddenly she leaned over, putting her ample cherry lips to the pink head and began to kiss it softly. Taking it partially into her mouth, she began to groan softly, intimately, as in a moment of private pleasure. The young Italian girl closed her eyes as if to darken her fulfillment. Tattania slowly began moving her head up and down, up and down, when suddenly she heard the squeak of the large oak door swinging open and saw Mother Columbo Fabiano, like a huge black crow, standing in the doorway.

APRIL 29, 1978, 4:20 P.M.

SANTA ANNA, ITALY

Obese, dark-eyed Mother Columbo Fabiano stood staring down at the frail body of Bephino Menesiero. She could not believe what she had witnessed that morning two months before. Mother Fabiano prayed for Bephino's soiled soul and for the soul of the young girl who had tampered with his body. The nun's veins in her temples bulged as she prayed to the Virgin Mary for forgiveness. "It was the act of Satan!" Mother Columbo shouted harshly in Italian, looking around the room. *"Il Diavolo,"* she groaned in a high-pitched voice, "is still living in this room!"

Many years before, the room's last patient, the strange, elderly mother of a paraplegic man who practiced satanism, had been found dead in the hospital alley below, her bed sheet wrapped tightly around her and her skull crushed from a fall. The blood found on the ground and the blood-smeared numbers 666 painted on the outside of the heavy oak door were both of the same type as that of the old woman. The mystery of it all was that the window of the room was still locked and sealed shut by very thick, old paint, and the roof exit was rusted and padlocked shut. No one could figure out how she had gotten out of her bed and out the window wrapped so neatly and tightly in the sheet.

Mother Fabiano was certain that after all these years Satan had acted once again and tampered with the innocent mind of the poor young hospital aide, who, as it turned out, had been the only person in the hospital on that particular day who had not been wearing the cross of Jesus Christ. Only the devil himself could have caused her to perform such a degenerate act on an almost dead man.

Bephino, lying locked up in his own body, watched and listened as Mother Fabiano carried on, shaking and actually suffering for Tattania, holding a large cross aloft and shouting at the devil as she prayed daily at Bephino's bedside.

Poor kid, Bephino thought, she got a tough break. What could have caused her to act as she did, what lured her into that terrible act of embarrassment? What a sad situation, he mused, to get caught kissing the cock of a nearly dead man. Now all the townspeople knew, not to mention the entire convent. Mother Fabiano, vividly explaining the scene to anyone who'd listen, as if compelled by God himself to speak out, had herself destroyed beautiful, young Tattania's life. Bephino knew she'd been his only ticket out of here; she was his only friend, his only hope to alert the doctors on the staff that he was truly alive—and now she was gone. He heard the nuns talking about Tattania, that she was now off working in an old wine café on the other side of town, serving a bunch of tough, old card-playing hooligans from the village. Poor Tattania, he thought, she probably had only wanted to explore the male body. She must have been too shy to approach Alfredo. Now she had no Alfredo and no job at the hospital.

But in fact, as the weeks passed, Tattania found that serving men at the café was not as bad as she might have thought. Most of them, having heard about her misfortune, had become quite protective toward her in a fatherly fashion, allowing no one to approach her for a date or even to suggest such things. But of course they whispered among themselves about the girl's unbelievable appetite—using a comatose man at the hospital for her pleasure! "And the man who they say is American still now lives and breathes!" a café patron emphasized to several wine-besotted gentlemen sitting around a table. The patron talked convincingly about the amount of cash originally found on the patient, and whispered his theory of the comatose man in the devil's room 666 coming back to life after the devil's girl had touched him. Some of the men in the café cursed and threatened the devil, and when enough wine had been consumed spoke convincingly of their intentions to march straight to the hospital and enter room 666 to see for themselves the comatose American man who'd been touched by both Satan and Tattania.

Later that evening, after Mother Fabiano had left Bephino's bedside to rejoin her sisters at the dinner table, three of these revelers made good on their inebriated promises and tipsily set off, holding one another up, to offer Satan their curses. "I'm gonna tell Diavolo to fuck himself," the smallest man, Abeno Puglia, whispered in a high voice to the others. "I gotta teach that Satan bastard a lesson!" Each man was shabbily dressed, their pea caps cocked to one side. They walked softly, as they sneaked through the corridors. When they reached the room in question, Abeno quietly and very slowly opened the door. All three men gazed in silence as they entered the room. A light bulb with a green plastic cover set off in the corner gleamed softly over Bephino's bed. The three men nervously, cautiously began to approach the still-frail Bephino. Little Abeno, the curser of the devil, suddenly removed his pea cap in a gesture of respect. Gino Salermo, the heavyset, red-faced man next to him, also removed his cap and held it to his chest. The third man, a self-exiled retired American Italian, merely stared down at the motionless man with a smirk. His name was Louis "Red" Biancesquardo, and he had once lived in Bay Ridge, Brooklyn.

"He's dead," Abeno Puglia whispered, looking up at the other men. "His skin looks almost blue. See," Abeno said, touching Bephino's thin face, "he's ice cold, feel him."

"No, he's still alive," responded Gino Salermo in his deep, wine-soaked voice. "He breathes; look at his stomach. It goes up and down, and the tubes they feed him in the arms, they still drip, and that means his blood still circulates."

"Circulates like *il morte,*" Abeno said, looking up at both men with a grin. "Where's Diavolo?" he giggled. "I gotta tell the bastard to fuck himself."

"Maybe he's hidin' in this guy's body and he's gonna jump out at us," Gino grinned, his round, red face flushing brightly with ill-concealed concern.

"Why you so quiet, Louis Red?" little Abeno asked in a low voice. "Whata ya, scared?"

"This guy looks familiar," Louis Red whispered in a thick voice. "He looks so familiar to me, but it can't be the guy I know. He can't be in Santa Anna. It's impossible."

"Are you the devil?" Abeno asked Bephino curtly. "Do you know Louis Red?" Abeno joked, holding his pea cap up to his mouth and speaking in a high voice. Hysterical giggles followed from him, in what sounded like a series of hiccups. At that moment, the light bulb in the lamp flickered and reflected a green glare from the plastic shade. Suddenly the room took on an intensely bright green hue, as if illuminated by an even brighter green bulb. The three men suddenly stopped talking. The room was awash in green, and even Bephino's face began to take on that color.

"Everything's turnin' green in this place! Let's get the fuck outta this room," Gino said hoarsely. "I see a shadow movin' around in the corner. I'm gettin' the creeps. Even this fuckin' guy's turnin' green. Look at him; now's the time for us to go." All three men turned abruptly and walked to the door.

Abeno opened it quickly and the men walked out. "*Aspetta uno momento.* Hold it," Louis Red said at the door. "Just a minute. I gotta check somethin' out." He turned and walked back into the room. It was still flickering green. Louis Red walked back up to the bed and stared down at the frail, skinny face lying in it. With his right hand, he turned Bephino's chin slightly from side to side as he examined the man under his neck. As a kid, Bephino had gotten slashed by Joey D's uncle in the schoolyard in Sheepshead Bay. Red had been there, and he always remembered that. As he moved Bephino's face, sure enough, the thin pink scar appeared on the lower right side of his neck. Louis Red's eyes widened at what he saw. "Bephino," he whispered incredulously, "it is you! What the fuck happened to you? What are you doin' here?"

Bephino heard Red speaking over his body and couldn't believe this could be happening. What was Red doin' in Santa Anna? he asked himself.

Red had once been his childhood friend. A Milanese, Red had always been bright and ambitious, and had become

Bephino's business partner in his string of Hero shops in lower Manhattan and in a betting operation. But before long Red had begun skimming a portion of the profits and bragging about his good fortune.

When Bephino learned about this, he decided to kill Red and his protégé, Johnny ("Mac") Macaroni. He lured both men into a cellar in a Chinatown laundry. Ignoring Mac's pleas for mercy, Bephino himself pulled the trigger, pumping a .38 bullet into Mac's forehead. Then Alley Oop and a huge Chinaman raised up the body and lowered it into a vat of acid, where it was dissolved, after which the liquidated remains were released into the city's sewer system.

Red, next up, was squirming with fear as he pleaded pathetically for his own life. And Red was smart: He prayed to Bephino's father's saint, the fisherman's saint, the Sacred Heart of Jesus, to let him live to see the birth of his unborn child. Bephino listened as Red prayed out loud to the Sacred Heart of Jesus. "Kill him!" Ben had shouted, "he's praying like a moron." Bephino didn't answer. Ben pleaded adamantly. But because of old childhood memories, and because Red's wife would soon have her baby, Bephino couldn't make the kill. He thought about the old Sicilian ways that had been taught to him as he watched Red pray. It was a pathetic sight. And so he spared Red's life, but ordered him to leave Brooklyn and never return. Ben had called Bephino mad. "Red will kill you someday," he had shouted. "You're making a big mistake. He will kill you!"

But Red did not kill him. Instead, he quickly skipped town, leaving his wife, Norma, and his young children for another woman. Bephino made Monkey his new partner in the Hero shops. Red was never heard from again.

And so now Bephino's righteous enemy was presiding over him in a godforsaken hospital in Italy. What would Red do? Bephino thought. Will he plunge his stiletto into my heart and take me out of my misery, or will he help me in some way? Red stared into Bephino's green face. "Bephino," he whispered again in shock. Suddenly the thick oak door opened and little Abeno peeked in.

"You OK, Red?" Abeno asked.

"Yeah, I'm OK," Red said sadly. He reached over to the flickering lamp and adjusted the green plastic shade that had slid over the bulb and made the room look so unearthly. He turned off the light and walked out.

"We gotta get out of here before we turn green," Abeno yelped, looking from Red to Gino as they walked down the corridor. "Everything's turning green in that fuckin' room."

After a couple of months of pondering and visiting Bephino's bedside, Louis Red, sitting and thinking at his farmhouse in Northern Italy, made his decision. He could not kill Bephino while he was in such an unhealthy condition. For old time's sake, he decided to help him. Red had changed over the years from a greedy, violent person to a passive man who desired very little in life; his anger and vengeance for Bephino had subsided with the passage of time. And so finally, for once in his life, Red made an honest decision.

"Hello, information? This is long distance. I'm callin' from Italy, and I need the number for an Aldo Pastrona. He lives on 9th Avenue, in Brooklyn—and if you find it, could you put me through?"

"Yes, sir, I have it; please make a record of the number: 212-689-9723. Hold on, sir, and I'll try to connect you."

The phone rang twice. A recording came on. "The number you have reached is no longer in service . . ."

"Your number had been recently disconnected, sir."

"Operator, try the Hero Corporation on Wall and Water streets in Manhattan. I don't have that phone number either, but it's important."

"Hold on, sir. We're allowed to make only two information calls. Please note that."

"OK, operator, I appreciate your help. This is my last try . . ."

"Hold on, sir. . . . OK, your number is ringing. Please make a note of it . . ."

"Hello, Wall Street Hero, Flakey Jakey speaking."

"Hey, Jakey, let me speak to Monkey right away. I'm calling long distance."

"Who's calling?"

"This is a friend of Monkey's. Put him on."

"Monkey's not here; Blubberhead's in charge now."

"What happened to Monkey?"

"He's gone on a trip. I have no idea where, so don't ask me."

"OK, put Blubberhead on."

"Blubber's busy talkin' to a chick. He can't be disturbed."

"Jakey, this is very important; put Blubberhead on the phone right away! I'm calling long distance from Italy," Red shouted.

Jakey hesitated. "What part of Italy?"

"Italy," Red answered. "Northern Italy. Just put him on; it's important!"

"It better be important. Blubber's been trying to corner this broad for six months. Hold on, I'll call him . . ."

"Yeah, this is Blubber," a deep voice said.

"Blubber, this is Red, remember me?"

"Not really. Which Red is this, Frankie Red?"

"No, Red the bookie, Louis Biancesquardo from Bay Ridge—you know me. I used to be partners with Bephino, remember?"

"Yeah, whata ya want? I thought Bephino chased you outta Brooklyn. Correct?"

"Where's Monkey? I gotta talk to him. It's very important."

"Monkey ain't around, he can't be reached. He's on vacation from Brooklyn for a while. I'm in charge now."

"OK, Blubber, now listen and listen good: You get in touch with Monkey right away and tell him I just saw Bephino Menesiero. . . ."

JULY 5, 1978, 10:00 A.M.

BOWIE, MARYLAND

"Hello, Dana, this is Ben. How are you? I want you to sit down. Are you sittin'?"

"What happened, Ben? Tell me."

"I got good news for you. Bephino has been located."

"Where the hell is he!" she screamed into the phone. "Where is he? How is my husband, Ben?"

"I can't talk too much over the phone, Dana, we can't take that chance, so don't ask me any questions. He's alive and he's in Europe, that's all I know. I'll tell you when we meet. Dana, you got a passport?"

"No, it expired years ago—Ben, how is Bephino?"

"He's OK, I got the story from Monkey. We can't talk on the phone, *a capisce*? Get a passport right away. It only takes two days for a renewal. Reissues are given very quickly. But you gotta have your old one when you go there. Take two new photos with you—two of 'em, don't forget—and your old passport also. We're leaving for Europe in three days, on Friday morning. Get to Kennedy Airport before 9:00 A.M. Take an early flight from Savannah. Make your flight reservations and call me back tonight. Friday, I'll be at the airport waiting for you, then we'll go to the international flight area. I'll have those tickets all ready."

"OK, Ben. I'll call you back. Oh, Ben . . . I'm gonna call my children right after I hang up, then I'll run to town to city hall and check on getting the passport reissued. I'm so happy, Ben. Thank God he's alive."

"Has Bubba Reed been near the farm again?" Ben asked.

"No, thank God," she answered. "Everything's fine over here."

"Are the boys doin' their job OK? Are they guardin' the place?

"The one they call Crazy, that Mikey fellow, he came down to check on them last week."

"Good! Mikey's doin' what I asked. We'll take care of Bubba Reed when I get back from Europe, don't worry."

"I'm not worried. You don't have to go after Bubba Reed. He don't come here anymore," Dana said. "Your men stay at the gate all the time. They take turns sleepin'. When Mrs. Roselli bakes lasagna, we send them some, otherwise they barbecue steaks or chops. They eat well. Don't worry about them guys. They're havin' a picnic down there. Yesterday they rode the horses."

"Good! OK, then I'll wait for your call. Get the earliest reservation for Friday mornin' and get the passport right away. Tell them it's an emergency, and they'll see that you get your passport right away. And call me back tonight. Dana, take care."

"I'm so happy, Ben!"

7

JULY 8, 1978, 10:00 A.M.

KENNEDY AIRPORT, NEW YORK CITY

"What is he doin' in Zurich? Why is he there?" Dana asked, as she and Ben trotted down an airport corridor.

"He's not in Zurich. He's in Milano," Ben whispered into Dana's ear. "We're gonna rent a car and drive through the mountains to where he's at. He's at a special place. You'll see when we get there."

"Why are you whisperin' about everything? I can hardly hear you with all this noise."

"I'm whisperin' because we have our enemies. You should realize that, Dana! Why are you actin' so naive about my whisperin'? Look at me." Ben rattled his two metal canes.

"I'm a cripple because of them guys. So now if they hear that I flew outta New York, they'll think I ended up in Zurich. I don't want anyone gettin' to Bephino before us."

Dana stopped for a moment as she took in the reasons for Ben's precautions. She was seeing him for the first time since his accident. She squeezed Ben's arm as they boarded the plane's front premier section. Watching his slow-moving, withered body, Dana remembered how Ben had once stood so erect and proud. Now he depended on his canes to carry him. "I'm so sorry, Ben, I'm so sorry. Sometimes I forget the business you guys are in. Please forgive me," she said as she sat down, raising his hand to her lips and kissing it humbly. "I'm so nervous, I lost twenty pounds in the last eighteen months," Dana said as she settled in her seat. After a few moments of silence, she asked, "Can you still drive a car, Ben? Those mountains in Europe are dangerous. Are you able?"

"No, I can't drive. We'll hire a driver with his own car. That's no problem. In Europe, everybody's a driver for rent," Ben answered wearily. "I just don't want to fuck up and have some of Boretti's people follow us right to Bephino's bed."

Dana began to whisper. "I thought that Boretti liked Bephino. He bought our house from us . . ." Ben looked ahead and did not respond. "You said that Red found him. How did you find that out?" she asked. "What is Red doing in Europe?"

"Red contacted Monkey's place of business and Monkey called me. I spoke with Red on the phone a few times, and he said it's Bephino all right, and he's in a coma. He's been in a coma for about seventeen months, according to Red."

"Oh, my God, Ben, I didn't know Bepy was hurt so bad. He's in a coma! What happened to him?"

"Look, Dana, I didn't want to tell you all this until we arrived. Please don't get upset, because you'll be no good to me upset. We got a rough time ahead of us. You gotta be strong and clearheaded. Just follow my commands. Move quickly and quietly whenever I talk, don't let me have to repeat myself. We gotta get Bepy to the best hospital in the world, and there's people who would not like to see this happen, so we gotta be strong. We've got a lotta work ahead of us."

"I'll do whatever you say, Ben, you know that."

"Good! Now let me take a nap. I'm tired. I didn't sleep all night." Ben closed his eyes and sat back.

"Is Bepy all right?" she asked softly.

Ben's eyes flickered open. "I don't know. He's in a coma, that's all I know."

"Will he ever come out of it?"

"We'll see what the doctors in Italy have to say, then I'll be contacting others in England and France. He'll get the best, I can assure you," Ben said. "I hope you brought your credit card along," he smiled.

Dana tried to smile. "How did Red find Bepy? That's such a mysterious thing, hah, Ben? Red, of all people," she groaned, shaking her head in wonder.

"Yeah, another million-to-one shot and we hit again," Ben grinned. "I understand from Red he lives on a farm near the village where Bepy is at, and through talk in the village he heard there was an American or Englishman in the hospital for a long time, so Red and his friends went to investigate, and after a while he realized the guy was Bepy. Unbelievable," Ben said, shaking his head. "Bepy's lost a lot of weight; he looks bad, Red said, so don't expect to see something special."

"Why does Bepy look that bad? Sounds like Red didn't recognize him right away," Dana said, her eyes filling with tears.

"Dana, Bephino is only about ninety pounds now. He's half of what he was."

"Oh my God, Ben, don't tell me this."

"It coulda been worse, Dana. At least he's still alive." Sobbing, she nodded and wiped her eyes with a tissue. Ben closed his eyes and fell asleep.

When the plane landed in Zurich, Ben made a deal with a driver to go along with them on a trip and stay for about a week or so. All they had to do was make a quick stop first at his house so he could pick up some clothes and things.

"No problem," Ben said. "We also gotta change some money into lire."

After the stops and errands, Ben was satisfied no one was

tailing them. He then gave the driver his first directive. "Lugano," Ben said.

"Ah, Lugano," the driver repeated. "Only a few hours from here. We must take the car on the railroad train," the driver continued. "We go through the mountains to Lugano."

"Can't we just drive?" Ben asked.

"No, the train; it's better with the train, and faster. The car stays with us right on the train," the driver explained. "There's a ten thousand lire fee for the car's platform service."

"It's OK," Ben said. "But ten thousand lire is, what, about twenty-six bucks? Here, take fifty thousand lire; keep the rest for tolls. Let's get going."

Several hours later, nearing Lugano, they had stopped and were now contemplating the remains of a roadside snack. "I don't believe we just had pigs' feet for dinner, on a roadside in Italy, no less. I hope that means good luck," Dana grinned. "The vinegar was so strong it made me drunk."

"Yeah, I asked for black coffee and cheese, and the guy brought back pigs' feet and wine. Welcome to Italy! We'll get a hotel later tonight farther in Lugano," Ben said. "Then tomorrow we'll go to Milan."

Looking over at the Swiss driver, Ben asked, "Can you speak Northern Italian?"

"I speak five languages, sir. Italian is no problem for me."

"Good, that's good," Ben said. "Because I'll need to make phone calls all over Europe to doctors and hospitals. You can speak for me."

"Fine," the driver said. "I can do that."

"OK, take us to a first-class hotel for tonight. We'll need three rooms," Ben said. "Then tomorrow morning we'll drive to Milano."

Dana grabbed Ben's hand in the car and whispered, "I'm so scared, Ben."

"Don't be; we're gonna get Bephino out of there as soon as possible. Dry your hand, Dana, you feel sweaty."

Later that evening at the hotel, Ben dialed Red's number. Red answered and agreed to meet them at the Shire Palace Hotel in Milan the next day at about 1:00 P.M., after which they would go to see Bephino at the hospital.

The next afternoon, Dana sat in her hotel room, nervously awaiting Red's arrival. At 1:35 there was a knock at the door. Dana got up and opened it. Ben observed from a large parlor chair, holding his aluminum canes. A man stood in the doorway wearing a pea cap and a worn, dark gray tweed jacket—the clothes of a small-village European. The man respectfully removed his cap from what seemed to be a balding head.

Dana looked at him. "Is that you, Red?"

"Yeah, it's me, Dana," he replied cheerfully. "Gee, it's been so long. . . . Since we were kids. How are you?"

Dana motioned for him to enter. "I'm as good as can be expected," she said, closing the door. "You don't look like yourself, Red. You're dressed like the townspeople. You look like a real Italian."

"I'm living like one of them, Dana. I have a little farm outside of town, a few pigs, about twenty chickens, and I keep strictly to myself these days. I have a beautiful wife and kid over here. My uncle died and gave me the farm. How are you, Dana? You still look as beautiful as ever." Red smiled broadly.

"Thank you, Red. That's nice to hear. I don't feel so beautiful anymore, but it's always nice to hear."

Ben silently watched and listened to Red and Dana renew old ties.

"You know Ben Del Ponte, don't you?" Dana asked.

"Yes, we met before." Red moved to shake Ben's hand.

"So, what are you doing living all the way in Italy, Red? It's a long way from Bay Ridge, isn't it?" Ben asked.

"It's peaceful here, Ben. You wouldn't believe my reason for leaving Brooklyn," Red said sarcastically. Ben looked away. "Like you may remember, the reason I left was you and Bephino," Red nodded with a glare, "and a million-to-one shot, Bephino winds up right here in my father's hometown with my own people. What a small world it is. Well, I'm glad, at least, I was here to help out." Red managed a meek smile. "Maybe it's my chance to regain my credibility with you and Bephino."

Dana was shocked to hear Red's words. She knew of no reason why Red should have left Brooklyn to avoid contact with Bephino. Then again, she realized, Bephino had never discussed business with her to begin with. "I'm sure Bephino will be grateful over your concern and help, Red," she offered, looking to Ben for confirmation. Ben merely studied the large window overlooking the local piazza.

"What happened to you, Ben? I see you holding those canes. Are you OK?" Red asked.

"I contracted polio," Ben said coldly.

"Well, if you're both ready to see Bephino, I'm ready to take you. But remember, before you see him: He's alive, but he looks dead. He doesn't look like the person he always was, but you'll know it's him. He's white as a ghost and in a coma. They feed him through the veins. If you're ready, let's go."

Two hours later they entered the dark, old-fashioned tiled-floor lobby of Santa Anna Catholic Hospital, about a hundred thirty miles outside Milano. A nun approached them, and Red spoke to her in fluent Northern Italian dialect. Ben swiftly reached into his pocket and handed her two American hundred-dollar bills. "Buy yourself a hat, Sister," he said. She thanked him, blessed him, and led the way to the room where Bephino lay. She opened the door, allowing Red to enter first. Ben followed. Then Dana, white as a sheet, half staggered in, holding the nun for support. Ben's eyes searched the semi-darkened room lit only by sunlight seeping through old curtains. He moved up close to the bed and rapidly scanned the body that lay, deathlike. Dana hung back with the nun. As Ben awkwardly moved up closer to the body, he began to inspect the inert form.

"Is it him, Ben?" Dana asked weakly. "What's that long hair around his mouth?"

Ben turned around to her, filled with emotion. "Yeah, it's him. They left his upper lip untrimmed, but it's him all right," Ben said. As Dana approached the bed, Ben grabbed her and whispered, "He's still alive, and he knows we're here. I can feel it. My senses tell me that he knows we're here, so don't crack up, OK?"

Dana reached out and touched Bephino's frail face. "Oh, honey," she whispered, tears dripping down her soft, white cheeks, "we're here to get you, we're here to make you well.

Ben's here, and your old friend Red's here with me. We love you, Bephino, and we're gonna get you outta here." Dana kissed his parched lips. An uneven bushy patch of hair crossed his lip. His face displayed small patches of unshaven hair. All four people in the room stared at Bephino's helpless and motionless body. Dana touched his hands and said, "He feels so cold. Can't we get him an electric blanket or something? He feels so cold, Ben, feel him. He's ice cold."

Speaking Italian, Red asked the nun about an electric blanket. She replied that all they had were the old army blankets, and the room had no extra electrical outlets to accommodate a heating blanket. Only the other wing had extra electricity, she said as she turned to leave the room.

Ben groaned, "It's 1978. The whole world has extra electricity but Italy."

After a long while Dana, who had been unconsciously clasping and unclasping Bephino's hands, looked up. "Ben!" she yelped. "His hand just moved in my hand! I felt it! I felt his hand move! Is that normal?" she asked Red. "Has this happened before?"

"I'll find out," Red said, and immediately left the room and called out to the nun. As she hurried in return and heard Red's question, the nun rattled back that she had never known him to have any movement. "Maybe the signora imagined it," she said, looking over at Dana. Dana and Ben both began to speak rapidly in Italian, Dana in Neopolitan and Ben in the Sicilian dialect. The nun shrugged. "The doctor comes tomorrow at 9:00 A.M. I'll mention it to him." She turned and left.

After several hours, there was no more to observe for the time being. As they retired to a nearby hotel in Santa Anna, Red said, "Call me day or night if you need me. You got my number, I'll be at home."

Later, during a late-night dinner, Dana told Ben, "You are right, Ben. Bepy knows we're here. He's aware, he knows. I felt his finger wiggle in my palm, Ben. I know he's aware of us!"

"I believe you, Dana," Ben said, sipping some wine. "I felt the same way. I could sense he knows we're with him."

"You know, Ben, we gotta figure a way to warm up his body.

Bepy hated cold—remember how he always wanted to go to Palm Springs for the winter? These bastards put him on ice over there," she mumbled. "We gotta figure a way to warm up his body," she repeated. "We gotta get him an electric blanket or somethin', or move him outta that room. It's terrible, the room he's in, did you notice?"

"Tomorrow we'll get him another room," Ben said.

The next morning they were at the hospital at 8:45 to meet with Dr. Salvadore Romano. The doctor, a pleasant old man, told Dana and Ben that the finger reaction could have been caused by her hands being warm and Bepy's cold. "The nerves are sensitive to the sudden temperature change. That could have caused the flicker," the doctor said. But he did not rule out Bepy's possible awareness. As for the electric blanket, he feared it would impose too extreme a change to the body's temperature; despite the blanket's thermostat, the sudden increase in heat could burden Bephino's weakened heart too much. "Your husband is taking intravenous feeding," the doctor advised Dana, "and that will eventually lead to death. Remember, he's still comatose and unresponsive, and a man in this condition should not be moved. So there is no sense to change rooms. At any rate, we could spare only this primitive room. The newer rooms are used for the ill who show promise of recovery. This case, I'm afraid, looks after all this time hopeless," Dr. Romano concluded, raising his eyes above his spectacles while shaking his head and patting Dana's shoulder in a clumsy attempt at comfort.

Soon after, Red joined Ben and Dana, having spent the morning with the cabdriver, phoning coma specialists all over Italy. The four of them sought lunch nearby in an outdoor café, where they considered their next move.

"I understand Bephino was bleeding pretty bad when they found him," Red related. "They managed to patch him up, but from the spinal shock he went into the coma. I understand his neck cords were torn apart pretty bad by a sharp object. That could have caused him to slip into the coma," Red mused, shaking his head.

"Did you see that Dr. Romano they got taking care of him over there? He looks like a guy who removed my tonsils when

I was a kid in Brooklyn," Dana said. "He's too old, he don't have the medical technology to get Bephino out of a coma," she complained. "We gotta move him, Ben. Let's make arrangements to take him to Milano or to Rome. Let's get an ambulance and move him. They must have more sophisticated hospitals in Milano."

Ben explained, "I'm waiting for Dr. Pastelli to call us from Rome. He's a specialist on this stuff. But one way or another, tomorrow, yes, we'll make some decisions or arrangements for an ambulance to move him," Ben agreed.

"Tonight I wanna go back and visit him again, OK, Ben?"

"Sure, of course, we'll go over and stay with him for a couple hours. Then later we'll have a late dinner at the hotel. They serve dinner real late here in Europe," Ben grinned. "Would you believe, at ten at night they're still seating people?"

"Right now we all better finish our lunch," Red interjected with a smile, "because come 2:00 P.M., they close for siesta time, and they'll be kicking us out of here."

Later that evening, Dana and Ben returned to Bephino's green-painted room and sat beside his bed. Dana immediately took her husband's hands into her own. After a while, she summoned the courage to pull the sheet and blanket back to view his naked body. "Oh, my God, he looks terrible," Dana whispered. "He doesn't even look like my husband. His body is so small," she wailed, turning to Ben.

"What did ya think he was gonna look like, King Kong? He's lying there for a year and a half. He's melting away," Ben replied.

Dana restored the covers, tucked her husband in, and once again took his hands into her own. "Sweetheart," she crooned, "the children are home waiting for you. They love you very, very much, and Mrs. Roselli keeps . . ." Dana broke off with a start, then turned excitedly to Ben. "Ben," she whispered, "I felt his finger moving again! I just felt it move right in my hands. I talked about the kids and he responded to me. Bephino," she whispered directly into his face, "if you can hear me, darling, move your finger again." Ben watched for Dana's reaction. Her warm, soft hands lay over Bephino's.

"Do you feel anything?" Ben asked.

Dana, crouching over Bephino, didn't answer; she waited and repeated her words to her husband. "Honey," she said, "if you understand me, please move your finger. Please," she begged.

Ben silently watched as Dana tried to exhume the little life that was left in her husband's body.

Suddenly, Dana jumped up. "Ben!" she yelled, "he moved his finger again! This time it was stronger than before."

"No shit," Ben exclaimed. "Let me try." He stumbled off his chair, placed his hands over Bephino's, and whispered to him, "Bepy, remember when we was Young Turks in New Orleans? Don Santoro? Remember, Bephino, how Santoro almost died? Remember the blond jig, and her cherry jubilee?" Suddenly, a finger flickered twice. "Dana, he understands us, he's aware. Bepy, do it again!" Ben yelled. "Come on, Bep, finger me again." The finger moved again. "OK, Dana, he's with us! Tomorrow we move him to Milan or Rome. I'll make all the fuckin' arrangements myself with an ambulance service and call the hospital!" Ben shouted with joy as he sat back down in his chair. "I'll have the best doctors waiting when we arrive. Dana, let's go back to the hotel. We'll rest and freshen up, have dinner and be back here tomorrow morning early to get him out of here."

"Believe me, Ben, all he needs is a heating blanket!" Dana almost shouted. "These stupid doctors over here are a hundred years behind the times."

"I know," Ben said. "Places like this are too primitive for us."

"Ben, you go back to the hotel without me. I'm not hungry. I'm gonna stay here tonight with Bephino."

"Dana, come on, get some rest; you're beat, I'm beat. Tomorrow we'll come back for him. There's nothing more we can do for him."

"No, Ben, please. I want to stay with him. He knows I'm here. I'm sure of that now. I wanna stay close to him tonight. You go back to the hotel. Come and pick me up tomorrow morning early, then I'll go back to the hotel to shower and pack."

"OK, Dana, if that's what you want."

She grabbed Ben's hands and said, "Yes, Ben. Tell the desk nun I'm staying the night and not to disturb me. I'll see you tomorrow."

"OK, first thing in the morning." Ben stumbled back up to his feet, set his canes in place and awkwardly walked toward the door. He turned and smiled. "Dana, get some rest, will you? You look like shit."

The sound of Ben's feet dragging down the cold tiled hospital hallway gave Dana a very lonely feeling. Turning to Bephino, she resumed her station beside him, her hands over his. After a few hours, close to midnight, she got up and walked out the door into the dark, lonely corridor and found her way to the ladies' toilet. After about fifteen minutes she returned to the room, sat down by the bed, and stared at her husband. "Bephino," she whispered, "do you love me?" Watching his hands this time without hers coupling over his, she asked again, "Bephino, do you love me?" His index finger moved twice. "Do it again, Bepy. Move your finger." And again he moved it. Now there was no doubt: The doctor was wrong. It wasn't a nervous reaction. The heat from her hand may have activated his muscles, but now he was able to move his own finger, without her hands empowering his. What if I were to press my entire body to his? she thought. Suppose I disrobed totally to give him warmth? He never could resist the warmth of my naked body, she smiled to herself. After a while Dana slowly, carefully began to remove all her clothes. Placing them neatly on a chair, she turned off the lamp, pulled back the covers, and crawled in alongside her husband. God, he feels ice cold, she thought. Pulling the blankets over them, she pressed her body closer to his with a shudder. After a long while, warmth was generated under the blanket. Oh, he felt so different, she thought. Bephino had always been so masculine and sexy. Now he was so frail and . . . Soon she fell deeply into sleep.

About four and a half hours later, at 5:00 A.M., sunrise, the door opened as Mother Columbo Fabiano entered the still-dark room to perform her ritual, to damn the devil. The mother superior, having been away for three days on a trip to

Rome, was unaware that Bephino had guests. Ever since finding Tattania, Mother Fabiano had not been herself. She had come to be obsessed with the image of the devil living in that room. As the heavyset nun approached the bedside lamp, she did not see Dana's long black hair loose and hanging freely on the side of the pillow. Her thoughts, as always, were of the way she had found Tattania that horrible morning with the near-dead man. When Mother Fabiano turned on the lamp, the green plastic shade slid once again over the bulb, plunging the room into an unearthly green. With a shiver, the nun turned to her patient, and it was then that she saw the tangle of black hair. No, she shook her head; Diavolo was playing a game with her. She leaned closer, but the image did not recede. And then she touched the hair. It was real enough. Dana, fast asleep, purred like a tired kitten. Mother Fabiano started, her eyes shifting around and down to take in Dana's shoes on the floor and her clothes lying neatly over the chair. For final, unspeakable confirmation, the nun slowly pulled back the covers—perhaps she was becoming mentally ill.

"Who's that!?" Dana yelped, exposed to the chill of the morning. "Who . . ." Dana turned and sat up, exposing her large, firm naked breasts.

Mother Fabiano, mouth agape, stared with mounting horror. *"Pazza!"* she screeched in Italian. "Are you crazy? What are you doing to this sick man? The man is dying and you're doing that to him! *Disgraziato!"* she yelled, biting her fingers. "Diavolo!" she screamed, looking wildly around the room.

Dana, hearing her yell to the devil, hobbled off the bed and tried to quickly dress herself, but the nun began to push and shove her. Dana was almost toppled over by the huge sister of mercy.

"Stop that," Dana pleaded in English. "Stop pushing me," she said, trying to put on her panties. The nun pushed at her again, and Dana fell to the floor.

Suddenly, a strange-sounding voice rang hoarsely through the room. "Leave her alone!" The voice of a man bounced off thick plaster walls.

The nun, still going after Dana, stopped dead in her tracks

and looked over her shoulder. Dana, still struggling to get up and into her panties, also stopped in her tracks and looked up in surprise.

Then the voice came again. "Leave her alone." Dana turned around slowly toward Bephino. The voice had come from him! The nun moved in what seemed like slow motion and began backing away, retreating from what was surely Diavolo himself speaking through Bephino's frail body. Dana, still naked, hurried to her husband.

"Bephino," she murmured, "is that you?"

"Yeah, it's me, sweetheart. I'm with you. I can talk now."

"Oh, Bepy, thank God, thank God," she cried, kissing his face all over. "Oh, honey, I missed you so much!" Bephino tried to smile. He even tried to kiss her back, but he was stiff as a board, and his lips were in very bad shape. Dana quickly slipped on her panties and grabbed her dress.

Suddenly the room's heavy oak door reopened, and Mother Fabiano came back in with her three sisters. Dana, still trying to dress herself, remained half nude, her bare breasts fully exposed as she pulled up her dress. Her bra was still draped over the chair. As she struggled to cover herself, she addressed a torrent of Italian to the invading nuns. They knew nothing about body warmth, she rattled to them; it was the warmth from her body that had brought her husband out of the coma. "He's awake, see? His eyes are open!" she gestured, speaking to them in Neapolitan.

The four nuns, easing up to Bephino's bedside, asked curiously, "Are you awake?"

Bephino grinned at the four nervous sisters hovering over him. "Yeah, I'm awake," he croaked in his strong Sicilian dialect.

One of the nuns, detecting the dialect, remarked *"Siciliano."* They all turned, smiling at Dana, who was still busy hooking up. The nuns began to hug her; Dana smiled with joy and hugged them back. Mother Fabiano quickly began to work on Bephino, bending his arms carefully so he wouldn't go back to sleep and possibly slip back into the coma. All four nuns moved him around and tried to get him to sit up. By 8:30 A.M.

he was up, drinking hot broth through a straw and sitting in a chair as he gathered strength for his first warm soaking in a natural hot spring that Santa Anna was renowned for. This was important to coax his body temperature back to normal as soon as possible. Bephino sat, very fragile, and sipped the broth docilely. He stared strangely and spoke softly to Dana in between sips. At 9:00 A.M., Dana heard the sound of Ben's feet dragging down the hall. Bephino's bed was empty and freshly made. The curtains were drawn and the window shade was up, allowing full sunlight into the room. Dana told Bepy, "That's Ben coming." Bephino meekly smiled at her, then asked, "What's he dragging?"

At that moment, the door opened and Ben stumbled in, hobbling and rattling his aluminum canes together, grasping the black rubber handles in one hand and pushing on the door with the other. As he awkwardly entered, his eyes took in the bed, freshly made and very, very empty. Fear flushed his face; then anguish. He quickly sought out Dana, whom he found standing to his left, smiling broadly at him. And then, directly behind her . . . Bephino, sitting in a chair! Then Ben saw his ninety-pound friend actually sitting up, and his eyes flew open in disbelief. He hobbled closer, as the smile on Dana's face widened and deepened. Ben looked at her, astounded, as he moved toward Bephino. Ben couldn't speak; his eyes brimmed over.

Bephino watched Ben's crippled body moving toward him—Ben, who'd always been healthy and perfect! His body had been lean and mean, a perfect woman's size 8, he always used to say. Ben stopped and stared silently. Dana moved quickly to Ben's side, put her arms around him, and kissed his face.

Ben stared down at Bepy with emotion, then asked, "Are you ready to go home?"

"Yeah, she got me out of it," Bephino half grinned.

Ben's eyes shot over to Dana, wondering what she had done to Bepy to bring him back to them. He didn't press the issue. Laying his canes aside, he bent over to embrace Bephino on both cheeks over and over. "It's so good to be with you again, my friend," Ben whispered.

Bephino's eyes focused on Ben's crippled body, his eyes moving up and down. "What happened to you?" he asked softly.

"I was hit with polio. We'll talk about it later, when you're well."

Bephino's weakness kept him from pressing further. At that moment, Dr. Romano, who had been summoned earlier, finally arrived. When he saw Bephino, he half circled the chair in astonishment. "I cannot believe my eyes," he sang out, waving his arms. "I'm so happy for you," he chortled, reaching out and shaking hands with Bephino. "Welcome back, my friend, welcome back. Do you feel all right to sit up?"

"I feel a little dizzy," Bephino replied.

"That's a normal reaction. You're very weak," the doctor said, turning to Dana. "Keep him talking all day," he advised. "Don't let him fall asleep. He's weak and can slip back into the coma very easily."

Raising his eyes to Dana and Ben, Dr. Romano said, "It's vitally important that he doesn't sleep for at least twelve hours. Continue the broth every hour, and he'll be getting a warm bath this morning. But no sleeping, OK?"

"OK," Dana replied, "we'll keep him up, don't worry."

Two weeks later, a 747 brought Bephino, Dana, and Ben back to New York. Ben's wife, Peggy, greeted them at Kennedy. Bephino was wheelchaired off, but Ben insisted on walking. All four soon boarded a connecting flight to Savannah, from where they would repair to the farm at Little Falls for a long, long rest.

"Is he home, Ma?"

"Yes, thank God. I only called you now because we've been so busy making him comfortable."

"Ma, I'm coming home right now."

"Patsy, listen to me; your father's home, but listen to me."

"Maa!" Patsy protested.

"Patsy, listen to what I have to say first, will you?"

"Go ahead, I'm listening."

"Your father's home, he's alive—but not well. He's gonna be OK, but if you see him now, you'll never forget it. And he himself thinks you and Rene should wait a few more weeks to give him a chance to regain his strength and appearance. He's so weak. He only weighs about a hundred pounds."

"Mom!" Patsy screeched. "Mom, I love him. I can't wait to see him. He's my father!"

"I know, darling, I know that, but you know how proud he is. He's a proud person, and he would be so unhappy to see your face change when you saw him. It don't even look like him. He's a skeleton, Patsy. Please give me a chance to build him up. Please stay in L.A. just for a few more weeks. Call him over the phone, talk to him, but respect his wishes; wait until he looks more like his old self again. The only people who are seeing him are Mrs. Roselli, Ben, Peggy, and me. Your sister was told he's still in Europe on business and is coming home next month. She'd die if she saw him in this condition. . . . Patsy? Are you OK?"

"I'm his son, Mom," the young man whimpered. "I'm supposed to be right with him."

"Give us a few weeks, Patsy, just a few weeks. Please, son."

"Mom, tell Daddy I love him and I can't wait to see him. Tell him I'm gonna kiss him on the lips when I see him."

"OK, darling," Dana said, wiping her eyes. "I'll call you every day and let you speak to him. Right now, he's sleeping. He's so weak, it's better we let him rest. I'll call you tomorrow morning when he gets up, and you can tell him you love him yourself, OK?"

"OK," Patsy whispered.

"Don't tell your sister anything that may upset her. And don't tell Alan Stone your father's home, because he'd be over in a minute. Right now, we're in a mess over here, what with Ben being crippled and your father so weak. It's like a nursing home. It's a good thing I got Peggy and Mrs. Roselli to help me."

"OK, Mom, I'll talk to you tomorrow. Thank God he's home. I love you, Mama."

"I love you too, son."

"OK, come and get it," Peggy called out to the men two days later. "We got pasta fagioli for lunch. There's a lot of iron in beans," Peggy reminded Ben and Bephino as she walked toward them.

"Here we go again with them fuckin' beans," Ben scoffed as he hobbled to his feet, trying to position his canes. "We're Italians, not Puerto Ricans! Beans are supposed to be fed once a week, not every day. Forget about what Bepy's doctor said. I'm still gassed up from the lentils we had yesterday for lunch, now she's got beans." Turning to Bephino, Ben groused, "My wife can't make a plain cheeseburger, there's always gotta be *iron* in the food." Bephino grinned as Peggy rolled his wheelchair onto the patio.

Several weeks had passed. It was a beautiful Sunday on the farm. The hot sun, burning off the early-morning dew, gave the meadows a pure, clean smell. Bephino Menesiero sat alone in his wheelchair in the shade of a giant elm tree. His deep, sunken eyes looked as if they had come from the dead. Mrs. Roselli and Dana were busy in the kitchen, cleaning up after a breakfast of pancakes and scrambled eggs. Bephino, on his way to recovery, still looked frail and unbalanced; his thin face, with teeth now too large for his mouth, reflected an uncharacteristic vulnerability. Bephino sat thinking of his children and how terrible it was that he couldn't allow them to see him in this condition. He'd been forcing himself to eat so that recovery in appearance would come as quickly as possible. His hands seemed long, delicate, and weak. He stared around the farm, breathing in the country aroma of clean life, while thinking sorrowfully of how many men he had murdered over the years. A gun for hire, a hit man since his boyhood in Brooklyn. Anything for a buck. Now he had it all: money, wealth, power, and his own private paradise, a world of his own. But deep down inside, he knew it was all a lie. He was facing hell on Earth and probably hell after Earth for his unscrupulous sins. He knew he had to settle up with New York, after which the piper would invariably settle up with him. He knew he would be ready when the piper called for him; he believed that. And there was no peace ahead; he knew that also. New York would never rest until he and Ben were dissolved into ashes. It was the way of the Mafia; no one rests until the ones you once respected are placed under the sod. Bephino's thoughts flashed from his children to the dons of New York. He remembered the words of Emilio Morrano, the old Mob boss from Bay Ridge: "The same dons that are here today respecting you," he had said, "will be the ones someday to destroy you." Bephino bit his lip. Boretti, Gaeta, and Tony Boy—they are the ones who will destroy me, he thought. They are the ones who caused Ben to be a cripple and me to be sent to Europe to become invalid as a man and to nearly see my grave. What I have ahead of me is God's way of reminding me of my past and what's in the future for me, Bephino mused. He thought of Ben struggling to walk. He knew Boretti had to be put to death for that.

"Bephino-o-o," Mrs. Roselli called from the kitchen patio, "do you want something to drink, some juice or milk?"

"No, thanks. Maybe later," he waved back to her.

Mrs. Roselli returned to the kitchen. "He don't want anything now," she told Dana in broken English. "And what time are the other two getting up? My God," she huffed, "they sleep all day. We serve breakfast two times a day over here. Well, I'm gonna start the sauce, I don't care if that Benny don't like the smell of garlic in the morning or not. I gotta mix the chopped meat and soak my hard bread for the meatballs. I'm gonna fry all the meat now for my gravy. Two o'clock, we eat!" Mrs. Roselli declared. "They wanna sleep, let 'em sleep," she said while opening three cans of Italian plum tomatoes. "She's gettin' fat as a horse, that Peggy."

Dana burst out laughing. "Go ahead, Mrs. Roselli, start your sauce. It's Sunday; when they get up, they get up! They're very dear to us, and besides, they're our houseguests. Let them do as they please."

"I always let them do as they please; they do it anyway," the old lady mumbled. "He thinks I put oregano in my sauce, that Benny. I never put oregano in my sauce! He's *pazzo,* that guy."

Two hours later, Ben and Peggy strolled sleepy-eyed into the breakfast room. "Good morning," Peggy sang out.

Mrs. Roselli kept her back turned and attended to her simmering sauce. "Dana went outside to be with Bephino two hours ago!" Mrs. Roselli snapped. "We gonna throw the pasta in the water at two o'clock sharp, ready or not," she mumbled still with her back to them.

"All we want is coffee and a slice of toast," Ben replied. "Don't bother with the eggs today."

Mrs. Roselli silently turned and stared. "The toaster is out of order, have a cookie. It's almost 12:30, it's time to fry the meatballs."

"That's fine," Ben agreed, "a cookie is perfect."

"I'm starting a diet today; all I want is coffee and juice," Peggy said as she poured a glass of juice from a jug. "You want juice, Ben?" she asked her husband.

"Yeah, I'll take some juice if it's OK with Mrs. Roselli," he grinned.

"Me?" Mrs. Roselli grumbled. "It's OK with me, have all the juice you like. You can sleep all day, for all I care," she snorted. "When I gotta cook, I gotta cook. If people don't like to smell garlic in the morning, they should get up earlier, that's all. Me, I'm up at six o'clock," she whined, rotating two soaking spring chickens in a pot of cold salted water.

"Don't worry, Mrs. Roselli; if we sleep late, we can help ourselves," Ben answered. "We won't bother you . . ." At that moment the sound of an aircraft buzzing the house tore through the room.

"What's that?" Peggy asked excitedly.

Ben hobbled with his canes to the sliding patio door, opened it, and looked outside. "It's a helicopter!" he yelled. "The fuckin' guy looks like he's gonna land in the pasture. Look at this shit!" Ben shouted. "I don't believe it; who the hell is this?" Ben began to walk toward the pool, with Peggy and Mrs. Roselli following. Dana, leaving Bephino in the shade, also walked toward the hovering aircraft.

"Who could it be?" Dana called out to Ben.

"I don't know," Ben replied. Then the realization set in.

Ben yelled, "Go get the shotgun quick, Dana, and get a few shells; *quick*, I wanna get the jump on them just in case!"

Dana and Peggy ran to the house and returned in a few moments with a five-round automatic Browning shotgun and a box of shells. Ben stood waiting for them. Bephino, still sitting in his chair away from the center of excitement, was not entirely aware of the concern. Ben grabbed at the weapon quickly, opened its chamber, and began loading the shells. The helicopter, a large one, finally settled on the grass. The blades and engine continued to cause high winds for some time before the engines came to a halt. The side door slid open and a loading ladder was lowered. Ben took aim. A young woman dressed in slacks began to disembark. She smiled and waved at the small crowd.

Dana screeched out, "It's Rene, it's my daughter!" Dana quickly turned to wave to Bephino, left sitting alone under the elm tree about three hundred and fifty feet away. Dana waved, "It's OK" to him, her face bright with smiles. Then Dana looked back at the helicopter to see her son, Patsy, also coming down the stairwell greeting his mother and the others. Ben lowered the shotgun, his face also wreathed in smiles as the kids helped a third person come down the ladder. It was Alan Stone, a nervous smile pasted on his tanned face. His gray hair sparkled in the bright sunlight along with his diamond rings and gold chains with their luck charms. Alan, unsure and worried, now seventy-two years old, was definitely not the same smooth Las Vegas tycoon of the old days. The children walked slowly alongside Alan toward the shotgun-bearing residents. Dana's emotional radar antenna spun back and forth from the kids to her husband, her face a mass of emotion at having her loved ones together at last. Patsy, who had promised to stay away for several weeks, simply hadn't been able to. Bephino, sitting alone in the wheelchair, sensed something joyous. Everyone began laughing, hugging, and kissing; the kids were screaming as they hugged and kissed their mother and Mrs. Roselli and then Ben and Peggy. Alan Stone, caught up in the wave, was also like a child, hugging everyone in sight, laughing and saying, "How you gonna keep us away?

How you gonna keep us away?" Alan's eyes then settled on Ben, who was smiling with lowered shotgun in one hand and his two metal canes in the other. Alan rushed to Ben, grabbed him warmly, hugged him tightly—very tightly—and kissed him on both cheeks with the utmost respect. And he whispered in Ben's ear, "I'm sorry, I'm so sorry, please forgive me. If I only knew they would do this to you . . ."

Ben hissed, "Don't be sorry for me, it's OK; everything's OK. Be sorry for them. They're the ones you gotta be sorry for, because we're gonna do the worst things you could imagine to them. Believe me, Alan, they're gonna pay dearly for this! You better start selling wheelchairs in Brooklyn; there's gonna be a hell of a market there."

"Where's Daddy?" Rene called out. "Where's my father? I wanna see him!"

Dana was at Rene's side, grabbing firmly on her daughter. "OK, honey, he's right over there, but let's do it easy, sweetheart, and don't get upset when you see him. It'll only make him feel worse." The children approached their father slowly, holding their mother tightly. Alan Stone, also walking along with the kids, was wrought with emotions. It had been one and a half years since he'd seen his friend. Ben, Peggy, and Mrs. Roselli quietly returned to the kitchen.

Bephino's weary eyes set upon his approaching loved ones. The tears of love were impossible for him to hold back. Even for a man so accustomed to presenting a strong face to the world, there was no way. . . .

SEPTEMBER 18, 1978, 3:00 P.M.

BENSONHURST, BROOKLYN

"What's that noise?"

"What noise? I didn't hear anything."

"Downstairs, Pauli, I heard a noise!" Marie insisted. "Be quiet for a second, let's listen," she said, waving her hand for him to be silent.

"There's nobody downstairs," Lil Pauli whispered back. "You must be hearin' things." Pinching her cheek, he said softly, "Put your clothes back down. Come on, baby doll, get your panties off. I got somethin' nice and big for you," Pauli grinned.

"I thought I heard a noise downstairs," she repeated, her eyes darting to the mirrored door leading to the first floor below. "I'm scared, Pauli!" the tiny, dark-haired, fifty-year-old wife of Jimmy ("the Geap") Dondaro, a local Brooklyn mason, said in a choked voice.

"Your husband's at the track, right?" Pauli asked.

"Yeah, but I get nervous, Pauli. I never let anyone come to my home. The neighbors on this block are all nosy. They watch everything I do," Marie worried, her eyes moving from Pauli to the mirrored door. Marie stood uncertainly, scantily dressed in her undies, while still holding her neatly folded dress before her. "I gotta be careful what I do; Jimmy's nuts when it comes to me."

Pauli smiled. "He's nuts all right, for leaving you home alone when you're so horny. Come on, take ya panties off and get on the bed."

"Is that why you came here?" she asked in a low voice. "Because you know I feel horny today?"

"Whata ya think I'm here for? Don't play games, get those bloomers off," Pauli answered briskly.

"You know, Pauli, you're here twenty minutes already and you haven't even kissed me once, you know that? Whata I got, the plague or what?" Marie asked, looking herself over in the mirror.

"I'm gonna kiss you, don't worry, baby. You watch how I'm gonna kiss you." Pauli leaned closer, touching her at the small of her back. But he did not kiss her.

Marie placed her dress neatly across a velvet lounge chair. "I must be nuts, doing this right in my own house," she groaned. "If my husband loses on the daily double, he's gonna come home early, and if he finds you here, we're both dead. Jimmy's like a beast when he gets nervous."

Pauli smiled and narrowed his eyes. "What, ya wanna talk about your husband losin' at the track and comin' home early, or you want me to make you cream—which is it?"

Marie quietly removed her panties and spread herself on the bed. Her hawk-nosed face watched Pauli as he stripped naked.

"This is the second time I'm gettin' fucked without a kiss; I don't believe this," she complained. "Not even a smile," she continued. "Baby doll, yeah, some baby doll; the guy's at the foot of the bed, staring at my feet. I don't believe this," she mumbled, shaking her head.

"Hey-y-y, *zitto*!" Pauli hissed in Italian. "Why don't you keep quiet; you'll get all the kissin' you want when your husband comes home. Let the Geap kiss ya!" Pauli said.

"My husband loves to kiss me," she snapped.

"Yeah, but he's got that expression on his face like he's gotta take a shit, right? So what good is it?" Pauli snapped back.

"Don't be funny, Pauli, you ain't any better looking. Look at that expression on your own face, *morto di fame*," she mimicked an Italian expression at him. "Look in the mirror; you're so hungry you look *morto di fame* today," she laughed. "All you kiss is pussy. Am I right, Pauli? You wanna eat and no kiss." She smiled tolerantly at him as she spread her thighs wide, exposing herself to him. "I think all you want is my body," Marie sneered. "If I recall, Pauli, you did this the last time too, the night I was coming home from bingo—remember, in your car? You were on your knees all night," she laughed.

Pauli stood at the foot of the bed, his large penis thickly hanging down. Then he moved to her, starting downward, kissing her feet and legs slowly, then licking up her thighs. "Gee, you have a beautiful body," he whispered huskily. "No stretch marks or nothin', you're unbelievable, the way you're built," he murmured, his tongue probing softly at the Y of her body. "You smell so clean, baby," Pauli whispered. "I'm gonna lick you silly; I'm gonna make you climb the headboard, before I give you what you want. You're gonna come right in midair," Pauli urged. Marie smiled and raised her body to his mouth in an inviting fashion.

"Make me climb the headboard, Pauli, I'm in a delicious mood today, very delicious, and I love to be licked before being screwed," she whispered, reaching forward and touching his head with her right hand, rubbing his neck affectionately. "You got some big prick, Pauli," she moaned. "I can't wait to get it." Suddenly, Marie's eyes flew open as she heard something again. "Did you hear that noise?" she asked, raising her head up from the pillow. "Now I'm sure, Pauli, I just heard it again," she gasped. "It sounds like someone downstairs. I'm scared. Pauli, maybe it's my husband," she whispered fiercely. Sitting up, she listened tensely and stared at the mirrored bedroom door. In it was reflected Pauli's exposed body, still pursuing its quest enthusiastically. The mirror displayed his large organ hanging down between his thighs like a big tail set beyond the cheeks of his heavy buttocks, as Pauli continued thrusting his large tongue directly into her black, hairy womb. Marie stared at the door mutely, listening for sounds, but as Paul's licking became more insistent she gradually began to succumb. Spreading wider despite her uncertainty, she lay back down and settled in. Placing her hands on Pauli's head, she began allowing Pauli's tongue to enter more deeply. Marie rolled her head from side to side and began to whimper. "Oh, that's so good . . . Pauli, what are you doing to me?" Pauli's moist tongue began to flicker wildly over her clit. "Oh, Pauli, it feels so good. Do it to me, Pauli . . . do it, do it," she called out passionately, as Pauli's flicks persisted.

"I'm gonna make you climb, bitch. I know what you like," he breathed, as his long, lusty licks became more and more rapid.

"Oh yes, oh yes," she screamed. "Oh yes-s-s," she shuddered, as she pressed her thighs tightly around Paul's head. "Oh . . . Pauli," Marie gasped, closing her eyes and grabbing and tearing at the pillow. "Oh, Pauli, I'm coming . . . I'm coming. Oh, Pauli, I'm coming. Oh, my God, it feels so good."

Suddenly the bedroom door swung open and two men entered abruptly, waving snub-nosed pistols.

"Get up, Pauli!" the heavyset one shouted. "We wanna talk to you. Get the fuck up, now!" the man shouted louder, leaning over Pauli's trembling body. Pauli staggered up, in shock, his moist face soggy and exhausted. The man then roughly shoved Pauli to a corner of the small bedroom while the other put a gun to Marie's head. Both men glared at Pauli's nakedness. "If you move, lapper, you're a corpse," the big man warned. "We followed you here, right to Jimmy the Geap's bedroom. Still up to your old tricks, humping everybody's wife, hah, Pauli," the man grinned. The other man slowly pulled a sheet up over the still orgasmic woman. "And in bed with Jimmy the Geap's wife," he chuckled.

At that, Marie was up with a start. In a trembling voice she pleaded, "Don't tell Jimmy!"

"Shut up," the big man shouted. "Get back down or I'll whack ya fuckin' nose for ya. We only wanna talk to your boyfriend, so keep ya funny face under the sheet. If you make a sound we'll kill both of you. Come on, Pauli, get your pants on, let's go downstairs," the big man said sternly. Marie stayed under the sheet, peeking out quietly.

"I'll stay with her," the smaller, younger man said. "Give me a yell when you're ready," he sneered to his partner.

At gunpoint, still barefoot, Pauli, wearing only his pants and holding the balance of his clothes under his arm, moved through the doorway and headed downstairs.

"Whata you guys want with me?" Pauli asked nervously as he lurched down the steps.

"Pauli, the old man wants you to give your friend Bephino up to us. We know he's back from Europe and probably living on his farm. We heard it from the street. He's avoiding us. Rocco wants to talk to him. If you're smart, Pauli, you'll do what the man wants, *a capisce*? If you say no, you go down in history as a bare-assed lover, *a capisce*? If you do the right thing, Pauli, you join our family and live happily ever after with everybody's wives," the man said with a sly wink.

"You're Porky Capeto, right?" Pauli asked.

"Right," the fat man replied. "And that's Nello Longello upstairs."

"That's not the right thing you're asking me to do, Porky," Pauli said. "Bephino's a sick man, he's ill. He don't want no trouble with the old man." Pauli lowered his head. "I've been with Bephino since we were kids. Don't ask me this . . ."

"You got no choice, Pauli. Either give him up or get your business in order."

* * *

"Hello?"

"Marie, this is Pauli. Can we talk?"

"Why are you calling me at home?" Marie hissed, covering the phone with her right hand. "My husband's home," she whispered. "It's raining today. Brick masons don't work when it rains," she said as she cupped her hand tighter over the phone, her eyes nervously darting toward the basement door.

"I only wanna talk for a few seconds, Marie. Where's your husband now?"

"Down in the basement; he's working on his fishing reel. I can't *talk,* Pauli. I gotta hang up; he may come upstairs any minute," she whined.

"How'd that guy Nello treat you yesterday, the kid that stayed upstairs with you? Did he act respectful?"

"Pauli-i-i," she murmured low, trying her best to cup both hands over the phone. "Why do you care?" she whispered harshly into the receiver. "What's the difference? It's over now!"

"What did he do? Did he act right or not? Did he show respect?" Pauli insisted.

Marie shook her head, looked at the basement door, and exhaled impatiently. "I don't believe this, Pauli. Sure, he acted right," she growled. "The kid was a hellava kisser! I gotta go, I can't talk! Good-bye . . ."

Pauli started at the sound of the click. He stood staring at the phone, his mouth agape.

ONE WEEK LATER

LITTLE FALLS, SOUTH CAROLINA

"Boy, it's a beautiful day today. Would you believe it's almost October and it's still warm down here?" Bephino said to Ben while basking in the South Carolina sunshine. "The heat really feels good to me."

"We still look like shit," Ben replied to Bephino. "Look at us. We're home eight weeks already and all we got is a good tan." Both men were sitting poolside, wearing bermuda shorts. "We look all broken up," Ben said, shaking his head. "We look like two fuckin' zombies and Boretti did this to us, Bep. Boretti laughed when they dragged me up to the roof. They flicked me off like a piece of shit. I came flying down grabbing at the air. I'm lucky I'm alive, Bep."

"We're both lucky to be alive—both of us," Bephino repeated. "We're coming along fine day by day," Bephino said, spreading suntan oil on his face. "Every day we're improving. I feel much better now that I'm out of that wheelchair. I gained forty-seven pounds since I'm home. I'm feeling stronger and I'm getting my head back too, and Rocco Boretti's life is coming closer and closer to an end—not because of me so much as for what he did to you." Bephino sat up in his lounge chair and adjusted his sunglasses. "That," he said, pointing at Ben's crippled body, "that he dies for." Bephino frowned. "Today we talk some business," he said to Ben.

"Good," Ben said. "I been waiting. How did the hit go?"

"It went OK, up until I got hit with a slug in my neck, and passed out in the snow, and then the coma—the rest is history. That poor man is dead for no reason. The guy was a real count, a distinguished man. I killed him. I cut his throat."

Ben changed the subject quick. "Boy, did you look *morte* when I saw you in Santa Anna," he grinned. "You were laying there like a dead body. Could you really hear everything that was going on?"

"Yeah," Bephino nodded. "It was unbelievable; I heard them nuns talking and praying every day. I even felt their touch but couldn't respond. What a locked-in feeling! I was so cold, but my body couldn't shiver. I was freezing. They prayed every day over me. Listen to this," Bep grinned. "The young girl that used to wash me up began fondling me, and they caught her . . ."

"Whata ya mean, fondling you? You were almost dead, what was to fondle?"

"The cleaning kid," Bephino laughed, "would you believe, she played with my dick and the boss nun caught her."

"Hey, Bep, this is me, Ben—not Mikey or Pauli or Monkey.

Don't expect me to sit here and believe that bullshit," Ben laughed. "I saw you; you were practically dead."

Bephino's face flushed with embarrassment, then he grinned sheepishly. "I'm not kidding. The kid got caught by big sister, the head nun. They chased her out of the hospital after that."

Ben's eyes were almost popping out. "You mean a cleaning girl played with your prick in the condition you were in?"

"Yeah, I think she even sucked it a little, and the boss nun walked in on her," Bephino marveled. "I heard the whole fuckin' thing like an amplifier in my ears. I felt sorry for the kid. I'm telling you the truth, Ben, the kid musta been horny or curious or somethin'. I couldn't believe it myself, but what could I do? I was at her mercy. She sounded so cute every day, talking to me like a child."

Ben's eyes rolled. "I don't believe this. If it wasn't you telling me this story, I'd laugh forever."

"That's nothing. Then the boss nun went *pazza,* she blamed the devil for it, kept yelling all around the room at the devil. Every day she came in and called out to the devil. And I had to listen to that shit day and night. Then who shows up a few weeks later with a coupla greaseballs—Red, from Brooklyn! Red was probably hiding in Milano from us, and I'm hearing his voice talking over my body one day calling me Bephino and saying what are you doing here. I thought I was hearing things, I thought for sure he would stick a knife in my heart and finish me off. There was a few times I heard his blade click open, then later I heard it click shut."

"It was Red who saved you, Bep," Ben said. "He called downtown to the Hero shop and spoke with Blubberhead. Blubber called Monkey and Monkey called me. Monkey wanted to come to Italy with me, but I said no. I figured it was best to come with Dana just in case you were *morte* when we got there. Dana could have seen you for the last time. Red told Blubber over the phone that you were half dead."

"I know. Red really had a lot of heart to help me. I owe him for that," Bephino smiled, "and you wanted me to kill him, remember, in that fuckin' *acid* in Mr. Fat's laundry down in

Chinatown. Hah—remember, Benny?" Bephino joked. "It's a good thing I make my own decisions." Ben rolled his eyes and smiled a cobra smile.

"Speaking of Red," Bephino said, "I want you to send him fifty grand. Send it via the Swiss accounts directly to his house, with a note that if he ever needs any more just call us. Red didn't look too good, he was getting bald and fat. I think he lost his spirit. Oh, and I also want you to send twenty-five grand to Tattania Greco. She's the kid that got fired from the hospital. Send it to her along with Red's check. She lives in Santa Anna also. Send her a note that says, 'Thank you for the blankets,' and sign it 'Puco.' She'll know who it's from," Bephino said seriously.

"Puco?" Ben asked, "Who the hell is Puco?"

"Just send it as I say. She'll understand who it's from."

"Yeah, I know, you just said that, but I wanna know who the hell is Puco," Ben chuckled. "Sounds like a fuckin' pet chicken or monkey or something."

"The kid was innocent—and naive," Bephino explained. "She began calling me Puco, she . . ."

"So, *you're* Puco?" Ben asked with a broad grin.

Bephino smiled, shook his head at Ben's ribbing, and said, "I'm Puco, yeah, and if you ever call me Puco I'll break your legs, *a capisce*?"

"How ya gonna break my legs? They're broke already—see, look at them, they wobble. My legs wobble, thanks to Mr. Boretti," Ben sneered, and then he changed the subject. "Go look in a mirror," he smiled. "You look half dead yourself, you look *mezzo morto,*" Ben chuckled. "Whata ya think, that suntan makes you look good? It makes you look Jewish," Ben grinned. "You're a real sport—was I hearing correct? You're gonna pay this kid twenty-five grand for a blow job?" Ben asked.

"The kid gave me a coupla blankets when I was freezing to death. She also played a big role in my life at the time. *Just send it!*"

"Consider it sent," Ben replied. "Twenty-five grand is in the wind—I mean, the mail."

"Now, tell me about Alley Oop's son," Bephino said. "I heard you took him to Bay Ridge to see his grandmother and aunts."

"Who told you?" Ben asked.

"Monkey told me, when he called last week. He said he went with you to Brooklyn to the old neighborhood a few weeks before you got dropped from the roof. Monkey and I didn't talk too much about it because I wasn't feeling too good at the time. So tell me about it. I understand it was a riot."

"A riot? It was unbelievable, you shoulda seen Alley Oop's old mother and his two fat spinster sisters screaming like nuts. It was unbelievable. The kid actually got scared at first, the way they were screaming. They thought it was Alley Oop as a kid coming back from the dead. It took me twenty minutes to convince them it was Alley's son and not Alley himself. Then when they were convinced, they began hollering again and hugging him, touching him, squeezing him. Then, of course, like true Italians, they began feeding him. You never saw three women so happy," Ben grinned. "The old lady with her wooden cane and her high boot-shoes almost fell out of the fuckin' window. She began screaming to the neighbors. *'Figlio mio,'* she screamed, *'figlio mio e figliooo,'* she called out to the people in the alleyways. Even the police showed up. Somebody thought there was a murder taking place with all that yelling going on." Ben rolled his eyes and smiled. "They love that kid. They kiss, they touch, they love him to death. They have gifts waiting whenever he goes to see them. He goes there every Sunday to eat pasta." Bephino curled his satisfied lips, wiped his eyes quickly, then smiled at Ben.

"The kid forgot he used to be a Murphy, hah?" Bephino said, beaming at Ben.

"Yeah, and you should of heard the two fat spinsters, the mouths on them," Ben said briskly, trying to hold back a laugh. " 'Where's Bephino? How come he hasn't come to see us?' they kept asking and asking, taking turns back and forth like two nuts, and the old lady chimes right in, '*Esta* Bephino? *Esta?* Why he no come-a?' I told them you went to Sicily to visit your people in Sciacca. That finally quieted them down."

"I'm glad they're reunited," Bephino nodded, "it was important to me for Alley Oop's sake. Now he can rest in peace. OK," Bephino said, lying back in his chaise lounge, "let's talk about Alley Oop's money. We got a lotta interest piled up from deals he would have been in on if he lived," Bephino said. "And we don't need it, so the kid gets it all. It belonged to his father, so it's his. We gotta transfer it to a trust fund for the kid, to protect him from his mother. *A capisce?*"

"*Io capisce,* the money is just like you set it up," Ben answered. "Fat Arty got it nice. He always kept Alley Oop's account intact; remember, we gave his mother and sisters a quarter million draw from the stock deal on our Mexican company, International Amex, when Alley passed away, and you were gonna give them the balance if they got married or if they ever needed it. Right?"

"Yeah, that's right, but they never got married, they got no kids, and they don't need it. They're old. I want the kid to get it all," Bephino insisted. "The kid should have it; he's the only one in the world who should get it."

"I agree with you," Ben said, looking at Bephino. "When you're ready, we'll sit down with the kid and Fat Arty and make the account transfer and set up a trust fund for him. Right now, we better not scare him with all that cash. He's gotten hit with a lot already all at once. The kid will go nuts with all that dough and forget about his training." Ben shrugged. "He's got a few more tough fights comin' up in Atlantic City. I want him to fill a goal in life for his father's sake. If we see he's gettin' hurt, we make him quit the fight game. Right now, he's 12 and 0, all by knockouts."

"You're right." Bephino nodded. "OK, we'll wait a few months, then talk again about it. Now let's talk about Joey D. Let's discuss him," Bephino said. "What happened with him? Why did he leave the farm?"

"Dana called me and said when Joey D heard you were missing in action, he packed his bags, called a cab, and left the farm without saying a word to anyone. Nobody saw him or heard from him since. I got an open contract on him: twenty-five grand, dead or alive."

"Whata ya, nuts? Open contract! Why you wanna kill him?" Bephino asked his friend, nervously passing his hand over his chin.

"Because he left your wife and Mrs. Roselli cold turkey; he turned belly-up on us and ran."

Bephino frowned. "Joey D was never a stable guy," he whispered, opening his eyes wide at Ben. "I always knew that! Call New York, tell our people to cancel the hit now, today. I don't want Joey D killed. A guy like that we have to pity. He's a mutt, he's probably hanging around Yankee Stadium with the scalpers. Leave him be, let Joey D live his life out in peace. Call it off," Bephino repeated. "He served us well, I don't wanna hit him." Bephino nodded as if to himself. "I can't kill a guy like Joey D, he's been with us too long."

"OK, it's cancelled out. Now, let's talk about Bubba Reed from Savannah, Georgia," Ben said grimly.

Bephino's eyes raised up and stared at Ben. "What about Bubba Reed? How do you know about him? You never met Reed."

"Dana called me in New York. This guy Bubba came on the farm one night and . . . annoyed her."

"Whata ya mean, annoyed her; what did he do, try and bang her?" Bephino asked, staring hard at Ben.

"Yeah, he was drunk and he came over the horse fence and all the way up the hill to the house. He heard you were gone so he tried . . ."

"What happened?" Bephino quickly interrupted.

"The girls ran his ass off with a shotgun. Whata ya think happened? Mrs. Roselli was with Dana when he came up to the house."

"Did he hurt them?"

"No, they were OK. Although I don't think you should mention it to the women again. Let them forget it. Soon as Dana called me, I sent two of our people to live at the gate house."

"I was wondering why them guys were living there when I first got back. I thought it was just because of Joey D leaving. I never dreamed that fuckin' wacko Bubba Reed was the main reason, that he would have the balls to come to my farm and go for my wife. This is the first I'm hearing of this," Bephino said, nodding slowly.

"He did," Ben nodded back, lowering his eyes, "he went for Dana. I waited for you to get well, Bep. I know you wanna be with us when we put him to sleep. Just say the word when you're ready and we'll leave for Savannah," Ben said coolly, looking up at the sky.

Bephino exhaled deeply, then sat back, lost in thought.

Two weeks later, several men sat relaxing on Bephino's ranch. "Boy, it feels good to be back together again," Monkey said.

"Are you comin' to New York?" Pauli asked, smiling at Bephino.

"No, I'm not, Pauli; nobody's going into their domain yet, and neither are you. So don't be sneakin' around, *a capisce?*" Bephino said, looking to Pauli for confirmation. "That means forget about the broads for a while, OK, Pauli?" Bephino teased.

"None of our Old Blood is allowed to go into Brooklyn!" Monkey said, reaching for a cigarette and looking directly at Pauli. Monkey turned to Bephino. "I gave specific instructions to Pauli and Mikey both to stay out of the city."

Pauli looked sheepishly at Bephino. "They're asking all over town for you, Bep. They know you're back. They really seem concerned," he lamented. "I was back in Brooklyn a few weeks ago, visiting my aunt. I heard from the street they wanna sit down with you."

"They seem concerned? They're not concerned, Pauli, they're worried," Bephino answered sharply. "And Pauli, for your own good, stay out of the city until we make our move. Let your aunt use a vibrator, OK, Pauli?" he winked.

Pauli, sipping a piña colada and chewing nervously on a piece of coconut, mumbled after a moment, "I think they wanna have a sit-down to clear the air."

"Too bad!" Monkey interjected sharply, surveying all the men sitting under a gazebo. "You were told to stay out of the city, so tell all your aunts you're outta action for a while. Understand, Paul?"

"Tell these schmucks about your son," Alan Stone said,

nodding to Bephino while flicking the ashes from his cigar over the railing and into the shrubbery.

"Who's the schmucks?" Ben asked, leaning forward. "Who are you referring to?"

"Yeah, Alan?" Mikey chimed in. "Who's the schmucks? I don't see any schmucks over here. It's only us. Are you referring to us?" Mikey asked.

"Come on, stop bustin' balls," Monkey yelled. "You know Alan uses schmucks as a joke. Whata ya pickin' on him for? You are schmucks, so shut up and keep quiet." Monkey smiled.

Alan nodded, "Thank you, Monkey, that was very commendable of you, coming to my aid."

"No problem," Monkey said.

Bephino pulled back his lips and dragged on his cigar. "My son called me from L.A. and said two men came over to him last week in a West Hollywood restaurant near Beverly Hills. The kid was dining with his girlfriend. They asked him, 'How's your father doing?' The kid was surprised when they came up to his table like that, because he never saw these guys before. He didn't know them from beans, and they shouldn't have known him. They had a shitty grin on their faces, he said. So it's gotta be a message from Boretti, and he's fuckin' with my kid's mind, so we gotta prepare to take him out."

"Bephino," Pauli offered again awkwardly, "I think they want you in Brooklyn. They even stopped at Mikey's sister's house and told her to get the word to Mikey all they wanna do is talk. No hard feelings, they said. Why don't we see what they have to say?" Pauli asked, looking to the men for support.

Bephino raised his brows at Pauli's persistence, then shifted his eyes to Mikey. "Mikey already told me that story last week about his sister. It's old news, Pauli. That's just the way they would do it," he explained softly to Mikey while still keeping an eye on Pauli. "They'll go all around us—first to Mikey's sister, then to my son." He turned to stare at Pauli. "Then to whoever is the weakest. That's the way they do things, Pauli. They sneak from person to person dropping messages all around, and then they move in for the kill."

"I heard from the street they say they only want to break bread with you," Pauli insisted.

Bephino's eyes focused hard on Pauli. Slowly dragging on his cigar, he puffed thoughtfully. Then turning to Monkey, he asked in a naive-sounding voice, "Do you believe that, Monkey, they only wanna break bread with me?"

"You gotta be kidding," Monkey replied. "No question about it, they're trying to bring you and Ben out in the open. They wanna make contact with your hearts. They got that fat bastard Porky Capeto on the street," Monkey said.

"It's a fuckin' shame," Bephino said, shaking his head, to Ben and Alan Stone. "Boretti couldn't leave well enough alone. He's always gotta stir up still waters. Everything was so quiet for once in our lives. We beat the feds in court so beautiful, and now we got a total, all-out war in front of us."

"You can't blame them, Bep," Pauli said. "They know you still got bad blood over your European vacation and because of what they did to Ben. Now they wanna talk about it. It makes sense."

Mikey turned to Pauli. "Yeah, and they wanna have a table and kill us all, right at the fuckin' table, right? You don't make sense, Pauli! They wanna do a Valentine Massacre on us, like Al Capone did. Whata ya, nuts or what, talkin' like that?" Mikey exclaimed while staring at Pauli, "and don't go near my sister's house anymore, *a capisce*?" Mikey stated. "She's got three kids, she don't need no more problems."

Bephino heard Mikey's complaint and tried to calm things down. "The only problem I could see is they may get to us before we get to them. That's the problem," Bephino said, looking at Ben and Alan Stone. "That's the problem," he repeated. "First they visit my son to let me know their capabilities, and then they even go bother a civilian, Mikey's kid sister." Bephino shrugged while shaking his head and eyeing up Pauli. The remark about Pauli getting near Mikey's sister bothered him. "I need a little more time before I do what I gotta do," Bephino said. "So just stay out of New York City for a while."

Pauli looked at Bephino. He knew Bephino was bothered.

Pauli smiled meekly and said, "I think they realize you're gonna go after them, and they wanna bring you out in the open somehow, maybe to make peace before a war starts."

Bephino stared back at Pauli, momentarily confused. "I thought you already understood that, Pauli. Whata we been, talkin' in fuckin' circles here or what?" Pauli became quiet and instinctively ducked his head. Bephino watched him for a long moment, then he said, "Come, let's eat. The girls are starting up the barbecue. Enough of these piña coladas. They're making us talk stupid. Let's have some cold beer and steak." Bephino's eyes darted around at each of his friends' faces while directing the group of men toward the pool bar.

About an hour later, after Bephino had finished eating, he caught Ben's eye. Both men walked slowly from the crowd across the lawn to a large water fountain exhibiting a giant nude statue of David. As they sat on a stone bench, Ben focused on Bephino. "What's the matter?"

Bephino hesitated, then the words came out unevenly, softly. "It's Pauli. The guy's . . . he's not the same. For some reason he looks *sciupato,* he's strange. Something's wrong with him."

Ben turned and looked back toward the swimming pool and barbecue area where all the guests were still eating and drinking. "Now that you mention it, he does look kinda funny. I thought maybe he was all fucked out from his orgies," Ben said.

Bephino frowned, then looked up at the large statue of David's massive form. "Pauli's usually like that statue, strong and handsome, but now Pauli's *a bianco,* he's pale. He has dark rings under his eyes and he don't make good conversation anymore. He comes out with things that are old news or don't make sense. He repeats himself and joins in the conversation late or too soon, like a man that's been touched by someone. I want Pauli under surveillance. As a matter of fact, I'll make it easy for you, Ben. Tell Monkey that Pauli will work the numbers again. Let him work out in the open. Give him the betting and numbers out of the Hero shop on the Lower East Side. If he's been touched by them, they'll call on him or perhaps someone will even visit him right there at our restaurant. Tell him he's gotta hit the mattress for a while. Let him live in the little apartment we got over the store until further notice. If and when they make contact we'll know for sure. Tap all the phones, upstairs and down, in the restaurant. We gotta know. Pauli's Old Blood. We gotta be sure before we come to any conclusions on his behalf. We owe him that much respect."

"How long you want this bug to stay in force?"

"A few weeks at least. Tell Monkey if they got to him already, they'll be back at him—you know how they operate. If they know he got scared and he's weak, they'll stay close to him to keep the fear of God in him. I noticed he's been looking around this farm very carefully. Maybe he's making a map for them."

"You think Pauli would do that to you, Bephino? He's Old Blood. He knows you got women here and your kids sometimes come on this farm."

Bephino smiled at Ben and then said, "I'm surprised at you, my friend."

"Whata ya mean? Surprised at what?"

"They could never get that kinda info from the others. They have to make direct contact with Old Blood. New Blood has never met with me since I'm home, and they'll never be allowed on this farm." Ben slowly puckered his lips and moved his head in agreement. "So keep Pauli well covered. I haven't dreamed of him yet. I hope I'm wrong because I always liked Pauli, he's been my friend for thirty-three years." Bephino looked away with emotion. "How's Alley Oop's kid doing?" he asked, changing the subject with some effort. "How's his training coming along?"

"The kid's doing good. Of course I haven't been around the gym myself, but I hear he's in top shape. He crippled a top contender, Tiger Cruise, in a sparring match a few months ago. The kid punches hard. I told you he's 12 and 0, all by knockouts and TKOs. We got him fighting every two or three weeks; we took all the baby fat off of him. We're keeping the pressure on him. I wanna make sure he'll be ready for the tough guys when he meets up with them."

"Good, get the kid ready in six months for a contender

fight. I want him to fight the champ in the next year or two, while he's young and cocky. After he's champ he's gonna retire young and cocky, with dignity. I don't want him to get punchy. Alley Oop is counting on us to look out for his kid, *a capisce*?"

Ben's face expressed surprise at Bephino's thoughtfulness. "Yeah, you're right, Bep, absolutely right. I never gave it much thought, but you are absolutely right. We gotta look out for Alley Oop's boy. I been so busy with you, I haven't had a chance to go see him."

"Here comes Alan," Bephino said, "let's go back to the others now; Alan's gettin' a little restless. He'll be over here in a minute, wantin' to know what's up." The men started walking toward their friend.

"What about them guys visitin' your son on the West Coast?" Ben asked.

"I'm glad you mentioned that, Ben, because I got them on my mind right now. I want two of our funny-faced people to visit Boretti's daughters, just to say hello. I understand they're both in college on Staten Island. Make sure they look hard at them, and ask how their father is. Give it to Monkey to handle. I wanna show Rocco our capabilities."

OCTOBER 21, 1978, 12:03 A.M.

LOWER EAST SIDE, MANHATTAN

Pauli sat alone in a very dim room in downtown Manhattan. A small TV screen flickered in the corner. He now lived in the one-room apartment over Nero's Hero shop. Wiping the sweat from his forehead, Pauli got up from his chair. Despite the late October night, it was hot in Pauli's room, and the steam from the downstairs boiler wouldn't shut off. Pauli, disturbed and restless, walked from the bed to a small sink in the corner of the room and back again. After a few turns about the room, he began to wash his unshaven face with cold water. He looked himself over in the mirror, then carelessly threw a towel down to the floor. He walked past the TV, slamming his hand over the top of it to stop its flickering. Pauli couldn't stop perspiring. Finally, he settled back down at a small table and began reading a newspaper. The whistling sound of the rising steam from the boiler below echoed through the small room. Pauli's feverish eyes were shifting back and forth from the newspaper to the TV when suddenly the phone rang. Pauli stared, afraid to answer, and allowed it to ring at least five times. He finally reached over to the wall and picked up the receiver.

"Hello."

"Hello, Pauli, this is Guido De Luca. How are you?"

"I could be better, Guido, thanks to you and Porky."

"Pauli, what time can we see you?"

"See me for what?"

"About the layout of your friend's farm. The old man told me that Porky said you got the specs ready for us."

Pauli began breathing heavily, took a long pause, and then, looking up at the ceiling, breathed out, "Yeah, I got it. I thought Porky was comin' himself to get it . . ."

"He is," Guido assured him. "We come together."

"OK, park outside my apartment building at 1:00 A.M.; park across the street, Guido, and when nobody's around just flash ya headlights once. I'll open the window and wave a white towel. Then send Porky upstairs. I'll give him the drawing I made for Mr. Boretti."

"Pauli, why we gotta do all that shit, waving towels like in the movies, hah? All we wanna know is exactly what the layout is and how many guys he's got guarding the place."

"Just do it my way and send the Pork Chop up alone, one guy, OK?" Pauli said, his voice rising. "I wanna make sure none of my friends stop over. If I don't wave the towel, that means I got company, don't come up. I'm sticking my neck out!"

"Hey, Pauli," Guido whispered, "we hear he's got people living all around him. Make sure you give us all the details, *a capisce,* Pauli?"

"Yeah, I *capisce.* Just don't be seen coming up here."

"OK, we'll be over at your place 1:00 A.M. Don't fuck up."

"Flash your lights, I'll be waiting," Pauli said coldly.

"OK, Pauli, we'll do that," Guido said after a moment's pause.

* * *

1:00 A.M.: Headlights blinked on and off on Water Street; Pauli waved his white towel. Porky climbed out of a new four-door black Lincoln. His huge body lumbered across the street and up the dark stairs to Pauli's room over the Hero store. Porky climbed the long flight of stairs to the first and last landing, breathing heavily all the way. Pauli opened his door to him. "Is that you, Porky?"

"Yeah, you got the blueprints?" he asked, huffing past Pauli the way he would the least significant doorman in the world. Pauli closed the door. At six-foot-two, Pauli looked small next to Porky, whose attitude was as overblown as his girth.

"Let me take your jacket, Porky," Pauli said politely. "Have a cold beer. It's hot as hell in here. The fuckin' downstairs boiler won't quit tonight. After a beer we'll go over the plans together carefully so you'll know exactly where each road on the farm is and where it leads."

Porky was packing steel and reluctant to remove his jacket. "I'll take the beer, Pauli, but let's make it quick; Guido is waiting down in the car. We gotta go downtown to the club; Rocco's waiting for us."

"Yeah, I know, but sit down over here at the table, Porky," Pauli insisted. "You gotta have a beer first. Make yourself comfortable, and look over the prints. I'll pour you a nice cold Lite." Pauli grinned, making a chug motion of drink, then moved toward the fridge, which was directly behind Porky. Porky sat down, took a deep, exhausted breath, and exhaled noisily.

"You did the right thing, Pauli," Porky said. "Boretti and the other dons all know of your cooperation with us. They all think you're . . ."

"A fuckin' yellow rat!" Pauli screamed and lunged forward. At the same moment he quickly stuck a seven-inch stiletto in the back of Porky's lower neck between the shoulder blades and began twisting, Sicilian fisherman style, enlarging the hole and damaging the spinal nerves. The blade went deep into the lower neck muscle. Pauli twisted hard, using both hands. The white cream of bone marrow mixed with blood and began to ooze out of Porky's thick neck, dripping easily down his back. Porky remained in a sitting position, very alive, his eyes wide open and bulging, speechless at the table. He knew what Pauli had done to him. His body was paralyzed. He just sat and stared straight ahead with the knife still stuck deep in his neck. Pauli had stuck Porky with the old Sicilian neck blow that paralyzes the enemy, not killing him instantly but keeping him alive and aware. Pauli reached into Porky's jacket and removed the steel, a .38 Magnum, from the holster. Pauli then sat at the table across from Porky. Porky just stared straight ahead, his eyes spread wide in utter shock. He didn't move or even moan. Pauli's eyes seemed very different. They didn't belong to the same man, the once beautiful Pauli of the smooth jawline and face that all women, married and unmarried, loved. His unshaven face now seemed wild and mad and dirty.

"What were you saying, Porky?" Pauli asked. "Please continue where we left off. The dons are fully satisfied with me? And they're aware that you have succeeded in making a fuckin' rat bastard out of me! And that you brought me to a level in my life where I could not face my friends anymore, and because of that, Porky," Pauli grinned, his face full of sweat and anger, "you're gonna die a real fat man's death tonight. I promise you that." Pauli got up from the table, walked around Porky and pulled the stiletto slowly out of his very broad neck. Porky's eyes widened farther as the knife was being removed. Pauli then, with one quick stroke, plunged it into Porky's right ear, where it entered all the way to the brain. The fat man lunged over in a thunderous fall. Pauli moved quickly to the window and began waving the towel wildly. The car lights blinked once, and after a few moments Guido removed himself from behind the wheel and proceeded walking toward the apartment house. Pauli met Guido at the top of the stairs. "It's Porky," Pauli whispered. "I think he had an epileptic fit or something; his tongue was hanging out like a real pig. He just keeled over on the floor and started chewing on his tongue," Pauli continued excitedly. Guido looked Pauli over, then slowly entered the room, walked up to Porky's body, bent over, saw the pool of blood, and turned around, wide-eyed, just in time to see Pauli smirk and pull the trigger of the Magnum pistol, firing once into his chest. Guido landed in a sitting position staring at Pauli, his back resting against the wall. Pauli instantly jammed the nozzle of the Magnum into Guido's mouth and pulled the trigger once again. The blast shattered Guido's head all over the wall.

Pauli sat on the edge of the bed holding the still-smoking short-barreled pistol. Blood was pooling all over the floor. Pauli walked to the table, ripped up the map, and flushed it down the commode. Returning to the room, he reached into his pocket and took out a white envelope and laid it on the bed. Then, quickly, without hesitation, he put the barrel of the gun to his own head and pulled the trigger. . . .

The envelope was addressed to Aldo Pastrona:

Dear Monkey,

The fuckers tried, they failed, they got nothing from me. I love you guys. You were all I had.

Lil Pauli

P.S. Tell Bepy I took two scumbags with me. I hope I regained my respect.

Little Pauli's funeral was crawling with FBI agents. Undertakers Joseph Sapacci and Sons had so many flowers delivered, they had to line them up outside on the sidewalk in front of the building. Swarms of unescorted women trailed through the chapel. The combination of the endless stream of women and the elaborate flower arrangements amused the FBI, as their long-range video cameras secretly zoomed in from the nearby cars and rooftops of Brooklyn.

Watching from one of those rooftops was Matthew Puland, the newly appointed New York state regional FBI chief, fresh from Seattle to head the New York task force. Puland stood peering down to the street, puffing on his cigar. After a few minutes, he turned and addressed special agent Jason Stuart. "How come the guy in the coffin's so important? They got flowers and broads all over the place down there."

Stuart smiled. "I only know that this guy Pauli, also known as Little Pauli, was very well liked in Brooklyn. He had more broads than Rudy Valentino. Even the wise guys liked him, in spite of the sneak-around guy he was."

"No shit, he was that good with the broads?" Puland asked.

Stuart nodded. "He was that good. We been watching him on and off for a coupla years now. Believe me, he had them all," Stuart said, scratching his head. "He's been laying in more bedrooms than Sealy."

Later that evening, around 7:00 P.M., the FBI agents still observing from the rooftops watched anxiously as two silver stretch limos with South Carolina license plates pulled up slowly to the front of the Sapacci funeral home. People crowded the sidewalks to view the occupants of the extended-out cars. The tough-looking driver of the first car got out and opened its rear door. News reporters began snapping photos of the arriving Sicilians.

Jason Stuart raised his binoculars and mumbled, "Ahh, what have we here? It's Menesiero and company," he said to Puland. "See the first guy getting out with the canes? That's Ben Del Ponte, underboss; he's a.k.a. 'Don't Call Me Benny.' He's a cripple now; that's the guy that got thrown off the roof." Still looking through his binoculars, Stuart nodded with a grin. "Yeah, last year the Mob flipped him off a roof. We tried to get him to open up. No dice. They handle things their own way."

"Who's the other one with them?" Puland asked.

"Ahh!" Stuart groaned, raising his glasses once again. "That's the big boss, Bephino Menesiero; he's the famous hit man also known as Bepy Dante. He's the guy that beat us in court by swallowing up Frank Caputo, our pigeon, remember?"

"I heard all about that in Seattle," Puland answered. "Unbelievable!"

Bephino looked great again. He had regained his handsome

appearance and was strong and sound. He moved with confidence as he entered the lobby of the funeral home.

Stuart continued. "The other two with him are probably just bodyguards," he said, as he refocused his lens on the people moving down below in the street. "Those guys getting out of the second limo look like what they call the Old Blood members. Aldo Pastrona—they call him 'the Monkey'—and then Mike Lastrano, 'Crazy Mikey.' The guy next to him is the Jewish hotel owner from Las Vegas, Alan Stone. He's got the El Banco Hotel, on the Vegas strip."

"What the hell is he doing with them?"

"He's connected with them. Everything at the El Banco is comp for this crew. It's their skim hotel. It's all in the files," Stuart nodded. "We got tapes. This guy Stone calls from Vegas and makes soft-spoken, intelligent suggestions. He's very involved in this family. He gives them a lot of advice, but we've never heard him say a miscalculated word yet. Not a word wrong yet!" Stuart repeated, shaking his head.

"Oh, he's . . ."

"Yeah, he's considered Old Blood too; they refer to each other as Old Blood because their regular soldiers came along years later, when Menesiero became a don. This guy Stone's sharp as a tack. He never slips. But sooner or later he'll slip up; they all do. See those guys standing off to the left, by the wall of flowers? Take a look," Stuart suggested, handing over the glasses.

Puland took the binoculars and focused. "Yeah, what about them?"

"Those guys are top guns of Rocco Boretti, the Boss of Bosses, *Capo di tutti capi,* as they say in the gutters of Brooklyn. You know, they lost two of their strongest enforcers the other day to Menesiero's man that's lying in the box, Lil Pauli. Pauli made the kill, then knocked himself off. It's all in your file to read. We hear there's bad blood between Boretti and this guy Menesiero. We also hear there's bad blood between the Boretti people and Louie Young Chow ('Bad Louie') from Chinatown and his cousin, the Woo Man. Two Orientals were found dead in a cellar locker room on Mott Street yesterday. The bodies were at least six days old. They were Bad

Louie's people, and it's whispered the Italians made the hit. The Italians claim that the Orientals are crossing Canal Street." Looking directly at Puland, Stuart nodded. "So you arrived today, your first day in New York, and you're gonna have an exciting new position here in the Big Apple, I can assure you," Stuart smiled. "It will be exciting."

Puland, still watching the Boretti people through the binoculars, crunched his cigar and with a wet mouth answered, "Beats Seattle." After a few moments, Puland turned and spat. "This Louie Young Chow guy you mentioned. I've had dealings with him before," Puland said. "He lived in Seattle's Chinatown about eight years ago. He's believed to have slaughtered twenty Chinese in one sitting. Some were only kids, ten or twelve years old. I hope I get him this time here in New York. I couldn't nail him in Washington. So tell me, Stuart, how come there's bad blood between Boretti and Menesiero?"

"We don't know for sure. What we do know is Menesiero was hiding away from New York at his ranch down South for about a year or more. The word on the street was he was *morte,* as they say—you know, dead, crushed in a car or something. But we got on record from customs, July of this year, that someone renewed an old lost passport of his. A rush request. The next thing we know, he's rolling through Kennedy's customs in a wheelchair at 6:00 A.M., and no one recognizes this guy because he lost about eighty pounds. So he doesn't match up with his passport photo. Customs calls us to question his reentry and says his signature matched up perfectly and his wife is with him. But the passport wasn't valid at a previous time when he probably left the country. So Burt Jenkins, who you replaced, told our customs department agents to go ahead and let him in, because there's really nothing we could do to stop him. I mean, he was an American citizen with a valid passport. Plus, we'd rather have him here so we can watch him. The only thing we maybe got on him now is how did he get out of the country in the first place?

"Menesiero had been picked up on his ranch about three years ago, I believe, by agents Vanders and Guilderson. He went through the arrest and pretrial arrangements like a champ. We got nothing out of him. Then on the third day of his trial, Frank Caputo—our star witness, the guy we pampered for a year—disappeared, and that ended our case against him. I mean, this guy Menesiero actually had gone unnoticed and unquestioned by the bureau for about thirty years, and it turns out that like Caputo, our talker, said, Menesiero was responsible for plenty of hits. And he slips through our fingers. Man, the guy is deadly."

Puland nodded. "We'll have to keep a better watch on this man before he makes Boretti disappear and we lose our opportunity for central promotions."

"You're right," Stuart nodded. "He's the best, they say. We gotta get him."

Meanwhile, back on the streets and inside Joseph Sapacci and Sons, Bephino and his crew paid their respects to Pauli's sisters and brothers, as a great flow of people continued past Pauli's coffin. "He looks so good," Frank the neighborhood barber said to Pauli's older brother. "I gave him a haircut only two weeks ago," he whimpered emotionally. "They did good work patchin' up his head," he commented as he moved to let people pass. Woman after woman slipped by, glancing awkwardly at the coffin to confirm that it was really Lil Pauli who was gone.

Bephino sat by the family, deeply mourning his old childhood friend. "Pauli died like a real man," he told Pauli's brothers and sisters. "He's a true Sicilian," Bephino whispered seriously. Monkey's eyes studied the line of mourners and counted the unescorted women.

Then turning to Ben, Mikey, Alan, and Bephino, Monkey grinned right at them. "Would you believe Pauli banged all these broads! I understand this has been going on all day. Pauli's sister told me," Monkey chuckled. "She said, 'Broad after broad's been sneakin' in to pay respects to my brother.' "

Bephino grinned, shaking his head. "Pauli sure had the talent with the ladies. He beat us all out."

"That's for sure," Mikey said.

"Don't look now, Bepy!" Monkey hissed. "Rocco Boretti's on the line to pay respects to Pauli. How do you figure that shit? He's got two of his pigs laid out also, and he shows up here at Pauli's wake!"

Bephino looked over at Boretti and then turned away. But Ben stared steadily at the Boss of Bosses until the two made eye contact, and continued doing so until Rocco nodded gently with a soft, welcome-back-from-the-dead smirk. Bephino, having conspicuously turned his back on Boretti, began a conversation with Alan and Monkey. Ben, still staring, whispered, "I can't wait to get that son of a bitch. I'm gonna cripple him just like he crippled me. He's gotta be delimbed at his kneecaps before I allow him to die."

Monkey made eyes at Mikey and motioned for him to join him outside. After a few minutes, they returned and Monkey whispered into Bephino's ear. "Boretti's got about six of his people outside," he said softly. "I don't recognize all of them. But they're his people."

"That's good," Bephino replied. "Go pay some newspaper guy outside with a camera to take their pictures, make them feel uncomfortable. Then tell the photo guy we'll pay a thousand bucks for every photo he gives us of those six Boretti people. We'll keep their pictures in our album," Bephino grinned. "Later on we make sure we visit all six of them."

Suddenly, a shabbily dressed gray-haired man came rushing into the funeral home, clearly looking for someone. He then pushed his way through the crowd until he found Monkey, who seemed to know him. After a few urgently whispered words, Monkey put his arm around the man's neck and the two stepped away to a quiet corner of the chapel in deep conversation. Bephino and Ben watched from a distance as Monkey's mild expression darkened and erupted. Monkey, close to losing control, headed quickly back to Bephino and the others, and said harshly to them, "Let's go, we gotta get outta here."

"Why?" Bephino asked.

"Just listen to me," Monkey said, grabbing Bephino's shoulder. "It's time for us to go."

Bephino glanced over to Boretti, who was talking to some people across the room. Boretti, taking in Monkey's agitation, watched as Bephino was evidently being told exciting news. "I'll be seeing you," Bephino nodded calmly to Boretti, then turned to his men and said, "OK, let's go. Let's say good-bye and leave slowly, not abruptly," he ordered. Each man said good-bye to Lil Pauli, then walked over to the Segura family, kissed the sisters, and said good-bye to the brothers. Bephino made excuses in a low voice for their early departure, after which there were more hugs of condolence and understanding. Then Bephino and his people left the building, climbed into their waiting limos, and drove off.

"They're leaving." FBI agent Stuart nudged Puland, who was taking a break. "I'm surprised they left so early. It seems like they don't wanna be in the same room with Rocco Boretti—soon as he showed up, it looks like they left." Puland stared down to the street, biting his now short-stubbed cigar, and did not answer.

As the limos drove toward Staten Island and New Jersey, Monkey turned violently to Bephino and Ben. *"They killed the kid!"* he blurted out in a choked voice. "They murdered him!"

"What kid?" Bephino snapped.

"Alley Oop's kid," Monkey spat out, sick with grief.

"What?" Bephino screeched. "Who told you that?"

"Tony Papa; he lives near Alley Oop's mother's house. He heard it on TV about an hour ago. He said the police stopped over at the kid's grandmother's house; Tony figured we all would be at Pauli's wake, so he came right away. They put two bullets in the kid's head—a message for us," Monkey said bitterly.

"The rotten motherfuckers," Bephino yelled in anguish.

"Them cocksuckers," Ben cried. "Why the kid? They're gonna pay through their asses for this!" Ben's voice quavered through clenched teeth. "They're gonna bleed forever, them bastards!"

"A poor, innocent kid they kill, for no reason at all," Bephino groaned. "I don't believe this!" he fumed, banging his fist on the limo bar. "It's gettin' totally outta hand! Now they're takin' the lives of innocent kids! The kid was so naive; he was a fuckin' teddy bear."

"We gotta burn their houses down tonight, with all their families in 'em!" Ben swore grimly. "We gotta act tonight, while they're sleepin'! They took my legs, now they took my soul," he grieved. "Them rat bastards! You don't know how much I enjoyed helpin' that kid. He was the nicest kid you'd ever wanna meet. What about his mother and his grandmother and his aunts? They must be dead themselves after hearing this thing!" Ben tried to kick his lame legs in anger. "Them cocksuckers!"

Bephino became deadly quiet as the car crossed the Verrazano Bridge and the Staten Island Expressway toward the Goethals Bridge to New Jersey. Everyone joined him in silence.

"And that's not all," Monkey finally muttered unsurely into a handkerchief. Ben and Bephino's eyes turned quickly to him. Monkey struggled with the words for a moment. "They cut the kid's balls off."

"Turn this fuckin' car around!" Bephino yelled to the driver over the limo's intercom. "Turn back to Brooklyn, *now*!"

"Where to in Brooklyn, Bephino?" the driver asked.

"Take us to Black Augie's house on Shore Road. Then you and Sonny take these limos back to South Carolina and return them to the dealer. Stay at the gate house and wait for further instructions from us. Tonight we're taking one of them out," Bephino vowed in a voice choked with anger and passion. "One by one, we're gonna murder them all. Them cocksuckers gotta pay for this," he said with deep sorrow. "They were all in on it, all of them. All the bosses had to condone such a fuckin' fretful act. A civilian, they hit!" he yelled. "They're trying to tell us something at the expense of a beautiful boy's life. God! We gotta give them bastards deaths that are unheard of. What they did to that boy," Bephino held his head, "a civilian, no less. . . . The kid shoulda never been touched. He shouldna been touched. He was only a kid."

"Yeah, he was only a kid," Ben uttered, weeping.

Everyone in the car resumed their silence. They knew what they had to do. After a long while, Bephino said, "Gataneo Gaeta, the old pimp—he was a pimp all his life—he's the second-strongest boss in New York: We kill him first. He's always been a nasty old fuck, he's a man known to be without an ounce of mercy, a no-conscience bastard. He probably seconded the suggestion made by Boretti to kill our boy. First we kill Mr. Gaeta, then all the others, one by one. Boretti will be last; he's gonna experience the worst shameful death you could imagine."

Ben and Bephino sat alone on a sofa in Black Augie's apartment in Bensonhurst, while the others watched TV in the next room. "You're right, Bepy, to hit Gataneo Gaeta before the others," Ben said. "He's the scumbag that instigated the whole European hit fiasco. He's the bastard that caused the entire situation that led to my becoming a cripple, that led to Alley Boy's mutilation. He's the demanding one. I wanna fix him first before he dies of natural causes, the old bastard! We should bust in his house early tomorrow morning, when he's still groggy and in his fuckin' pajamas," Ben said, looking to Bephino for acknowledgement.

Bephino looked up, holding his chin. "I agree, Ben; it's time for us to act like that, take them from their houses in their fuckin' pajamas. We'll do it in the early-morning hours. It's time we showed them rat bastards who they're playing with. I want Monkey to call up my friend Johnny the Safe from Bay Parkway. He's listed under John's Locks and Safes. Tell him to come over right now. We gotta talk to him. Tell Monkey not to tell him anything. I'll do that. And, Ben, tomorrow you ride with Johnny in his car. Mikey and Monkey ride with me in Augie's car. We're gonna use Augie's car for this—tell the boys to change the plates just for tomorrow. Send them over to a bar-and-grill parking lot to lift a set of plates. We'll hit Gaeta bright and early."

"Gaeta's an early riser," Monkey said, entering the room. "He's from the Old Country, he's probably up at 5:30 every morning watching his tomato plants grow. He's usually having espresso coffee by 8:30 at the club on Mott Street. I know 'cause I used to see him when I was a kid on my way to the James Center to train."

"Good, then he should still be home about 6:00 A.M., probably cracking open a boiled egg," Bephino said.

"Suppose his wife's there or he has company," Mikey said, joining into the conversation.

"We'll deal with that when we get in his house," Bephino replied, looking up at Mikey. "Where's Alan?" Bephino asked.

"He's in the bedroom asleep," Mikey replied.

"Gataneo Gaeta has ruled with an iron fist for years. He and Rocco had no mercy. He killed the kid when he had the power to save him. Now he's gonna pay the piper. It's his turn to die, he's old; it's a shame he already beat the system. The only way we could even the score is to give him a real slow, ugly, decapitating-type death, something that will make his blood run crazy through his body and pop his fuckin' head off from the pressure. They killed Alley Oop's son," Bephino said, his voice thick with sorrow. "Alley's son was like our son. Next it will be my son they kill. I have no mercy anymore. If he's got houseguests and they're in our way, we'll have no choice, we'll take them out too."

Don Gataneo Gaeta sat quietly at his kitchen table at 5:30 in the morning, wearing a white T-shirt and light-blue undershorts. Licking his anxious lips, the old man began spreading butter on a slice of warm toast. He then folded the toast and began to dunk it in a large cup of hot coffee.

"Gatt!" his white-haired wife called out loudly to him from across the room at the cooking range. "Your eggs are almost ready."

"You know what causes this crazy unusual hot weather and them heat waves?" Gataneo asked loudly back to his wife. "It's the damn nuclear testing!" he yelled. "It's the testing going on between Russia and the United States! That's why we can't stand the heat anymore, it's always hot!" he shouted, looking over his shoulder to his wife for an answer. But Mrs. Gaeta, who was partially deaf and wore hearing aids in both ears, walked silently to the table and handed her husband another slice of toast. Then in a loud voice she repeated, "Your eggs are almost ready, Gatt," as she smoothed her housecoat and walked back to lower the flame on the boiling pot. She shuffled sideways over to the kitchen sink and opened the faucet. Gataneo buttered his fresh slice of toast and began to dunk. As he sopped up the coffee and then bit into the bread, his lips quivering as he swallowed, the sink water rapidly ran over the boiled eggs.

At this moment the front door of the brick Westchester one-family house was being picked open by Johnny Ramola. As Johnny stepped aside, Bephino and Crazy Mikey quickly and quietly walked past him and entered the living room. They stopped at an archway leading to the lighted kitchen. Gataneo's loud voice carried across the room in his conversation with his wife. Bephino peeked in the kitchen through the arched doorway and saw his mark sitting at the table in his underwear and an old woman in a housecoat with her back turned. The kitchen faucet, running full blast, was partially drowning out Gaeta's conversation. Bephino saw the woman busy cracking open the eggs and spotted her hearing aids. He signaled to Mikey that they were going to grab him and take him out of the house fast. Gaeta's voice became louder as he tried to compete with the running water. The men moved lightly and swiftly behind the old man. In one motion Mikey covered Gataneo's mouth tightly—so tightly that he immediately winced in pain. Mikey, squeezing hard, swiftly picked the old man's frail body right out of the chair. Hurrying, he soundlessly carried Gataneo out the front door, Bephino moving along with him to hold the man's dangling legs. As they reached the car they had waiting in the alleyway, Mikey threw the old man roughly into the backseat like a laundry bag. Gataneo yelped in pain as his knees and ankles banged against the sides of the automobile. Bephino and Mikey quickly got in on each side of him and told Monkey at the wheel to move out. Each man quietly sat beside Gataneo and did not acknowledge his presence any further. Monkey pulled out and turned left at the corner as he headed for the highway to Bensonhurst—the old neighborhood, and Rocco Boretti territory. After a few moments of silence, Bephino passively glanced over at the half-dressed man sitting bewildered and confused. Gataneo's sunken eyes briefly met Bephino's.

"What's this for?" the old man asked with a tremor of fear in his voice.

"For Ben, for Pauli. But mostly for the eighteen-year-old kid you ordered killed, and for the balls you removed from his body."

Gataneo remained silent. After a few long moments, he asked awkwardly, somberly, "Will you make it quick for me?"

9

OCTOBER 25, 1978, MORNING

NEW YORK CITY

New York's newspapers were quick to scream the news. MOB RUB-OUT! the headlines called. Publications of a more sensational nature were happy to oblige with the pertinent details:

> Reputed underworld crime czar Gataneo Gaeta was found dead in Brooklyn in a corner of a city asphalt-vehicle storage lot yesterday afternoon. The eldest asserted Mafia boss, alleged to be number two in New York's crime syndicate, Gaeta was discovered under a twelve-ton pavement roller. His body had been crushed flat up to the neck. The only part of his body untouched

was his decapitated head, protruding from beneath the large rear roller, lying in a pool of blood. The seventy-eight-year-old Gaeta, born in Palermo, Sicily, was believed to control New York's Pleasure Palaces, among other similar entities in Las Vegas and Atlantic City. Mr. Gaeta's seventy-five-year-old wife told police that the last time she saw her husband he was sitting at the kitchen table of their home in Yonkers, waiting for his breakfast. The soft-boiled eggs she was cooking were still lying on his plate when police arrived that afternoon to notify her. "I thought he went for a walk," she told homicide detective Pat Rogers. "I turned to serve my husband, and he was no longer at the table."

The deceased man is survived by his wife, Louise Gaeta, two married daughters, Joan Navarra and Marie Strombetto, and one son, John G. Gaeta, a Yonkers physician. Funeral services will be held at the Minelli Funeral Home on Marcus Avenue in the Bronx, and religious services at St. Luke's Church in Yonkers. The coffin will be closed.

NOVEMBER 16, 1978, 6:00 A.M.

LITTLE FALLS, SOUTH CAROLINA

Bephino sat alone, watching the mares and their foals graze in the plush green fescue and clover pastures. The redness of dawn began to appear in the east. He knew it was over. His life of peace and happiness had ended. Sitting out on his bedroom patio, he waited for faithful Monkey to get back from a trip to Los Angeles. At 9:00 A.M., Monkey pulled up the farm road.

"How was your vacation?" Bephino asked his friend, embracing him warmly. "Did you enjoy Hollywood?"

"I had a nice time. I saw my cousins. They live in Tarzana. The weather is so beautiful in California. I wish we lived there," Monkey said with a gleam in his eye.

"I'm glad you enjoyed yourself. You deserved a good time. A lot has been done in the past two weeks. My family's already gone," Bephino said. "So you and I are all alone on the farm."

"Gone where?" Monkey asked.

"Ben and I sent Dana, Rene, Patsy, and even Patsy's girlfriend to Mexico. And Ben's Peggy, Mrs. Roselli, and Alan Stone all joined them today in Cancun, where Alan's rented a large place on the beach. They gotta stay away until our business is finished in New York."

"Even Mrs. Roselli?" Monkey asked.

"Yeah, just until we finish what we gotta do," Bephino said, rubbing his chin. "If they came here on the farm, they'd even kill Mrs. Roselli. I can't take that chance with people's lives. They killed Alley Boy, they'll kill anyone. I feel sure of that."

"I thought this farm looked kinda vacant when I drove up. I got a strange feeling," Monkey said.

"We had no choice, they would all be targets. Rocco's gonna go after anyone he can to get to me. He couldn't get me at Pauli's funeral because there was FBI agents all over the place. So he killed Alley Oop's son to make his point. God! I can't get over it, him losing his life because of us. He was only a kid. He had nothing to do with our business. His life was just beginning for him, and they ended it in a minute. How could they agree to such a degenerate act of vengeance? They dismembered the kid! I'm sick over that boy. I'll never forgive it, I'll never forget it. I feel so terrible, Monk, it's eating me up inside. And Pauli . . ." Bephino frowned. "They drove poor Pauli so mad he committed suicide. Pauli was a harmless guy, all he wanted was broads; he wasn't a threat to anyone. He just took numbers and bets for us. The guy never made a hit until the night he murdered them animals, and he couldn't live with that so he killed himself. And now Pauli's gone. They made him ashamed of himself. God, do we have problems. . . . So I been up all night, thinking, Look at what I'm leaving—a paradise. I love this place," Bephino said sadly. "Well," he sighed, "we got Gataneo Gaeta out of the way, and yesterday Mikey said our soldiers took out more of his top capos, so nobody's gonna be looking for Gataneo's job for a while."

"Bephino, I really enjoyed my trip to the West Coast. I'm

glad I'm back and I'm ready to work, but how about after we clean up New York we retire? Let's leave New York permanently—maybe for California," Monkey smiled. "New York's becoming a fuckin' nightmare, dealing with those people. They never quit, it's always problems—do you realize we gotta kill half of New York to square this thing?" Monkey asked, shaking his head in frustration.

"They're our people, Monk, we're the same kinda low-life, murderous bastards, we're no different. We were in it from day one. We may be smarter, because we realize you can't go on and on killing and you can't squeeze every penny out of New York; them guys intend to keep squeezing the eagles' balls all the way to their graves. We have no choice; they're our people and we gotta do the honors. We gotta put them bastards to rest before they put us to rest. That's the only way I know of to deal with it. It's beyond sit-downs, it's beyond negotiation; they went too far. They gotta pay for that kid's life with blood. They gotta pay for Ben. They ruined him." Bephino stared at Monkey, then put his hand on his shoulder. "This time we can't stop and make peace. If we don't do what we gotta do, they'll kill us all, and our families—they'll kill my children, Monk. I know that for sure.

"There's no one on the farm but you and me, and we're leaving the farm in two days for good. I'm selling out. We're gonna live very quietly in New Jersey for a while until we kill them all. The next boss we hit, it's gonna be like a showcase. It's gonna be exotic; his balls will be all over Brooklyn. They'll never dream we're living in New Jersey right under their noses. We're hitting the mattress for a while. The farm will be sold to the highest bidder next month. After the war ends, we'll decide what to do. I'm working on a plan of total destruction of Boretti and his family. I wanna make model parents out of their children." Bephino pounded his fist. "I can't believe Boretti would stoop that low, to kill a kid the age of his own sons and daughters. Doesn't he realize he's putting us in a frame of mind that could hurt his own kids? I'm having very bad thoughts. I have that blood-taste in my mouth. He's gotta suffer bad, that bastard. He's gotta have grief before he dies. Do you know I can't face Paula Murphy, the kid's mother? I can't face her! As far as I'm concerned the kid is dead because of me." Bephino looked up at the sky. "I thought I was strong enough to live with anything. I thought I could handle any death."

Both men remained quiet for a moment, then Monkey spoke. "We need more men than what we got to do the job. We don't have enough people to win an all-out war with the families. They got hundreds and hundreds of soldiers in New York."

"I know, I know; but once we eliminate the dons and perhaps the first top ten or twenty in each family, they'll be all fucked up and confused. They'll start going to church again. Believe me, they'll change quick, very quick. We'll probably have to scare a few wives and kids to keep 'em scrambling. They'll be so busy tryin' to keep their wives and kids calm and sedated, they'll become exposed to us without realizing it, you know that; but it's us or them, and they killed the first innocent."

"Does your wife and kids know about all this?" Monkey asked.

"All they know is that the farm will be sold as is. I told them, Take your toothbrush and leave. They got the message. My family knows I made a decision. They realize it's too dangerous for them to stay. They whined and whined, but they know I gotta do what I gotta do. We all have to relocate after this is over. It's gonna be messy for years. Let's hope we're still alive when it's over." Bephino shrugged. "Alan Stone's gonna stay in Mexico with them," Bephino said. "He'll keep them well, he'll be our contact. Ben and Mikey are in New Jersey right now making sure the house we purchased is fully secure and totally private. It's about fifteen acres in the country. We bought the property last week in the name of Paula Murphy, Alley Boy's mother. When we finish with it, she can have it for her and her father to live out their lives. They're gonna need solitude after losing their son like that."

Monkey stared, speechless. He knew Bephino was grieving for Alley Oop's son. His eyes were different. The killer was in his face once again, and Bephino was fighting it. He hated to give up his paradise to go to New York for war. "You're unbelievable, Bephino," Monkey said. "It's just like old times, you're thinking of everything. I've been away from you for not even two weeks and you're moving like lightning. Everything's in motion. You think of everything—even the kid's mother and grandfather you think of."

"I didn't think of everything, Monkey; if I had, we wouldn't be in such a fuckin' turmoil. Rocco hurt us bad, he's got us scrambling to stay alive. He's got me running out of my house. I'm selling my farm, a place I love, I'm on the run. He's got me worried, Monk; we could lose the whole ball game to him, and if someone tips him off that we're living in Jersey, he'll send a crew over with machine guns to destroy us, and if he finds out my family's in Cancun, he'll hit them right on the beach. Rocco's a sick man. He'd slaughter even the kids. He's proved himself already."

"Maybe we should slaughter his kids, see how he likes that. We'll attack him right on his own beach in Staten Island," Monkey said. "You know the house, you lived in it for years. Maybe that's where we should stage our war, right in his fuckin' bedroom. We'll hit the fuckin' beach like the marines and kill all his family for what he's done to Ben, Pauli, and Alley Boy."

Bephino frowned, then pulled back his lips at the recklessness of the suggestion. "Pauli and Ben were people involved. I could understand that he moved against them. Pauli and Ben were soldiers. But they hit Alley Boy, a civilian, shot him twice in the head then mutilated him just to let us know they mean business." Bephino scratched his head. "I can tell you, Monk, I have not made a decision to kill his entire family. Those daughters of his are so young, they're innocent and beautiful. I don't know if I can do such a thing," Bephino shrugged, shaking his head. "I don't believe I could live with myself after such an act. I'd be no better than that Manson guy."

"What about Boretti's son, he's bad news. Believe me," Monkey insisted, "that kid will come at us forever." Monkey waited silently for an answer, but Bephino just stared, his eyes sunk deep and thoughtful.

After a few moments Bephino said, "His son we'll have to think about. A decision will have to be made later on. He's only a kid."

"Kid, my ass!" Monkey said. "He's got three notches on his belt."

Bephino answered, "In any case, we're gonna bust their asses wide open. They killed our kid for no reason. They're all gonna die a very messy death. Rocco's son is only twenty-one. We gotta give him some thought." Regaining his composure, Bephino frowned. "So, let's deal with today's business. The reason I had you come to the farm is . . . you and me gotta go to Savannah. We got business in Savannah, so let's go."

The next day the cobblestone streets of Savannah, Georgia, echoed with the news of the Top Hat nightclub's owner having been found brutally slashed to death in the old slave-market auction barn. Bubba Reed, reputed drug dealer and nightclub owner, was found facedown in a pool of blood, gutted from stomach to throat. Police believed a drug deal may have gone sour. There had been reports of feuding among Texas and Georgia crime families.

NOVEMBER 21, 1978, 6:00 P.M.

FORT LEE, NEW JERSEY

"OK, gentlemen, here's our plan," Bephino said to Ben, Monkey, and Mikey five days later at their headquarters in New Jersey. "You know we're radically outnumbered by the power of the five families. And now that new guy Frankie DePasquale got his own crew, so we gotta deal with him also. They're all gonna stick together like shit and turn thumbs down on us. They'll use DePasquale to make the hit on us. They figure we won't figure that. But they're wrong. Just the way they used me as a kid to take out people, they'll use Frankie to take me out. So it's important that none of our men know where we are holing up. Boretti will try to grab a few of our boys to squeeze information out of them to find out where we're at; that's the way he operates. He did it to Lil Pauli, but Pauli was Old Blood and fucked Boretti in his ass. Pauli took out their two best guns. Now this week the Gaeta family also lost two good buttons. We're doing good and we haven't even gotten started. Them guys woke up a sleeping lion.

"Alan Stone got us an address of a vacant house in Bayview. That's the only location all our soldiers will know of and meet us at. And when they meet us at the Long Island house, they'll think we four are staying there. We'll put four toothbrushes in the bathroom and food in the kitchen—also clothes in the closets—so they'll think that's our home base. They are never allowed to call us. We call them, remember that. If and when one of them sings to Boretti, Boretti will have DePasquale or his men storm the Bayview place. And we'll know we got a fuckin' rat in our crowd. We'll seek him out, pluck out his eyes, and put him in Boretti's garbage can to set an example so the others walk the line."

Bephino sipped a ginger ale slowly, then looked up. "OK, so you guys already got that part. The other is we need about a hundred fifty more hit men working the streets of Brooklyn, Staten Island, Long Island, Manhattan, Queens, and the Bronx. We gotta be able to hit all the social clubs, union halls, candy stores, coffee shops, bars, even their houses. Places where they all meet, congregate, like in Little Italy; all the cafés gotta be hit. I wanna hit every fuckin' club room and coffee joint on the East Side. The key is it's gotta be done on the same day and about the same time. All at the same time!" Bephino repeated. "We gotta hit the clubs on Cherry Street, Houston Street, East 15th Street; then later that night, when all the family members we missed begin to crawl back to their clubs and hangouts to assess the damage, we clip a few more here and there. They'll never expect such a large-scale assault. Brooklyn's gonna be empty for a long time. When we get through with them, every fuckin' soldier that we missed who's working for the five families will be heading home to take cover, and when they arrive home, the ones with rank like capos and buttons get priority. We'll have people waiting for them when they arrive in their driveways, and the minute they park their cars and head up the steps to their house our boys'll open fire."

"Where you gonna get a hundred and fifty men to fight for us?" Monkey asked. "We need an army of trained men, lotsa trained men, for this kinda operation," he insisted. "We only got about twenty-five good soldiers in our group. How we gonna pull this thing off?" Monkey asked, shifting his eyes to Mikey and Ben. "Where we gonna get another hundred twenty-five loyal guys to make hits all over New York in such a short time for us?"

"Chinks," Ben injected quickly. "We're gonna use Freddie Woo—they call him the Woo Man—and that other chink from Seattle, his cousin, Bad Louie Young Chow from down Chinatown, as pawns to help us in this war, and if we have to we'll go to the Bronx and recruit Gasper and his band of Puerto Ricans."

"Gasper!" Mikey laughed, "Who the fuck is Gasper?"

"He's a boss spick from Fordham Road in the Bronx. For two hundred bucks a hit, his spicks would kill Santa Claus. I understand from good people in the Bronx that all we gotta do is target the person and they open fire—like I said, they work cheap. Two hundred a whack for whoever they kill. And you wanna hear it all? They got their own Uzis and ammo," Ben grinned.

Monkey and Mikey listened hard and swallowed slowly, then locked eyes and nodded in agreement. Bephino remained silent. "It could work," Monkey said, "but how you gonna get the chinks to cooperate with us and organize such a big operation? You got a list of locations to hit a mile long."

Bephino looked up. "We already contacted Bad Louie and Freddie Woo. We're gonna see them tomorrow. We'll spend a few days with the leaders of the Chinese group. It's gotta work. We'll take them from fancy Chinese place to fancy Chinese place—even in Little Italy, perhaps—to eat. We'll make them feel real important, then we'll take something from them of value so they don't turn on us. After we got them by the balls we give accurate instructions and addresses and tell them what they gotta do at a certain time and day. Then they'll open fire and hit the targets three days before Christmas Eve. Every hit man's got a time and location. We tell them that all males who look over the age of, say, about twenty-two who are in the club rooms or bar hangouts gotta be hit. All women and children, of course, can't be touched. Within two days of Christmas Eve we should make a good impression on all the families. They'll respect us," Bephino nodded.

"What about Jersey? They'll get involved, won't they?"

"The Jersey and Philadelphia crews are too busy watching each other's moves in Atlantic City. They'll never consider getting involved or helping New York. They'll stay nice and quiet, play dumb, and wait until the smoke clears. Then they'll grab another casino or two, and when Boretti shows up dead they'll grab some more. But before these targets are hit we got our own work cut out for us: We gotta make the kill ourselves on all the dons and their top capos. That's our job. Then after a few quiet days after the shocking news of the hits, all club rooms will be filled with soldiers talking and bullshitting about who went down and how. When they start to huddle in the hangouts and the coffee shops to talk about the possible new dons being elected, we cut the fuckin' chinks and spicks loose. After that massacre, forget about New York. It's gonna become a nice place to live. Concrete's gonna be cheap again, houses will cost less, it's gonna be nice," Bephino grinned. "And they all gotta thank Rocco Boretti for this. Him we kill maybe on New Year's Eve or Christmas Day." Everyone smiled; Bephino was talking like old times.

"You make it sound so easy," Monkey grinned. "Who's gonna keep count of how many hits the spicks and chinks make? They gotta get two hundred a hit, you said, so how you gonna keep score?"

"What's the difference, we pay them by the head on whatever they turn in. What could it total up to, ten or twenty grand at the most, even a hundred grand—what's the difference? That's cheap for the kinda service we're gonna get."

"Whata ya gonna take from them?" Monkey asked. "I

heard you say you're gonna take something of value from them so they don't jab us."

"We'll take their girlfriends or maybe their mothers for a while, something like that," Bephino smirked. "Leave it to me, OK? Tomorrow we're gonna meet up with them.

"Hand me the telephone, Monk, I gotta call the real estate lady that's gonna represent me at the auction sale of my farm this month." Bephino was handed the phone, and he began to dial long distance. After a few seconds of dialing, his eyes glanced easily around the room and finally settled on Ben, Mikey, and Monkey. Waiting for a pickup on the other end, he rolled his lips and smiled at the men watching him. The phone rang three times. The Realtor answered.

"Hello, is this Pat?" Bephino asked. "This is Mr. Menesiero, how's everything? Are the auctioneers finished listing all the merchandise on the farm? Don't forget the tractor and the pickup truck . . ."

"Mr. Menesiero!" Pat interrupted, "I'm so glad you called. You left without giving me a phone number."

"I'm sorry, Pat. At the moment I can't be reached. I'm on the road for a while."

"Mr. Menesiero, we had a terrible experience at your home today."

"What happened? What kind of terrible experience?" Bephino asked, his face paling.

"I don't know how to even begin to explain. I'm filled with tranquilizers and I'm still shaking."

"What happened, Pat? Tell me!" Ben and Monkey's eyes focused on Bepy; they both realized something was wrong. Mikey was out of the room for the moment.

The Realtor began to explain. "As you know, we were at your house yesterday and today, listing and tagging items to be auctioned off. John Sims and his wife, Donna, the auctioneers, were busy in the master bedroom tagging the lamps and fixtures when two men rushed into the house and killed them both. I mean shot them both dead! Harold and I were in the laundry room, inspecting the washer and dryer, because we thought maybe we could use them at our summer home.

Suddenly we heard shooting at the other end of the house. When we finally got the nerve to stick our heads out to look around, we saw two men running out the front doors to a car that was parked in the front of the circle drive, and John Sims and his wife were both shot in their heads. I can't believe this," Pat cried. "My God! They shot them four times in the back of the head. The police are looking for you, they want to speak to you."

Bephino stared into the phone.

"Mr. Menesiero, are you there?"

"Yes, I'm here, Pat. Tell the police I know nothin' of the shooting. I've been away on business. They should contact my attorneys—Higgins, Bell, and Flynn—in Savannah, for further details. I will be away on business for a while, and I'm not gonna be available until sometime in March. Tell the police to catch the bastards who did it, because they probably wanted to kill me and my wife."

"I know! That's precisely what the police said," Pat replied.

"Pat, lock up the house and take it off the market till you hear from me. I'm sorry about the incident. I feel terrible about the Sims people gettin' killed. Good-bye. I'll be in touch."

Surveying his friends, he slowly updated them. "Boretti hit my house. He had two hitters bust in the place. They killed the wrong people. They killed the auctioneer and his wife. Would you believe what's goin' on in my life? Two innocent people got killed for no reason at all. Rocco's goin' fuckin' crazy. Innocent people are dying. The rotten bastard's gotta pay for this. I knew he would try that. I smelled it, that's why I sent my family to Mexico. I knew he was gonna make a desperate move."

"You said it, Bep! You told me that the minute I got back from California," Monkey said.

"That rat bastard! He killed two fuckin' totally innocent people," Bephino continued. "The fuckin' auctioneer and his wife! Would you believe that shit? Two simple bastards, who hung around wearin' sneakers all day together. They didn't even look like me and Dana. They walked around wearin' jeans and tennis shoes, smiling at each other all day, like two country hicks. Christ! I feel terrible over this. Two innocent people killed!"

"I told you!" Ben shouted. "He's gotta die a horrible death! It's gotta be the fuckin' worst death anyone could imagine! Limbs we gotta remove—limbs, from that bastard!"

"My life is becomin' a fuckin' nightmare!" Bephino exclaimed. "That fuckin' bastard Rocco, he killed people right in my home . . ." Bephino looked up at the ceiling. After a moment or two he collected himself. "Let's get back to business," he said grimly. "We can't let what happened on the farm fuck up our heads; it's a shame two fine people had to die, but what can we do? All we can do is get these bastards as quick as possible. Boretti's death will be precisely timed. I promise you guys that it'll be right!" Bephino said with dead calm. "Tomorrow it's chop suey in Chinatown. Like I said, you and me, Monk, are meetin' with Bad Louie and his 'girlfriend,' Freddie Woo. I can't believe both these guys are nephews of our old friend, the late Jimmy Lee. They're both male cousins, and I hear they make it with each other."

"Yeah," Monkey replied, "and we better make a nice, strong impression on them, because they sound like they're both sick in the head."

The next day at noon, Bephino and Monkey entered the famous Golden Rice Bowl Cantonese Restaurant in Chinatown. The owner, Christy Soo Ling, a full-faced smiling Oriental woman in her early forties, greeted both men and escorted them to the bar where Bad Louie Young Chow and his troop were waiting. Introductions were cool and casual, everyone reluctantly shaking hands, keeping up the pretense. Freddie Woo blinked his false eyelashes coquettishly, then turned his head away when introduced. After a few moments the group was directed to a private dining area in the rear. Bad Louie acted as leader; his cousin and associate, Freddie the Woo Man, also seemed to command respect. Little Tommy ("Itchy Balls") Sing stood close by the Woo Man; Sammy Foo Wan and Billy the Kid Chan were also present. These men were the latest wild bunch of New York's Chinatown and the top capos of the Bad Louie Young Chow gang. Bad Louie, sly and tough-looking, did not smile, though he seemed casual and relaxed. Itchy Balls kept a hard, firm face. Billy the Kid Chan kept grinning; he was glad to meet Bephino and Monkey. Sammy Foo Wan kept picking his teeth. And Freddie Woo . . . well, he was definitely a horse of a different color. He wore his hair teased up in thin strands, puffed up wild and high. Large gold earrings dangled from both ears. Along with his pretty face, blue eye shadow, and pancake makeup, he chose to dress in full black leather. A weird, impatient smirk often crossed his face; a deadly glare flared lively in his eyes. All the Orientals moved like kung fu experts. Bephino rolled his eyes to Monkey over Freddie Woo, whose own piercing eyes picked up on it. Bephino pleasantly offered everyone a round of drinks. They all nodded to each other in the utmost refusal. Bephino then asked if they wanted to have some lunch.

At this, Freddie Woo screamed out, "Why you ask for meeting? We no eat with you, we no drink either; tell us what you want!"

Bephino cleared his throat and glanced at Monkey in surprise at Freddie Woo's outburst. He nervously scanned the group, settled momentarily on Bad Louie, then went back to Freddie Woo. Finally directing his reply to Bad Louie, Bephino took a deep breath and began. "As I told you, my name is Vito Torrelli, and my partner here is Joey Pantora. We both work for Angelo Marandala and Johnny Tortoricci. They got their social clubs over on Mulberry Street and Mott Street. Mr. Marandala and Mr. Tortoricci are both very important people. They want you to join them as friends in a war, an all-out takeover of New York." Bephino let the words sink in as he prayed the Orientals would take his bait.

Bad Louie's eyes opened wide, while Freddie Woo's expression changed from bad to worse. Both men seemed to be getting upset. "Why do you need us to win war?" Bad Louie demanded.

"Because we know you have bad blood with Rocco Boretti and our people also have bad blood with Mr. Boretti, so it's better for you to join with us against Mr. Boretti." Bephino hesitated, then said, "And if you don't join with these men in their war, they will take over Chinatown like in the old days. Remember Jimmy Lee," Bephino nodded, "your uncle. Well, he refused to cooperate, and he sings with the Chinese angels now."

The Orientals looked at one another and then began screeching loudly to each other simultaneously in Chinese. Sometimes it sounded as if they could be laughing, then suddenly as if they were crying and cursing. Bephino and Monkey's eyes flicked back and forth, then flashed at each other without expression. What had they done, Bephino wondered.

Freddie Woo screamed to them finally, "What name of club do these important men stay?"

Bephino thought for a moment, then said, "The Pal Eddy Social Club on Mulberry Street and the Red Eagle Social Club on Mott Street. Why?"

"How about the big Italian club on Elizabeth Street?" Freddie Woo asked.

"No, that one belongs to the old Sicilians. Them guys are not involved in this. They're all old people in that club. It's only Marandala and Tortoricci, they're the bosses that want you in with this thing."

"And so they the ones who killed our Uncle Jimmy Lee?" Freddie asked in a high-pitched voice. "Is that right?"

"Yeah, that's right!" Monkey snapped. "And if you guys are smart, you won't let that happen to you. A coupla weeks ago you lost two good men on the other side of Canal Street. So if I were you, I'd cooperate, and then you can keep your territory."

"Keep territory!" Freddy Woo screeched, his teased, sprayed hair standing up stiffly, his powdered face wry and fierce, his eyes deadly blue. "We keep our streets and we keep yours too," he said with a large, insincere smile. "You tell your big-shot Italians that we no help you in your war, we keep what we got and we kill every Italian that crosses the big street into Chinatown. And for the two people we lost to them last month, we will take out ten of their people this month," Freddie Woo sneered, looking to Bad Louie for acknowledgement.

Bad Louie smiled wisely at his men, then spoke quickly across the table to Freddie Woo. Freddie Woo replied to Louie in harsh, strange sounds. Then turning sharply to Monkey and Bephino, Bad Louie said calmly, "Don't be too confident in yourselves, my friends; you should be more unpredictable and wise when you ask to meet with me. I have carried the burden of revenge asleep in my heart for many years. The death of my Uncle Jimmy Lee and my grandfather, Chin Lee, who also died in the Dragon's Nest years ago at the murderous hands of you Italians, will be revenged!" At that moment the Chinese began to confer seriously among themselves. A few short moments later, Louie turned to Bephino. "Please be cooperative and follow us out the rear door through the kitchen. Please be relaxed and don't make unnecessary unpleasantness." Louie stared seriously. "You are being observed by three automatic pistols. Get up slowly and walk with us to backyard. We must make small impression on you."

"Hey, look fellas, we didn't come here to offend you—" Bephino said.

"Quiet! Please do not make terrible situation more terrible," Bad Louie interrupted.

Bephino glanced at Monkey, whose wide eyes signified they were in for it. Everyone got up and walked quietly through the Chinese kitchen. The busy cooks, dressed in white aprons, continued chopping precooked roast pork butts, keeping their faces down but watching the procession from the corners of their eyes, hanging onto their meat cleavers with passion and respect.

Once in the yard, Freddie Woo tossed his head, turned left, and hurried to a steel door at the rear of the building directly abutting the Golden Rice Bowl Restaurant. Freddie unlocked the steel door, turned, and spoke in staccato to the other three men, who were covering Bephino and Monkey with pistols. Suddenly the three men rushed forward and searched Bephino and Monkey for weapons. Finding none, they pushed Monkey face forward down the steps leading into a dark cellar. Freddie Woo lunged at Bephino and swiftly chopped at his chin with a nine-inch boning knife. When Bephino quickly grabbed at his chin, his hand came back full of blood with a half-inch hunk of flesh in it. It felt as if a dimple had been cut right from the bottom of his chin. "What was that for?" he asked Freddie Woo incredulously.

"I made a small impression on your face," Freddie replied. Bad Louie burst out laughing. The other men grabbed Bephino and sent him flying, also face forward, down the narrow open cellar steps. The steel door crashed closed. Bephino grabbed desperately at the dirty walls of the stairwell as he tumbled to the dark bottom, landing hard on the concrete floor. The place was pitch black. The only light seeping in came from a small, steel-barred window about head level at the far end of the room. Bephino and Monkey moved slowly, Bephino holding a handkerchief to his chin. Neither could see a thing; their eyes still had not adjusted to the sudden darkness.

"Holy Christ!" Monkey yelped, "what's that squealing sound? It sounds like rats!"

"Yeah, I hear them," Bephino answered. "Sounds like they're all over the place."

"There must be hundreds of them down here. Holy shit!" Monkey yelled. "They're on my feet. I'm stepping all over them. Holy Christ!"

"Just stay put, don't rouse them up any more than they are. I feel them too; maybe they'll calm down."

"I can't stand rats!" Monkey wailed. "I shake when I see a fuckin' mouse."

"I know, me too, I'd rather find three niggers under my bed than a fuckin' mouse. The thought of rodents turns my stomach. Let's keep still for a few minutes. Maybe they'll stop squealing at us. I hurt my leg falling down them stairs. It's beating like a drum," Bephino whispered.

"Them fuckin' chinks are mean bastards," Monkey complained. "Did you see the fuckin' crazy blue eyes on that Freddie Woo—he looks crazy, that bastard, he looks worse than Bad Louie. He's all made up like the Queen of Sheba. He's like a wild, painted woman with death in his eyes. I never saw a chink with blue eyes before. They say these fuckin' chinks chop heads off people. Whata ya think, Bep, ya think they'll go for our scalps?"

"Who the fuck knows? All I know is he just cut a fuckin'

hole outta my chin—I'm bleeding, I feel a piece of meat missing. My chin is bleeding bad. We gotta try to get outta here fast. Hey, Monk," Bephino whispered, "I feel a large thing nibbling on my feet, like a cat. Can you see it?"

"Yeah, it's as big as a fuckin' cat but it's a rat! God, is he big!" Monkey kicked hard at it. "Scat, you bastard!" he yelled. *"Scat!"*

"Soon as our eyes get used to the dark, we'll move around. But for the moment, let's stand still and be quiet," Bephino said, soaking up his blood with his handkerchief.

"Christ!" Monkey screamed. "Now something's nibbling on my leg. The rats are running over my shoes. I feel them. Bepy-y-y, get us out of here. I can't take this shit. Oh, God!"

"Stay calm, Monk, don't panic . . ." Bephino's voice echoed flatly off the thick cement walls of their tomb.

"God," Monkey yelped, "I can't, Bep, I can't help it, I can't take rats, they're all over the place. Look at 'em. Listen to the sounds they're making. I can see them now. There's thousands—look at them! They're crawling all over the place."

"I see them, it's unbelievable how big they are."

"I never dreamed there was a cellar like this still existing in New York City. Listen to them squeal, they're turning my stomach. It's like they're telling each other we're in here. I saw a movie like this one time with thousands of rats. But these are even bigger. Look at them over there. Bep, they're as big as cats. Let me see your chin, take that rag away," Monkey said. Monkey leaned forward and looked at Bephino's face. "You gotta fuckin' hole right at the bottom. What'd he *do* that for?"

"I don't know, he just grabbed me quick and chopped at me once. Come on, let's try that door, maybe they didn't lock it." Monkey quickly ran back up the stairway. He began pushing hard on the steel door but couldn't get it open. "They got it locked up tight!" he yelled.

Bephino walked up the stairwell. "Let's both push hard, maybe we can bust it open."

"How's your leg?" Monkey asked.

"It's OK. Come on now, let's both push hard; at the count of three, let's push all we got. One, two, *three.* It's shaking but it seems to be attached to a steel frame on the building. I see some daylight on the sides." Bephino turned and looked back down into the cellar. "Hey, Monk," he whispered, "there's a guy moving around in the darkness down there, see him? He's watching us. What the fuck is it, he looks small with a lot of long hair."

"I see him, but what the fuck is he doing down there?"

"I don't know, but look at him. He's circling us, waiting for us to come back downstairs. Listen, the rats are getting quiet all of a sudden. Keep your eyes trained on him; don't lose him. It seems like the rats are afraid of him. Listen how quiet it is now," Bephino said.

"Yeah," Monkey whispered, "all of a sudden they stopped squealing."

"Like they got respect for him," Bephino said, staring into the darkness.

"Maybe he eats them," Monkey whispered back, also staring into the darkness.

"He's coming closer to the staircase, Monk, he's crouching down like he wants to leap up at us. We better get ready; this bastard looks hungry."

"He's starting up the stairs—look at the fuckin' long hair on him! This bastard's nuts. What is he, a chink or what?" Monkey asked. "He smells like shit. I can smell him from here."

"He's small like a chink," Bephino whispered. "Look at him, he keeps coming closer, look at the fuckin' hair on this bastard. The motherfucker smells bad—God! He smells like a fuckin' goat. Monk, we better get ready. Let's kill him! It don't pay to fuck with him. He's probably eating all the rats, he must be nuts. We better punch his brains out."

"Holy shit, Bep, here he comes, he's gonna leap—Bep . . . Bep . . . Bep . . . he's got me by the throat, he's on my back!" Monkey and the thing fell tumbling down the stairs, causing the rodents to scream and squeal like a flock of crows. Bephino jumped down the steps, three at a time. "Help me, *help me!*" Monkey screamed. "He's chewing on my throat. I can't break him loose. I'm bleeding . . ."

Bephino grabbed the thing by his neck and tried to pull

him off Monkey. The thing was strong and turned himself around in Bephino's hands, then began chewing at Bephino's hands in the darkness like a wild dog. Bephino landed a sharp kick to the thing's throat and it began to sag to the floor. Stepping back, Bephino kicked hard at the beast, who growled in pain and rage. Monkey recovered and also began to kick. They both kept kicking until the hairy thing fell in a heap. They kicked at his head for a long time after, to make sure he was dead.

Two days later, the door of the cellar opened. The light from outside flashed down. Monkey and Bephino were half out of their minds. No food, no sleep, and they reeked with the dead man's wild odor. The dead Oriental lay off in a corner covered with hungry rodents. The stench was unbearable. Both men were weak, smelly, dirty, and covered with their own dry blood. At least the dead Chinaman's body seemed to occupy the rats and distracted them from Bepy and Monkey. The steel door remained open.

"Stay next to me, Monk, and don't make a sound," Bephino whispered. "We don't know what's next with these guys. Maybe they'll come in shooting at us. Stay quiet, let them make their move. The only thing we got going for us is the darkness; it's our only weapon. They can't see us but we'll be able to see them."

At that moment three gun-toting men appeared, dragging a man to the top of the stairs. They began kicking him down the stairwell into the dark hole below. The guy came tumbling down like a ton of bricks.

Monkey and Bephino stood in the darkness, quietly waiting for the man to get up. After a few minutes, the fellow began to rise. His image in the darkness looked familiar to both Monkey and Bephino. They watched for a while, then Bephino said, "Holy shit—Mikey, is that you?"

Mikey spun around. "Who's there?" he hollered.

"It's us, Bepy and Monkey. Whata ya doin' down here?"

"I was lookin' for you guys. I went to the Golden Rice Bowl

and asked the bartender if you'd been in there about two days ago. The next thing I knew, I got a gun in my back and they took me in a room and about five chinks attacked me. They even took my gun! What happened?" Mikey asked. "Why are we here—and what's runnin' around? What the fuck's that squealin' noise?" Mikey yelped.

"Rats!" Monkey yelled, "thousands of rats. We're livin' with rats the size of cats and small dogs! They're all over the place! We can't sleep, Mikey. They crawl on us when we're asleep! Then we were attacked by a crazy man livin' down here. We killed him. He's in the corner under them rats. We smell like him now; we touched him, we had to handle him. Now we stink like him. The rat bastard tried to *eat* me, Mikey. I'm all cut up. My neck is raw from his teeth. We looked all over this cellar for a way out, but it's all locked up, like a tomb. We found two piles of bones with skulls in the back corner. He musta ate them people."

"Where's Ben?" Bephino asked.

Mikey's bewildered eyes were still locked on the corner where the rats feasted on the dead man. Turning to Bephino, Mikey said, "He's over in New Jersey, at the house, waitin' for us. He's been waitin' for you to come back. He got kinda worried. He sent me to Chinatown to the restaurant to peep around. Oh, yeah! Listen to this! Mott Street is in a fuckin' turmoil. All hell broke loose yesterday in Little Italy. We thought you were involved in it.

"Eighteen guys got slaughtered including Angelo Marandala and Johnny Tortoricci. Both their clubs got bombarded last night by hit men with Uzis. It's all over the TV and in all the papers. They got blasted while playing cards. According to the TV, it was a mess down there. They showed the club rooms—bodies all over the place, heads on the floor. We thought you did it."

"Heads on the floor?" Monkey asked. "Whata ya mean, on the floor?"

Bephino looked up. "You gotta be kidding. It must of been Bad Louie and the Woo Man that made the kill. The chinks really went into Little Italy? Unbelievable," Bephino groaned.

"That's exactly what I was trying to get them to do! Attack Marandala and Tortoricci. I wanted them guys out of the way by using chinks. What I didn't figure on is that the fuckin' chinks would turn on us and cornhole us down here like this. They'll probably clip us too after we suffered enough. Or maybe they figured the madman living down here killed us already."

"Yeah, that's it," Monkey said. "They send people to their death in this cellar. That's why those skeletons are down here. They feed them to Toe-Jo." Mikey's eyes flashed around, looking for the skeletons.

"Whata ya looking for?" Monkey asked.

"Where's them skeletons you're talking about?" Mikey asked, his eyes still searching around.

"In the corner on the other end. They're in a pile. These chinks are bad," Monkey groaned to Mikey. "They're gonna kill us, Mike, I'm sure of it. They're bad, these bastards."

"So are we," Bephino sneered in the darkness, "so cut the shit, OK, because we're gonna kill them rotten bastards the first chance we get, just for kicks."

"Yeah, if we ever get out of here alive," Monkey whined.

Bephino shook his head disbelievingly. "The yellow bastards really killed Marandala and Tortoricci? Unbelievable! I'll tell you one thing, these chinks got no respect for nobody. They threw us down here like shit," Bephino said. "They didn't even think about it. Looks like they're tough, all right. I gotta say that for them."

"Yeah, and I thought we were gonna take something of importance from the chinks! You know, like their mothers or their girlfriends?" Monkey smirked. "Your plan sounded good until they fed us to these fuckin' rats."

Bephino looked coldly at Monkey. "This is bullshit, whatsa matter with you? No one's perfect, we can make a mistake, so we go on to the next thing. That's our only chance. You're always hopping on the shit we do wrong. We gotta get outta here before they come to see if Toe-Jo ate us up. Now that Mikey's here, maybe all three of us can pull the bars off the windows and crawl out." Bephino moved toward the little cellar window. "Look," he said, pointing to the steel bars.

"They go into the side of the building, into the brickwork. If we all pull together and yank hard, maybe we could make the bricks come loose and the bars will drop out. Then we could open the window that's farther beyond it and get the fuck out of here."

Mikey reached up and began to pull hard. "These fuckin' bars ain't budging," he said.

"OK, let's raise Monkey up. We hold him up and let him kick hard. Maybe something will happen. Let's try," Bephino said.

Several hours later, Monkey had kicked the last bar loose.

"OK, we're back in business!" Bephino yelled. "Let's climb out one by one and get back to the world."

"Unhinge the window, fast!" Monkey yelled.

"Hold it!" Mikey snapped. "Let's move easy-like, and hope we don't get blasted when we get up in the alleyway. Them guys were all packing 9mm automatics, even the fuckin' cooks have cleavers in their hands. Did you see them? They walk around the kitchen cutting up nothing, holding big meat cleavers."

"OK, I'll go first," Bephino said. "If they're out there, I'll tell you."

"Yeah, if you're still alive," Monkey warned.

Leading the way, then, Bephino was lifted up, and he climbed out into the alleyway. He heard the beautiful sound of car horns and people moving about the streets. His heart began to beat excitedly. He pulled up Monkey and Mikey, who followed quickly. All three were out of the cellar. An Oriental cook was standing about forty feet away by the Chinese restaurant's rear screen door. He seemed to be smoking. His back was toward them. Suddenly he must have heard something, because he turned his head and saw three men coming toward him. The Oriental quickly turned and jumped back into the kitchen of the Golden Rice Bowl. The three men began to run fast out of the alley into the busy streets of Chinatown.

"Oh, my God!" Monkey said about two blocks later, as they slowed down to a brisk walk. "Look at these beautiful, crowded streets. I thought we'd never get outta there. I never realized how much I loved the dirty streets of New York.

Listen to the cars, the horns, look at the people; they're beautiful. Them fuckin' rats, they made me sick. I'll never forget it."

"Let's get back to the house and regain our senses," Bephino said. "It's a good thing Mikey wound up with us, otherwise we'd never have gotten out. A fuckin' million-to-one and we win again," Bephino laughed.

"He's laughing, I'm still crying!" Monkey shouted. "I'm starving. We smell. We didn't eat for two and a half days. We smell like rats. Let's go get a pizza or something before we fall down."

"OK, let's cross on Mulberry Street—see Bella Pizza over there? That's Nicky Polumbo's place. Let's wash up in Nicky's bathroom. We gotta wash this blood off us. Your neck, Monk, needs cleaning. There's dark, dry blood caked on it. After we clean up, we'll call Ben to tell him we're OK, then we'll eat."

Later, devouring a pizza, the three men were quiet. They'd washed up and by now felt more comfortable as they sat in a corner booth. Mikey asked Bephino, "What happened to your chin, you got a hole in it?"

"That fuckin' crazy bastard Freddie Woo jumped me and chopped my face with a fuckin' boning blade."

"You look like that movie actor now," Mikey laughed.

The men lapsed into silence once again. They did not want to speak or think about the rats or the thing they had had to kill, or the horrible smell still wedged in their noses and on their clothes. Monkey ate with a most unusual expression on his face.

"Nothing tastes right," he said. "I keep smelling Toe-Jo, and thinking of that little rat bastard biting into my neck. A fuckin' Chinese Dracula." Monkey said. "What a nightmare!"

"You're right, I'm having my own little nightmare. It's been a fuckin' bad year," Bephino said, looking at his men. "First I'm in a coma, then I'm in a wheelchair for a few months, then I gotta eat like a horse to gain seventy pounds. My family's worried stiff about me and I have to send them away to Mexico, they're all wondering what I'm doing. I had to move outta my beautiful farm to keep my family alive. I loved that farm. I was so happy living there. It was a dream come true for me. Boretti put me on the run. Alley Oop's kid got killed because of me. Ben's a fuckin' cripple because of me. Everything's going wrong, my destiny is on the wrong track. Sometimes I wonder, was it all worth it? It's all going down the drain sure as shit, it's going down right before my eyes. Emilio Morrano tipped me off before he died. He said, 'Follow your destiny.' If I turn and run after all this has happened to me, what kind of man would I be?" Bephino asked his friends.

"I'd say you were a smart man," Monkey said, sipping his beer and looking at Bephino. "It might be worth it to fuck everything and retire in California or Mexico. It's only a matter of time before they knock us off. In this business nobody lives to retire. You got a short shelf-life in this racket."

Bephino stared for a long moment, then breathed out. "I figured the chinks right, up to a certain point. I fed them the bait, about the boys wanting their help against Boretti. I figured out whether they would join us in a phony war or whether they'd act on their own and go after Marandala. And I was right; they acted on their own and killed two of the most powerful enemies we have. They saved us a lot of work. The only thing I never figured on was them throwing us to the rats. What a nightmare; nobody would ever believe this story."

"So now we're back to square one," Monkey said. "Now we gotta hit the chinks to get even for what they did to us. We were better off doing our own work and clipping Marandala ourself. If you wanna know the truth," Monkey glared, "I would have rather dealt with Marandala and the other scumbag ourselves. At least we know what to expect from Italians; the chinks are full of mean fuckin' tricks. It's like being in Vietnam; if you get captured they don't kill you, they serve you to rodents the rest of your life. Me, I'd rather die than live like that."

"Don't worry," Bephino warned, "after we take control, we're gonna turn our thoughts to those two maniacs, Bad Louie and Freddie Woo, that sick-looking bastard. They're gonna live with all our men sleeping on their doorsteps. I want our people to earn," Bephino said. "They haven't been active for a long time. We gotta give them an incentive, let them earn when they kill."

"Whata ya mean, take control?" Monkey asked. "I thought we were gonna retire out of New York."

Bephino turned to Mikey. "Tell me, Mikey, I wanna hear the details of the attacks on Marandala and Tortoricci's clubs. How'd the chinks make the hit, and how did the police know they were chinks?"

"You mean slaughter, not hit," Mikey said. "It was a fuckin' slaughter. They killed everyone. The chinks who done the damage wore ski masks. They ran into Marandala's club while the guys were relaxing and playing cards. First they shot a few guys; then, to make a good impression, one guy with a fuckin' long blade went from table to table and decapitated three or four guys' heads. The exact same thing was going on at the same time over on Mott Street at Tortoricci's place, guys were losing their heads. The papers say the hit men were small guys, about five-foot-five, but no one lived to really describe them. The police say it must have been Bad Louie Young Chow, but they really don't know; they got no proof, because at that time he was supposed to be having dinner at the Rice Bowl with Christy."

"Would you believe they got away on foot—like deer they ran. No cars were used because the traffic moves so slow in Little Italy. They had to be chinks," Mikey said.

Bephino frowned. "It was Bad Louie and the Woo Man, no doubt about it. We know because we were next in line to be decapitated if that animal didn't eat us; they were gonna take our heads. There's no doubt in my mind about that anymore. Them chinks know the streets like the alley cats know it, and Woo Man is known to chop off heads. But, I wonder, why didn't they kill us right away?" Bephino sat thoughtfully for a moment. Then he said softly, "Maybe they wanted to make us know their capabilities. It's probably their way of making an impression on us. The Chinese have strange ways, it's hard to figure them out.

"Well," he announced with a sigh, "now that Gaeta, Marandala, and Tortoricci are dead, we only got Boretti and Tony Boy Cafaci and that DePasquale guy from Bath Beach to deal with." Bephino took a slug of beer.

"Your Chinese scheme worked halfway," Monkey said. "Now whata ya gonna do, go to Spanish Harlem and wind up in the Puerto Rican's banana cellar for a few more days?" Monkey began to laugh heartily at Mikey and Bephino.

Bephino snapped back at him. "Stop laughin'! You look like a fuckin' ape when you laugh like that." Monkey's face changed. "I was wrong, I admit it. We can't deal with these kind of people. I know it now. It was a big mistake. We gotta go it alone. We'll only take out the dons, maybe a few capos. Then we'll turn all our people loose in the city, clippin' soldiers left and right. Then we make a stand in Little Italy and see if we get respect. As a matter of fact, startin' tomorrow, all our soldiers go to the mattress. Fuck it, let's do it! Tell them to start knockin' off any of the five families' soldiers they run into—any of them. The fat lady's gonna sing again in New York City! It's open war as of tomorrow. Give our men a ten-thousand-dollar bonus for every capo they take out. I want action! Five thousand for buttons, and twenty thousand each on Bad Louie and Freddie Woo's fuckin' heads. I want them Chinese bastards dead in ten days. Let our boys earn the money we were gonna give to the Puerto Ricans and the chinks, right? So we pay the boys well! It's worth it," Bephino said. "I won't be wrong this time—and don't forget we gotta contact Gaeta's man, Nimo. He owes us a hundred grand for the European hit. Nimo was supposed to be holdin' the cash. We'll make him pay up before we kill him. We're gonna settle our accounts with everyone. Next year this time, New York's gonna be a swell place to live. People are gonna have respect for one another again. Maybe we'll even buy a condo on Long Island." Bephino grinned at Monkey. "Ya want a condo, Monkey?" Bephino winked at his childhood friend.

"Yeah, in L.A.," Monkey winked back.

10

THANKSGIVING DAY, NOVEMBER 26, 1978, 12:30 P.M.

FORT LEE, NEW JERSEY

"Hello, Alan, are you people up? Bephino laughed into the phone.

"Bepy! Yes, we're all up. We're sittin' around the patio by the pool. We just finished breakfast. Bep, you should be here with us! Cancun is so beautiful, every day it's eighty degrees. Why don't you forget what you're doin' and fly here? Give the schmucks New York! Let 'em have it all. Fuck 'em," Alan said, speaking closely into the phone. "I've been seein' it via satellite TV. It sounds horrible over there. Let 'em all drop dead. Get outta there! They should keep New York, they deserve it!" Alan said.

"It's work that's gotta be done. We have no choice at the moment," Bephino replied. "How's Dana and the kids?"

"Fine! Everyone's fine. They're bein' looked after by me, you shouldn't worry."

"I know, Alan. That's why you're there, so I shouldn't worry," Bephino laughed at Alan. "Let me speak to Dana. I'll see you soon, Alan. Stay well, my friend."

"Hold on for Dana! Stay well yourself," Alan whispered.

"Bepy?"

"Yeah, baby. How's everything?"

"Everything's OK. How are you doin'?"

"I'm OK, honey. No problem, everything's fine."

"Are you eatin' OK?"

"Of course I'm eatin'! I had a calzone last night. It must of weighed ten pounds. Don't worry, I'm fine. I'll be with you for New Year's. I already got my plane tickets. I'm takin' the Mexican airline out of Kennedy on New Year's Eve."

"Why can't you come for Christmas? The kids want you here for Christmas. Last year they spent the entire holidays without you. . . ."

"Dana, I can't be there for Christmas, so forget it. Explain that to the kids. And Dana, listen: Don't let the kids leave that location—under any circumstances! Don't let 'em come back to the States until I say so. It's important, OK?"

"Bephino, whata ya doin' on Christmas Eve all alone? When is this all gonna end? You're sellin' the farm, now where do we go? Whata ya gonna do with our lives? Tell me! I wanna know!"

"Don't worry, OK? Everything will be fine. Just stay put. I need a little more time. Christmas Eve I'm booked solid; I'm gonna sing Christmas carols to an old friend. I promise you, this will be the last holiday we'll ever be apart."

"Then will you call it quits?"

"Yes."

"I love you, Bephino! I miss you. I had a rough two years."

"I know, honey. Just take care of the kids. I'll be with you for New Year's, I promise. Say good-bye to Alan for me. Tell him I'll be in touch. Kiss the kids for me, and tell Peggy and

Mrs. Roselli that Ben's fine. Ben and I will both be there for New Year's. Take care, Dana! I gotta go."

Bephino, Monkey, Ben, and Mikey were sitting around two hours later, reading the newspapers and watching the football game.

"Where we gonna eat?" Mikey asked. "It's Thanksgivin' today, or doesn't anybody give a fuck?"

"We're gonna eat in Little Italy, at Casa Bernado, on Elizabeth Street," Bepy said.

Monkey propped himself up. "Are ya nuts? All the wise guys downtown are gonna see us. The word's gonna spread like wildfire that we four are in town. And the FBI's got everybody under surveillance since Pauli's funeral and Gaeta's funeral. I hear the good guys and the bad guys are goin' nuts lookin' for us. If we go to Little Italy, they're gonna pick up our tail again."

"No shit!" Bephino shouted. "Then they'll all know we don't give a fuck for any of 'em, includin' the FBI."

Monkey looked over to Ben and asked, "Do you agree with what he's doin'?"

"Yep," Ben answered. "Are you ready to go eat, Bep?" Ben asked, looking over at Bephino.

" 'Are you ready, Bep?' " Monkey mimicked Ben's question. "You fuckin' guys are nuts!"

Bephino smirked, "Get yourselves ready for dinner. First, we're makin' a short trip to Bay Ridge," he said. "Let's go, Monkey, get yourself ready. I'm gettin' hungry," Bephino smiled. "I want the word to get out to Boretti we ate like men in Little Italy after we blew away his goombada, so he knows what to expect from us."

"Why we stoppin' in Bay Ridge?" Mikey asked. "It's shorter if we take the Holland Tunnel straight over to Little Italy."

"We're gonna stop and clip that fuckin' big-bellied bastard Tony Boy. I'm gonna do it this afternoon. His day has come. Would ya believe I heard he was actually present when they killed Alley Oop's kid. Petey Lumps told Blubberhead that

Tony Boy, the fuckin' animal that he is, was watchin' the kid Alley bein' killed and cut up. Imagine that, a fuckin' don doin' such a thing to a kid! So I decided I wanna hit him today while he and his family are enjoyin' Thanksgivin'!"

"You're gonna do it in front of his family?" Monkey asked.

"What about Alley Boy's family?" Bephino replied. "Did Tony Boy give a fuck for the kid's family? Tony is goin' today, with the drumstick up his ass, not in his belly," Bephino said bitterly. "Let's get ourselves dressed for dinner. Let's look sharp for the people in Little Italy. I wanna make an impression on them. Let's go, sad sack, say a prayer for Tony Boy," Bephino said, pushing at Monkey, "because Tony Boy is on his way to the Promised Land!" Bephino nodded to the men.

"The FBI is tryin'a tail ya, and you're gonna make a hit on Thanksgivin' Day!" Monkey grumbled as he headed for his bedroom.

"Casa Bernado got good food," Mikey said, walking alongside Monkey. "The pasta fuzilli is fantastic."

At 4:30 P.M., a black four-door Chrysler driven by Monkey pulled up slowly in front of Tony Boy Cafaci's home on Cropsey Avenue, Brooklyn. Bephino checked out the area and opened the car door. "Park around the corner," he said. "I'll be right back."

"Where ya goin' alone?" Ben asked. "Take Mikey with ya. Suppose ya run into trouble, suppose people see ya? Suppose he's got people in there with him?"

"Just park the car right there, off the corner. I'll be back in a few minutes. I gotta do this myself, for Alley Oop's sake." Bephino hopped out of the car. The Brooklyn streets were as quiet as a Sunday afternoon, when everyone's home having their Sunday dinner and watching the games. Bephino knew holidays in Brooklyn were usually quiet, so it could be a good time to take out Tony Boy. Bephino walked up to the front door of the Cafaci home, slipped on a pair of cheap cotton work gloves, opened the front door to the two-family home, and entered the vestibule. He then rang the inner doorbell and waited until he heard heavy footsteps coming toward the glass-paneled wooden door. Bephino stepped to the side.

"Who is it?" a man asked, sounding as if he had food in his mouth.

"It's me, Nimo. I gotta talk to Tony Boy."

"Nimo who?"

"Nimo Guiliano. I work for Gaeta's people. I'm from the Bronx. Tony knows who I am. Tell him it's important!" Then Bephino asked, "Who are you?"

"I'm Julio, Tony's brother-in-law," the guy answered from behind the closed glass-paneled door, chewing hard. "Wait a minute, I'll tell 'im ya here."

"Thanks," Bephino said in a strong-sounding voice, at the same time reaching into his coat pocket and taking out a 9mm automatic pistol with a silencer attached to the end.

A few moments later, Bephino heard another set of footsteps approaching the door again. He stepped farther to the side and stretched out his arm. The door opened and Tony Boy asked, "Nimo?"

Bephino didn't answer. He hugged the wall. Tony, wearing a sleeveless white summer T-shirt, leaned forward cautiously, so that just his head protruded out the glass-paneled door about five inches. "Nimo!" he called out softly. Bephino had the tip of the silencer at ear level. He watched Tony's baldness peek out curiously, slowly leaning forward, extending farther and farther through the doorway, inch by inch. When Bephino saw enough meat, he pulled the trigger two times quickly. Tony caught both slugs just above the temple. The big man fell forward heavily on the tiled vestibule floor, completely blocking the vestibule's exterior door. Bephino was blocked in, unable to pull the door back inside the small room for his exit. Hopping over Tony's big belly, Bephino proceeded to pull at the door, but Tony's huge, dead body would not budge. Bephino nervously looked back into the house and saw people far off in the rear rooms talking loudly and sitting around a table at the far end of the dining room. The noise from the people's laughter and the loud football game on TV must have covered Bephino's activity. He began to roll the body to one side, holding it back with his left foot just enough to get the door open about twelve inches for him to squeeze out. Reaching the outside air, Bephino slipped the warm pistol back in his coat pocket, removed the work gloves, looked around briefly, took a few deep breaths, and made his way to the parked car waiting for him. Looking back over his shoulder he then climbed into the backseat and the car pulled out.

"How'd you make out?" Ben asked. Bephino didn't answer, but turned and looked back once again as the car drove away heading toward the Belt Parkway north for the Lower East Side of Manhattan. Ben asked again, "How'd you do?"

Bephino, exhausted, rested his head to his left side and stared straight ahead. "Tony Cafaci can't dismember any more kids, that's for sure," he whispered. Those in the car exchanged looks, but did not speak any further. During the ride the car went along the highway and over the Brooklyn Bridge towards the city. Bephino dozed off. All was quiet, when suddenly Bephino began to mumble, "How was I supposed to know? . . . How would I know that?" seemingly still in his sleep. Monkey and Mikey turned to the backseat where Bephino sat slumped, his eyes closed. Ben shook Bephino.

"Wake up, Bepy!" Ben said. Bephino's eyes opened; he seemed dazed. He began to sit up and shake his head. "You were yelling," Ben said. Bephino rubbed his face.

"I was dreaming of Alley Oop like he was alive and real. He was mad about his son getting killed. I was trying to explain to him. How was I supposed to know they would do such a thing to the kid, I told him." Everyone exchanged glances. Obviously, Bepy was still suffering greatly over Alley Boy, perhaps more than they thought.

Upon arriving on Elizabeth Street, the four well-dressed men entered the Casa Bernado Italian restaurant. The maître d' immediately recognized them, and he began bobbing up and down, showing respect. They were smoothly, smilingly escorted to a large round table in the rear. The restaurant patrons began eyeballing and whispering over the four new arrivals. Heads turned and eyes signaled from table to table that these were top-echelon Mafia bosses. After a few minutes, the owner, Salvatore Bernado, a seemingly nervous man, came out and embraced Bephino Menesiero. They laughed and talked about their families being Sicilians from the Old Country. Elizabeth Street, the original, traditional Sicilian territory in New York, had been known to rear some of the toughest Mafia bosses that ever reigned over New York.

The men all ordered the homemade fuzilli pasta and breast of veal stuffed with ricotta cheese. "Does it feel like Thanksgiving to you?" Mikey asked, buttering up a piece of bread and looking around for a reply. No one answered Mikey's question. They just grinned slightly at one another while avoiding eye contact with any other patrons of the house.

During dinner Bephino leaned over and whispered to Mikey, "I want you to take out Frankie DePasquale soon as possible—next week, at the latest. He lives on Bath Avenue with that divorcée, Kitty, the one with the big knockers that was caught humping a delivery boy in her neighborhood, remember, by her husband, Joe, the pork store guy. He's got the store over on Avenue U."

Mikey was thinking.

"I'm sure you guys remember her, Mike; she always wore them tight clothes?" Bephino smiled.

"Yeah, I remember hearing of her from Lil Pauli. I never saw her, but I heard of her—big, sexy ass, big tits. As a matter of fact," Mikey grinned, "that's the broad that was crazy over Lil Pauli at one time. Pauli got into her pants before Frankie DePasquale grabbed her."

"Is that right?" Bephino asked. "I never knew Pauli had her."

"Pauli had 'em all," Mikey grinned, "from Bath Beach to DeKalb Avenue—even the niggers and the spicks from Fulton Street, if they were knockouts. Pauli sniffed them out and banged them."

Bephino scratched his neck as he thought about Lil Pauli. "DePasquale lives with her now. He watches her like a hawk, so be careful, Mike. Keep an eye on her and you'll get DePasquale with his head up her fat ass," Bephino said. "I want DePasquale out as soon as possible; he's a definite threat to us. He's Tony Boy Cafaci's brother-in-law, and he's bad people. I want all bad people in coffins before the end of this year. We're gonna start the New Year nice this time," Bephino whispered.

"How about Boretti?" Mikey whispered back. Ben's eyes

looked up from his plate to focus on Bephino and hear of Boretti's fate.

"Maybe I'm gonna take care of him personally," Bephino replied in a low voice. "I'm not sure about him yet. I gotta think of something pretty for Rocco. . . . Yeah, I gotta give that one some special thought, Ben," Bephino replied. "Maybe we'll do it all together on Christmas, somethin' nice and Christmasy," Bephino smiled. "He's gonna be the hardest to get to, since his donkey buddies are all gone. He don't go to the club much anymore. He stays outta sight now. I understand he keeps good strong people around him. The only time he may be alone with his family could be Christmas Eve. I'm thinkin' on it. In any case, however which way we go with it, Rocco Boretti will be checked out by Christmas Day, because Ben and I gotta leave for Mexico to see our wives and my kids later that week. I wanna be with my family for New Year's. Oh, yeah, I got two extra plane tickets for Mexico," Bephino grinned. "You two guys wanna come with us?"

"Does a duck like water?" Mikey asked. "Of course we wanna be with you. Whata we gonna do hangin' around New York, wave hankies at all the funeral processions?"

"OK, great! We'll go to Mexico together for New Year's. We start the New Year right! We'll all get the fuck away from the bullshit."

Mikey suddenly looked at Bephino. "Whata ya gonna do about Rocco's kid, Carmine?" he whispered. Leaning closely over the table, Mike whispered, "If Rocco checks out, the kid's gonna keep comin' at us. No question about it, the kid's gonna come."

"That's what I already told him," Ben said, agreeing with Mikey. "I told him the kid's already got three scalps hangin' on his belt. We should take him out of his fuckin' misery now, while we're givin' the attention to his father." Ben nodded reassuringly over his own suggestion.

Monkey also nodded in agreement. "I agree with Ben and Mikey, Carmine is a crazy kid. He'll always be a threat to us. He'll never lay down and roll over. He's too close to his father. He's gonna go nuts. He should be put to sleep now, perhaps even first. While we're workin' on one, we do the other. Then we can have clear heads for a while."

"He's so young," Bephino hissed. "I know you're right, he should be eliminated, but it really hurts me to wipe out the kids. I knew Carmine when he wore short pants. I always admired that boy! He was always tough. Givin' him the attention at this point in his young life is hard for me to swallow. It's somethin' I never thought I would have to do in my life. We got time, we'll think about it," Bephino said.

"It's gotta be done, so just do it," Ben insisted to Bephino. But Bephino just stared, he did not reply.

Later on, when dinner was over, the waiter came over singing an Italian song to the four men. He carried a tray of pastries and a pot of Italian coffee. Everyone gave the waiter center stage and enjoyed the humorous singing. Finally the waiter left.

"Mikey," Ben whispered, nodding, "when you go pay respect to DePasquale, you better be careful. DePasquale's been number one in New York since Bephino Menesiero. He's an unbelievable hitter. I hear they pay him big bucks, so big they had to make him; they gave him a button and his own crew. He's a made man now."

"That's why he's gotta get our attention right away," Bephino said with emphasis. "I know all about Frankie since he was a Young Turk in Williamsburg. He's bad, no question about it. He'll always be a threat to us. And that reminds me: That short bastard Nimo Guiliano keeps comin' to my mind. He's holdin' that hundred grand for our services on the European caper. Let's collect our money and do him in the next few days. We'll take the cash to Mexico for play money. Nimo musta thought I forgot the fee, or else he's prayin' we forgot, or hopin' we get knocked off so he can pocket it."

"If Frankie DePasquale is so good, why didn't the commission send him to Europe to see the prince instead of Bepy?" Monkey asked the table in a whisper.

"Because he's Tony's brother-in-law," Ben answered in a low voice. "DePasquale is Cafaci's wife's maiden name. He's her brother. Like Bepy said, he originally comes from Williamsburg, and Cafaci brought him to Bensonhurst. The guy is good, he's young and fearless," Ben said, widening his eyes. "He's just as good as any of us—maybe better. You better be careful, Mike, he's got a very bad crew behind him. They're all trigger-happy. They hang out near Cropsey Avenue by the Italian club."

"Tony Boy's old club," Bephino said. "I think they call it the Cropsey Club. I used to stop in to pay my respects to Tony when I was a kid. I was always trying to pick up a certain job or some work that had to be done from the big guys. But Emilio Morrano was the only guy who gave me work; Tony Boy would chase me."

Mikey watched everybody's face. "If DePasquale is that bad, I gotta make it real exotic, something nice for him. Maybe I'll stick a carrot up his ass and leave it hanging out. That should make a good impression on the world, wouldn't you say?" Mikey grinned.

Bephino merely nodded. "You know, Mikey," Bephino grinned, "fall weather in New York was always something special to me. I remember when I was a kid I used to watch the fruit-store guys making their displays of apples, California navel oranges, peppers, eggplants, mushrooms, walnuts . . ." Then looking at Monkey and Ben, he said seriously, "Everything smelled like fall season. It was so colorful. The red wine-grapes were being delivered to the old winemakers in the neighborhood. What a smell of fresh wood and grapes! I used to help carry the wood boxes down to the cellars, and there were always chestnuts roasting on the outside flames. It was so beautiful when we were kids."

"Yeah," Monkey said. "How about the sweet-potato man coming with the roasting oven and selling sweet potatoes for only a nickel apiece?"

"Yeah," Mikey joined in. "He used to yell out in the streets, *Garbede garbe!* Remember?" Mikey grinned. *"Garbede garbe!"*

"And when fall began it always made itself known, like right now," Bephino said, looking around the table. "Like today, Thanksgiving Day, the streets are loaded with garbage from the week's business, but for some reason the cold, brisk air blowing in blankets New York's foul odor and gives it a unique smell. I only smell the cooking in Little Italy. The fresh fish being sold by the chinks, the fresh cheeses hanging in all the pork stores, the salamis curing from the rafters, and the provolone cheese being cut by the pound."

"How about the sweet smell from the pastry shops?" Monkey asked.

"Yeah, that's what I mean. The pastry shops, everything, smells so beautiful in New York in the winter months."

Monkey's eyes darted around the table as he realized Bephino's words were rooting themselves in a plan.

Ben, seeing Monkey's face drop at Bephino's words, quickly changed the subject. "Be careful, Mike," Ben warned, "Bephino makes a lot of sense. It's wintertime; everything smells nice. People like Frankie DePasquale sleep later in the wintertime. He's lying in bed with that sweet-smelling puttana, fucking her brains out. I understand she's a real nymph, can't resist sex, but I also hear that if anybody even looks at her, DePasquale goes botzo and then he's all over the guy's ass. So be careful, OK?" Ben said.

"Yeah, I'll be careful. I'll make a plan to fit DePasquale's day, and when he rises the carrot goes in; then his day ends, and so does the problem. Consider him a fucking corpse," Mikey assured him confidently.

Bephino grinned at Mikey, then at Ben and Monkey and whispered, "Come on, friends, let's go home; we ate enough. Thanksgiving is over, there's a good football game going on tonight. Mikey can handle it. He's been doing it longer than Frankie. Oh, yeah! That reminds me," Bephino said. "We gotta discuss Freddie the Woo Man and Bad Louie. Them two chinks I also got on my mind. They're still walking, and I wanna turn every available guy we got loose in their direction soon as possible. I want everyone directed at them two bastards; I wanna hit them in their cribs when they're in each other's arms. Let's make sure we get around to Freddie Woo," Bephino said, shaking his head and holding his now dimpled chin. "I'm really gonna think about him for a long time. Even when he's dead. Them bastards really gotta pay for feeding us to rats; I keep dreaming of that fuckin' cellar."

"*You* keep dreamin'!" Monkey said. "You should sleep with me in my bed. I scream all night long, I wake myself up from it. 'They're all over me!' I wake myself up yelling. That's how loud I scream," Monkey grimaced.

Two days later at 9:30 A.M., Mikey drove by the Cropsey Avenue Social Club. He continued around the neighborhood streets to Bath Avenue by Bay 58th Street and back again to Cropsey. After a few spins, he spotted Frankie DePasquale in the street being picked up by a driver in front of his two-family apartment house on Bath Avenue. Mikey eyed up the house and parked down the street on the other side. He walked along the avenue looking in store windows, then crossed over and ducked into the building that Pasquale had left from. He studied the buzzers. One read EUGENE RAFFALINO, first floor; the other read KITTY GEMA, second floor. He pressed Gema's buzzer and shortly a buzz back allowed the vestibule door to open. Mikey swiftly moved toward the stairs. A dark-haired woman in a nightgown appeared at the top of the stairs holding a man's terry-cloth bathrobe in front of her to block the caller's view. "Frankie, is that you?" she asked.

"It's me, Tommy White," Mikey said, hustling quickly up the stairs. Reaching the landing in a few seconds, Mikey hissed excitedly. "I work for DePasquale. He just told me to stay with you for a while; there may be trouble in the neighborhood today." Kitty was caught sleepy-eyed and off guard.

"I thought you were Frankie," she mumbled, rubbing her eyes. "I thought he was coming back for something. He just left," she said, her eyes focusing on Mikey's face. She finally noticed Mikey's strong, dark, neat face, his dark, wavy hair and black, piercing eyes. Mikey stared at her beauty. "What do you want?" she asked. "Frankie would never send a man like you to stay with me." Mikey quickly grabbed her robe from her and pointed his gun at her face. Then, grabbing her, he laid his powerful right hand on her soft, delicate white neck and squeezed her throat. She was scared and slow to move away.

"You're hurting me," she groaned. Mikey squeezed her harder and held her tighter. Every time she tried to speak he held her tighter until her eyes began to bulge and her voice disappeared. Slowly her tongue dropped out of her mouth and hung there, rendering her totally speechless. Mikey was strong; with one hand he easily moved her back into her apartment and closed the door behind them with his foot. She was a tall, large-breasted beauty and Mikey could see her voluptuous body through the nearly sheer nightgown. Under it she was completely naked. Mikey looked her over, then whispered, "I'll let your neck go, but if you make one sound I'll kill you quick. Understand?" he said harshly, close up to her face. Kitty nodded, her tongue now drooling and still hanging out of her head. Mikey eased his hold but raised his silencer-tipped automatic to her chin.

"Don't be smart, understand, bitch, because I'll pump you full of bullets if you do the wrong thing. Now wipe your fuckin' mouth, you're all wet," he ordered.

"What do you want here?" she whispered to him, rubbing her neck and then reaching for the man's robe to dry her mouth.

"I want Frankie. When will he be back? And be truthful, bitch, because believe me, I'll snap your fuckin' neck if you say one thing that don't jive."

"Frankie went to his sister's house. Someone killed his brother-in-law two days ago on Thanksgivin' Day. They're layin' him out today on Bay Parkway. Frankie just left; he went over there to see if he could be of help to his sister and her kids. They're goin' nuts over at the sister's house. Someone killed him while he and his family were all eatin' dinner."

"What time will he be back?"

"He should be home by five," she said, still rubbing her neck. "He's comin' to pick me up at five o'clock for dinner, then we're goin' to the funeral parlor later tonight to pay our respects."

"What's the chance of him comin' home early?"

"There's always that chance, you never know with Frankie," she said, flinching her shoulders. "You really hurt me, you know that?" she said, touching her throat. "My neck is still hurtin'."

"Does he come alone or with people; answer my questions," Mikey growled.

"Sometimes he comes with Teddy Tangello, his driver."

"Anyone else?"

"No, usually only Teddy."

"Are they packin'?"

"Only Teddy carries a gun. Frankie's still on parole. He can't take the chance of carryin' one."

"There any guns up here?"

"There's one in the left nightstand in the bedroom and two in a shoe box in the closet. He only carries a gun if he's got work to do."

"OK. So far you're doin' good. If you continue to be a smart girl and cooperate, you're gonna be around tomorrow. If not, I'll twist your fuckin' neck off that beautiful body, and you can leave Brooklyn in a box with Frankie today."

"Are you gonna kill him?"

"You can forget about him as of right now. Today his life is *finito.* Don't even waste your time thinkin' about him; he's a fuckin' corpse. Now sit over here on the couch and be quiet and don't move. I'd rather not hurt you, so don't make me, *a capisce*?" Kitty stared silently into space. "If your phone rings, be cool; don't fuck up, because the guy on the other end goes on living and you lose your face to a bullet, *a capisce*?" Mikey nervously repeated while peeking out the window.

"I *capisce.* Can I at least wash my face and brush my teeth? I just got out of bed, I feel messy. I wanna place a hot towel on my neck, maybe it'll feel better."

"OK, but I'm staying with you. So don't fuck up; you're too beautiful to wind up without a face."

Kitty moved into the bathroom, lowered her nightgown to her waist, exposing her large, plump breasts, and began to wash her face and neck. Drying off, she raised her nightgown back up. Mikey stared at the half-naked woman so calmly exposing herself. She then began to brush her teeth. Drying her face, she asked, "I gotta use the bowl, can you wait outside?"

Mikey thought for a moment and then asked, "Whata ya gotta do?"

"I gotta sit!" she whined. Mikey looked around the bathroom, opened the vanity cabinets, then a few drawers.

"All right, go ahead and sit, but I'm staying outside, and the door stays open. So whatever you gotta do, do it fast."

After a few minutes she reappeared in the bathroom doorway, a relieved look on her face. Her hair was combed neatly, her mouth was fresh and clean. She held a hot wet towel to her neck. "Can I put some clothes on?" she asked. "I'm half naked in this see-through nightgown."

"No, stay the way you are, you look fine. Sit down on the couch and stay put."

"But I'm half naked, you could see me."

"Tough shit! Sit over there and shut your ass, don't mess with my head if ya know what's good for ya." Mikey glared convincingly at her.

Kitty moved quietly across the room and sat down. "Can I at least make a pot of coffee?" she asked. Mikey went to the window and peeked out. His eyes flashed back at Kitty, but he did not answer her. After a few minutes, he sat in a comfortable sofa-chair opposite Kitty. "Can I make some coffee?" she asked again.

"No, I didn't come here for coffee. Just sit there and be quiet."

They both stared at each other until she finally turned away. "Why can't you do your business away from my home? Why do you do it over here?" she complained.

"Hey, look lady! If I was you I'd keep my fuckin' mouth shut and hope to God you live through this, OK? Because if you turn me off, you're gonna be stretched out tomorrow over at Bay Parkway in a his-and-hers box. You be nice, lady, because I'm not a man with patience." After about twenty minutes Mikey moved to the couch and sat next to her. Kitty looked away toward the window. "You're a pretty broad, you know that? Whata ya, Jewish?"

She turned and half grinned. "No, I'm not Jewish, I'm Italian. Why do you think I'm Jewish?"

"I don't know. I thought maybe you married Joe Gema, the

pork store guy, for his dough, and then when he caught you fuckin' around, you ran to Frankie DePasquale for protection." Mikey raised his eyebrows at her. "You're built like a Jew, you got nice big breasts, you gotta nose job. You're well kept for your age," Mikey said, moving his mouth around his thoughts.

"Well, I'm sorry to disappoint you, but I'm very Italian, and I don't have a nose job. My father was Calabrese."

Mikey grinned for the first time, resting his hand on her thigh. "Calabrese," he whispered. "Calabreses got thick heads, they're stubborn people. You gotta thick head?" he whispered. She turned away from him. "Your thighs are nice and smooth, you know that? Like silk. You got a very sexy body and nice thick lips. I like lips like yours, they're very sexy."

"Thank you, Frankie likes them too."

"Yeah, but Frankie ain't gonna be around to kiss them no more!" Mikey paused. "You remember a guy by the name of Lil Pauli?" he asked.

Her eyes opened wide. "Are you a friend of Lil Pauli?"

"Yeah, I was a friend. He was one of my best friends. He's dead now, thanks to DePasquale and Tony Boy's crowd."

"Pauli was a beautiful guy," Kitty said softly. "I really liked him. He was a real gentleman."

"A thousand other women thought he was a gentleman also," Mikey snapped. "But no more, thanks to your Frankie." Mikey got up and walked to the window, moved the curtain a few inches, and stood quietly watching the streets, his eyes darting back to Kitty.

"Everybody liked Pauli," Mikey sneered at her, "but now he's dust, he's gone; it's a shame, I really miss Pauli." After a few minutes, Mikey turned to her and smiled.

"How about if I give you something special while we're waiting for the corpse to come home? Let's make believe I'm Pauli," he said huskily.

"What is this, a joke? Did you come here just to see if I'd screw you, or did you really come here to kill Frankie?" she said with a smile. Then, her face clouding suddenly: "Did Frankie send you up here to see if I'd . . ."

Mikey walked up in front of her and unbuckled his pants. "You call this a joke?" he asked as he opened his pants wide and dumped out a huge penis directly in front of her face. Her eyes widened.

"What are you doing?" she asked. "Put that away!" Looking up at the ceiling, she started to giggle. "I don't believe this man!" she whined warmly. "He's got his pants wide open!" she tittered, as she looked toward the window.

Mikey grabbed her head and said, "Don't play games, bitch; there ain't no saints named Kitty that I know of. So lick it real nice, and if you're good at it, maybe I'll let you have it all. Now go ahead, Kitty girl, show me how much you really love a good fat cock."

"Just don't call me bitch! I don't like that!" she said. "And don't force me, I don't like to be forced." After a brief turn away of her face, Kitty reached over and touched Mickey's prick with her hand. Slowly she began to squeeze it and roll her hands over its fast-growing flesh. Looking up at him, she said, "He's kinda chubby, isn't he?" Mikey pushed his torso forward as a cue for her to suck it. Kitty moved forward and took it, slowly putting it into her mouth. She began to give Mikey warm, tender head, licking the sides, then up and down and over the throbbing head. Mikey's legs tightened. Kitty became more rapid in her movements and rhythm. After a while of intense sucking, Mikey said, "You certainly don't have to be forced, honey, you really love it. Look at your face, you're in heaven when you're licking it. Lay down, open your legs wide, I wanna stick it in your cunt." Kitty laid back and sprawled wide on the couch. A thick, dark, spreading patch of hair caught Mikey's eyes. He began to look at her approvingly. She was frightened but excited. His eyes glared down on her. Mikey was impressed at the way she spread herself, waiting for him. "God, you're a hairy bitch," he whispered. "Your hair spreads all down your thighs." Mikey's eyes roamed her ripe body up and down. Her face was flushed and hot. She beckoned him with a beautiful grin, a jest, rubbing her own pink nipples and breasts, swollen with passion. She glared feverishly, waiting for him, then she licked her lips passionately at him. Mikey robustly mounted her like a unicorn probing his horn at her, with one knee on the couch and one slipping to the floor. He began to line himself up, holding his huge dick and probing cautiously into her dark, hot womb. She was moist but still tight for him. He poked a bit and then began to enter her hard.

"You're some cunt," he whispered to her in a thick voice. "You were made to be fucked," he said, staring at her. Mikey pumped deeper and harder into her. "You're some hairy bitch, you know that?" he whispered. He kept reminding her what she was. Mikey stared down at her as he pumped hard. She whimpered deliciously in response.

"God, your cock is so thick—oh! Oh, my god, I could feel my sides busting," she moaned as Mikey bolted wildly, ramming harder and harder. In the midst of his deep, thrusting movements, he pulled her limp upper body directly up close to his chest. Kitty began flicking her tongue at him wildly in the air; meeting with his handsome face she began licking and kissing him wildly. "Open your shirt!" she ordered, grabbing at his shirt. "Open your shirt, I wanna lick your tits," she called out to him. "I like a man's breast," she said in a fever. Mikey ripped open his shirt and Kitty began sucking his hairy chest. After a long while of her sucking him, she lay back down and squirmed around, staring into his piercing dark eyes. His strong hands roamed excitedly over her huge breasts. Her nipples were pink and taut and voluptuous. Kitty moved her body around sensuously as he fondled her, then Mikey moved his hands to her face, touching her lips tenderly with his fingertips. She felt a taming come over her. The couple suddenly pumped hard, kissing each other's faces wildly.

"I'm fighting it," she gasped. "It feels so good to me. I don't wanna come too quick, your cock is so big, I want it to last all day," she moaned.

"You really know how to roll that big ass around," Mikey moaned back as he pumped deeply into her body. "Oh, shit! I'm . . . I'm coming," Mikey yelped. "Ohh Christ, ohhh! What a feeling," he groaned as he moved about furiously.

"Give it to me, honey, give it to me," Kitty urged simultaneously as she grabbed the thick, muscled cheeks of his buttocks. "Come on, baby," she said, digging her fingernails into them, "give it to me-e-e," she screamed. Kitty pumped with long, deep thrusts to him. "Come on, baby, come on," she repeated breathlessly, "give it to Kitty, come on!" she screamed passionately.

As they both shuddered and became still, Mikey awkwardly raised himself up off the couch and began to fix his clothes. Kitty lay quietly, staring at the ceiling, her nightgown hanging off her body. Her eyes settled and focused on Mikey. "You have beautiful eyes, do you know that?" she smiled.

"You got a beer?" Mikey asked. "I'm dry."

"In the fridge," she answered.

"You want one?" he asked, walking toward the kitchen.

"Yes, please," she answered in a voice still swollen with postclimactic aftershock.

Mikey twisted open two beers with a dish towel and returned to the living room. He handed her one, still using the towel. He began wiping things, even going back to the bathroom to wipe the cabinets he'd touched earlier. Mikey was careful not to touch anything at all in the apartment, not even the beer bottles. Holding his bottle still in the dish cloth, he began to drink in big gulps.

Resting briefly in between swallows, he looked over her again. "You're some great piece of ass, you know that?" Mikey smiled. "You got a cunt that's covered with hair like I never saw before, it's spreading up your ass and down your thighs. You're really something different," he said, rolling his lips over the bottle to sip again.

"You're not bad, yourself," Kitty smiled. "You're really stout in your pants. You're unbelievably large; I've never felt this way before, maybe because I've never seen one that thick before," she grinned, raising her bottle to her lips.

Mikey smiled at her and walked over to the window. He turned and went back to the couch and bent over her. "So you never saw a great prick until today?" he smiled. "See, and at first you thought this was some kinda joke," he said, kissing her again, tonguing her, kissing her beautiful face all over. He whispered, "You're such a fuckin' hot broad, you love it, don't you?"

"I do, I really do," she sighed. "I love to be fucked, I can't help it, I gotta have it. Once I see it, that's it, I'm finished."

"How old are you?"

"I'm forty-six," she replied, kissing Mikey's lips tenderly like old friends would. "How old are you?" she asked pecking a kiss on his nose.

"I'm . . ." Suddenly they both heard a car door slam shut in front of the building. Mikey leaped to his feet and ran to the window. There were Frankie DePasquale and Teddy Tangello, walking toward the building. "OK, get the fuck up!" he yelled. "Get over here by the door, it's post time," Mikey screeched urgently. "Stand right over there by me by the kitchen door," he ordered, "and be cool, baby, because I wanna take you home with me tonight." He stared at her. "Does he have his own key?"

"Yeah, he'll use his own key to come in," she whispered nervously. "I'm so scared," she said. "Please, fella, let me stay in the bathroom, please," she begged, "don't let me see this."

"Stay quiet or I'll kill you," Mikey snarled, grabbing her hard by the neck. "Be cool, lady, it'll be over in a minute. Don't fuck up, it'll cost you," he warned.

The rumbling sound of men's feet climbing the stairs grew as they approached the apartment door. DePasquale tried the door. It was locked. Mikey heard the keys jingling around outside the door, then a key being inserted to open it. The door opened slowly. "Kitty!" DePasquale called out. "Kitty! You dressed? I got Teddy with me." DePasquale entered first, his back toward Mikey and Kitty, who were behind the door. Tangello also entered and attempted to close the door. Mikey began shooting. *Sip-sip,* the silencer hissed. DePasquale took two in the back of his head. Tangello, unaware and caught off guard, heard the whispers of the silencer first, then saw Mikey. He turned around to run and grabbed Frankie's falling body. In the same motion Tangello, realizing death was stalking him, quickly pulled out his own gun. Holding DePasquale up like a shield, he started shooting wildly into the walls. His gun had no silencer. The blast noise was loud and terrifying. Mikey began shooting back, putting more bullets into DePasquale's body. Tangello backed into a corner like a wild man, dragging DePasquale's collapsed body with him. Mikey dragged Kitty with him toward the bathroom to gain cover. Tangello became terrified, trying unsuccessfully to hold up the heavy body as a shield. He fired again wildly at Mikey, putting two .38 bullets directly into Kitty's chest. Mikey, holding Kitty's body, took careful aim and caught Tangello twice in the throat. Tangello's head fell forward as if hanging from his body. The small room was full of gunsmoke and smelled of raw blood. Kitty slumped over in Mikey's arms. DePasquale wound up in a prone position on the floor in the far corner of the kitchen, his head virtually split in two. Tangello was lying on his back with blood pumping profusely from his throat. Mikey looked around in the now silent apartment, still holding Kitty's dangling body by her waist. He rolled back her head and looked at her eyes. They were open wide. She was dead, blood gushing out of her large breast. He dropped her to the floor and left quickly.

CHRISTMAS EVE, DECEMBER 24, 1978, 11:00 P.M.

STATEN ISLAND, NEW YORK

A short-bodied yellow school bus belonging to the Holy Covenant Church of Lynbrook, Staten Island, pulled slowly along Sea Horse Drive and into the snow-filled circular driveway of the Staten Island estate of Rocco Boretti. Snowflakes the size of nickels were falling into piles at least eight inches deep. The bus moved slowly through the snow-packed driveway, heading toward the front of the house. Bare-limbed trees carried an extra white layer, and plush branches of the blueish spruce pines hung white and low to the ground. Christmas Eve had the look of a wonderland. Santa Claus sat quietly in the rear of the bus.

"It's a good thing we put on the snow chains," the bus driver said, turning to Santa. "It's deep as shit out there!" he nodded, pulling up directly to the front double doors of the Boretti house. Twelve teenage children sat quietly on the bus, bundled warmly in winter clothing. "OK, we're here!" the bus driver announced.

Santa Claus got up and moved toward the front. "All right, kids, now you all know what to sing. Keep singing the beautiful Christmas songs we talked about before, and don't stop until I tell you to stop; remember that. I give the signals, watch me. And when I wave at you with the sign to quit, you move fast and get back on the bus. Each of you has a hundred bucks apiece waiting when you get back to the convent, plus a nice gold watch. So let's make it beautiful," Santa said, lifting his sack to his shoulder. "Now unload and form a row in front of those double front doors." Santa followed the twelve departing children off the bus toward the house. The house was lit up for Christmas but seemed very quiet. The children began to form a row in front of the house's double doors.

The bus was parked to the rear of the standing children. Santa quickly walked back to the driver and handed him a roll of money. "When I give you the cue, Jimmy, you get these kids out of here and fast, get them back to the school quick as possible, *a capisce,* and make sure they get their cash and their watches."

"Io capisce," Jimmy answered.

At that moment the curtains on the large front bay window moved; a face watched the children's movement as they prepared themselves to sing. "The first Noel . . ." they began. Santa Claus stood facing the right side of the house near the front double-doors, holding his sack of gifts at his feet. The house was enchantingly covered with beautiful blue Christmas lights, trimming the overhang and down the corners of the exterior siding and around the windows of the mansion. A few minutes later, an overhead light directly above the front doors lit up. A young man in his early twenties appeared in the entrance wearing only a short-sleeved shirt exposing strong, muscled arms that were painted with greenish blue and red tattoos. Behind him was a beautiful young girl with long black hair hanging almost to her waist. Her body was broad, big-boned, but very beautiful and sexy looking. The girl stood directly behind the young, powerful-looking man, grinning widely at the sight and sound of the singing children, not to mention the robust Santa Claus ho-ho-hoing and waving at them.

"I don't believe they still do these Christmas things on Staten Island," she said softly to her boyfriend, Carmine. "In Brooklyn they never do these things. It's so beautiful! I always love Christmas carolers on the eve, don't you?" she asked, lowering her right hand from her boyfriend's waist down to his buttocks and squeezing him in an arousing fashion. "I can't wait to get you later," she said affectionately, kissing his neck softly. Santa Claus's eyes focused intently on Rocco Boretti's son. Suddenly two younger girls in their late teens appeared, huddling close to the others. Both young girls held their cardigan sweaters tightly wrapped around them. The air was filled with Christmas song. One of the young girls began smiling and stepped out into the snow. "Oh, look! It's Santa Claus," she said, turning to her brother.

"Get in here!" Carmine Boretti yelled out to his sister. "You're gonna get ya feet all wet." As the schoolchildren sang, Christmas carols rang through the air, an unbelievable, enchanting sound. Santa began handing out gifts to the Boretti children. Small boxes were being passed out to all at the door.

"Go call Daddy," young Carmine Boretti said to one of his sisters in a tough-sounding voice. "Hurry up, call him! He'll go berserk over this!" he said, walking out in the snow himself to receive his gifts.

"Daddy's on the phone," his sister replied. "He's talking to Uncle Petey."

"Daddy's gotta see this," Rocco's son insisted. "Go call him anyway, this is too beautiful," the young man said, watching the chorus and shaking snowflakes from his flimsy shirt. "He'll go wacko over this scene," he muttered to his shapely girlfriend, who was beginning to shiver from the cold air. He handed her both gift boxes. At that moment, a small, olive-skinned woman with a slight hook nose stood in the doorway holding onto a frail, white-haired lady, her ninety-one-year-old mother. Mrs. Boretti spoke in a loud voice. "Let Grandma see!" she called to her children. "Let Grandma see!" she repeated as the two young girls stepped aside, the older woman moving forward to better see the singing children.

"All ri-i-ight!" one of Rocco's daughters screeched, holding the small box and wrapper in her hand. "Santa Claus gave me a snake-skinned wristwatch for Christmas!"

"Me too!" her sister screamed with laughter.

"Che cazzo e' freddo!" Rocco's son grumbled to his girlfriend, who was still holding both wrapped gifts in her hand. "It's freezing. Come on, honey, I'm getting a sore throat standing out here," he said to his girl. "Let's go inside and get my father."

The two young people moved back into the house, shaking the snow off their bodies. Rocco's daughters followed, leaving the mother and grandmother in the doorway holding their hands out to Santa Claus, smiling and receiving their gifts. Suddenly Rocco Boretti appeared smiling at the front doors, slipping himself easily between his wife and his mother-in-law and putting his arms around both women. Rocco's smile broadened at what he heard and saw. "This is beautiful," he said. "Listen to the way these kids sing," Rocco said, shaking his head. "What voices on these kids, like angels! Honey, they're singing to us." He smiled at his wife and gave her a peck on the cheek. Rocco's small, mousy, sandy-haired wife smiled back up at him and pinched his chest, as she shivered a little under her green wool cardigan.

Rocco's mother-in-law began to complain. "Hey! Come on," she groaned, backing out of the cold breeze. "I'm freezing," she said. Santa Claus's piercing eyes watched Rocco Boretti closely from under his thick eyebrows and fluffy white beard. His eyes rested fiercely on the grinning, glassy-eyed Boss of Bosses. Rocco's face glistened red from his enjoyment of the finest imported Italian wines New York had to offer. He smiled broadly as the children launched into "White Christmas." The two women backed away into the house, but not before Rocco's wife admonished him in whispers to "give the kids some change."

"Of course, I will; go inside," Rocco assured her. "Let Mama sit by the fireplace, she's gettin' too cold out here. I gotta take care of these kids," Rocco said, smiling at Santa Claus as he turned back to the house to make sure the women had closed the large front doors behind them. Then he walked unthinkingly out into the deep snow, wearing only house slippers and a light sweater. Santa's eyes flared wide as Boretti neared him. Then Santa waved, signaling the kids to start getting on the bus and alerting the bus driver to prepare to leave quickly. Rocco stood before the children, handing each a ten-dollar bill. From the bus, the driver poked his head out the door and grinned greedily at Rocco, who reluctantly handed him a bill as well. Then, turning from the driver, Rocco said, "Ah, we can't forget Santa Claus." Walking toward Santa, Rocco said, "*Buon Natale,* Saint Nick."

"*Buon Natale,*" Santa Claus replied. Santa's eyes watched the last child board the bus. The doors slammed shut, the bus started up, and a large puff of exhaust clouded the air. Rocco jumped away as the smoke began to cloud around him. Losing one of his slippers in the deep snow, he bent over to retrieve it. Rocco's eyes followed the bus as it pulled away, then quickly flashed at Santa, who was left behind.

Boretti walked toward Santa, shaking his head. "Would you believe it? I'm standin' in eight inches of snow with my slippers on," Boretti smiled foolishly, handing ten dollars to Santa Claus. Then he asked awkwardly, "How come you ain't on the bus with them kids? Didn't you arrive with them, or you got a reindeer hid around here someplace?" Boretti laughed, waiting for a reply.

Santa smiled, reaching into his sack as if feeling for a gift. He pulled out a longshoreman's baling hook, and in one quick, thrusting motion plunged the hook deep into the nape of the Boss of Bosses' neck.

Rocco, wading in snow, stood speechless and confused. He just looked at Santa as the hook took hold of him. His eyes flashed back toward his house as if looking for help, but the main expression on Rocco's face was that of utter surprise. His fear became more apparent as Santa Claus, in his bright red suit, began to drag him right out of his house slippers through the deep snow toward the end of the circular drive, using only one strong hand to do it. The old-time longshoreman's hook sank deeply into Rocco's neck and the circuitry of his nervous system. With each twist and turn, the heavy, sharp-pointed steel hook with its stout wooden T-shaped handle settled deeper and deeper into Rocco. The immediate, paralyzing blow, long used by the ancient Sicilians and passed on in modern times by the elderly Sicilian fishermen in Boston's North End, was still greatly effective. Rocco was awake and fully aware but completely helpless as Santa Claus dragged him from his little wet slippers, hauling him like luggage farther up the long drive, away from his house and into the rural South Shore darkness of Staten Island. Rocco's body left blood and drag marks, and it carved out a human-made pathway around the circular drive to a car waiting at the entranceway.

Bephino and Ben waited in the backseat, while Monkey sat at the wheel. They had all followed Rocco's progress. Bephino quickly got out to help red-suited Mikey dump Rocco onto the floorboard at Ben's feet. It was 11:30 P.M. Christmas was almost here. The car pulled out slowly, wheels spinning in the heavy snow, and made its way onto the highway and over the Verrazano Bridge to Brooklyn. Crossing the bridge, Rocco lay still and alive but completely silent, his head resting on the floorboards, while Ben and Bephino's feet rested in turn on his body. Ben told Bephino he wanted to perform the coup de grace. "I want his fuckin' limbs first," Ben growled. "I wanna cut him up in small pieces and drop him all over Brooklyn." But Bephino did not reply. He patted Mikey's head for the great job he'd done out there. Soon the car was driving slowly through the snowy winter streets of Bay Ridge in Bensonhurst. Mikey began removing his Santa suit. There was no traffic; it was nearly midnight. Bephino stared quietly out the window.

"You're not answering me," Ben cautioned Bephino. The windshield wipers thumped back and forth rhythmically, keeping the heavy snowflakes from blocking their view.

Mikey turned from his front passenger seat as Ben repeated carefully and a little more loudly, "Do you understand what I'm saying, Bep?"

"I heard you," Bephino answered, staring at Ben. "You can kill him, that's what he's here for; but we're not gonna cut him up."

"Why not?" Ben shouted. "Look at what he done to me. I'm a cripple, and the kid—what about the kid, he cut up the kid, didn't he? He took the kid's balls off. Whata ya think of that?" Ben demanded.

Rocco lifted his head slightly, his eyes alert to the method of his death being negotiated. Blood continued to drop down his neck and pool on the rear floorboard of the stolen car. Bephino and Ben's feet still rested atop his paralyzed body.

"This guy's scum! He's scum!" Ben shouted, waving his arms and pounding his fist on the back of the front seat.

"Forget it, Ben! I ain't gonna cut up anybody for anyone. I am not resorting to total insanity, barbarian tactics. It's gonna be done my way," Bephino said looking hard at Ben, "so keep yourself under control. A decision has been made."

Boretti managed to raise his arm and touch Bephino's knee. Looking up, he whispered, "Sciaccitano," calling Bephino by his youthful nickname. A name all Mafia mobsters had used when he was a Young Turk running round the streets of Bay Ridge. "Not on Christmas," Boretti whispered, pulling at Bephino's pants. "Not on Christmas."

The beautiful black-haired girl ran her fingers over Carmine's crotch and around his thick thighs. The two young lovers sat downstairs in a dark room on a leather couch facing a fifty-two-inch TV screen, which was displaying the antics of Laurel and Hardy. Rocco's wife and mother sat upstairs in the living room snuggled up close to the warm fireplace. Rocco's two teenage daughters had repaired to their bedrooms, where they busily chatted on phones to their girlfriends. "It's 11:50," Carmine Boretti whispered to his purring girlfriend. "We better go upstairs, it's almost midnight; they're gonna make the sausage and peppers in a little while. You better help my mother in the kitchen," he said, nudging the groping beauty who reluctantly pulled her hands out from between his thighs. "We'll play later when they all go to sleep," he said, kissing her heavily made-up face.

The couple got up and walked upstairs to the living room. Carmine grinned broadly as he approached his mother and grandmother. "So you saw Santa Claus again, hah, Grandma? At ninety-one you're still playing around with St. Nick," the young man jested.

"Yeah, play around with St. Nick, my neck," the old woman replied. "I'm too old to play around with anybody."

The young man inhaled and expanded his chest in a stretching motion. He breathed in and out, looking around. "It's almost midnight, where's Daddy?" he asked his mother.

"I don't know, he's probably in the toilet. You know him, he falls asleep in there. Go bang on the door. Tell him it's almost Christmas, we're gonna start the sausage in a few minutes for good luck." Then turning to Carmine's girlfriend, Mrs. Boretti asked, "How's your mother and father? Are they staying home for Christmas?"

"No, they went to my aunt's on Long Island, they're staying all week."

"Hey, Ma!" Carmine yelled a short while later. "He ain't in none of the bathrooms. I checked every one—upstairs, downstairs, all over the place."

"Look outside, go ask your sisters where he could be," Rocco's wife said, struggling to get up from the couch while holding her back as if in pain.

"Whatsa matter, Rosie, your back bothering you again?" her mother asked.

"Every time I sit on that couch my back gives me trouble. It's too soft, I sink too low," Rocco's wife moaned as she awkwardly walked toward the kitchen.

"He ain't nowhere!" Carmine yelled a few minutes later, walking nervously through the house. "He ain't nowhere!"

"Did you ask your sisters?" his mother asked, her voice rising.

"I asked them—they're on the goddamn phone, talking like two bananas. They don't know nothing and they could care less, the little bitches."

"Hey-y-y! That's your sisters you're talking about," the grandmother yelled across the room. "Watch your mouth! They're angels, those girls."

"Go look in the garage," Rosie pleaded to her son, "maybe he's in the garage, go see . . ."

Rocco's young son quickly left the room. A few minutes later, he came running back full of snow, holding up his father's slippers. *"Something's happened!"* he yelled. "Something happened, the snow is all fucked up out there, there's blood, somebody was dragged all over the place out there . . ."

"Did you hear what Rocco just called me? Sciaccitano," Bephino said, smiling. "It's been a long time since capo di capi called me Sciaccitano," Bephino said, looking down at Rocco as he stepped on his face. "In spite of the cruel death he gave Alley Boy, I decided this scumbag's gotta die with respect. First of all, he's the Boss of Bosses. If we tear his balls off him, it would prove to all New York we had no respect, and respect we must always have. Second of all, all the remaining New York soldiers and buttons would look down on us for such a mutilation of capi tutti. So what you wanna do, Ben, is not the way we're gonna kill him. Third, Ben, I'm thinking of his family tonight. I could picture their eyes right now, when they realize he's gone. The last time I saw his kids, they were small kids, when I sold him the house, remember? And you saw them grow yourself, you lived near him for three years. Now the kids are big, they love him. He's their father! We must give him a death with dignity, for the children's sake!"

"Give him dignity? I'll give him shit!" Ben raged, grabbing at the hook still stuck in Boretti's lower neck. Ben pulled hard; Boretti moaned. Ben yanked the handle a few times more. "Let me hear you moan, Rocco! Come on, ya bastard!" Bephino did not object to Ben's tantrum. "You fucked up my body, Rocco, but I'm here tonight to kill you, you rotten bastard!"

"So that's my decision," Bephino continued, "that's what I decided. Either you put two bullets in his head or I do it." Bephino cleared the fogged window with his gloved hand. "We're in Bay Ridge. We're comin' to his club headquarters in a few seconds. I wanna get it over fast, it's Christmas already. We're gonna whack him out and dump him right in the street in front of his headquarters. That will tell the world what his people thought of him. All the New York families will know we meant business, and they'll know we showed respect for his Sicilian blood." Bephino pulled out a .38 pistol from his coat pocket.

Ben leaned toward Bephino. "Give me that goddamn gun!" he scolded. "I'm gonna fix this bastard fast before you change your mind and let him walk outta here." Bephino frowned at Ben but understood. Ben took the gun quickly, grabbed Rocco by the scalp, pointed the barrel to his forehead and said, "You rotten bastard, you got off easy, you know that?" Rocco felt the cold steel, and his frightened eyes flew open wide. Ben heard the nervous gastric sounds beginning to release from Rocco's body.

"Nooo!" Rocco moaned, "I wanna live, let me live, please God, let me live!" he begged. "Please, God," Rocco whimpered, "please," he repeated like a man who had seen the face of God turn and walk away from him.

Ben yanked Rocco's head farther upward, looking directly at him. "You talking to God?" Ben asked. "Ya wanna live, ya rotten bastard? After what you did to the kid, you got the balls to ask God to let you live? Jesus, you rotten bastard, this is too good for you!" Ben swore as he recklessly banged the nozzle of the gun over Boretti's mouth, breaking off the man's front teeth in the process. Boretti's bowels suddenly released from his body, and his belly moved in sharp, heaving spasms. "Look at you, the big boss shittin' all over himself. You can't even have the dignity to die like a boss, you scumbag," Ben taunted. "This is too good for you!" Ben shouted, looking at Bephino. "Thank Menesiero for this pleasant death." Bephino turned to look out his window, allowing Ben to complete his act of vengeance without comment. Ben fired once into Rocco's mouth. The back of Boretti's head broke loose, leaving a four-inch flap hanging. Pulling the gun from the limp dead man's mouth, Ben stared for a moment, watching Rocco's eyes bulge from the impact. Then came the coup de grace, as he rested the nozzle on Boretti's forehead and fired once again, giving the Boss of Bosses a Mafia-style send-off.

The car was fully stopped in front of Rocco Boretti's Bensonhurst social club. The club was closed; all the members were home with their families. Monkey and Mikey got out in the deep snow and opened the car doors. Everything was strangely silent in Brooklyn, and completely white. The men dragged Rocco's body from the car and dumped him facedown in the snow. The area around the body quickly became steeped in bright red. Mikey and Monkey then threw the Santa suit next to Boretti, jumped back into the car, and pulled away.

None of the men looked back. Ben and Bephino were silent. Monkey turned left on 75th Street. Glancing over at Mikey, Monkey nudged him. "He's not retiring," he whispered. "Otherwise he would have done it different."

Almost exactly four weeks later, Bephino Menesiero, Ben, Monkey, and Mikey arrived in Little Italy late one morning and entered the old-time Sicilian headquarters on Elizabeth Street, the club that years ago had been the most important among Italians in New York City. The crowded room was busy with movement, everyone still buzzing about the Brooklyn murders and the killing of Rocco Boretti, the Boss of Bosses. Bephino entered first. Ben struggled behind him, hobbling and dragging his feet, walking with both canes. Everyone in the club room became still as they watched the men enter. Monkey and Mikey followed, studying everyone's reaction and watching their eyes. The weather was cold, only thirteen degrees above zero. The windows were wet on the inside and iced over on the outside. All the men wore fedoras and fitted dark blue or gray sharkskin overcoats. As they entered, all the patrons looked up and became silent. Bephino motioned his men to a table in the corner, and then all four sat down. After a long pause, a man serving as a waiter came to their table.

Four cappuccinos were ordered, with anisette doubles on the side. A very old man observed from the far corner of the room with a group of other elderly Sicilians. They all quietly sipped homemade wine and watched Bephino Menesiero. The old man, wearing a gray pea cap, squinted and stared intently at Bephino. After about twenty minutes, he walked carefully if unsteadily straight over to the Menesiero table. Bending over and removing his cap to show respect, the old man embraced Bephino and kissed him on both cheeks, signifying to all at the club that the new Boss of Bosses was present. "El Padrino," the old man whispered in a harsh, worn voice, obeying a time-honored ritual from the Old Country. The room suddenly resumed its movement, as Sicilian after Sicilian lined up to embrace Bephino Menesiero. Ben, Monkey, and Mikey stood watching. Good fellows and soldiers of other New York families approached Bephino with respect, whispering in Italian words of good wishes in his ear. "Padrino, Padrino," they murmured in respect, embracing him and kissing him on both cheeks. "El Padrino."

"Well, we finally made it to the top," Mikey chuckled.

"Yeah, but for how long?" Monkey said, speaking out of the side of his mouth as Bephino busily accepted the embraces of Little Italy. "We can all run now," Monkey said with a grin, as the Young Turks from Mott Street now appeared and entered the club room to pay respect to Bephino.

Ben laughed shortly. "These same guys who are kissing the shit outta him today will be the ones to accept a contract on him next year."

Across the street in a van, the FBI anxiously watched the movement in the club room. The club doors opened frequently as members entered and left. The word was flying in whispers through Little Italy. Men, young and old, rushed up the street to other clubs, calling for others to pay respect to the new capo di tutti capi. Mikey grinned at Ben and Monkey. "I don't give a fuck what you two guys say. We're in charge of this country as of today." He shook his head at both the men.

Over the next several weeks, Bephino Menesiero's name

rang out across America as cities everywhere acknowledged him as the new "man of respect."

Bephino's wife and children returned to New York on March 14, 1979. Dana, Bephino, and Mrs. Roselli took up residence on Long Island. The children both went to Los Angeles. Things were quiet for a little while.

12

APRIL 23, 1979, MIDNIGHT

BENSONHURST, BROOKLYN

The Bensonhurst Social Club of the late Emilio Morrano and the recent late Rocco Salvatore Boretti was crowded with card-playing Brooklyn cowboys. Tobacco smoke clouded the air and mixed evenly with the loud voices of tough-speaking men. Off in their usual far corner sat the big four, Bephino, Ben, Monkey, and Mikey. Monkey sipped easily on a double scotch.

"Well, we finally did it! We slipped right back into the past, didn't we?" Monkey said sarcastically, looking around at his friends. "We're all back where it started, on 13th Avenue, Brooklyn—and I was under the impression we were going to

Hollywood," Monkey observed with mock innocence. "With all the dough we accumulated over the years, this is where we wind up, back in Bay Ridge. I don't believe it. It's like *Twilight Zone* on TV," he chirped, lowering his eyelids and gulping at his scotch. "The four of us sitting here look like the missing freaks from the rogues' gallery."

"You better make that your last drink tonight, Monk, because you got work to do," Ben said, "and you don't sound too kosher."

"Work? It's just after midnight. I'm ready for bed," Monkey chuckled.

"So was Nimo Guiliano in bed when we paid our respects to him," Ben reminded him. "Now he's with the angels." Monkey laughed at Ben's warning.

Bephino waved over the woman who served the drinks and sandwiches. "Angie, bring me a large pot of coffee and four cups, please."

"You want some buns?" Angie asked. "We just got a fresh delivery. We got hot crumb-buns and jelly and cream doughnuts from the German bakery on 75th Street."

"She's got buns," Bephino told his group, looking to see if they wanted any.

"Yeah, I'll take two crumbs," Mikey said.

"I'm a little hungry," Ben said. "I'll have one jelly." Monkey said nothing. Bephino looked at him.

"Come on, Monkey, you're the one who needs it. You gotta soak up the booze, you got work tonight." Bephino leaned over to him. "Like the old days, Monk, we're back in action," he said, patting Monkey's head.

"All right," Monkey relented, "gimme two of them fuckin' cream buns, Angie, but they better be fresh, because when I throw up, I don't want stale shit comin' back up at me."

"They're cream doughnuts," Angie corrected him, "not buns. And they're so fresh they're still warm."

"What's the difference—buns, doughnuts, they taste the same," Monkey joked, giving Angie's waist a squeeze as she walked by. "What kinda work we gonna do tonight?" Monkey whispered then to Bephino.

"Chinks!" Ben answered, exposing his front teeth. "Chinks," he repeated. "We're gonna clip them fuckin' lowlife chinks tonight, the guys who fed you to the rats." Ben smiled. "Our people claim they were unable to make contact with them, so you gotta supervise it tonight, *a capisce*?"

Monkey looked at Bephino. "Is he serious? You gonna do this tonight?"

"Yeah," Bephino replied. "It's Thursday, and Chinatown is quiet. The Woo Man is still breathing. Nobody was able to corner him. We gotta put him to sleep tonight. It's been on my mind," Bephino said with a nod.

"It's Friday morning, actually," Mikey said with a chuckle.

"Yeah, it's Friday morning," Ben sneered.

"But it don't matter, we want you and Monkey to take four of our guys with you. Take Chicarelli, Charlie Fontana, Joey G., and Joe Bruno. They're all bad boys that need airing. I want those fuckin' chinks chopped up good before they die. I can't stop thinkin' of them," Bephino whispered. "This is Freddie Woo and Bad Louie Young Chow's address. They live together in those new condominiums on Bayard Street. I want you guys to go along with our boys and make sure Joey G. don't fuck up with his chain saw. I want the fuckin' gooks split in half. Tell him to use the big chain saw on them. Leave in about a half hour. Joey G. is all set and waiting for you; just give him the eye when you walk out, and the boys will follow you. They got the cars waiting, loaded with the equipment. Explain to Joey G. clearly who they gotta hit so he don't do like he did last time and whack the wrong guys. Let them go upstairs and do the work. You two wait downstairs for them in the car. The doorman of the condo building is a little guy with a uniform, he wears a big hat, he's a chink too." Bephino said in a whisper. "So, this is how it's gonna go. . . ."

Late the next morning, Bephino was still lying in bed in his Long Island condo as he rubbed his eyes and consulted his dresser clock. When he saw it read 11:30, he flipped up a switch on the nightstand that brought his bedroom television to life. Finding the midday news, Bephino listened intently, moving closer and closer to the TV until he was finally at the end of the bed. Dana and Mrs. Roselli could be heard moving throughout the other rooms.

"This is Dan Baker," the man on television announced, "reporting for channel 3 news. Early this morning on the outskirts of Chinatown, four masked men allegedly forced their way into a luxury building and murdered seven people in one apartment before dismembering them and then escaping. According to doorman Sam Chin Sin, the men broke into the security condominium at 180 Bayard Street at about 2:50 A.M., took him hostage, and dragged him to unit 19H, registered in the name of Fred Woo, an Oriental businessman known to be part owner and operator of the Woonsong Noodle Company at 210 Mulberry Street in Chinatown. At the apartment door the intruders coerced Mr. Chin Sin into announcing to Mr. Woo that he had an important package for him. When Mr. Woo opened the door, the masked men rushed into the apartment and began machine-gunning the entire group of men and women inside."

At that moment, Bephino's bedroom door swung open as Dana entered from the sitting room. "Bepy," she exclaimed delightedly, "you're up!" Bephino, frozen still at the edge of the bed, hissed at her, "*Shush,* honey! I got the news on now!"

Dan Baker continued. "According to New York City Police Chief Fieldmore Breslin, three of the victims have been identified as figures in Chinatown's underworld: Louis ('Bad Louie') Young Chow, Fred Woo, and Mr. Nicky Lee. They had been dragged out into the hallway and cut in half with a gas-operated chain saw. Fred Woo was found decapitated and in three parts. Several bodies were flung at the sole neighbor's apartment door. When Sy Mitchell of apartment 19G opened his door to see what had caused the powerful noise, he saw bodies being cut in half by a hooded man wielding a bloody, gas-puffing saw. He was informed by the intruders that if he called the police they would return and use the chain saw on him. Sy Mitchell says he then locked his door, piled furniture against it, and turned his TV on full volume. Mr. Chin Sin, the doorman, was pushed across the landing into a closet by the hit squad and allowed to remain there."

"My God!" Dana pouted. "We move back to New York to listen to this shit. Why didn't we move to Florida or Palm Springs to live? These Chinese people are nuts over here, they kill each other with chain saws," she said in disgust.

Bephino turned off the TV, got up from the bed, put his arm around his wife, and walked her slowly and silently into the kitchen. He opened the refrigerator and poured himself a glass of orange juice. As he drank he stared quietly at his beautiful companion, the best friend he'd ever had.

"Don't you think I'm right?" Dana asked, looking steadily at her husband. "Aren't we better off somewhere else, at least closer to the children?" His silence did not discourage her. "If we lived in Palm Springs, honey, we'd be closer to Patsy and Rene—they're both working in Los Angeles now. It seems like it's gonna be a permanent situation for them. I thought you couldn't stand New York. Remember saying when we moved down South how you hated the cold, you hated the garbage in the streets? You couldn't stand the rubbish piled up on the sidewalks—'Everything smells,' you said, remember?"

Bephino gulped down the last of the orange juice, breathed in hard, and said, "New York is New York. It won't change, and we have to accept it as it is. Look: I'm gonna take a shower. When I come out, I'll take you for lunch over at the Sea Grove Pier. We'll eat fresh tuna steaks in the glass room overlooking the ocean, OK, sweetheart? It's just as nice as anyplace in Palm Springs or L.A."

Dana's eyes focused on Bephino. She wanted to smile. Instead she said, "Bepy, you never told me how you got that cleft in your chin. I can't believe you're that vain that you went for plastic surgery while I was away in Mexico, because if you did, the guy was a butcher. He ruined your chin." Dana moved closer. "It looks all chopped up," she said, touching the scar. Bephino backed away and rubbed his chin, then modeled it playfully at her as he approached again and kissed her beautiful oval face. Then he turned and walked toward the bathroom.

"Hey!" she called out to him as she used to in her younger days. "Was that chin supposed to be a Park Avenue plastic surgery?" she asked flirtatiously. "Because, honey, if it was," she continued with a sly, pretty smile, "I'm afraid you got gypped somethin' awful."

Bephino smiled at her persistence and ran his fingers slowly through his thick black hair as if in thought. As he began slowly unbuttoning his pajama top, he said, "You really wanna know about my chin? OK. I got this cleft from them chinks you saw on television this morning—the ones without the heads, the dead ones," he explained patiently. He then raised his eyebrows once and nodded curtly at her. "Them chinks did it."

"That's almost as good as your Moby Dick stories," Dana chuckled. "Go take a shower, I'll settle for the tuna steak you promised me."

The years passed. It was now 1986. Bephino Menesiero continued to reign quietly over all New York families. People busily went about their business, and concrete in New York was cheap again.

On Friday, January 17, at 4:00 P.M., a long gray stretch limo made its way slowly along the Avenue of the Americas in Manhattan's snow-filled streets. Sunk deeply in the backseats were Ben, Monkey, and Bephino. Driving was Sonny Garbo from the coffee shop on Park Row near Foley Square, the man who had helped Ben during Bephino's 1977 trial. In bad financial shape, he'd gone to Ben for help. Ben had kept his word and made Garbo a good fellow in the Menesiero family. The limo continued through Manhattan's heavy traffic.

Bephino leaned forward. "Find a place to park, Sonny," he said. "Park over there in front of Madison Square Garden. I wanna get a newspaper before we stop for dinner." Sonny swung the big car into a bus stop area and backed up.

"You want a paper?" Monkey asked. "I'll get it, which paper do you want?"

"I'll get it," Bephino replied, removing himself from the backseat.

"The fuckin' streets are full of snow," Monkey snapped. "You're gonna get your feet all wet."

"And how about you?" Bephino said. "Ain't you gonna get your feet wet?"

"Yeah, but . . ."

"But what?" Bephino asked, putting on a gray-rimmed fedora. "I can get my own paper and get my own feet wet. Why should you get yours wet?" he smiled, moving out of the car. Suddenly, he moved back in, looked at both Ben and Monkey, and said, "You know who I been thinking about all day?"

"Who?" Ben asked. Then Ben, answering his own question said, "The FBI, probably, because I want you to know they're still following us. I see a fuckin' van marked Carol's Florist two cars behind; when we stop, they stop."

"They been following us for years," Monkey said. "We ain't doin' nothin'."

Bephino shook his head. "I was thinking about the poor bastard I had to clip in Europe. The fuckin' guy actually died for absolutely nothing that concerned us." Bephino shook his head and got out of the car. He puckered his lips and raised his eyebrows at his friends, then shut the car door. He walked about thirty feet to a closed-in newspaper stand that was set out on the sidewalk directly in front of the Garden. About five people were standing in line. Bephino also stood in line, as snowflakes fell hard and began to thicken on his hat and overcoat. Finally, reaching the newsstand, Bephino asked for a *Times* and a *Wall Street Journal*. The paper man serving him wore a thick, heavy navy wool pea coat and a soft wool cap pulled over his ears, down to his eyebrows. His brown wool work gloves had the fingertips cut off so he could handle the cash. Bephino picked out two papers and handed him a five-dollar bill. The man kept sniffling nervously, wiping his nose on his cut-off wool glove. "That's $2.25 outta five," he said, opening a wood cash box to retrieve his change. The man kept sniffling and staring at Bephino, wiping his nose with his glove while counting out the money. He looked up and grinned meekly at Bephino while he handed over the change with his wet, mucus-soaked glove.

"Keep the change," Bephino said, eyeing the man with a mixture of pity and disgust.

"Thanks a lot, buddy," he said, "thanks a lot. Happy New

Year." He reached out to shake Bephino's hand. As Bephino and the pathetic man exchanged looks, a memory chimed in.

"Happy New Year," Bephino replied, tucking his papers under his arm and turning to go. After ten or so steps, realization dawned. Bephino stopped suddenly and whirled to look back at the small green wooden newspaper stand. He glared for a long moment through the heavy-falling snow. The paper man's head stretched way out over the counter, peeking out to find Bephino. Their eyes met again. People in line became impatient, but the newspaper vendor kept stretching his head out, seeking Bephino. Bephino stood stock-still, his back toward the limo. Monkey, Ben, and Sonny Garbo watched Bephino stand in the wet, slushy snow, staring at the newsstand. The paper guy, darting his head in and out, suddenly smiled and shouted to Bephino in a friendly, familiar voice, "Happy New Year, mister," waving his right hand with the cut-off glove. Bephino reflexively waved back, staring straight and thinking hard while slowly backing up toward the car.

Monkey lowered the window. "What the hell are you looking at?" he shouted. "You're getting soaked out there, it's turning to rain!"

Bephino then turned and walked to the car, glancing back at the man one last time before getting in.

"What the fuck was all that about?" Ben laughed, once Bephino had finally settled back into his seat. "You were standin' in the snow for ten minutes. What the hell were you lookin' at? The FBI must think you're goin' nuts. They must have videoed that fuckin' scene just for laughs, you standin' in the snow with ya hat all white."

"I thought I knew that newspaper guy," Bephino answered. "The guy looked very familiar."

"Who was he?" Monkey asked. "You musta known him. You stared at him long enough."

Bephino raised up his newspaper and opened it to the stock market section. Monkey asked again, "So who was he?" Bephino still didn't reply. "Who *was* the guy? Ya gonna tell us or what?" Bephino raised his brows, lowered the paper, and grinned. "Whata ya keepin' secrets now, or what?" Monkey demanded.

Bephino shook his head from side to side, puckered his lips for a moment, then burst out laughing. "Would you believe the fuckin' newspaper guy was our Sabu? It was Joey D, would you believe it? Joey D was sellin' the newspapers," Bephino laughed. "He had a little gray beard, his hat was pulled down, coverin' his ears. It took me a while; I knew that I knew the guy, but I wasn't sure. He kept snifflin' like a mutt."

"Ya gotta be kiddin'," Ben said, holding his chest as if to contain its laughter. "The bimbo's sellin' newspapers! I told ya he was a fuckin' bimbo from day one, I always told ya so."

"Maybe he's doin' all right for a bimbo, sellin' newspapers," Monkey laughed. "At least he's one bimbo that's gonna live to a ripe old age, because we ain't."

Bephino laughed. "I knew he recognized me, but he was afraid to really say hello to me. Christ, I can't believe he left us after so many good years together."

"He's a fuckin' bimbo, that's why he left," Monkey spat. "A bimbo with probably a good, safe job."

Everyone burst out laughing.

May 7, 1986, 3:00 p.m.

Little Italy, New York City

Ben and Bephino sat outside a café on Little Italy's Grand Street, both sipping demitasse coffee under a green-and-white awning. The streets were full of people hurrying by, women walking with bags of groceries and little children playing on the sunny sidewalks. Traffic along Grand Street as usual was bumper to bumper, moving slowly to the corner traffic light. The Italian elders walked by tipping their hats to all the neighborhood merchants and to the important people of New York who were sitting outside their respective cafés. Walking by, a beautiful, elderly lady approached Bephino's table, smiled, and handed him a rose. She bent over, kissed him, and touched his face. *"Buona fortuna,"* she whispered in her Sicilian dialect.

"Grazie," Bephino replied, reciprocating her respect by smiling and touching her hand as she turned to walk away. Then two old men walked up to Bephino's table, both smoking twisted black cigars and wearing pea caps. These gentlemen, real Sicilian old-timers, had never left Elizabeth Street's Sicilian colony. They stood around all day on the block, talking and watching things happen. "It's a nice day, Padrino," one of the old men said, tilting his head to one side and speaking in broken English. "You know, I was a fisherman too in the old days," he said. "I was friends with your father, Pasquale, and your Uncle Joe," the old man said. *"Io Sciaccitano* like you," he said proudly with a broad grin.

Bephino greeted him with a genuine smile. *"Qual' à vostro nome?"* Bephino asked the old man. But the old man, changing the subject, motioned with his eyes at Bephino. Standing before him, he glared wisely at Bephino, raising his eyebrows and signaling urgently in the Sicilian sign of awareness, a signal used in the old days as sign language. The old man blinked away like a Western Union telegraph machine. Bephino looked around curiously, receiving the sign of alarm. The old man moved up closer, hovering directly in front of the table, seemingly purposely to block any possible view of him from the streets. The old-timer whispered in Italian, "Over there." His eyes flickered again at Bephino, then toward a young man now approaching from the center of Grand Street toward the espresso café, carrying a newspaper under his arm. Bephino looked around. He saw the old man's eyes darting back and forth crazily in the direction of the young man crossing the street. Bephino nodded to him with gratitude. *"Grazie bene, Papa,"* Bephino whispered. He touched his hands with respect, then quickly alerted Ben, relaxing, as if sunning, in a sprawling position, holding his two canes in one hand, the other hand in his jacket pocket. Ben seemed preoccupied, smiling at two small children playing on the sidewalk nearby with a puppy.

"It's Carmine, he's makin' his move!" Bephino snapped.

"He's crossin' the street over by the pastry shop. He's got a newspaper under his arm!"

"You just realized that? I been watchin' him for the past hour," Ben said in a low voice, removing a .38 pistol with a short silencer already attached to it from his coat pocket. "And he's got a backup standin' on the corner of Mott Street, see him?" Ben asked. "I been watchin' both of 'em all mornin'." The traffic on Grand Street continued to be heavy. Carmine Boretti was now about halfway across Grand, waiting for a slow-moving car to pass in front of him. The car's driver began blowing his horn. Pedestrians turned to look at the car that was being so noisy. Traffic in front of it was at a stop. The light changed to green, then back to red, before the driver could make enough progress. Impatient, he leaned out the window and cursed, blowing his horn again at the traffic ahead of him. Bephino's eyes flashed from the Mott Street corner to Grand Street where Carmine was crossing. Bephino carried no gun. Ben's cobra eyes were awaking, darting around as he waited for people to clear his view. But Ben seemed awkward and off-balance. Bephino thought briefly about reaching out and grabbing the gun from him, but could not do that to his friend who had been so loyal to him. He watched Ben. Could Ben handle this? Bephino wondered. The light changed from red to green. Horns were blowing. Then suddenly, for some reason, Carmine Boretti turned around and walked away. Making a right on Mott, he became lost in the crowded streets. Ben turned and looked for the backup on the Mott Street corner; he was also gone. Ben smoothly and casually returned the gun to his pocket. He then stumbled to his feet, setting his two canes in place. "Come on, we better get the fuck outta here."

Bephino burped and got up, handed the waiter twenty bucks, and with eyes scanning everyone crossing or approaching his path, he walked with Ben toward their waiting car. Sonny Garbo, parked by a hydrant, sat relaxing at the wheel. The car pulled out and turned down Mulberry Street toward the Brooklyn Bridge. Ben spoke first.

"I was watchin' him all mornin'. I didn't want to upset

your stomach, you were enjoying your demitasse, so I didn't say nothin'. The fuckin' kid was finally gettin' ready to make his move. I'm sure he had an automatic pistol wrapped in the newspaper. I think the FBI watchin' us from the roof scared him away," Ben said. "I think I saw a video camera over the furniture store's rooftop, scannin' down on the streets."

"I think the whole neighborhood saw him preparing himself but me," Bephino said. "The old people warned me. Would you believe I never saw Carmine watchin' us?" Bephino said, pulling his lips back and allowing his eyes to close in thought. "He coulda got us that time for sure. I was too relaxed."

"The kid's a true Sicilian," Ben sneered. "He has to do what he has to do."

"I know," Bephino whispered in a quick reply, "and I admire him for what he's out to do, for his father's sake. The kid's got honor and respect. And *il rispetto* comes before anything, we know that. And I always knew someday Carmine would try to pass the blood. This time it's not business. This time it's personal, blood to blood. It's like a blood clot that's gotta be removed, one way or the other."

"I always told ya that," Ben said, shaking his head. "This kid's gotta be dealt with. He's dangerous, I'm tellin' ya."

Following four cars behind, in a light brown van, were FBI agents Carl Vanders and Burt Stapleton and their driver, John Higgins.

"Listen to this shit," Vanders barked excitedly, facing Stapleton. Both men, riding in the van's back compartment, wore earphones and watched a tape recorder spin slowly. "Mensiero's gonna make his move—I could feel it comin'. Listen to the way they're talkin'," Vanders whispered. "Yeah," he groaned, holding his hand to his earphones. "I could smell it comin'; he's finally gonna let Benny talk him into makin' the fatal decision, one that we could play openly to the grand jury. Here it comes—" Vanders yelped. "Listen, we got the bastard! Did you hear that?! It's all on tape. They ordered Carmine Boretti dead."

Stapleton nodded, then reached across to shake his partner's hand. "We got all of them cold turkey—all except

Monkey Pastrano and Mikey What's-his-name," Stapleton grinned.

"Mikey's the only dangerous guy that's not in the car. I wanted him too," Vanders said. "Lately he's becomin' too respected for some reason."

Driving up ahead, and unaware of the bugs planted in each rear stereo speaker of their car, Bephino sat quietly as Ben reassured him that murdering the young Boretti was the right thing to do.

After a long silence, Bephino turned to Ben. "I'm leaving for Bel Air in the mornin'. I'm gonna stay with Alan Stone for a while. He's not feelin' well. He's outta the hospital now, convalescin' at the movie star's place in L.A. I'll give you the phone numbers over there. We're stayin' with Frankie Martin." Bephino looked at Ben. 'It's important I spend some quiet time with Alan. We gotta make some moves in Vegas very soon."

"How you want it handled about Carmine?" Ben asked.

"Put Monkey on it with at least four buttons. Blow the kid outta his crib and do it right away." Bephino raised his finger to his upper lip in thought, then said, "Don't hurt his family. He's married now and got a baby. I hate to take out a kid like that, he's still so damn young. I guess I put if off long enough; I was hopin' he would take up some kind of hobby, like tropical fish or somethin'." Bephino nodded while rubbing his chin. "Kill him tonight, before he kills one of us," he said softly. Then turning fully to Ben: "Don't let him know what hit him. Make it right for him."

Ben turned away and stared ahead. "It'll be done right," he nodded. "Don't you worry. I'll even buy the little bastard a mass card."

"You better buy more than a mass card, Ben, because after we kill this boy, it'll take Rocco Boretti in his grave more than a hundred years to forget us."